Shandril strode toward the tower, ignoring the dark-armored warriors who stood at its gates. They frowned and reached for their swords—and then shrank back away from her, moving hastily sideways along the wall. Shandril stared at their frightened faces and then glanced behind her to see what they were staring at.

All around her, in a dark and deadly ring, beholders were rising up silently. She'd teleported into a trap.

THE HARPERS

A semi-secret organization for Good, the Harpers fight for freedom and justice in a world populated by tyrants, evil mages, and dread concerns beyond imagination.

Each novel in the Harpers Series is a complete story in itself, detailing some of the most unusual and compelling tales in the magical world known as the Forgotten Realms.

THE HARPERS

FANTASY ADVENTURE

CROWN OF FIRE

Ed Greenwood

The action of this novel occurs in the Year of the Prince (1357 Dalereckoning), immediately after the novel Spellfire, *and before the Coming of the Gods.*

CROWN OF FIRE

First Printing: April 1994
Printed in the United States of America.
Library of Congress Catalog Card Number: 92-61094

9 8 7 6 5 4 3 2 1

ISBN: 1-56076-839-8

TSR, Inc.
P.O. Box 756
Lake Geneva, WI 53147
U.S.A.

TSR Ltd.
120 Church End, Cherry Hinton
Cambridge CB1 3LB
United Kingdom

**This one's for Jenny and for the Knights,
for waiting in patience for so long—
even though you were waiting for different things.**

Dulce est desipere in loco currente calamo

Acknowledgments

Thanks to J. Robert King, for walking shield to shield on this journey—and to Jim Lowder, for keeping faith.

Prologue

Something flashed as it moved—aye, there! Brann stepped up to the grassy crest of the hill where his flock was pastured and looked east, shading his eyes against the bright forenoon sun. Whatever was moving caught the light again, flashing against the dark, tree-clad lower slopes of the mountains opposite him. Out of habit, Brann looked quickly around at his flock, counting without thought. He found nothing amiss and peered back to the east again, looking for that moving glint to show itself again.

The mountains stood high and dark, like a row of stone giants frowning down on easternmost Cormyr. The Thunder Peaks, men called them, named for the fierce storms that often rolled and broke among them. They were hard and grim and splendid, and sometimes Brann just sat and watched them for hours.

Much as he was watching them now. They towered over him like a dark, many-spired fortress wall, forever hiding Sembia from the high meadows where he stood. Rich, splendid Sembia, a land where fat merchants lay at ease among piles of gold coins, glittering like that spot on the mountains. Ships full of coins from all over the Realms —even far, sinister Thay, where wizards kept slaves— came to its shores every day.

He'd not always be just a shepherd. Someday he'd go to Sembia's docks and meet with adventure, Brann promised himself . . . not for the first time. He sighed at that thought, shook his head with a wry smile, and glanced about at the sheep again. His count was right, and none of them was straying, shifting, or even looking particularly awake. Brann stared at the sheep in growing exasperation. They ignored him, as usual. Oh, for a little excitement! Nothing here seemed amiss—also as usual. He sighed again, and looked east.

The sky was bright and clear, and every boulder and stand of trees on the familiar flanks of the Peaks was as it had always been, unchanged—except . . .

Except for that little winking flash of light, far away over the rolling, grass-clad hills near the Gap. Something shone back the sun at him again, something descending through the high meadows, where he spent most days alone with his flock. It was something—or someone—that wore or carried metal. It wasn't on the road through the Gap, so it couldn't just be another trading wagon hung with pots and pans. Perhaps it was a knight of Cormyr— perhaps even one of the Dragon Knights, who were the personal swordguard and messengers of Azoun, the Purple Dragon, king of all this land. With quickening interest, Brann watched for another flash.

There it was again. Metal, surely, and bobbing in short, choppy moves—so it wasn't a horse, or someone riding. It looked . . . as if some splendid knight in gleaming armor were marching afoot across the hills toward him. Brann leaned on his staff and shaded his eyes for a better view.

Then his mouth fell open. A dwarf—a *real* dwarf, with an axe and a beard and a mail shirt, and all! Brann stood frozen in wonder. A tiny voice inside him chuckled at his awe and reminded him that this was what he'd wished for. Adventure was striding to meet him, after all.

Staggering, actually. The dwarf stumped along on one side of a girl who was being carried, and a slim young man struggled along on the other. The dwarf was bearing most of the girl's weight on his broad shoulders, but he was so much shorter than the man that the two were having trouble moving straight forward with their burden.

* * * * *

"Keep on, lad," Delg grunted. "There's a guard post not far ahead . . . two hills ahead, and we should see it." Sweat dripped from the dwarf's dusty beard as he spoke.

Narm nodded grimly, saving all his breath for carrying his lady. Shandril was slim and shorter than most; she *couldn't* be this heavy. She hung loose between them, senseless. Narm stumbled, caught himself with a wordless hiss of apology to Delg, and shook his head impatiently; stinging sweat had run down into his eyes again. He looked ahead—and stiffened. Through the blurring of sweat he saw dark, moving blobs on the grassy hills ahead. " 'Ware—" he panted.

"They're sheep, lad," the dwarf said dryly. "Right dangerous, if ye're a clump of grass, I suppose. Aye? Just sheep."

Narm shook his head wearily. His legs felt hollow and weak, his strength draining out of them with every step. He had to—to rest. "Stop, Delg—just a breath," he panted, wiping sweat away with his sleeve. "Just a—"

"*No*," the dwarf said in tones of cold iron. "If you stop

now, boy, you'll never get on again in time. They'll catch up with us and run us down out here like boar, and Shan will have cooked twenty-odd Zhents in vain. Keep moving! We're almost there."

* * * * *

Brann watched, astonished, as the bristle-bearded dwarf in armor and the young man in mage robes staggered past him, panting under the weight of the girl they carried. Her long reddish-gold hair dangled along one limp arm as they strode doggedly and unevenly on, up the last hill before the village.

Brann looked east again, a view he knew very well. There was no sign of anyone following them. He turned and stared curiously at the sweat-darkened back of the young wizard as the strangers went over the hill and began to descend out of sight.

His mouth was suddenly dry. His hands, as they dipped to his belt, trembled; he almost dropped the horn. So this is excitement, he thought. Brann shook his head, and blew. The horn call wavered and then grew steady, high, and clear.

* * * * *

The high song of a shepherd's horn was ringing off the walls of houses as the three tired adventurers came down into Thundarlun. Before them rose the watchful stone bulk of the guardhouse, where Delg had known it would be. On benches along its wall, Purple Dragon soldiers sat alert, watching with interest in their eyes as the three approached.

Delg guided Narm down onto the dusty road, and the soldiers frowned and rose, catching up halberds from where they leaned against the guardhouse wall. One shouted into the building as the weary travelers came close enough to see wary faces and ready weapons. A Purple Dragon with a hard face and a gray mustache appeared from within and strode out into the road to block their way. The sword of a guardcaptain gleamed high on the shoulders of his surcoat.

"Halt, travelers!" His voice was deep and level, but not unfriendly. "You seem in some trouble and are come to Cormyr, Realm of the Purple Dragon. State your names and what you seek here."

Delg looked up at him and silently and imperiously gestured at a soldier to approach. The man glanced toward his commander. The guardcaptain appraised the dust-covered dwarf and then nodded. Holding his halberd warily, the soldier stepped closer.

Delg shifted the limp girl he held into Narm's grasp, staggering just a bit as the burden left him. Under her full weight, the young wizard sank to his knees in the dust. The soldier moved to help; Delg ignored them both. Keeping his hands well away from his axe, the dwarf strode forward to confront the Cormyrean commander. His beard jutted defiantly as he looked around at all of the guards, raising his hand to show them its emptiness before reaching slowly to his throat. He drew something out from under his mail, something that hung from a silver neck-chain, and cupped his hand around it as he showed it to the Purple Dragon guardcaptain.

The man frowned down at it, and then slowly raised his eyes to meet the dwarf's steady gaze. They looked at each other for a long, silent moment, and then the guardcaptain waved to the soldiers on his right. "Take her in, fast." He added, to Delg, "Our wizard's within."

* * * * *

Shandril's head swam. The light had changed; she was
inside a building somewhere, being bumped and scraped
along a rough stone passage and through a door. Then
hard, smooth wood was under her. She slumped down on
the seat, too exhausted to even be thankful, and heard the
soldiers who'd brought her here go out again, sword-
scabbards clanging against stone. Then she saw the flickering blue glow ahead and forced herself to focus and be
alert. She was in the presence of magic.

As her gaze cleared, she saw a man sitting at a table in
front of her—a stout, fussy-looking man with a wispy
beard. He seemed to be alone in this gloomy, bare stone
room. Alone until she arrived. He was looking irritably
over his shoulder at her, a shoulder that bore the purple
robes of a war wizard of Cormyr. The flickering blue radiance—the only light in the room—was coming from a
thin, gleaming long sword floating horizontally in the air
in front of the wizard.

Shandril let her eyes close to slits and her chin fall to
her breast. After a moment, the wizard shrugged and
turned back to the floating blade. Murmuring something
to himself, he reached toward the blade and made a certain gesture. Blue lightning crackled suddenly, coiling and
twisting along the gleaming steel like a snake spiraling
around a branch. Then there was a brief, soundless flash,
and the reaching, blue-white tongues of lightning were
gone. The wizard nodded and wrote something on a piece
of parchment in front of him.

Then he tugged at his beard for a moment, spoke a
single, distinct word Shandril had never heard before,
and made another gesture. This time there was no
response from the magical blade. The wizard made
another note.

* * * * *

Delg squinted up at the Purple Dragon commander. "In a breath or two, I'll tell you all that," he said, "if you've time to listen by then. There's near thirty Zhentilar riding on our heels—they'll be here very soon."

The commander stared at him, saw that he was serious, and said, "Zhentil Keep? 'Twill be a pleasure, Sir Dwarf, to turn them back." He made no move to call his men to arms, but nodded his head at the guardhouse into which Shandril had been taken. "So speak—what befell?"

Delg turned to look east. His hand glided swiftly to the reassuring hardness of his axe. "She won time for us to escape, blasting a score of Zhents out of their saddles. Unfortunately, there are more, and all her—ah, magic is gone."

The captain was not a stupid man. His eyes widened for a moment as the dwarf spoke of magic—younger than most spell-hurlers, that lass. His eyes narrowed again an instant later as he too turned to look at the horizon. His face changed, and he shouted, "Down! 'Ware arrows!"

A hail of shafts answered him, thudding into the turf many paces short of them. Up over the nearest hill bobbed many dark-armored heads, rising and falling at a gallop. The Zhentilar, riding hard and with arrows to waste, had come.

Faces paled and jaws dropped. Then the men who wore the Purple Dragon were scrambling for crossbows and cover. As the minstrels of the Dales say, they scarce had time for last wistful wishes before death swept down on them.

* * * * *

Shandril heard a faint yell, then another. Somehow she found strength and was on her feet, her head swimming. The world rocked and swayed. There was nothing in her but sick, helpless emptiness. Sweat glistened on her hands with the effort. She swayed and caught at the back of the wizard's chair for support.

Astonished and irritated, the mage looked up into her face. She pushed past, leaned on the table for support, and reached out with weak, trembling fingers. The blade was cold but tingling as she touched it; trembling with weakness and relief, she felt the magic it bore begin to flow into her.

"What're you—that's magic, lass—no—*don't!*" the wizard blurted. Then he stared in surprise; the blade flashed with sudden light and seemed to waken. Pulses of radiance ran down it and up the arms of the young girl, who grasped its hilt in both hands and gasped. She closed her eyes and shuddered as small arcs of lightning leapt from the blade and spiraled around her.

From outside came sudden tumult: thudding hooves, screams and yells, and then, very near, a horrible, gurgling moan.

The wizard tore his gaze from Shandril just long enough to roll his eyes and snarl, "What *now?* Oh, Mystra *aid* me!"

Snatching a wand from his belt, he strode out of the room. What in the name of all the gods was going *on?* The sudden reek of something burning came to him as he flung wide the oaken door of the guardhouse—and stopped in astonishment, again.

Across the threshold, he saw Guardcaptain Ruldel's face twist in pain as he sagged back into the arms of a young man in mage robes. Many arrows stood out of the dragons on the warrior's surcoat and shield, and already his armor was dark with blood. Above him stood a dwarf, face grim, bloody axe in hand. The war wizard goggled at them all from the doorway, frozen in disbelief.

As the commander sank into the boy's arms, he groaned,

struggled to speak for a moment, and looked up at the dwarf.

The words came in a rough hiss. "Tell Azoun, I . . . we were togeth . . ." The rest was lost forever in a last rush of blood.

Delg shook his head as he tugged the shield out of the man's lifeless hand; the fool had not even had time to get it properly on his arm. Now he was past needing it. Delg crouched, holding the shield—it was as tall as he was—up to protect Narm. The young mage was drenched with sweat, exhausted from deflecting far too many arrows with a feeble, invisible magic meant for hanging cloaks on pegs or fetching small things from across a room. The spell had failed in the end, and Narm barely clung to wakefulness.

Arrows hissed and hummed past them, reaching hungrily through the air close by . . . toward the open door of the guardhouse.

The war wizard stood there, still looking astonished as the shafts tore into him. Irritation joined puzzlement on his face before he gurgled and toppled slowly sideways, an arrow through his throat. Errant shafts cracked off the stone wall beside him.

There was a barked command from whence the arrows had come. Through the sudden stillness that followed, one man came riding, trotting up to confront the young man and the dwarf. The frightened faces of villagers peered from windows. All around the Zhentilar, the soldiers of Cormyr lay sprawled in blood, pinned down by many arrows. One warrior hung limply out the open window of a cottage that was already crackling into rising flames.

As he reined up in front of Delg, the dark-armored Zhentilar swung a drawn long sword lazily through the air, trailing drops of fresh blood. He looked down at the grim dwarf, over at the sprawled wizard in the guardhouse doorway, and then around at the frightened, watching faces, and his cruel face brightened in satisfaction. He rose in his saddle with insolent grace and brandished his bloody sword again.

"Come out, wench!" he bellowed at the open guard-house door. "Come out, or we'll burn this village, and you with it!"

A murmur of fear went up. The bewildered folk of Thundarlun could not believe so many strong, capable Purple Dragons—a soldier for every three villagers—could be slain so quickly and easily. In numb silence, they looked down again at the still forms and the blood. Had the gods forsaken Thundarlun?

The Zhentilar beckoned impatiently without looking behind him; one of his men obediently rode up with a blazing torch in hand. With a cold smile, the Zhent swordmaster looked around at the stunned, fearful faces of the watching villagers. Slowly and deliberately, he wiped his blade on the flank of his horse—it snorted and shifted under him—and he sheathed it. Then he reached out, took the torch, and brandished it like a blade, trailing rippling flames through the air.

His horse rolled its eyes in fear; the Zhent pulled back sharply on the reins to prevent it from bolting and swung his new weapon in arcs of flame. "Come out!" he snarled, "or taste fire!"

Silence fell . . . and lengthened, hanging heavy on the smoky air. Villagers murmured in fear as the wait continued, and the swordmaster's face grew stony. He raised the torch and sat his saddle like a statue of impending doom. The silence stretched. The fire he held on high spat and crackled.

The dwarf stood watching it, eyes narrow and shield raised over the kneeling form of Narm, who had grown pale and seemed to be having trouble swallowing.

And then a slim girl in dusty travel leathers stood in the doorway. Yellow-white fire seemed to dance around her eyes and hands, blazing like the torch in the swordmaster's hand.

"You called for me, Zhentilar?" The words were calm and cool, but flames flickered from her lips as she spoke. At the sight, Zhents and villagers alike murmured and fell back.

Then the girl shuddered, and her face creased in pain. It cleared again. She straightened almost defiantly, looking up at the Zhent swordmaster, her hands going to her hips.

An arrow sang toward her. The swordmaster's furious order was too late to halt its flight—but Shandril looked at it calmly, not moving. Under her gaze it caught fire, blazed like a tiny, leaping star, and was gone in drifting sparks and smoke.

The moan of awe and fear from the watching villagers was louder than the startled oaths some of the Zhentilar uttered.

"You called me out," Shandril said in a terrible, hoarse whisper. Her eyes, blazing with fire, fixed on the Zhentilar swordmaster. As she glared, flames roiled around her face—and then lanced out.

The Zhentilar's face paled as hissing flames leapt at him. He flung up an armored arm to shield his face. The flames swelled to a sudden, savage roar.

Then the swordmaster cried out in sudden pain, twisting in his saddle. Smoke rose from the half-cloak about his shoulders. His mount reared under him, neighing, and the torch fell from his smoldering hands.

Shandril raised one blazing hand, and in her eyes he saw his death. "By all the gods," she said in fury, flames rising around her hair in a leaping crown of fire, "you'll wish you hadn't."

One

A COLD CALLING

Tongues wag their ways on great adventures with ease. Feet oft find it harder to follow.

Mespert of Baldur's Gate
The Book of the Coast
Year of the Talking Skull

 Most of the long, high hall lay in chill darkness. Here and there, lamps shed eerie, feeble glows into the cold vastness. Menacing shadows swirled where this lamplight was blocked— by a long stone table, the many high-backed seats drawn up around it, and the robed men who sat in them.

"So you have all come," came a calm, purring voice from one end of the table. "Good. The Lord Manshoon will be pleased at your loyalty—and eager ambition. We are looking for those who in days to come will lead this fellowship in our places. It is our hope that some among you will show themselves suited to do so. Others here, I fear, will reveal just as surely that they are not."

Sarhthor fell silent. The men around the table knew his

slim, graceful form would remain as still and as patient as stone until he wished to move a finger or change his expression. Right now, as the silence stretched, his calm, keen-eyed face was—as usual—expressionless. It might have been carved from the same gray stone as the pillar behind his seat.

Sarhthor's dark eyes, however, glittered with cruel amusement, a look familiar to many seated there. They were the most ambitious and daring of the apprentice magelings of the Zhentarim, and had all been trained or inspected by this man.

Many long, tense breaths were drawn as quietly as possible in the dimly lit cold as the wizards sat and waited, trying not to show their fear, their personal hatreds of each other—and their mounting impatience.

At length, one of the seated men spoke. "Teacher Sarhthor, we have come to hear High Lord Manshoon's will of us, and to serve. May we know his plans?"

Sarhthor smiled. "But of course, Fimril. Lord Manshoon will tell you what you are so eager to hear." He added a little smile, and then let it slide slowly and coldly into calm inscrutability. In the mounting silence, the men around the table regarded his face for a long time, trying to match the calm, unreadable expression Sarhthor wore. Some came close to succeeding.

Someone coughed, and heads turned, glaring. The heavy silence returned and slowly grew old. Sarhthor sat at the end of the table as though he was the tomb statue of some dead king and watched them all with cold patience.

Finally one of the magelings stirred in his seat. He was a handsome, fine-featured man whose upswept beard was scented and adorned with small, highly polished moonstone teardrops. They glistened here and there among his beard's curled hairs as he spoke. "I am patient, Teacher— but also curious. Where is the high lord?"

"Why, here, as it happens," said a new voice, full and rich and only gently menacing. Heads turned all down the table.

At the far end of the table from Sarhthor sat a regal, dusky man robed in black and dark blue. A moment before, there had been no man and no chair in that spot. The High Lord of Zhentil Keep smiled at all the turning heads. Before him on the table sat a serving platter covered with a silver dome, steam rising gently from around its edges.

"I've only now escaped from the pressing business of governing this great city"—the voice dipped only slightly in silken irony—"to meet with you all. Well met. I trust the patience taught by Sarhthor and wise others among us has kept you all occupied, and I beg you to excuse my not offering you any of my evenfeast. I am"—his voice dipped in soft menace—"*hungry* this night."

Then the Lord Manshoon flashed his teeth at them all in a smile that shone very white, and he uncovered the platter before him. Wisps of richly scented steam rose from the deep red ring of firewine sauce. It lay in a channel in the platter, surrounding the lord's evening meal: a dark, slithering heap of live, glistening black eels from the Moonsea, lying on a bed of spiced rice. A slim, jewel-topped silver skewer appeared in the lord's hand from the empty air before him. Smoothly, he stabbed the first coiling, twisting eel, and dipped it delicately in the hot sauce.

"Despite my apparent ease," Manshoon said, waving his laden skewer as he looked down the table, "our Brotherhood—nay, the world entire—remains in peril. You have all heard of the recent commotion among our fellows of the Black Altar, and of the matter of spellfire."

He paused for a moment. The silence of the listening Zhentarim wizards had changed subtly, and Manshoon knew he had their keen interest now. He smelled the sharp edge of their fear as they faced him and tried to look unmoved and peerless and dangerous. He almost chuckled.

"That matter remains unresolved. A young lady by the name of Shandril walks Faerûn somewhere south and west of us, guarded only by a dwarf and her mate—a knave by the name of Narm, who is weaker in Art than the least among you has been in some years. This Shandril alone commands spellfire, imperfectly as yet. She seeks training from Harpers and can expect some Harper aid along her way."

The quality of the listeners' silence changed again at the mention of the Harpers. Manshoon smiled and, with slow bites, emptied his cooling skewer.

"Sarhthor will tell those of you who are professionally interested all about the known strengths and subtleties of spellfire. Such professional interest will be exhibited only by those who have volunteered for the dangerous but fairly simple task of seizing or destroying this Shandril, and bringing what remains of her in either case here to this hall.

"You all know that something wild and uncontrolled has crept into the Art of late. This chaos may or may not be linked with spellfire—but it prevents us from surrounding the maid and overwhelming her with spells. We can, however, take her deep in the wilderlands, where we can act unobserved, and the unintended effects of such a confrontation can be curbed without much loss or concern.

"All knowledge of her powers and anything you learn or take from her will be placed entirely at the disposal of the Brotherhood. Hold nothing back. Those who fail to exhibit such probity will earn an immediate and permanent reward. Those who merely fail against the girl Shandril will have as many chances as they feel they need to impress us. We *will* be watching. As always." His eyes smiled merrily at them as he devoured the head of an eel, touched the bowl casually, and vanished with it in a flickering instant.

The end of the table was utterly empty again. Only faint wisps of spiced steam remained behind, curling in slow silence.

The magelings stirred, shoulders visibly relaxing here and there down the table. Heads turned, throats were cleared—but these stirrings came to a hushed halt an instant later as Sarhthor's purring voice came again from the near-darkness at the other end of the table.

"So who here volunteers to seize or destroy spellfire for us? Yield me your names, or"—he smiled faintly—"recall urgent business elsewhere and take your leave of this place . . . and also, I fear, of the Lord Manshoon's favor." He looked around, meeting the wary eyes of several wizards too brave or foolish to look away. "Your patience we have seen this night. We have also taught you to be decisive; show me the result of that teaching now."

In the clamor that followed, a smile slowly appeared and crawled across Sarhthor's face like an old and very lazy snake. But as each man there volunteered, Sarhthor's eyes met theirs briefly and bleakly, like a sudden, icy lance-thrust in a night ambush. In his dark gaze, the magelings saw that he expected them to die in this task. Sarhthor felt he owed them at least that honesty.

* * * * *

"What's wrong with you, then?" Delg asked, drawing himself up as much as his four battered feet of height allowed. The dwarf stood over Shandril, beard bristling as he squinted down at her. A pan of fried onions, mushrooms, and sausages sizzled in his hand. "Or don't you like an honest panfry?"

Shandril smiled wanly up at him from the bed of cloaks and furs she'd shared with Narm, and she raised a warding hand.

"I—I'm seldom hungry these mornings." Her slim face was as white as the snowcaps of the Thunder Peaks behind her. She shuddered and looked away from Delg's steaming pan, wondering if she'd ever arrive at far-off Silverymoon. To reach it, they still had to cross half of Faerûn. The ruined village of Thundarlun was only a day behind them, and even draining the fallen war wizard's wand had not fully restored the spellfire that smoldered within her.

On the other hand, twenty more Zhentilar would ride and slay no more; she'd left them twisted bones clad in ashes. Shandril shivered as she heard the screams again. Then Delg brought the pan so close to her nose that its sizzle jolted her back to the chilly morning. She pulled away from the smell, biting her lip to keep from gagging. She clutched the furs closer around herself.

"Well, why?" the dwarf demanded, frowning fiercely. "Are you ill?"

"No," Narm said gently from behind him, "she's with child."

The dwarf almost fell as he lurched and tottered about speedily to face the young mage. "She's *what?*" he demanded. "Did *you* have anything to do with this?"

Shandril giggled. "We *are* married, Delg," she added sweetly.

"Aye. But—but—what of the babe, with you hurling spellfire about, an' all?"

"I—" Shandril began, then fell silent, spreading her hands in a gesture of helplessness. The dwarf saw something almost desperate in her eyes, and he whirled about again to face Narm. The young wizard also spread his hands anxiously but said nothing. Then he shrugged.

"You *don't know*," said the dwarf heavily. "You truly don't know what you'll give birth to after all this hurling fire and collapsing and hurling fire again. . . ." Delg let his words trail away as he looked at them both challengingly, but the two young humans were silent.

The dwarf sighed heavily and tossed up his arms in resignation. Mushrooms and sausages left the pan to soar into the air, still steaming.

Narm leapt forward but missed catching one. Most of the others landed on Delg's head or back in the pan. The dwarf stood a moment more, looking down at Shandril and shaking his head. Sausages shifted in his tousled hair. "Ah, well," he said, rather sadly. "Ah, well . . ."

Narm brushed off the sausage he had picked up. "Delg Hammerhand," he asked softly between bites, "have you been so lucky—sorry, favored of Clanggedin—as to have gone your entire life through always knowing exactly what you're doing and what the right thing to do is and what everything means and the consequences of all?"

Delg glared at him, beard bristling. "D'you mock me, lad? Of course not!"

"Well, then," Narm said mildly, "you will understand how we feel, doing our best with what the gods have given us, beset by foes and wandering lost in the wilderness, far from aid and wise advice. Uh, save yours."

Shandril laughed helplessly. Delg turned back to look at her, sighed theatrically, rolled his eyes for good measure, and said, "Right. I stand corrected. Thy panfry awaits, great lord." He bowed to Narm, waving with the pan at a nearby rock. "If you'll be seated, herewith we two can sate our hunger and discuss how best to feed your lady without having her spewing it all back at us."

* * * * *

The morning sun shone down bright and clear through the trees of Shadowdale, leaf-shadows dappling the rocks on the rising flanks of Harpers' Hill. Storm's blade flashed back its brightness as she slid the steel edge along the whetting stone. The Bard of Shadowdale sat thoughtfully under a tree, putting a better edge on her old and battered long sword. She kept silent, for that was the way Elminster seemed to want it, this morn.

The Old Mage stood looking east, whence a cool breeze was rising. His eyes flashed as blue as the sky as he raised the plain wooden staff he bore, and the staff seemed to glow for a moment in answer. The wind rose, and the wizard's long white beard and mane stirred with the rustle and dance of the leaves all around. Elminster was muttering things under his breath, using his old and deep voice, and Storm knew that her sister, on her throne in far-off Aglarond, heard them and was whispering words back. None other was meant to hear them. Storm took care that she did not, for that was the way she was.

Elminster stopped speaking and smiled. The wind died away again, and birds rose from the trees around, twittering. The Old Mage stared eastward, unmoving. Storm watched him, frowning a little. She knew him well enough to see the sadness hidden behind his eyes. The Old Mage stood silent and motionless for long minutes.

When Storm began to grow stiff and the edge on her sword threatened to become brittle and over-sharp, she slid her shining blade softly into its sheath and went to him.

Elminster turned to her thoughtfully. "I thought," he said slowly, his eyes very blue, "I'd put such love behind me, long ago. *Why* do I keep finding it again? It makes the times apart from her"—he turned away to stare into the green shadows under the trees—"lonely indeed."

Storm put a hand on his arm. "I know. It's a long walk

back from Harpers' Hill. That's why I came."

In silence one old, long-fingered hand closed over hers and squeezed his thanks, and together they went down the twisting trail through the trees.

* * * * *

"Ready? We'd best be off, then. Even with spellfire to fell our foes, it's a long way to Silverymoon, an' we're not out of the Zhents' reach yet." As he spoke, Delg hoisted a pack that bulged with food, pots, and pans onto his shoulders.

Shandril put on her own pack, but said softly as she came up beside the dwarf. "No . . . we haven't any spellfire to fell our foes. I'm not going to use it again."

Delg's head jerked around to look up at her, but it was Narm who spoke, astonished. "Shan? Are you—crazed? What—*why?*"

His lady's eyes were moist when she looked up at him, but her voice was flat with determination.

"I'm not going to go through my life killing people. Even Zhents and others who wish me ill. It's . . . not right. What would the Realms be like if Elminster walked around just blasting anyone he chose to?"

"Very much as it is now for you—if everyone he met tried to kill or capture him," Narm said with sudden heat. "Folk have more sense than to attack the mightiest archmage in all the Heartlands."

"But not enough to leave alone one maid who happens to have spellfire—'the gift of the gods.'" Shandril's tone made a cruel mockery of that quotation. She looked away into the distance. "I . . . hate—all this. Having folk hate me . . . fear me . . . and always feeling the fire surging inside. . . ."

"You're not the first maid who's been afraid of things, you know," Delg said.

Shandril's head snapped up. "Afraid?"

"Aye, afraid," the dwarf said softly. "You're afraid of what you wield. Afraid of how good it feels to use it, I should say . . . and of what you might do with it—and become in the doing."

"No!" Shandril said, shaking her head violently. "That's not it at all!" She raised blazing eyes to glare into his own. "How can *you* know what I feel?"

The dwarf shrugged. "I've seen your face when you're hurling spellfire. One look is enough."

Shandril stared at him for a moment, open-mouthed, and then buried her face in her hands. The small, twisted sound of a despairing sob escaped between her fingers, and they saw her shoulders shake.

Then Narm's arms were around her. "Shan, love," he said soothingly, trying to calm her. "Shan—easy, now. Easy. We . . . both love you. Delg's telling truth, as he sees it . . . and truth's never an easy thing to hear. Shan?"

His lady said nothing, but her sobs had died away, and Narm knew she was listening. He kissed the top of her head, stroked her shoulders soothingly, and said, "I know how you feel. We both do . . . and we . . . know well how hard it is for you to use spellfire. But our lives depend on it. We'll both die if you refuse to wield it—or hang back from using it until too late. Our foes won't wait for you to wrestle with any decisions." He stroked the hair back from her temples, and then added quietly, "And I'd hate to die because you chose a Zhentarim over me."

Shandril stiffened in his embrace. Narm caught Delg's eyes, saw the dwarf's expressionless nod of approval, and went on firmly, "That's what you'll be doing, you see, if you don't use spellfire as fast as Delg draws his axe or I work a spell—you'll be choosing the life of a Zhent wizard over ours." He smoothed her hair, and added softly, "And then you'll be alone before you die."

"Which won't be long after, if I know Zhents," the dwarf grunted. He lumbered forward and dealt Shandril's rear a gentle blow. "Come on, lovejays. You can cry while you walk, lass: we haven't time for you to stand here and find all the wrinkles in your soul. Zhents are after us—and the gods alone know who else—so we must be on our way. Unless, of course, you're really fond of this particular spot . . . as the site of your grave."

Shandril raised stony eyes to glare at him, tears glistening on her cheeks. Delg nodded approvingly. "That's right, lass—hate me, just so long as you do it while you're moving. *On!*"

"My spells and my love are yours," Narm said quietly. "Use them as you will . . . all I ask is that you use spellfire when we need it."

Unspeaking, Shandril looked at him and nodded. Narm smiled. His lady reached out, took hold of his chin, pulled it close, and kissed him firmly. Then she sighed, turned, and set off in the direction Delg had been heading. The man and the dwarf exchanged silent glances, then followed.

* * * * *

Elminster was still melancholy when he reached his tower. A handful of days ago he'd watched Shandril Shessair and her half-trained lad Narm set out from the dale, heading for Silverymoon in the North . . . and, the Old Mage feared, for their deaths. Even with all the Knights of Myth Drannor misdirecting agents of the Cult, the Brotherhood, Thay, and the gods alone knew who else— Narm and Shandril were probably doomed.

Aye, doomed. Elminster of Shadowdale might have commanded the experience great age brings, as well as magics powerful enough to tear apart castle keeps and dragons alike—but such things did not give him any right to tell young folk what to do or to shape their lives for them. Even though the girl commanded spellfire with power enough to rival Elminster, he could not directly intercede. Perhaps his hands were tied *especially* because she held such power.

The choice had been their own, the trail theirs to take, the consequences their tutors . . . and the chances of their making it alive to Silverymoon slim. Very slim . . . even if a certain Old Mage raised a hand to aid them from time to time. Aid them, but not dictate their fate. That would hurt, too, when in the end he heard whatever doom had claimed them.

This sort of dilemma had come up too many times over too many years. It grew no easier to take. Not for the first time, Elminster felt the weight of Mystra's burden and wished he could just grow old as other folk did, laying aside all cares as he sank into gray, endless twilight. Or perhaps he could call out one of his mightiest foes and go down fighting, hurling spells linked to spells and sealed with his own life energy in one last magnificent spell-battle that would reshape the Realms anew; it would give folk such as Shandril a new morning to walk into, fearless and happy, a new world before them.

Maudlin fool. The death such a spellstorm would cause! Entire realms shattered—folk and trees alike twisted for years to come . . . no. Get out and have a pipe and think more useful thoughts.

As always, Elminster's feet led him to the rocks beside his pool. Their familiar ledges, smoothed by his backside over many hours of sitting, were solid and reassuring beneath him as he looked out across the still waters and made smoke.

Blue-green and thick, it coiled up out of his pipe, sparks swirling in its heart as they sought the sun high above.

Elminster watched them leap and spiral; his eyes saw
Shandril hurling spellfire instead, and he wondered how
far she'd gotten by now, and if worse foes than bumbling
Zhentilar had found her.

Two stones at his feet clicked together, a tiny enchantment that told him someone was coming up the path to
his tower. Elminster did not turn to look—not even when
they clicked again to tell him his visitor had turned down
the short run of flagstones that led to the pool. He merely
let the pipe float out of his mouth, and said calmly, "Fair
morning."

"Oh. Ah, aye. That it is." The voice was high and uncertain. Elminster looked into eyes that were very blue; they
belonged to a young boy he'd never seen before, a lad in a
nondescript tunic and gray hose. He came hopping down
to the edge of the pool and kicked at a half-submerged
stone at the water's edge. He looked back over his shoulder at the Old Mage, and asked, "You're Elminster, aren't
you?"

The Old Mage regarded him thoughtfully. "I generally
answer to that name, aye."

The boy grinned at him with the impish confidence of
youth; an older person would never have dared utter the
next question Elminster heard. "So why're you just sitting
here, an' not making blue dragons turn cartwheels, or the
sky go black, or—or—you know?"

"I'm thinking," the Old Mage said simply. There was a
silence, but the lad waited patiently for him to say more.
Surprising, for one so young. After a breath or two Elminster added, "It's a harder thing to do than hurling dragons
around or bringing down night during the day."

"It is? So what're you thinking about?"

Elminster looked warily into those guileless eyes. They
stared back at him with no hint of unsavory motive—
clear, direct, and innocent; deep, brown, and steady.

Elminster watched a golden light growing in them, smiled inwardly and, without a word or gesture to betray his intent, called into being four balls of writhing fire.

Trailing sparks, the spheres of flame roared away from him, smashed into the boy, and hurled him far out over the pool. There was a ground-shaking blast as the morning exploded into bright flame. The noise was followed by a mighty splash.

The pipe glided to the Old Mage's lips again. He smoked, sober eyes fixed on the roiling waters of the pool, waiting.

He did not wait long. Something smoldering and tentacled rose up out of the pool. The plumes of smoke rising from it thickened as it broke clear of the waters. It no longer looked anything like a human boy. Its mottled, bubbled skin seemed to flow and shift as Elminster watched it grow two limbs that became humanlike arms, the ends parting and melting into fingers. As the coalescing hands waved, butter-colored eyes swam into view in the thicker bulk below, fixing him with a hard stare. The skin parted in a gash that shaped itself into a mouth, that—

The spell the Old Mage hurled this time tore the very water out of the pool. Fish, startled turtles, and slimy plants flapped and spun in the air—and in their midst, bright blue flames raced over the tentacled form as it rose into the sky, screaming and twisting frantically. It struggled, arched a spine it hadn't possessed a moment earlier—and then fell limp, a-dangle in midair.

Elminster's eyes were hard as he watched the tentacled mass drift toward him, held fast by his spell. Beyond its smoldering bulk there was a terrific crash as all the water fell back into the pool. Startled birds called, and then flapped hastily away from the trees around.

Elminster frowned. His pipe had gone out.

He guided the dead, tentacled thing to the grass at his feet. It landed with a wet plop, still enshrouded by flickering blue radiance.

The Old Mage snapped his fingers, and a long black staff inset with runes of silver appeared in his hands. He pointed one end of it at the ganglious bulk and waited, eyes never leaving the monstrous form. He raised his chin and said clearly to the empty air before him, "Torm. Rathan. Come to me, by the pool. I have need of ye."

He peered around warily, sniffing the air. Such otherworldly foes seldom hunted alone.

It seemed a very long time before he heard thudding feet and the warning clicking of the stones near at hand. The two summoned knights skidded to a stop when they saw the dead thing. They were breathing heavily in their haste, and they held weapons ready.

The slimmer, younger knight in the lead was Torm—a black-haired, green-eyed charmer with a fine mustache. Torm's shoulder was currently being used as a support by the stout and puffing cleric Rathan, whose brown hair and stubbly mustache were disheveled from the run, and whose strong features had gone quite red.

Torm looked down at the dead monster, then back up at Elminster, and he raised an impudent eyebrow. "Been fishing, have we?"

"This is a shapeshifter," Elminster replied calmly, "of a very powerful family who call themselves the Malaugrym. The glow denotes a spell of mine that holds it powerless to work magic."

Before Elminster could stop him, the thief Torm kicked one still-smoking tentacle. There was no response. Torm shrugged and said, "Looks dead to me."

"And that will stop it from using Art?" The Old Mage's voice was sarcastic. "My thanks for thy assurance; as one so learned in magic, thy judgment cannot help but be correct."

Torm shrugged. "Your blade hits home, Old Mage; I stand corrected."

Elminster held out the staff, keeping its end pointed at the fallen Malaugrym. "Take over my binding, Rathan. I must work a spell to seek out any kin of this one who may lurk near."

The stout priest took the staff, and Elminster turned away, making complicated gestures and murmuring many odd-sounding words that the two knights could only half hear. Then the archmage paused, raised his hands, and turned slowly around. He nodded with a satisfied air.

Torm raised an eyebrow. Elminster saw it, and explained, "There was another Malaugrym present—the sister of this one. My Art has entrapped her; she cannot use any spells while she remains in Faerûn."

Torm glanced at the trees and meadows around them. "She fled?"

"For now; she'll return to take revenge on me. Spells I may have denied her, but she can still shift her shape."

"Revenge for this?" Rathan asked, nodding his chin at the dead bulk of the tentacled thing.

"Aye, but there's an older score," the Old Mage said. "I slew their father, long ago. I wonder why they dared to come here, after all the years between." Then he stiffened. "She's after Shandril," he snapped. "Of course."

"Well, slay her, then. With your own spell laid on her, tracing her should be easy enough," Torm said. He looked around at the grass, trees, and muddy waters of the pool—and then, reluctantly, his gaze fell again to the dead monster at Elminster's feet.

Elminster shook his head. "I can only trace her when she takes her own form."

"That?" Torm asked, gesturing toward the rank heap on the ground.

Elminster nodded. "When she takes the shape of a creature of Faerûn, she's hidden from me. Without magic, and given all those already hunting Shandril, her own hunt will cost her some time and care—and during it, she'll spend most of her time as a human, of course." He looked at the two knights, and the ghost of a smile crossed his face. "That's where the two of ye are called again to glory."

Two sighs answered him. "Why is it always us?" Torm asked the rock beside him. Wisely, it chose not to answer.

* * * * *

As the light of Elminster's last spell faded in the spell chamber high in the Twisted Tower, Rathan sniffed at a burnt smell that seemed to cling to him. The gaze that he turned on Elminster was rather sour. "What have ye done to us *this* time, Old Mage?"

"Cast a fog of forgetfulness on ye; it'll make folk forget they've seen ye. It will also slightly alter thy looks from time to time, while it lasts."

Torm sighed. "Will I look human most of the time? Male? As handsome as usual?"

"As usual," Elminster agreed in dry tones. "I can't trace the Malaugrym herself, but I *can* find Shandril. I'll send ye to her—but mind ye keep back from the lass; if ye stand guard with her, she'll relax, and ye'll have no hope against the Malaugrym. Thy only hope of besting this menace in battle is to strike when she's already battling spellfire and those who stand with Shandril to defend her."

"This Malaugrym is that powerful, eh?" Rathan asked quietly, out of habit touching the silver pendant of his goddess. Tymora was said to grant luck to her faithful when it was truly needed—and Elminster was nodding his head rather grimly.

"Her name is Magusta, and she's one of a powerful clan who walk many worlds, shifting their forms to whatever best aids them in seizing all the power they can. We are very old enemies, they and I."

"If these folk are so old and powerful, how is it that we've heard nothing of them before?" Torm demanded, eyes narrowed in suspicion. "Are you sure this isn't another of your little plots?"

Rathan turned his head patiently to look at his longtime friend. "Would ye like me to tell ye what an idiot ye are, or shall I save the breath?"

At the same time, Elminster said with a dry smile, "Of *course* this is one of my little plots." He snorted. "Thy mastery of diplomacy forbids me from involving ye in any of my big ones."

Where she sat in the dimness against one wall of the chamber, Storm Silverhand smiled and spoke up for the first time. "It is another 'little plot,' to be sure—but these Malaugrym are old indeed, Torm. Most folk in the Heartlands, if they've heard of them at all, know them as 'the Shadowmasters.' Individually, their mastery of magic is about as powerful as that of an experienced mage. They are ruled by venom and pride, and practice at magic—or anything else—is foreign to their nature." She stretched, and added soberly, "It may be your only advantage against them."

Rathan had nodded in recognition at the name 'Shadowmaster.' Now he rumbled, "We two are poor weapons indeed to use against such a foe. I know that Those Who Harp are even busier than the Knights of Myth Drannor . . . but will we have no aid from thee?"

Storm spread her hands. "The Malaugrym—for there may be others in Faerûn, mind—know us, whatever guise we take; someone not known to them will fare better, seeking to strike at them unexpectedly."

Elminster nodded. "Look into the eyes of any creature ye meet, from squirrel to horse, and every man. If ye see a golden light there—or the blue glow of my spell—ye're facing a Malaugrym. Strike then to slay, speedily, and stop not until all has been burned away." He waved his hands, and an oval of flickering blue light appeared in the air before the two knights—a magical gate that would transport them to the region where Shandril Shessair toiled on.

Torm sighed. "You make it sound simple enough . . . but simple orders have found their ways onto tombstone carvings often enough before. What if it happens that we really need you—will you come?"

"Soon enough to save thy life, if ye are beset?" Elminster's eyes were sad. "Ye're old enough to know that no answer I give ye will serve as a sure shield. Death watches always, waiting, and has a swifter hand than I."

The slim, handsome thief waved a hand with a theatrical flourish. "Granting all that—are we on our own in this?"

Elminster looked up at the ceiling of the spell chamber, where an old enchantment made the stars wink and glitter as they drifted across an illusory night sky. "The gods above know I am a busy man," he told the stars innocently, pretending not to hear the resulting snorts of the knights, "and am beset at present with matters even weightier than spellfire—but I should not be overmuch surprised if I find myself sparing time for a charge over the hill or two, when my business takes me that way. What say ye, Storm?"

The bard inclined her head and patted the hilt of the well-used long sword scabbarded at her hip. "I, too, will do what I can—and there are my fellow Harpers along the way. One of them does nothing but wait for Shandril and Narm. To say nothing of Delg the dwarf; I'll be surprised if he has not caught up to them already. We will all of us do what we can."

As the knights nodded and started toward the gate, checking their weapons, Elminster added quietly to Rathan, "Ye might pray to Tymora that our efforts will be enough."

Torm rolled his eyes. "Don't tell me," he said, putting the back of his hand to his brow in a mock swoon. "The future of all Toril hangs in the balance. Again."

Elminster raised one of his own eyebrows in a parody of the thief's own manner. "Of course."

Two

MUCH TALK, AND EVEN SOME DECISIONS

*Try as we may, none of us can be in all places at all times.
Not even the gods can do that. So we do what we can and
measure our success, if we are wise, by what our hearts tell
us at the end of a day, and not what our eyes tell us of how
much we have changed Faerûn.*

Storm Silverhand
To Harp at Twilight
Year of the Swollen Stars

 Their last glimpse of Thunder Gap,
far behind, was blocked by dark, sinis-
ter winged shapes in the sky. Narm
watched them flapping out of the mountains, found his mouth suddenly dry,
and swallowed with some difficulty.

"Delg," he managed to croak. The
dwarf did not even turn to see where he was pointing.

"I've been ignoring them," Delg told him sourly. "It's
easiest."

"Ignoring them? That's *all?*" Shandril asked incredu-
lously, looking back at the dark, hunting shapes as they
grew ever larger, ever closer.

"You've a bright scheme of some sort, lass?" The dwarf's tone was sharp as he hastened on, an errant skillet banging on metal somewhere inside his pack.

"Well, we've *got* to hide," Shandril said hotly. "I haven't spellfire enough to—"

"That's why I've been saving my breath and not stopping to look back," the dwarf said in dry tones. "It brings the trees closer, as fast as I can make them move. . . . See the little dip ahead there? It's a ravine: the branches'll be thick, and there'll be a stream to hide our own noises— arguing with wise dwarves, for instance. . . ."

Narm and Shandril exchanged glances, then hurried after the dwarf toward the ravine he'd indicated. Only after they had reached cover did any of them speak again.

"What are they?" Narm's voice was low. He'd never seen such ugly things before—huge, fat, scaled things with bat wings, claws, and horselike heads that ended in two probing, twisting snouts. Each snout held sharp jaws; even down here Narm could smell the rotting reek of their breath.

"Foulwings," Delg said. "Well named, aye?"

Narm watched the heavy, ungainly things flap over them, wheel, and dart this way and that, searching along the road and the edges of the forest for signs of a maid, her man, and a dwarf. He shivered as a foulwing turned overhead, and the head of the robed and hooded rider pivoted, scanning the forest. For a moment it seemed that the foulwing rider looked right at him. Fear rose in Narm. Frantically he searched his mind for some spell that wouldn't reveal their location to the foes above.

And then the foulwing wheeled in the air, belching and snorting angrily as its rider struck it cruelly with a metal goad. In the man's other hand, a wand glinted for a moment before he flew onward, out of sight. His companions, some ten or twelve others, followed afterward.

"Who rides foulwings?" he asked, trying to sound calm.

"Evil folk," Delg said brightly. When Narm looked at him in disgust, the dwarf added a savage grin. Narm folded his arms and waited for further explanation.

Delg rumbled, "If you must know, lad: the Zhents; the Cult of the Dragon; I've heard the Red Wizards of Thay do, too; I saw the private army of a lich riding 'em once, in the Vilhon—and the tavern-talk in Suzail, when last I was there, had some lord or other of Westgate using them, in league with a pirate. For all I know, half the rich merchants in Sembia keep 'em as pets."

"If they're as common as all that, why've I never heard of them before?" Narm protested.

Delg rolled his eyes. "D'you know how many folk I've heard say that down the years, lad? Most of 'em had been adventuring longer than you have, too—and the things they hadn't met with before killed 'em just as dead as if they'd been old friends. Had you seen or heard of spellfire before you met with your lady? D'you think I could stand in the midst of it, protesting I'd never heard of it before, and thereby escape being burned?"

Narm opened his mouth to reply, but another voice spoke first: Shandril could move very quietly when she wanted to. They'd left her lying silent and still under spread cloaks in the ravine—but neither Narm or Delg was surprised to find her beside them on their perch on a low, gnarled bough of an old phandar tree. Her eyes smoldered a little as she asked softly, "Could these foulwing riders be the darker, greater foes Elminster warned us about back in Shadowdale, do you think?"

Narm spread his hands. "He never said enough about 'Those Who Watch' to tell us how to recognize them."

Delg shrugged, and added, "I'd rather not call those bat-horses down to ask." He squinted up at them and asked, "Does it matter? Whoever they are, they're bold enough to fly openly into Cormyr in broad daylight. Just one of those foulwings could tear all of us apart if it catches Shan by surprise, with no spellfire ready. It's the forest for us, from now on."

And so it was that the only known wielder of spellfire and her companions turned off the road into the vast and deep Hullack Forest. They rested after several hours of struggling through thick stands of duskwood. While they sat, Shandril managed to eat some cheese, preceded by some rather old milk, and followed by some rather wine-strong broth. Delg insisted on doing all the cooking. "I'd probably *starve* if I left the food to you or your husband there" was the gentle way he put it when she'd protested. Shandril was just as glad not to handle their provisions—too much had been salvaged from the ruin of Thundarlun, bringing memories of its slaughter back into her mind. She was growing tired of the killing—and of seeing fear in the eyes of folk she was fighting for, or alongside, when they looked at her.

None of the three wore smiles this day. None had been eager to enter the dark, tangled forest. It stretched on for miles, sprawling over most of eastern Cormyr, a wild and forbidding place. Foresters and hunters seldom ventured far into its dim depths. Long before night stole up to cast its cloak over Cormyr, the three had come to the end of the last, fading forest trail—and plunged on into the track-less, shady depths of the heart of Hullack Forest.

"We can't see far enough or move fast enough for my liking," Delg said, axe in hand. He glared at the trees all around them in the gathering gloom. "I'm beginning to hold the opinion that we'd have done better to have stayed on the road and faced whatever your enemies had left to hurl at us."

"*I'm* beginning to hold the opinion," Narm replied in a

low voice, "that your words are wiser now than when you led us off the road."

"Belt up, lad!" Delg put little anger behind his words; he peered tensely around them as if expecting an immediate attack.

"Wherever wisdom lies," Shandril said softly, "we can't find our way back now. We must go on. Night comes swiftly—we daren't travel blindly about in it, for I've heard of boars and worse hunted here. We must find a place to rest, before dark."

"Aye. A safe place," Delg grunted. "A place one of us can defend while the others sleep. A place with rock at our backs is best."

"Assuredly," Narm agreed. "I'm sure I've several such places just lying about here, somewhere . . . now where did I leave them, I wonder? Cou—"

"You," Shandril told him severely, "have been listening to the nimble tongue of Torm too much of late. Let's hurry, ere the light fails entirely: we must seek high ground and hope we find a cliff, or perhaps a cave."

"One *without* a bear," Delg added, hastening on in the gathering darkness. They could hear him puffing as they hurried on over leaves and tangles of fallen, mossy logs. More than once he slipped or stumbled and broke branches underfoot with dull cracking sounds. "I never liked forests," he added gloomily on the heels of a particularly hard fall.

Shandril and Narm both chuckled. They were climbing a tree-clad slope toward a place of slightly greater brightness in the deepening twilight; a glade, perhaps, or rocky height where trees grew more thinly. The forest around them was coming alive with mysterious rustlings and eerie, far-off hoots and baying calls. The three hurried onward and upward over tumbled stones, racing to find a refuge before nightfall caught up with them.

The trees thinned, and then the weary travelers came to an open space. Looking up, Narm saw stars winking overhead in the gathering night. A huge shadowtop tree had toppled here, perhaps a season ago, its vast trunk smashing aside smaller saplings to clear a little space in the thick, tangled forest. The three wanderers looked around for a moment, met each other's eyes, and nodded in unison. This place would have to do.

Delg caught Narm's elbow. "Gather firewood," he said. "You and me. One each side of her, while Shan unpacks. Don't make noise you don't have to."

"A fire?" Narm said. "Won't that draw anyone who's searching—"

"They've *magic,* lad," Delg told him dryly. "They could find us if we stuffed leaves in our hair and stood like trees 'til morning. The big beasts, too—an' the smaller ones'll come to look, but not dare approach too near. We may as well have some comfort."

* * * * *

"Dear, dear," Gathlarue said, not very far away, as she looked into her softly glowing crystal, where three tiny shapes moved and spoke. Her slim lips crooked in a little smile. "I was *so* looking forward to seeing you stuff leaves into your mouth, Sir Dwarf. Now I'll have to stare at your fire—and looking into dancing flames always makes me sleepy."

"Wine, Lady?" Gathlarue's older apprentice stood over her, a dark shape against the trees that rose all around them. The slim, raven-haired girl held a silver-harnessed crystal decanter in her hands.

Gathlarue looked up at her, smiled, and took the goblet she offered. "My thanks, precious one. You know my needs so well."

Mairara twisted her mouth in a wordless, affectionate reply, bent to kiss her, and glided softly away. Gathlarue grinned faintly into her scrying globe; the blood-spell she had woven long ago let her listen to the thoughts of both her apprentices whenever she chose, unbeknownst to them. For all her kisses and kindnesses, Mairara meant to work her a painful death one day soon.

Before that day came, Gathlarue meant to use her well. To rise in the ranks of the Zhentarim would take more magic than Gathlarue could wield alone. A few days back, while in Zhentil Keep, she'd seen afresh all the cruel striving that would oppose her. The magelings had been gathered to hear Manshoon, and so much cruelty and aroused magic had hung barely in check in that room that the smell of it had almost made her afraid.

Almost. She'd have to be careful, as always; the other mages could bend their wills entirely to hurling destruction, but she always had to spare some Art when in their midst for cloaking herself in male guise. Her Zhentilar warriors respected her, but no women, it seemed, rose high in the robed ranks of the Zhentarim.

That could well change—soon. She had a spell that might handle even Lord Manshoon. More than that, she had one that might just foil spellfire. Gathlarue's smile deepened as she recalled finding the spell: she had discovered a place high atop a leaning, roofless tower in ruined Myth Drannor where a certain word and touch of a certain stone brought a portal into being in midair. The oval, shimmering door had led into some ancient wizard's long-abandoned hideaway. It was a cozy room tucked away in nothingness—a room whose walls were covered with shelves groaning under the weight of spellbooks. More spells than she'd ever have time to learn. Yet she'd taken away enough, if the gods smiled on her, to rule any corner of Faerûn she chose. Not that anyone but her knew that, yet.

Gathlarue had learned patience down the years, and now it was an old, comfortable friend. She nodded, sipping the wine, and looked out into the gathering darkness of the forest depths. Her amulet made the drink safe, whatever drugs or poisons Mairara or others might have added to it. She bent her concentration again to the stone.

Ah—the three had their fire lit and their cooking begun. They'd relax soon and talk. She'd listen and learn, not rush in to find death from the maid's spellfire. Even the great Shadowsil had perished in Shandril's flames—and Manshoon himself had been forced to flee. No, she'd watch and wait, to strike when the chance shone brightest. As she always had.

Gathlarue took another sip of the warmed, spiced wine, and stretched like a languid cat. From behind her, across their forest camp, came the faint but unmistakable sounds of Tespril entertaining one of the guards in the deepening night. Gathlarue made a face in that direction. Really—the quality of apprentices one was forced to settled for these days . . .

* * * * *

Delg had produced a rather strong-smelling bundle from the bottom of his pack, and at Shandril's wrinkled nose and raised eyebrow had said only, "Yes, it's Zhent stuff. From Thundarlun. Owner past needing it. Handy, carrying an axe—everyone should."

The meat, whatever it had been, made a flavorful stew. Delg tossed liberal handfuls of onions into the little blackened pot. The warm, sharp smell that followed made Shandril think of Gorstag's onion-heavy stews back at *The Rising Moon*, the inn where she'd grown up. Her eyes were suddenly wet with tears. She'd been happy there—how happy, she hadn't known until too late. Now all that was lost forever; she dared not go back for fear her foes would slaughter her friends and burn the old *Moon* to the ground. She bit her lip and turned into Narm's arms, burying her face against his chest just before the hot tears came.

"What's wrong, Shan—" Narm began anxiously as she sobbed and shook against him.

Delg stumped up to him, shook his head to stop Narm's words, and reached out one brawny arm to stroke Shandril's heaving back. His stubby fingers moved gently, lovingly, as his other arm took hold of Narm's wrist, and guided the young mage's hand firmly to Shandril's back. Narm obediently began soothing his lady, and the dwarf stepped back, nodding in satisfied silence.

Shandril cried, seeing again the clutching claws of the gargoyles in ruined Myth Drannor, the cruel, mocking smile of the Shadowsil who'd captured her, the chilling eyes of the dragon who'd lived beyond death, and the burning, roasted men she'd left behind her in Thundarlun. Why, oh why, couldn't she just go back to Shadowdale or Highmoon and live in peace among friends—and never see a Zhentarim wizard or Cult of the Dragon fanatic again? Gods hear and answer, she thought, if you have pity—*why?*

Delg let the fire die low as he stumped around the clearing, peering watchfully into the dimness of the woods around him. It would do the lass good to cry awhile—past time for it, for one so young. He stroked the familiar curves of his axe head as he went, remembering Shandril's anger in battle, her eyes turned to blazing flames as she dealt death to the Zhents. He shook his head to banish those sights from his mind. More power than was good for anyone, this one had—more power than most could carry, and stay good folk.

A little chill went through him as he stopped and looked into the night—and thought about how he might have to kill her, for the safety of all in the Realms. His superiors had been grimly insistent that he never lose sight of that.

It was not the first time he'd had this dark thought. Delg stroked his axe again. It *was* the first time his mind had envisioned his axe leaping down to cleave Shandril's head, her long hair swirling amid blazing spellfire . . . the dwarf shook his head angrily and stumped back toward the fire with unnecessary violence. Enough of such fell dreams! They're for folk too idle to pay full heed to what's around them right now. . . .

Shandril lifted bright eyes to him as he came up, and she managed a wavering smile. Delg nodded at her, and asked roughly, "More stew?"

Narm smiled, shaking his head slightly; Shandril did the same. The dwarf shrugged and sat down beside the fire, shifting the burning branches and adding a few more.

And then there was light where no light should be, touching his face on the side away from the fire. Delg spun, hand going to his axe. Narm and Shandril scrambled to their feet behind him.

In the air above the fallen shadowtop, a patch of light had appeared. It hung at about the height of a tall man's head, an area of spinning, silvery radiance that pulsed and sputtered. As they watched, it brightened and seemed somehow to *look* at them.

"Be not alarmed," came a faintly echoing voice from it. A man's voice, sounding somehow dignified and elderly, speaking from a long distance away.

A wizard, no doubt. Whatever the voice said, Delg *was* alarmed. Damn all magic, anyway! Honest folk couldn't—

"Hold, Shandril of Highmoon!" The voice had grown louder, and stern. "In the name of Azoun, I bid you make answer to me! I am Vangerdahast, Royal Wizard of Cormyr, and by this magic can only speak to you, not cast magic on you or do any harm to you and yours. Shandril, do you hear me?"

Three pairs of startled eyes met. Delg shrugged. Impulsively, Shandril leaned forward and said, "I am here, Lord Wizard." Her voice quavered; for some reason, she felt guilty and weak and in need of approval from this far-off wizard she'd never met. In Highmoon, she'd heard often of the mighty Vangerdahast—and by all accounts, he sounded less good-natured and forgiving than the far mightier Elminster she knew. The patch of radiance pulsed and grew brighter.

"That is good, Lady Shandril. I repeat: I mean you no ill, and this sending of mine can do you no harm." The light drifted nearer, and Narm's face darkened in suspicion. He raised his hands, ready to cast a spell, and stepped between Shandril and the wizard's glow, waving to Delg to keep watch on the woods around them. The dwarf gave him an approving, mirthless grin and did so.

"What would you, then?" Shandril's voice was steady now, her tears forgotten. It seemed they were under attack once more. Her fingertips tingled as excitement rose within her, and her spellfire awoke.

"I would know what you intend to do within the borders of Cormyr, and where you are bound. More: I must know what befell at Thundarlun, and your part in it." The light dwindled slightly, danced, and then strengthened again. "What say you?"

Shandril trembled in sudden suspicion. Just who was listening? Was this really the great Vangerdahast? And who might be listening from the dark woods all round them? She caught Delg's eyes; the dwarf had turned to look at her levelly, his face expressionless. Shandril took a deep breath and made her decision.

"I intend no harm to the folk and land of Cormyr, nor any challenge to the authority or property of the king," she said flatly. "I am fleeing enemies who would destroy me—among them, the warriors of Zhentil Keep, who followed me into your land through the Gap and caught up with me at Thundarlun. I can trust no one enough to tell where we are headed, but I assure you that I do not intend to settle or tarry in Cormyr. Let us pass in peace, I ask you."

"What happened at Thundarlun?" The voice was calm and level.

"Zhentilar troops, on horses, attacked us at Thunder Gap. We—escaped them, and got as far as the guard post at Thundarlun before they caught up with us. Their arrows killed all the soldiers and the war wizard there. They set fire to houses and threatened to burn all the village if I did not come out to them. So I did." Shandril paused for a moment, and then added simply, "When they were dead, we took what food and drink we needed from the guard post, and went on."

"You slew them all?"

"You know what I bear," Shandril said sharply, more cold anger in her tone than she really felt.

"I do," came the voice. "I do not question your words, but I must know if any Zhentilar still ride free in eastern Cormyr."

"All that I saw are dead," Shandril said wearily, "but again and again they find me with magic—as you have done. Zhents may listen to us even now; I feel they are near."

"How many did you kill? And how many soldiers of Cormyr did you see dead in Thundarlun?"

Shandril fought down sudden tears, struggling to speak.

Her voice, when it came, was a fierce whisper. "I don't count the dead any more, wizard. *I can't bear to!*"

"Have you heard *enough?*" Narm could no longer contain his anger; his shout echoed back at them from the nearest trees.

"Peace, lad!" Delg said gruffly, and tromped closer to the floating light. "As near as I can tell," he told it without introduction, "Shan burned about a score from their saddles at the Gap. That many and a dozen more at the hamlet where we fought. I saw near two dozen more Purple Dragons lying dead there. And I have a question for you, wizard: Is it Azoun's will that we pass freely through Cormyr, or are we going to have to fight every soldier and war wizard we meet? Tell us now—or that's just what we'll have to do, for the sake of our own hides."

The light shimmered. "I cannot speak for the king," it said, after some hesitation.

Delg bent closer. "He's there with you, though, listening, isn't he?"

A heavy, waiting silence hung in the glade after those words, and the light slowly grew brighter.

Then a new voice spoke from it, younger and more melodic—and yet somehow heavier with authority. "I am. I have heard of you, sir, and have heard now three voices speaking; how many of you are there?"

Delg said promptly, "I'm no longer young enough to willingly wear the cloak of a fool. Would you make true answer, in our place?"

"I understand," the king's voice replied. "There is a harp rhyme, known to some, that begins with the words 'I walked in the woods and dreamt I felt the kisses of maidens'—do you know it?"

"I do," said Delg roughly, breathing hard. Narm and Shandril were both aware that a great tension had suddenly fallen from the dwarf. "The song is well chosen.

I've heard harps, more than once. You have good taste in ballads."

"Thank you," said King Azoun, and they could tell he meant it. Shandril also sensed more than one meaning lay behind those two simple words—something only Delg would understand. She glanced at the dwarf, but he had turned to peer alertly into the forest about them, his battered, bearded face expressionless.

The king went on. "Word has come to me of all of you, then. Shandril, know that Cormyr has no designs upon your powers or person. Yet, I warn you never to forget this: whatever the challenge, I *will* keep peace in my realm, no matter the cost. My knights and armsmen will do what they must to defend the good land and folk of Cormyr. We will not seek you, or offer war to you and yours. Pass in peace—and let us hope that we can one day meet openly, as friends, and give no thought for battle or danger."

"Pretty speech," Delg grunted, in a low voice.

Shandril rushed to cover the dwarf's words. "I—I thank you, Your Highness. I mean no harm to any in Cormyr, and—I hope to know you as a friend, too." She paused for a moment, and added, "I'm growing impatient for the day when, gods willing, it won't be a dangerous thing to be my friend."

The light drifted a little closer to her, sparkled, and then drew back. "If it's any strength to you," the king's voice said gently, "I have known that same feeling. Gods smile on you, Shandril of Highmoon. You have our blessing to pass through our land."

"My thanks," Shandril replied. "Farewell."

As she spoke, the light was already dwindling and fading. She watched until she was sure it was gone before sighing her relief.

Narm turned to embrace her, smiling, but she thrust

him aside and ran. She managed to get several strides away before she fell on her knees and emptied her stomach into the moss and dead leaves.

Delg stalked over to stand above her heaving shoulders. As she choked and sobbed, he said dryly, "Perhaps it's a good thing we didn't seek the palace in Suzail straight off to have audience with the king. His carpets might not be overly improved by your visits."

Shandril choked and shook and then found herself laughing weakly, still on hands and knees.

"Shan! Shan? Are you all right?" Narm asked fearfully.

Shandril felt the forest damp beneath her palms and the searing ache in her ribs. Despite it all, she smiled.

"I think I am. Yes." She reached out, got a hand on Delg's belt buckle, and dragged herself upward. The dwarf stood like a rock as she climbed up him, hand over hand. Upright, she steadied herself, wiped at her mouth, and then brushed some errant hair out of her face. She saw a smile playing at the edges of his lips.

"Thanks, Delg," Shandril said to him and hugged him. "I'm right glad you're with us." She stepped into the shady gloom of night under the trees, and they saw her eyes catch flame for a moment before she added softly, "I'll be happier still when we reach Silverymoon and the safety and teachings of Alustriel." Spellfire danced in her hands for a moment before she added in a frightened whisper, "Help me get there—before the Zhents make me too accustomed to killing."

* * * * *

"Have they begun?" There was cold amusement in Lord Manshoon's voice as they turned through an archway guarded by two stiffly alert guardsmen.

"Of course," Sarhthor replied. "Some took bold leave of

me, with grandly sinister half-promises and hints of dark plans. Others simply slipped away."

Together they stepped into a large, empty chamber, then turned sharply right into a dark alcove. Its dusty, cobwebbed back wall was an illusion; as they strode through it, Sarhthor added, "You know they've started, Lord. Once you spoke of spellfire, you could have forbidden them to seek it—and still they'd have tried. Magelings who last this long are ruled by their lust for power, however much they might pretend to command wisdom and shrewd reason."

The two archwizards squeezed past a motionless golem and strolled down the dark passage beyond it to a featureless door. Sarhthor drew it open, and Manshoon strode through, his black cloak swirling about him.

The room beyond was small. Two closed doors faced them, and in the center of the room stood a wooden plinth; on it lay a small gold key. Manshoon ignored all these features, turning sharply left to a door beside the one through which he had entered. He strode forward as if that dark wooden door did not exist—and as the toe of his boot touched its surface, he vanished, leaving Sarhthor alone in the room.

The Zhentarim archmage carefully closed the door they had entered through and looked around the room. Death awaited those who touched the key or the other two doors, he knew—for he had helped arrange it so. Smiling faintly, he followed Manshoon.

One of his boots left the floor in that dark room deep inside Zhentil Keep as the other clicked down onto glass-smooth marble in a grand, high-vaulted chamber in the heart of the Citadel of the Raven. It took hurrying warriors two days or more to make the trip they'd just covered in a single step. Sarhthor hoped it would never be necessary to reveal the existence of the magical gate to the Zhentilar. They'd not be pleased, and he hated unnecessary violence.

Ahead, Manshoon ignored the faintly glowing tapestries that hung in midair all around, like the vertical war banners carried on the spears of Zhentilar horsemen. He looked only for what shouldn't be there—and found nothing out of place. He strode across the vast, high hall to stand facing one of the elaborately painted windows, then halted, watchful and coldly patient. The window was as large across as three stone coffins placed end to end. It depicted a scarlet dragon coiling around the pearly-hued moon, its emerald eyes glittering and jaws opened to devour the pale orb.

Manshoon stood impassively and dispassionately regarding it as Sarhthor made his own way across the gleaming marble to stand behind and to one side of the high lord. As he came to a halt, the window began to slide aside.

Their arrival had been watched, as usual.

Still glowing with false sunlight, the window slid open, revealing a dark hole behind it, like the eyesocket of a gigantic skull. Out of that darkness floated two spherical creatures, their dark bodies surrounded by sinuously coiling tentacles that turned restlessly to point in one direction and then another. From the end of each stalk, a cold, fell eye looked out at the world.

Each beholder slowly turned on end to gather all ten of its eyestalks in a sinister, watchful cluster: a forest of eyes stared at the two Zhentarim wizards as the beholders drifted into the room.

The eye tyrants floated on in silence until they hung above the wizards, well out of reach and comfortably separated from each other. Then they rolled slowly upright, revealing their many-toothed mouths and large, central eyes. One was slightly larger than the other.

"Something is amiss here," the larger one hissed in its deep, echoing voice. "Strange magic is present."

Manshoon turned wordlessly to Sarhthor, who frowned, shook his head doubtfully, and said, "If you'll allow me a few breaths and a spell, Lords . . ."

"Proceed," three cold voices said together, and the archmage had to hide a smile at how like the eye tyrants Manshoon sounded . . . how like an eye tyrant he had truly become.

Slowly and carefully, Sarhthor made the gestures and mutterings of a powerful and thorough detection spell. Thousands of tiny motes of light erupted from his robes, swirling around the chamber like a school of startled fish, prying into every corner. The conspirators waited patiently as the lights swooped, darted, hung in corners, and finally faded away.

Sarhthor shook his head again. "Many enchantments adorn the tapestries, walls, ceiling, and floor—as always, and some of them have been laid so as to shift and change, over time—but as Mystra is my witness, I can find no trace of scrying, spies, or magical traps in this place. There are, however, two spiders alive here, and a scuttle-bug—by your leave?"

Manshoon nodded, and the beholders blinked all their eyes, once. Sarhthor strode across the floor to crush the three intruders underfoot. "Done," he said simply, then walked back to stand with his lord.

"You called for me with some secrecy," Manshoon said flatly, looking up at the beholders, "and I have come. Speak."

Eyestalks curled, and many glances flickered silently back and forth high above the two men; an unspoken agreement was swiftly reached. The smaller beholder drifted slightly lower. "We have become increasingly mistrustful of the loyalty of Fzoul and his underlings to any

causes and authority but their own. Prying priests are
everywhere in Zhentil Keep; we dared not meet with you
there."

The other, larger beholder spoke. "We have also," it
rumbled coldly, "begun to despair over the ineptitude of
the current crop of magelings. Many of us would like to
see wizards firmly in control of our Brotherhood again,
wielding spellfire so as to rule or destroy the priests. But
most of the lesser wizards lack the self-control to govern
themselves, let alone control anything else."

"Aye, this spellfire is the key," said the smaller eye
tyrant eagerly. "If you are to keep our support, Manshoon,
your hand must come to wield it, or hold a firm grip on
whoever does."

The High Lord of Zhentil Keep shrugged. "Tell me
how, with the losses we've suffered so far trying to seize
spellfire, I am to ensure our wizards will be powerful
enough to win it at last—and still be strong enough to
tame the priests."

The rumbling reply sounded a little triumphant, and
somehow amused. "With the unlooked-for aid we have
brought you. Meet Iliph Thraun, a lord among liches, as
you are a lord among men."

Something small and white moved in the dark opening
from whence the beholders had come. It turned and rose.
A yellowed human skull drifted into view, looking down at
the two wizards.

Both of them stared expressionlessly up at it, thinking
the same old saying of Faerûn: *surprises seldom grow more
welcome as one gets older.*

The skull drifted to a halt in midair, floating below the
two beholders. Two pale, flickering points of light hung in
its dark sockets; its gaze was cold but somehow eager as
it looked down at the two mages.

"Well met," it said formally, in hollow tones punctuated

by the faint clattering of its teeth. "In life, long ago, I had the power of spellfire. I can drain it from this Shandril, if I can catch her asleep."

"And if she wakes before you are done?"

The skull drifted closer. "Once enough of her spellfire is gone, the lass will lose control over what is left. She will become a wild wand whenever she unleashes spellfire—a menace to allies and those she holds dear. Soon she will destroy them . . . and, in the end, herself."

Lord Manshoon nodded slowly. "I thank you, lich lord. Your powers may bring victory for us all." His words held the finality of a farewell.

As the skull made a polite reply, the smaller beholder turned and drifted a little way toward it. Obediently, the skull drifted out through the opening it had entered by. When it was gone, Manshoon calmly asked the beholders, "What good is this? I trade a young, reckless girl who scarce knows how to use spellfire for an old, wise, mighty-in-Art lichnee who is sure to defy my orders? Where's the gain in that?"

The larger beholder's mouth crooked in a slow smile. "In becoming a lich, this Thraun used a flawed process; its unlife is maintained by magical energies provided by magelings whom it tutors, then destroys when they grow too powerful. It feeds on certain spells cast for it—if you modify them in the right way, you or any wizard can command the lich lord with absolute precision."

The other beholder spoke. "Would you know these magics?"

"Of course." Manshoon did not even look at Sarhthor as he added, "Speak freely."

"The energy can come from any of the spells that drain lifeforce, or from those that create fire or lightning. Thraun needs them modified so their effects form a sphere, the energies spiraling to its heart—where this lich lord waits. If you work a governance over undeath and a masking charm employing the name 'Calauthas' in your modifying incantations, you can control Thraun from a distance—an absolute control that compels the lich lord's nature. If you choose to do this through a lesser mage whose mind you control, you can even command the lich lord without its knowing who you are."

"So Thraun, who doubtless intends to destroy us all when it regains spellfire, becomes our helpless pawn. A nice twist." The High Lord of Zhentil Keep took two thoughtful paces across the gleaming marble, and then looked up again.

"The time to use Thraun is not yet," he said. "To gather our mages or to have the lich lord widely seen will arouse Fzoul's suspicions. If you agree, I'll send a mageling to serve Thraun, a wizard this lich lord believes it can easily destroy—but one whose mind I control. We tell Thraun our difficulties in capturing Shandril continue, and it's best not to reveal a lich lord whom others may fear and attack, unless we have the maid in hand."

"I have noticed," the larger beholder observed, "that the priests of our Brotherhood regard all undead as things to be either their slaves or swiftly destroyed."

Manshoon nodded. "That is why there have always been very few liches in the Brotherhood." He began to pace again. "If Thraun grows restive, or Shandril eludes us for too long, we allow it to go after her—exerting our control only when necessary."

The beholders drifted toward the dark hole, and the false window began to slide out over it again. "We are agreed," the larger eye tyrant said simply. "This meeting ends."

"We are agreed," the two wizards echoed, "and this meeting ends." They stood together in silence and watched the dragon window settle back into place.

Manshoon looked at Sarhthor. "Useful news."

"If kept secret, Lord. As it shall be." Their eyes met for a long moment—dark, steady eyes set in expressionless faces.

Then Manshoon nodded and turned away. They strode together across the marble to where the unseen gate waited to take them back to the High Hall of Zhentil Keep.

"One thing occurs to me," Sarhthor said thoughtfully, a pace or two before Manshoon would have vanished. The high lord looked back at him silently.

"Others use this place besides us," the wizard said. "If I were to leave a tracing spell behind to record changes in Art, we'd know precisely what castings had been done here between our meetings. No spying magic could escape our notice."

Manshoon was already nodding. "Do it." He turned away and disappeared.

Left alone in the chamber, Sarhthor took a few steps back the way he had come, and then cast a spell with quick, precise movements. A faint, sparkling radiance seemed to gather out of nowhere to coil around his wrists and then leap outward in all directions, streaming away until it faded back into nothingness. Wearing the faintest of smiles, the wizard looked slowly around the chamber, turned on his heel, took a few strides, and vanished in his turn. Silence fell.

Then the marble floor seemed to ripple and flow, like the farthest tongues of water that waves throw up onto the sands of a beach. Gathering in one corner behind a tapestry, the ripples rose up smoothly into a man-sized pillar, spun for a moment, and sharpened into the form of a tall, thin, bearded man in plain, rather shabby, homespun robes.

Elminster of Shadowdale dusted himself off, looked around with a critical eye at the glowing tapestries, and then stared thoughtfully up at the dragon window. Scratching his beard, he grunted, "'Tis high time, indeed . . . for certain folk to set down their harps and get their hands dirty. Again. Just as it's time old Elminster got walked all over, again. 'Tis not the first time, this tenday, the world's needed saving."

Three

SWORDS GATHERED IN THE SHADOWS

*Stormy weather is always with us, somewhere in Faerûn.
Beneath it, all too often, swords are out, the hand that
wields one seeking to bury it in the body that wields another.
Part of the way of things as the gods order, perhaps—or just
the way of all of us flawed beings who walk this world. I fear
I'll never see a day when no swords will be drawn—or
needed. But then, perhaps my sight fails too soon.*

Alustriel, High Lady of Silverymoon
To Harp and to Help
Year of the Deep Moon

 It was, as the minstrels say, a bright
and beautiful morning in the forest.
Birds sang and swooped in the branches
as three Zhentilar warriors, whose
faces and backs ran with sweat, bent to
their work. Grunting under its weight,
they lowered the stout frame of wooden
poles into the pit where they stood. The end of each pole
had been sharpened into a cruel point.

"How're we to know she'll come this way? Aye?"

"Not our worry, Guld." The swordmaster's voice came

from above them at the lip of the pit. "We're just sword-arms. When the cover's done, we just hide by it and wait with blades out—and that's exactly how Lord Manshoon said it."

The swordmaster had meant to awe them into silence with his last words, but the three sweating men—now climbing out of the pit and struggling to drag the dirt-and-brush-covered wooden lid properly onto the greased axle-pole—were young. They still owned tongues that wagged faster than the muzzle applied by prudence would allow.

"What makes high-an'-mighty Manshoon think we can do what he couldn't? Him with a dragon and all his spells and wands, too!"

"He obviously knows your true worth better than I do, Alorth." The swordmaster's tone was biting.

Guld bent to slide the thin twigs into the sockets provided for them, taking care. The branches would hold the trap-cover up until this Shandril's weight was on it. Giving the last one an extra tap, he looked up, wiping sweat and hair out of his eyes. "Seriously, Sir: what leads Lord Manshoon to send swords against this lass, where spells fail?"

Swordmaster Bluth bent his critical gaze on the finished pit trap, watching as Alorth spread a basketful of earth and leaves over its edges, kicking them into place with a practiced boot.

Then Bluth shrugged and looked up. "We're only intended to wear this Shandril down so she's tired and hurt and has used most of her spellfire before the mage-lings attack her. I'd like to surprise a few wizards, though, by capturing her ourselves."

"Ourselves being those of us who're still alive, you mean." Alorth's voice was hard. "Why attack her at all if we're just going to our deaths? Why not leave her for the wizards—tell them she's slipped past us somehow?"

The swordmaster walked all around the pit trap and nodded his acceptance; it was well-concealed. He stepped back to look at the trees around, searching for any signs they might have left of their presence, then replied, "Duty, lad. Duty to orders. It's what we live for—and die for."

"So lords can sit safe in their towers," Alorth replied bitterly.

Bluth turned a cold eye on him. "Dangerous talk, Alorth. Taking the venomed dagger of your tongue to the plans and deeds of your betters is a sport that was old— and deadly—long before you were born."

He looked around one last time, and then drew his sword and said to the other men briskly, "Best we get dressed again and ready. If the other lads do their work as well as we have, they'll be here soon."

* * * * *

"I'm done, Shan." Narm shut his spellbook with a snap. "Mighty magic once more up my sleeves."

"At least you're not as overblown about it as most mages," Delg said, looking up at him. "Though you're not much better than most of 'em at walking, or cooking, or digging latrines . . . or anything else much useful. . . ."

"Delg!" Shandril and Narm protested together. The dwarf laughed and settled his bulging pack on his shoulders. As usual, he carried far more than his larger companions.

"We'd best be off before some more Zhents find us," he said merrily. "North as before, then?"

Shandril shrugged. "You know better than I. Lead on."

Without further words, the dwarf set off into the waiting woods.

"How do you feel today, love?" Narm's voice was low.

Shandril gave him a smile. "Better than I have since we

left Shadowdale. About time, too—it's a long way to Silverymoon. From what Storm said, if we walk and have to avoid Zhents more than once or twice, winter could well find us before we're halfway there."

"See Faerûn," Narm said, gesturing at the trees around them. "Know high adventure. Meet strange and fearsome beasts, the like few folk have ever seen—"

"And slay them." Shandril's voice was wry. She seemed to be looking at something far away. "I never dreamt, back at the *Moon*, that when I finally got my taste of adventure, it would mean I went around burning powerful wizards and veteran warriors to ash—and that the Cult of the Dragon, the Zhentarim, and just about everyone else I met would attack me."

Narm hastened to head off her darkening mood. "Who else your age, though, has fought dragons—undead dragons, even—and lived?"

He caught his lady by the shoulders, eyes dancing, and went on jovially, "Has been rude to Elminster the Sage—and lived? Blasted Manshoon of Zhentil Keep and the dragon he rode out of the sky, and sent them fleeing for home? Blown up entire castles? Made friends with the Harpers, with Elminster, and with the Knights of Myth Drannor? Walked the ruined streets of Myth Drannor, that folk all over Faerûn talk of?"

Shandril smiled ruefully. "Yes, and hasn't had a spare moment to draw breath, yet alone enjoy any of it."

"You married me—and seemed to enjoy *that*," Narm protested in mock hurt.

"She must have been deaf, then," Delg put in, ahead of them. "The way you babble day and night through."

Narm favored the dwarf with a certain rude sputtering noise made by small children throughout Faerûn.

"You'll have to be a little closer to kiss me, lad," the dwarf replied, eyes twinkling. Then his face grew more grave. "Shan—are you having thoughts against this journey?"

Shandril shook her head. "No—whatever I do, danger waits for me or comes looking. At least if I'm going somewhere, I have the feeling I'm doing *something* rather than just running from the latest attack." She looked at them both and spread her hands. "If I wasn't trying to get to Silverymoon—even if it *doesn't* turn out to be a friendly haven—I'd be dead by now. I'd have surrendered, just to be free of always running and worrying and fighting. I'm so *sick* of it all—I could scream!"

Fire danced in Shandril's eyes for a moment, and then died away, leaving her expression empty, her eyes like two dark, despairing pits. "I do scream," she added, voice unsteady, "when I have to *use* spellfire—cursing the gods for playing this jest on me."

Delg squinted up at her. "Others have cursed the humor of the gods, lass, even among the dwarves—but I've heard elders tell them the gods jest with us all, and we are measured by how we deal with what befalls. Of *course* you want to be free of all who harry you. Who in Faerûn wouldn't?"

He shifted his heavy pack on his shoulders and added, "More than that: I'd be sad if one so young and inexperienced as you had already decided exactly what she'd do her entire life through . . . because she'd have to be a fool to be so certain about so little."

"My thanks, Delg—I think," Shandril told him a little stiffly.

And then she shrieked. Out of nowhere, something slim and dark tore through the air, leaping past her breast to crash into the leaves beyond.

Delg put his head down and charged bruisingly into Shandril. As they crashed into the damp, dead leaves together, the dwarf snarled, "Down!" in Narm's direction.

With the hum of an angry hornet, another bolt tore through the air close overhead, and then another. Narm rolled amid dead leaves nearby, cursing.

Shandril fought for breath as Delg wriggled and grunted beside her, shucking his pack, tearing his shield free, and getting his arm into the straps. His axe flashed past her nose as he hefted it.

"The Zhents again!" the dwarf hissed, peering into the trees. "There!"

He pointed. Shandril rolled onto hands and knees and came up beside his hairy hand, looking along the pointing finger—and into the eyes of a Zhent who was loading a cocked crossbow.

From the leaves beside them, Narm muttered something. Two pulses of light leapt from his hand, streaking through the trees. The man grunted as they hit, staggering and dropping his bow.

Shandril saw others behind him, and rose to her feet, pointing. Spellfire roared down her arm, shaking her, and white flames shot out through the trees like the breath of a furious red dragon. Leaves blazed and then were gone. Halfway to the Zhents a tree was burned through by the roaring flames. It toppled slowly, and crashed ponderously among the dead leaves.

Shandril snarled and raised her other hand.

Delg caught her arm from behind. "No, Shan!" Then he cursed and shrank back from her, clutching at his hand. Shandril stared at him in shock. Smoke was rising in wisps from the dwarf's fingers; he shook his hand, roared out his pain, and looked up at her, eyes bright with tears.

"Remind me not to do *that* again soon," he growled, flexing his burned fingers. Then he nodded at where she'd aimed. "You daren't do that in these heavy woods, lass—look."

A burnt scar stretched away through the trees from

where she stood, to where a tangle of trees had fallen. Shandril stared along her path of destruction, face bleak, and saw dark-armored figures moving amid the trees beyond it.

The dwarf hesitated, then reluctantly reached out and caught at her arm again. This time no ready spellfire burned him. "Too many. We must run from them, lass—if you use your fire freely, all these woods'll soon be ablaze around us."

They could see Zhent warriors, blades drawn, in the trees to their right and ahead of them. The Zhents were advancing cautiously, moving in as a group so as to arrive together, their blades a deadly wall of steel.

Delg couldn't see any foes to their left. He heaved his pack back onto his shoulders, hung his shield on it, commanded, "Come!" and broke into a lumbering run, heading to the left.

Narm and Shandril followed, hurrying through the trees. They heard shouts behind them and broke into a panting run. Narm skidded to a halt, waved his hands hurriedly, and then scrambled to catch up with his lady.

Close behind him—too close—Zhentilar soldiers cursed and struggled in the invisible spellweb the young mage had left for them to blunder into.

Shandril looked anxiously back every time her route through the thick-standing trees turned to one side or the other. Narm grinned at her between gasps for air as he closed the distance between them, sprinting and leaping as he'd done as a small boy—and never since, until now.

That invisible web Elminster had taught him had come in very handy. A few Zhents must have gotten around its ends, though—and soon it would melt away, freeing them all. By then, a certain trio of fools had better be long gone.

Narm reached Shandril's side. They crashed wildly through leaves and tangles, leaping over rocks and fallen

branches and slipping on mud and wet leaves underfoot
while the dwarf huffed along ahead of them, completely
hidden under his pack. The bulging rucksack looked like
it was running away by itself, leaping and scuttling
through the leaves.

With aching lungs and pounding hearts, Narm and
Shandril followed, plunging down a slope of old leaves
and soft mosses that gave way and slid under their feet.
Soon they reached the bottom of a leaf-choked gully, and
ran along it, gathering speed with the easier footing. Their
route looked like an old, sunken road hidden below the
overhanging trees, cutting through a ridge ahead and
then dropping out of sight.

The pack that hid Delg bobbed and wiggled as it fairly
flew along ahead of Narm and Shandril, but their longer
legs were beginning to close the distance to the huffing
dwarf. Now he was only thirty paces or so in front of
them. Narm growled and put on a determined burst of
speed.

Twenty paces ahead.

Ten.

There was a sharp cracking sound—and then another.
The ground in front of Delg rose suddenly, like the draw-
bridge of a keep, and the two puffing humans saw the
bulky pack slip back down its slope. Delg's axe flashed for
a moment as he waved it—and then the dwarf and his
pack fell out of sight.

Narm and Shandril came to a shocked halt on the very
edge of the pit Delg had fallen into, and they clutched at
each other for balance. Delg lay helpless like an upended
turtle atop a forest of wooden spikes that had pierced the
pack he wore. Shandril looked over her shoulder to find a
vine to drag Delg out, but just then, four Zhentarim soldiers with drawn swords rose from behind the trees, atop
the banks of the gully.

"Surrender to us," one said heavily, "or—"

Shandril didn't want to hear the choice, it seemed. With a scream very like the angry shriek of a harpy, she hurled spellfire in a fury. White flames leapt forth, roaring; when they died away, the Zhents around saw that the warrior's upper body had been blasted away.

The legs tottered for a moment and then fell. The two men beside the ash heap screamed in terror and ran.

Narm dropped to his belly beside the pit. Its lid was held open by Delg's booted feet; the red-faced, furious dwarf lay below, just beyond his reach, spitting curses Narm was glad he couldn't understand.

Shouts came from the trees behind them. The warriors they'd run from—who'd herded them here, Shandril realized—were following up their trail. Fast.

One man remained atop the other bank, sword drawn. He looked down at them uncertainly, his face gray with fear, his eyes wide.

"Drop your sword, or die!" Shandril told him. "*Now!*"

Alorth licked bloodless lips and looked across at what was left of the swordmaster. He threw his blade down, raising his hands to plead. "Please—"

"Get down here!" Shandril hurled spellfire back down the gully behind her without looking; a cry of despair, abruptly stilled, answered her. She glared at the Zhentilar. "Come down—or die!"

Almost weeping with terror, Alorth slithered down. Those burning eyes stared up at him from only a few feet away. They might belong to a young, frightened girl—but they held his death, and Alorth knew it. He trembled, sudden sweat running down his nose.

"Touch no weapons," Shandril said, biting off her words. "Reach down and get him out of the pit. If he's hurt, or if you leave the pack behind, you die."

Alorth stared at her for a moment, and at the young

mage who rose up from the dirt to glare at him. A crossbow bolt whistled past them.

"Move, or *die!*" Shandril hissed, eyes flaming. Spellfire
lanced out. The Zhentilar cried out at the burning pain
her gaze brought him, and fell heavily on his knees.
Behind him, he heard screams and a roar like rolling
thunder. He looked around—to find the forest lit by hungry flames, Zhentilar warriors shrieking and staggering in
the conflagration. The young lass stood defiantly facing
them, fire dancing in her hands.

Then something gleamed, very near, as it slid down
into his view: the point of his own sword, not a finger's
length from his eyes, the angry face of the young mage
behind it.

Sobbing in fear, Alorth turned and reached for the
dwarf. Too far. He'd never reach that far, without—he
frantically scrabbled at the edge of the pit, but harsh
hands were suddenly at his ribs and belt, heaving and
shoving.

With a cry of terror, Alorth Bloodshoulder toppled
headlong toward the spikes, those cruel points leaping up
at his face, and—there was a sudden pain in his knees as
he came to a wrenching halt. Alorth groaned. Sweat fell
past his eyes—and spattered on the sharpened wood only
inches below. The mage must be sitting on his lower legs.

The dwarf, still snarling dwarven curses, swarmed up
his arms, digging in fingers with cruel force. Then the
weight and the pain were both gone, and Alorth was
roughly hauled up onto the ground. Freed, he slumped
into the dirt, moaning softly.

The noise like thunder came again. Alorth looked up
with tear-blurred eyes, and saw a stream of white, roaring
flames rolling down the already blackened gully away
from him, the girl silhouetted against its brightness.

Crossbow bolts leapt from the trees to either side,

caught fire as Shandril looked at them, and crashed down in smoke and ashes. The dwarf, axe in hand, glared at Alorth from a foot or so away, and the Zhentilar fearfully snatched the dagger from his belt.

Shandril heard his grunt of effort and spun around. Spellfire roared, and Alorth found himself staring at the bare bones of his arm. The smoking remnants of the dagger fell from them an instant before they collapsed, pattering to the ground in a grisly shower. Alorth found breath enough to whimper for a moment before the world spun, and he crashed down into darkness. . . .

* * * * *

"Are there any left?" Narm was peering back through the trees as they stood gasping for breath in a little hollow deeper in the forest. They had run from the gully of smoking Zhentilar corpses for what seemed like an hour. The pursuing shouts and crossbow bolts seemed to have stopped—and far behind them, they heard barking calls that probably meant wolves had discovered waiting cooked meals.

"There're *always* more Zhents, lad," Delg puffed. "They're like stinging flies." The dwarf was glumly looking at his torn and punctured pack. Shredded clothing protruded from the rents the spikes had made.

Narm pushed the cloth back through the holes. Between gulps for air, he said brightly, "That could've been . . . far worse . . . aye?"

Delg rolled a severe eye around to meet his. "Many men spend their lives trying to get out of one hole or another. Just take care, Narm, that yours doesn't wind up being a pit with sharpened spikes at the bottom of it."

Shandril managed a weak chuckle, and then got to her feet. "We'd best go on while we can," she sighed. "Or they'll be on us again—and those crossbows can't miss forever."

Narm was muttering something and passing a hand over Delg's pack. Where he touched it, the worst rents and holes shrank and closed, the fabric smoothing out as if new. Narm, finished, probed at his work, and looked up at her. "How are you feeling, Shan?"

"Tired. When I said I was sick of endless battle," Shandril told him grimly, "I meant it."

* * * * *

The glow from the pool lit the face of the Zhentarim priest who stared into it, watching them from afar. He smiled a slow, cruel smile and said, "Oh, maid, if you're sick of battle now, you'll be at the doors of death over it, before long—I can promise that." The warriors standing with him all laughed. It was not a pretty chorus.

* * * * *

As they struggled through the endless green depths of Hullack Forest, and the day wore on, Delg felt the constant weight of watching eyes on them. More than once, he called a halt to peer around suspiciously, looking at the dim legions of tree trunks on all sides. "We're being watched," he said. "I can feel it."

"Magic?" Narm asked.

"Of course magic, stumblehead," the dwarf replied grumpily. "If a beast—or even a Zhent sneak-thief—was stalking along behind us, I'd have seen it by now."

"As you say, oh tall and mighty one," Narm replied, eyes dancing.

Shandril flicked a warning look at her husband as the dwarf growled something under his breath, and Narm raised his hands. "Peace! Peace, oh giant among dwarves!"

"A bit less tongue, youngling," Delg replied, "and we'd best be on our way again—unless Elminster taught you any clever spells that can ward off scrying magic."

The mage frowned. "No, no . . . but I'm trying to remember something Storm said, back in Shadowdale, about the goddess Tymora."

"Tymora?"

"Aye . . . Rathan gave us a luck medallion blessed by Tymora, and Gorstag gave us another. Storm said something about how such things can be used, but I can't recall—"

The dwarf snorted. "Of course not. You're a mage, and mages can't even remember their own names or ages. Let me look at these medallions."

Shandril obediently pulled on the chain around her neck, drawing her medallion out of the breast of her tunic. Narm brought his out of his robes. The dwarf squinted at them both and sighed.

"By the gods, you two innocents'll be the death of me yet! With these, we can be cloaked from magic, twice— each use will burn away one medallion."

"What?"

"Aye." The dwarf fairly danced in impatience. "There's a charm on these things." He swung around to fix Narm with eager eyes. "You can cast an invisibility spell, can't you, lad?"

Narm nodded. "Y-yes."

"Well, if you cast it on one of these medallions, the spell will last until the next morn, so long as the medallion isn't touched by a living being, or moved. The spell covers everyone within ten paces—or whatever, I forget exactly how far—and nothing can see, hear, or smell them from outside that space. Even sniffing beasts and wizard spells miss you. All the spells that detect things find all sorts of traces, aye—in the wrong places, and moving in the wrong directions."

"You speak truth?" Narm's astonishment overrode his manners.

"Nay, lad—I *want* to die under a dozen Zhentarim blades," the dwarf snarled, "after all we've been through thus far. So I'm lying to you both so Manshoon can walk right up to us while you think us safe. Of *course* I speak truth! One of these saved my life, once, when our company was too badly wounded to go on; with it, we bought time for healing."

"If that's so," Shandril said quietly, "I could use a rest from all this running—and time to practice a bit with my spellfire. I'm still burning things to ashes when I mean only to cook them gently, or send spellflame past them at something else. I've no wish to burn most of this forest down, or slay things I have no quarrel with."

"Let's go on until we find another clearing, then," Narm said. "And some water to drink."

"We're past highsun," Delg said. "We'd best be getting on."

It had grown late, the sun sinking low amid the trees, before they found another clearing. "Here," Shandril said, giving her medallion to Delg.

The dwarf set it on a stone near the center of the open, grassy space, and sat himself on an old stump nearby. "Your spell, lad," he directed. Narm carefully worked his magic and touched the shining silver disc. It flashed and then briefly sparkled, but nothing else seemed to happen.

"Is it working?" Shandril asked. The young man and the dwarf traded looks and shrugged in unison.

"I don't feel we're being watched anymore," Delg said. He turned to Narm. "Best study your spells, lad, while I get a meal ready."

Shandril sighed, relaxing, and then walked a few paces

away. She found some bushes and a comfortable moss-covered stone, and sank down thankfully. Yawning, she rubbed at her shoulders and aching feet. Then she stiffened. There was a tiny fluttering inside her; spellfire tingling faintly . . . building again.

She bent her will to calling the inner fire up, feeling it surge and roil about within her. When Shandril felt ready, she stood and hurled a tongue of flame between the two trunks of a forked duskwood tree. They smoked and creaked in the heat, but neither burst into flame.

Pleased, she threw spellfire again. This time her target was a small cluster of leaves: could she burn them off their branch without disturbing other leaves nearby? The cluster flared and was gone; a few flames flickered and then died in their wake. Shandril frowned; she'd burned more leaves than she'd meant to.

None of the three travelers saw the medallion begin to smolder. When the next burst of spellfire lashed out at a small patch of toadstools, the medallion pulsed with momentary fire. Drifting smoke showed that only a blackened patch remained where the toadstools had been; the medallion melted into a tiny remnant that crumbled and fell apart, unseen.

When next spellfire licked out—in a curving arc this time, reaching around behind a stout tree—malevolent eyes were watching, as before. . . .

* * * * *

"Watch well," Gathlarue said softly, looking into the glowing crystal, "and remember—this is not a fire spell. The maid's fire cleaves all spell barriers we know of and will scatter any wall of fire you or I might raise."

Mairara lifted an eyebrow. "I find it hard to credit that wench with wits enough to stand up to any mage of skill."

"She is said to have forced Lord Manshoon himself to flee," Tespril whispered. Her eyes were large and very dark; Gathlarue was pleased to see that at least one of her apprentices was smart enough to be scared.

She stretched, then favored them both with a smile. "We shall watch and learn much more before we move against Shandril ourselves."

She ran her fingers idly through a lock of Mairara's long, glossy black hair, and as its owner smiled at her, sat back from the crystal and told Tespril, "Order our even-feast brought to us, here. Tonight we'll have rare entertainment to watch; the main troop of Zhentilar are to try their luck at capturing Shandril. The idiot sword-swingers are such crude fumblers they've been assigned one of Fzoul's best priests in case they should kill Shandril by mischance."

The apprentices laughed merrily, and Tespril bowed and hastened away to give the orders.

"Lady," Mairara whispered, bending over her mistress, "is this spellfire really so much more powerful than the spells of, say, a pair of capable archmages?"

"Watch," Gathlarue murmured at her senior apprentice. "Watch what befalls tonight, in my crystal . . . and govern your own mind in the matter."

Mairara nodded, somber eyes on her, and then looked up swiftly as Tespril returned.

"The men are taking bets on how this night's battle will turn out," the younger apprentice said, chuckling. "They want to know who commands the Zhentilar."

Gathlarue smiled. "Karkul Memrimmon leads," she said. "A great beast of a man who fights with spiked gauntlets, and never stays out of the fray."

"You've met him, Lady?" Tespril's tone was teasing, her eyes bright.

"I kept well out of his reach," Gathlarue told her. "He's

the sort who'd get thrown out of taverns *I* wouldn't go
into. . . ."

* * * * *

Spellfire crackled satisfyingly around the stump. Shandril watched a small thread of smoke curl up from the
bark, and she nodded, satisfied. She could strike exactly
the spot she aimed for—and high time, too, as Delg would
say.

She sighed ruefully and looked at the dark, deep woods
around her. A branch snapped somewhere off to her left,
not far away. Shandril's eyes narrowed, and she backed up
to a tree, calling "Narm? Delg?" as loudly as she dared.

Her answer came swiftly—something large and hairy
emerged from behind a nearby tree, lumbering along like
a grotesque parody of a man. A cruel beak larger than
Shandril's head protruded from the dusty, matted feathers
on its face. Hungry, red-rimmed eyes glittered at her, and
it began a crashing charge through the leaves.

Shandril screamed and hurled spellfire at it in a frantic
spray. Sputtering spellflames raced out of her and wreathed
the huge monster—and it screamed. Shandril sent a bolt of
fire right into its face and backed hastily away around the
tree, as it roared and flailed blindly with its bearlike claws.

Her flames hit it again, and its cries grew weaker. There
were other crashing sounds behind her, now, coming
closer. Shandril looked up. Delg and Narm were bounding through the undergrowth. She sighed thankfully—
and the wounded beast charged toward the sound.
Anxiously Shandril hurled spellfire into that reaching
beak—and the thing recoiled, roaring again.

There was a sudden flash of light in front of Shandril. It
lit Narm's stern face as he guided his conjured blade of
force straight into one of the beast's eyes.

Light flashed again inside that monstrous head, and with a rough, despairing cry, the thing crashed to the damp leaves at her feet. Smoke rose from its mouth and then drifted away. The beast thrashed about briefly and lay still, its eyes growing dull.

"An owlbear!" Delg's voice was rough with worry. "You seem to run into the most interesting folk, wherever we go."

Shandril looked down at the smoking thing at her feet, her eyes empty. She suddenly shuddered and turned away with a sob, starting to bolt. A moment later, she ran straight and bruisingly into something large and hard—Delg's shield. The dwarf stepped out from behind it, letting it fall, and caught Shandril by the arm. "You can't run from it, lass—sooner or later, you've got to face it. As long as other folk in Faerûn want what you've got, you must kill to live—so, these days, killing's what you do."

Shandril stared at him. "And what if it's not what I want to do?" she asked very quietly.

The dwarf squinted up at her and then shrugged. "Then you'd best lie down and die the next time someone attacks. You'll save a lot of trouble—for yourself, not for the rest of the Realms."

Shandril looked back at the smoking corpse, and then fixed tired eyes on his. "I don't like killing. I'll never like killing."

Delg nodded. "If that proves true, 'tis good, very good, for us all."

Shandril frowned. "What do you mean, 'proves true'?"

The dwarf leaned on his axe. "Slaying's never easy, lass. When you're young, it's a shock—the smell, the blood and all. . . ."

Narm added quietly, "And when you're old, you see your own death in each killing . . . a part of you dies each time."

The dwarf looked at Narm in surprise. "Wise words for one so young; right you are, indeed." He stared off into memory for a moment, and added softly, "Much too right, lad."

"And between youth and old age?" Shandril asked quietly. "What then?"

Delg squinted at her. "Ah," he rumbled, "that's the time when one who must kill is most dangerous. They get good at the task—very good, some of them—and they also get so they just don't care about the lives they take."

Shandril looked at him. "And if that happens to me?"

Delg looked into her eyes and then turned away. "I'll try to kill you. So will Elminster, and the Knights—and, of course, the Zhents and everyone else in Faerûn who's been hunting you all this time."

"Tell me," Narm said to the dwarf, his voice like a quietly drawn sword, "what you'd say if I stood by Shandril then, even if—gods forfend—she did come to love killing . . . what then?"

Delg looked at him. "Before you died," he said gruffly, hefting his axe meaningfully, "I'd be very proud of you." Then he walked away over the edge of the ridge, axe in hand, looking very old and very alone.

Narm and Shandril peered at each other. "I hope I'm never that sad," Narm said quietly as he put his arms around her.

"I hope I'm never that short," Shandril said with a sudden smile. The mood broken, they laughed uneasily—and then heartily when they heard Delg snap the words, "I *heard* that!" from the other side of the ridge.

After their laughter was done, they walked back together and found the dwarf gloomily surveying a scorched stone in the center of the clearing where the medallion had been. Delg sighed, lifted his eyes to Shandril's, and said gruffly, "Just keep your fires away from my axe, lass.

Oh, aye—*and* the seat of my breeches."

Narm chuckled to rob those words of their sting, but Shandril did not manage a smile.

* * * * *

Not far away, men in black armor crept through the forest, their drawn blades blackened with soot. Their progress was marked by muffled curses and stumbling noises from time to time as rocks and tree roots disputed passage with the soldiers.

A swordmaster near the rear muttered, "A little more care and quiet, there!" Silence answered him, and after a few cautious breaths the officer turned his head and added, "Keep a good watch out behind, Simron—or you'll wind up owlbear-meat."

"Aye, sir," Simron replied, low-voiced, and laid a restraining hand on the shoulder of the man beside him. They knelt unmoving until they heard the swordmaster scramble away.

Simron turned and surveyed the night in all directions behind them. After being satisfied that they weren't followed, he turned back to his companion and said, "I'm in no hurry to move on yet and get cooked like an ox on a feast night. Have ye heard the one about the six dancing girls and the glow-worm? No? Well, then . . ."

* * * * *

"Enough, lass. It's too dark to keep hurling flames about, even down in this vale. Your fires'll draw the eyes of beasts—and worse—all around in these woods." Delg put a cautious hand on her elbow, which was about as high as he could reach.

Shandril let the smoldering spellfire in her hands die

away and then stood trembling, drenched with sweat. Managing a weary smile, she said, "Thanks, Delg. I suppose I got carried away—I even forgot about evenfeast."

"It's waiting," the dwarf said, leading her briskly back to where Narm lay against their packs, dozing. "If the flies haven't had it all by now—"

Whatever else he'd been going to say was lost forever in the sudden crack of a whip, very near in the darkness. A startled, tired Shandril watched light blossom here and there among the trees as lanterns were unhooded. More than one lamp was sent streaking through the air, borne by hurled spears—and in the light they shed, the horrified dwarf saw dark, sinuous shapes leaping at them.

"War dogs!" Delg swore. "Narm, 'ware! *Narm!*" He was running as he bellowed, axe flashing out.

In eerie silence the dogs bounded toward him. Their tongues must have been cut out, Shandril thought in horror, as she raised weary arms and sent killing spellfire into the night.

Gods, but they were fast! Dogs dodged and leapt, bared fangs flashing as they came. She struck again, and blazing hounds writhed in soundless agony, rolling over and over, smoke rising from their flanks.

She saw Narm's hands fall, a spell done—and a dozen or so dogs came to an abrupt, brutal stop, falling and thrashing about together in a confused mass. He must have conjured another spellweb. But many more dogs streamed around the fallen ones and toward them. Shandril hurled spellfire again, and in the midst of it, one dark form rose up, pawed the air for a moment, and then fell over on its back, dead. By the light of her spellflames she saw a score of leaping dogs still coming, snapping and snarling as they came.

Delg stood among them, axe rising and falling. The light grew stronger as torches were lit. Shandril saw the gleam of armor all around them in the trees as Narm, his dagger in hand, reached her—just in time to be bowled over by a leaping war dog.

Shandril screamed as fangs snapped at her throat. Frantic spellfire flared as she was struck by the beast, and the heavy, cooked dog bore her to the ground with the force of its leap. It left the stink of its charred, headless body all over her.

Shandril screamed again, rolling free, as a hurled spear hummed past her ear.

Amid the hissing torches, the Zhentilar warcaptain watched her crawling as fast as she could for the cover of a tree. He grinned cruelly and said to one of his officers, "Now."

The swordmaster whistled, and the air was suddenly alive with hissing crossbow bolts.

Four

GREAT MURDERING BATTLES—AND WORSE

It is one thing to face a rival with your blade in hand and make a bloody end to all rivalry between you. It is quite another to wage war with coins in the shadows and softly striking words in hidden chambers. The second way can kill just as surely—but no one who follows it is lauded as a hero, or grudgingly granted as brave even by one's enemies. There is something in us all that admires those who stand tall and bold in the bright light of day—even when they pay for this boldness with their lives.

Azlundar, Lion of Neverwinter
One Warrior's Life
Year of the Sighing Serpent

 Crossbow bolts hummed hungrily through the night around Shandril. She crouched low, looking around frantically for Narm and Delg. There they were, among what was left of the dogs. Shandril's stomach lurched and turned over uneasily at the bloody sight; she let her revulsion fuel the rage that was building in her. Spellfire flared and raced down her limbs. Her tattered

77

leathers caught fire, flaring up in bright flames that rose around her until they licked at her sweat-soaked hair.

Armored in spellfire, Shandril Shessair stood up and roared her anger into the night, flinging her arms wide. Spellfire blasted out of her in all directions, low over the heads of her loved ones, lancing into the Zhentilar warriors. The white flash of its striking was blinding.

Trees cracked and fell, blazing. Men screamed briefly amid the roaring. Crossbow bolts flared into flying cinders. Heat-shattered armor fell from blackened skeletons, which toppled slowly after them to the smoking ground.

The spellfire died slowly and raggedly. There was a last rolling burst, and then only a slow sputtering of flames, fading to nothing.

Shandril stared wearily around at the smoldering devastation, smoke rising slowly from her hair. She moaned, her eyes went dark, and she crumpled to the ground.

Delg struggled to his feet, hurling bloody dog corpses aside. "Lass!" he bellowed, face white, "Shandril! I'm coming!"

Bloody axe in hand, the dwarf staggered across the beaten turf to where Shandril lay. A few flickering lanterns were still alight, and by their dim glow the dwarf found her. She was breathing and apparently unscathed, though very pale. Moving as stealthily as he could, he dragged Shandril to cover behind a tree. Then Delg straightened to see what foes remained.

A few Zhent warriors were still standing in the lee of two smoking trees. They seemed dazed; Delg counted seven—no, eight: a huge man in cracked and blackened plate armor rose among them, sobbing and clawing at his helm with spiked hand-gauntlets that were each as large as Delg's own head.

Narm was moving feebly among the dogs.

"Narm!" Delg roared. "*Up*, lad—I've need of your spells! Hurl a few balls of fire at yon Zhents!"

The dwarf knew well that Narm's Art was too feeble to work such magics, but if he read them right, the Zhentilar soldiers might run like rabbits at the thought of facing more fire. If he was wrong—well, one doom was as good as another.

He was half right. Delg heard curses, and saw men running off into the night.

"Simron, come back, you craven dog!" A swordmaster bellowed. "The curses of Bane and the Brotherhood on you!"

"Rally them!" This hoarse voice belonged to the giant with the spiked gauntlets. "Rally them, Swordmaster—and spellfire shall yet be ours! Does the priest live?"

"By the grace of Bane," a cold and smooth voice answered him, "I do indeed. How fare you, Warcaptain?"

"My eyes, man! Cast a healing on me, by the Black Altar! I cannot *see!*"

As quietly as he could, Delg clambered over a tangle of grounded spears and the contorted bodies of dogs in order to reach Narm. With a grunt, the dwarf rolled a dead canine aside and dragged the still-groggy wizard to a sitting position.

"Up, lad!" he said sharply, slapping Narm's face. "Up, and take this!" He thrust his belt dagger into Narm's hand; startled eyes fell on it and then rose to meet his.

"Awake, lad? Good. Guard your lady; I've work to do." Delg pointed out where Shandril lay, clapped Narm on the back, and set off through the smoking ruin to where the Zhents clustered.

Only five still stood there—the priest, the blinded but still-blustering warcaptain, a swordmaster, and two warriors. The last three had swords in their hands, and the swordmaster was snapping orders at the men to gather lanterns and make ready to look for the lass.

The dwarf went forward slowly, keeping his axe low and behind him, lest its blade flash back light and warn of his approach. Smoke still drifted lazily amid the blackened trees, but it seemed Shandril was not fated to burn down Hullack Forest this night.

Good. Thank all the gods for that. Now, if they'd just spend a skybolt or two to deal with five Zhents . . .

Perhaps he'd not been devout enough. Or perhaps as a dwarf, he thought wryly, he was expected to act for the gods. Whatever, no bolt came from the sky. Delg grinned savagely at the thought of what spellfire must have seemed to the Zhents who'd run. Oh, there'd be tales of tanar'ri or gods making the rounds of the Moonsea North before long—unless the owlbears and wolves were thorough tonight.

Delg's boot found a stone, painfully. With iron control, he halted and bent to feel it. Small enough. Good. Setting aside his axe, he took up the stone, leaned back almost to the ground with the rock in his raised hand, and came upright in a throw sped by all the weight of his stout body. The hurled stone sailed up into the night—and crashed down in the brush behind the Zhents.

"Who's that? By Bane, answer!" Silence gave the warcaptain the reply he feared. "It's one of them, getting away—swordmaster, see to it! Bring him down!"

The swordmaster looked about helplessly, caught the priest's cold and level gaze, and reluctantly took up a lantern, tersely ordering the two warriors to his flanks.

A moment later, they waded cautiously into the brush, swords raised. Delg, axe held ready, used the noise they made to cover the sounds of his own cautious advance. He crept to the lit area where the warcaptain was pleading with the priest to heal him, and the priest was insisting that the helm come off first.

"It won't," said the big man, voice approaching a sob. "I've *tried* . . . it feels stuck to my skin. Gods!"

Keep sniveling, the dwarf thought savagely. Just a breath or two longer, and I'll—

The axe came up quickly as Delg rounded the last tree, but it was impossible to move silently in the bad light. The priest saw and heard—and was very fast. He shoved the warcaptain into Delg and fled cursing into the darkness.

The fearful Zhentilar felt the impact, heard the priest's fearful oath, and concluded something was wrong. He lashed out.

Delg had stumbled clear—but not quite far enough. One of those war-gauntlets caught him square in the ribs. He grunted and sat down with a crash. The stout dwarven mail held, but the breath had been driven out of him, leaving a searing pain behind.

The sightless man reached forward. He sensed where his foe lay. Delg dropped his axe and rolled aside, pivoting on his own knee to come in close to the warcaptain.

Those blindly grasping gauntlets triumphantly closed on the axe handle and used its blade to flail at the ground. Delg winced as his axe struck sparks from more than one rock—and then his reaching hands found the man's belt dagger and tore it free.

The Zhentilar turned at the tugging, and Delg climbed the arm that swept around to strike him, clambering up it to drive the short blade hilt-deep through the helm's eye-slit and the unseen and unseeing orb beneath.

Dark, hot blood splashed him as he leapt free, to the sound of startled shouts from the swordmaster and warriors, who saw the warcaptain topple dead with no apparent foe. Delg lay prone in the darkness and waited.

A moment later they were fleeing, crashing in head-long flight through the trees. Delg retrieved his axe and scrambled atop the warcaptain's corpse so he could see farther.

His hunch was right. The priest had fled back into the darkness only a little way, and then stopped to watch what befell—so as to return triumphant, should his side win. He stood alone, uncertain, between two trees. Delg smiled grimly, shook his head at the man's arrogant stupidity, and raised his axe.

Lanternlight caught the blade. It flashed once, and the startled priest half-turned to flee, peering through the darkness and trying to see what was happening.

That was time enough. Delg hurled his weapon, grunting as he threw his entire body into the attack. The blade whirled free, and Delg rolled on the ground. The spinning axe took the priest in the head, ending all his thoughts in one brief, bright moment of pain. The black-robed body crashed down into rotting leaves.

Only a pace behind it, a stout figure hid in the deep night-shadows. It held a drawn blade up and ready; if the priest had gone a pace or two more, he'd have impaled himself on the steel. The figure shrugged, grinned, slid his sword back into its sheath, and melted into the night, unseen.

Delg, panting, thought it prudent to retrieve the warcaptain's dagger before venturing out into the night in search of his axe. He had to tug the blade several times to tear it free of the helm. Turning, he set out, and had almost reached his axe when he heard Shandril calling his name, her voice soft with fear.

* * * * *

Fimril, mageling of the Zhentarim, smiled as he rose from his crouch over the dancing flames. The sweat ran down his pale, drawn face in sheets and dripped from his chin; the spell he'd just used was too exhausting to hold for long. Few mages—in or out of the Brotherhood—could call images from the flames of a campfire as clearly as he could. He shook with weariness—but it was crucial that he saw it all.

His voice, when he could find it, was warm with satisfaction. "Karkul and the priest are both dead, as are almost all of their men—and the maid's spellfire has run out. The time to strike is now."

He showed an eager, vicious smile to his frightened sell-sword bodyguards. None of them, however, saw the skull floating in the night gloom beyond the circle of firelight. Its smile matched Fimril's own.

*   *   *   *   *

The twin doors flashed and flared as various magical locks and bindings were released—and then ground slowly and ponderously open.

A handsome, cold-faced man in swirling black robes strode through the doors, onto a midnight sea of slick black marble. He walked to the center of this room, which was always dark, turned to face the doors, and halted. Tiny motes of light flickered and pulsed on his robes, rising slowly into the air. They winked and drifted in small circles, gathered over the man's head, and coalesced into a sphere of flickering light.

Under the gathering radiance of his conjured driftlight, Fzoul Chembryl waited patiently, like an impassive statue, in the center of the innermost sanctum. He listened to the familiar chants in the temple passages outside with the air of an old and jaded critic. In the growing light, his long red hair gleamed like new-polished copper.

The silence that then fell outside told Fzoul his guest had arrived. In moments, its massive shadow loomed up

in the doorway. It drifted in with slow caution, eyestalks
darting this way and that.

Fzoul lifted his head a little and said calmly, "Greetings, Xarlraun."

The beholder turned its pale eyes toward him. Xarlraun was dark, the chitinous plates of its outer skin covered with many old and ill-healed scars. The monster was
as large as a woodsman's hut, its spherical body as high
as three tall men standing on each other's shoulders. For
many years it had dwelt in its own high mountain valley,
feeding on herds of rothe that roamed the grassy slopes.
As the decades passed, it grew large, and its hunger had
grown with it. Finally the day had come when all the
rothe were gone from the valley, so the beholder had
descended into the world of men—and found far more
plentiful food. Men were bonier than their livestock—
especially those who wore bits of metal—but far tastier.
Xarlraun stayed, and grew wise in the ways of men.

Wise enough to ally itself with strength and come drifting down the dark night streets of Zhentil Keep to this
meeting—at a time when its lesser brethren were keeping Manshoon and Sarhthor busy in another meeting,
elsewhere. Wise enough not to trust the man standing
alone before him in the dark room.

"Greetings returned to you, Fzoul Chembryl," it said in
a deep yet hissing voice. "You know why I have come."

"I do. Spellfire, and our plans to seize it." Fzoul paused.
"I presume you don't want to listen to me speak of all our
failures thus far?"

"You presume correctly. Begin, if you will, with the passage of the spellfire wielder through Thunder Gap."

Fzoul nodded. "At the Gap, Shandril Shessair fought
the most powerful dracolich known to exist, Shargrailar
the Dark—and destroyed it. This act officially ended any
pursuit of spellfire by the Cult of the Dragon. We know of

six Cult agents who continued to pursue Shandril after
the council met in Ordulin. One, Thiszult, disappeared at
Thunder Gap, and we presume him to have perished by
spellfire. Another, Ghaubhan Szaurr, commands a large
permanent force in the Stonelands—too large and skilled
for us to eliminate at will, so we have suffered it to
remain and harry the patrols of Cormyr for us. Szaurr
will become a factor only if Shandril travels into his
grasp. The other four have been eliminated by members
of the Brotherhood."

The beholder kept cold silence.

Fzoul cleared his throat and went on. "Our efforts to
seize spellfire by magical force have failed repeatedly—
due to the power of spellfire and the intervention of
others, including Elminster of Shadowdale, the Knights
of Myth Drannor, Harper agents, and powerful archmages unfamiliar to us, whom we assume to have been
acting for their personal gain. The known Thayan agents
in Sembia did hear of spellfire, but either acted through
the Cult or were eliminated by us."

Fzoul took two slow steps and raised his hand. A glowing map of the Dragon Reach lands, from the Marsh of
Tun to the Vast Swamp, and the Neck north as far as the
Ride, began to form in the air. It was as large as the
beholder that regarded it and pulsed with red, moving
lines of light at Fzoul's bidding.

"Our magical failures have led us to the conclusion that
either creative uses of Art, or new spells, or both are necessary to deal effectively with spellfire. So for the first
time we have thrown the Zhentilar into the hunt in force.
The former Cult stronghold at Semberhome, and the old
bandit keeps of Alarangh and Tossril, south of the East
Way and just east of Thunder Gap—here and here—are
bases for our troops. Their open presence will goad both
Cormyr and Sembia to arms to protect their borders and

keep the trade roads open, so they have been instructed to act only in emergencies, when the prize is worth the cost." Fzoul paused to catch the beholder's gazes directly. "Spellfire," he added quietly, "was considered a prize worth any cost."

"Let us hope those words do not haunt you overmuch," the beholder replied, its deep voice sounding slightly wry.

Fzoul shrugged and went on. "From these strongholds, two groups of mounted lancers with crossbows set out. Twenty from Alarangh, and sixty from Tossril. The force from Alarangh passed through the Gap only a few days ago and caught up with Shandril—who is accompanied by a dwarf and her husband, a mage of no account—immediately."

"She destroyed them," said the beholder.

"Aye, with spellfire. It revealed clear limits to the energy she can wield. She collapsed when she had routed them—and her companions fled with her to the hamlet of Thundarlun, where there was a guard post of twenty-eight Purple Dragon troops."

"At the same time, all of our agents in Cormyr, Tilverton, and the Stonelands were warned of Shandril's coming. One of our forces in the Stonelands, under the command of Warcaptain Karkul Memrimmon, was ordered south into the Hullack Forest. With the aid of one of my upperpriests, they managed to cross the Moonsea Ride unobserved, east of Gnoll Pass, and rode by night to the headwaters of the Immer—here."

"By then, your warriors had slaughtered the garrison at Thundarlun and set some of it afire, but Shandril slew them all," the beholder added.

Fzoul sighed. "Aye. Either she recovers her powers very rapidly, or she found some sort of aid in Thundarlun that ah, renewed her spellfire energies."

He paused, cleared his throat again, and went on. "When the swordmaster of the force from Tossril did not answer magical queries, we assumed he was dead and his force defeated. Spies riding foulwings from Sember-home were sent to overfly easternmost Cormyr, and return before they could provoke any response in force from Azoun's war wizards. They found no sign of Shan-dril or her companions and concluded she must have gone into the Hullack Forest, seeking cover."

"Your spies in the court at Suzail and among the war wizards?"

"Reported nothing," Fzoul replied. "So far as we know, Shandril does not have the backing of Azoun—nor is he trying to gain spellfire for himself. He may not even know that it is within his borders."

There was a faint shriek from outside the chamber, and then another, louder one. The eye tyrant turned. "Sacrifices? At this time, Fzoul?"

"No," the priest replied. "We understand it is custom-ary for you to feed about now, each day."

The beholder's eyestalks began to whip and coil sinu-ously in evident pleasure. "My thanks for this courtesy," it said, drifting eagerly forward.

An instant later, they heard curses, sobs, and strug-gling noises just outside the chamber—and then a naked man was hurled into the sanctum, cartwheeling in the air. In the doorway, they saw a flash of moving metal from the staff that had struck him. It was still trailing motes of magical light as it withdrew.

Some of those same sparkling points of light clung to the body of the terrified man, who did not fall to the ground, but drifted to a halt in the air close to Fzoul.

The man saw the beholder looming over him, shrieked in terror, and lunged away, soaring through the air toward the doorway he had come in by.

"Sporting," said the beholder, as the man flew away, into the light spilling from the passage beyond.

An instant later, he struck an invisible barrier with a crash. The snapping of bones could be clearly heard, and the man sagged limply, drifting toward the ground.

"Not too sporting," Fzoul replied with amusement. At his words, the captive's head snapped up. His eyes narrowed with hatred, and he dived through the air, snarling as he swooped down at the unmoving high priest.

He never got there. An eye flared, and he was dragged inexorably sideways toward the waiting maw of the eye tyrant. Its jaws snapped; fine droplets of blood rained down, and the legless body jerked and spasmed in midair.

Xarlraun eyed the limp, hanging man disappointedly, then drifted in to gulp him whole. "I expected a better fight," it said between crunching noises.

"The next one may be better," Fzoul said smoothly.

The beholder belched, shaking the chamber and making Fzoul's stomach churn and his eyes sting. It licked its lips, considering. "That one had drunk much sherry, not long ago." Then it leaned toward the priest, and said in silky warning, "You won't be foolish enough to try poisoning any of these morsels, will you?"

"Of course not," said Fzoul. "That sort of behavior is beneath me." His tones were calm, even scornful, but a sudden dampness glistened on his forehead.

Outside the chamber, the screaming began again. The beholder listened and then said, "I'll eat again when we're done. Please give the necessary orders—and have all the priests who are listening just outside withdraw, as well." Its voice sounded coldly amused.

As the high priest came back from the doorway, the beholder spoke again. "Go on, Fzoul. I'll regard the map if I feel the need. Your aerial spies found no trace of the spellfire wielder and assumed she'd gone to cover in the

Hullack Forest."

"Aye," Fzoul said. "Manshoon felt that if magic was to succeed against spellfire at all, it must be by new spells devised to deal with spellfire or by some combination of spells or manner of attack that we, as experienced workers-with-Art, had missed seeing. I agree with this view. We had already sent out a summons to all our magelings, to a meeting in the High Hall. When they met, Manshoon invited them to go out and seize spellfire by whatever means they chose."

"Filling the field with a score or more of wild, ruthless, half-tutored mages? Was that wise?" The beholder drifted closer, fixing several disapproving eyes on the priest.

"It was necessary," Fzoul said, trying not to sound apologetic. "Our magelings need a weeding. We'd like some of them tested and all of them given experience, and there are one or two who have developed or found spells we'd like to see in action—before their owners have time to plan and properly prepare for an assault on us. The stability of the Brotherhood is better served if we remain in control of it for some time to come."

"So your force from the Stonelands is lost in the north reaches of Hullack Forest, various magelings are wandering all over the map, and Shandril's disappeared from view—in a sovereign realm with its own powerful band of organized wizards. *This* is your plan?" Its deep voice purred with sarcasm as it drifted lower.

Fzoul stepped back despite himself, but continued flatly, "The force under Karkul Memrimmon laid a trap for Shandril, which she fought her way out of. Evidently thinking herself free of enemies, she camped and practiced hurling her spellfire for hours. After dark, Karkul's force surrounded her and attacked."

"And were slaughtered in their turn?" The beholder sounded amused.

"Well, yes—a few fled, but Karkul, the upperpriest, and the rest fell. Shandril had to destroy a fair stretch of forest to do this and now, we believe, has exhausted her spellfire again—with two magelings moving in on her."

"Three I know of," Xarlraun corrected.

Fzoul raised an eyebrow. "You seem to have sources unknown to me," he said, his voice a soft challenge.

The beholder seemed to smile. "Have you any more of those flying bites?"

Fzoul nodded. "I'll see." He strode to the door of the sanctum, gave curt orders, indicated a guard at random, and returned to the beholder.

"Tell me more of your plans, should this Shandril escape from the Hullack Forest," the eye tyrant ordered.

Fzoul quelled a flash of anger and nodded, face expressionless. "Our agents in Arabel have orders to do whatever it takes—even revealing their loyalties by making open war in the city—to prevent Shandril from moving farther west into Cormyr. We hope to drive her to the Stonelands or Tilverton, where our forces are stronger. At that time, the more powerful members of the Brotherhood will take an active part in trying to seize spellfire—with the very real reward of rising to lead us all if they gain it."

"And what if you do gain it? What use is this power to blast men to ashes?"

"We see—" Fzoul began as the terrified guard, cursing and shouting, was catapulted naked into the chamber. When he saw Fzoul, he began to plead, offering money, mistresses, information about hidden treasure caches and the doings of Fzoul's rivals—Fzoul turned his back and walked away.

The temple guard flew at the high priest from behind, hands outstretched to grasp Fzoul's neck. The beholder watched with interest. When Fzoul made no move, it reluctantly reached out with its eye-powers to prevent murder. The diving guard tore through the map image, scattering it into sparkling nothingness—and then was tugged aside, jerking and thrashing as a fish struggles in a net.

Fzoul turned his head and smiled up at the eye tyrant. "My thanks," he said. "Primarily we are interested in spellfire to avoid having it fall into the hands of our enemies. If it is lost to all, we will not be utterly devastated. If it falls into the hands of foes, we *may* be utterly destroyed."

The high priest turned to meet Xarlraun's central eye directly. The guard was trying to flee, now, darting back and forth as ten eyestalks turned and twisted to follow him. The beholder rumbled, "Proceed. Tell me what the Brotherhood would do with spellfire."

"If we did gain spellfire," Fzoul responded, "we would use it first to enforce discipline in the ranks of the Brotherhood, until obedience was absolute. Here"—he waved at the sanctum around them—"we suspect Manshoon means to make us utterly loyal to him, whatever our god's commands."

He spread his hands in a gesture of resignation, and continued. "When Manshoon felt secure enough in his control of the Brotherhood, spellfire would be used to destroy key foes—Elminster of Shadowdale and the Simbul of Aglarond, for example—who often anticipate and ruin our plans."

Fzoul watched the doomed guard flying with frenzied skill, dodging and darting about the ceiling of the chamber. One of the beholder's eyes swiveled around to meet his, and he went on. "Thereafter, spellfire would be used carefully and covertly to remove strong leaders who oppose us—Azoun of Cormyr, Maalthiir of Hillsfar, and the rulers of Mulmaster, Calaunt, and then Thay. Our objective would be to advance our own agents to positions of greater influence in these places, to make them more amenable to our causes so we need not destroy or openly conquer them."

The high priest watched the guard swoop right at the eye tyrant, kicking eyestalks aside, then dart around behind its central body, making a desperate dive for the door.

"Experimentation with spellfire, to make it something we can preserve with breeding or nurture with training, would then follow," Fzoul added, as the guard plunged at the open doorway. At the last instant, the man swept his hands back to his sides and closed his eyes.

The snap of his breaking neck was softer and duller than either the priest or the beholder had expected. Silently the eye tyrant used its powers to raise the corpse to its waiting mouth, cheated of its sport again.

It idly rolled the lifeless guard over and over in midair as it spoke. "Will you take a direct hand in trying to seize spellfire now from this Shandril?"

"Not willingly," Fzoul replied. "I fear Manshoon has come to view this battle as a personal one after Shandril slew a lover of his—Symgharyl Maruel, the sorceress known as the Shadowsil—and sent him fleeing from battle. In that flight, he lost his favorite dragon steed, one long bonded to him and of unquestioned loyalty, and had to fight his way through baatezu to get out of the ruins of Myth Drannor. *He* will attack in person if he gets an excuse."

"I asked what the high priest would do, not how he expects Manshoon to behave," the eye tyrant observed coldly.

Fzoul answered it with a wintry smile—and the words, "I have learned the benefits of waiting until the battle-hungry and the foolish have worn a foe down, and then stepping in at the end. An open attack on Shandril would not be prudent, for the Brotherhood or for myself; if I fight her, it must be another way."

"We think so, too," Xarlraun replied. "And because of this, we have chosen to support you, Fzoul, over Manshoon. You seem wise enough not to act against him, or reveal our part, openly—for in a struggle between you two, both you and the wizard would be destroyed; the only question would be whether you would succeed in taking Manshoon down with you."

The beholder's jaws opened, and swallowed the temple guard whole. Fzoul inclined his head in a nod of agreement, and then waited for the crunching sounds to subside.

When they did, the beholder went on as if there had been no interruption. "You wondered as to my sources earlier. Most important among them is a creature Manshoon thinks he controls absolutely—a lich lord known as Iliph Thraun. He is mistaken; *you* now control it absolutely—with this."

The beholder's sides heaved, and it spat out something from an internal organ. Fzoul ignored the red saliva dripping from the thing as the beholder's eye powers brought it smoothly down to him. Before he had to foul his hands on it, it spun in the air, unwrapping itself. Soiled cloth fell away; Fzoul stepped back hastily when he saw the marble floor smoking where drops of saliva had fallen.

Out of the last wrappings floated a fist-sized black gem in a brass cage. From the stone, a neck-chain dangled. Fzoul put out his hand for it, and the beholder nodded approvingly.

"Put it on only when you wish to see out of the lich's eyes and work your will on it. Your identity and mind is shielded from Manshoon, the lich itself, and all others; use your will to break Manshoon's only when you deem the time is right—that will probably come when he tries to use the lich lord against you."

"What, precisely, is a lich lord?" Fzoul asked carefully, eyeing the gem in his hand. It felt cold and heavy and seemed to watch him menacingly, looking up from his palm and awaiting its chance.

"A failed lich, of an ancient sort. It needs to feed on spell energy to continue its unlife, and takes the form of a disembodied, flying human skull, able to see, speak, think, and cast spells. The gem you hold contains the soul of Iliph Thraun; through it you can control the lich lord absolutely, even to drive it to its own clear destruction. Your will prevails over all other spells, items, and inducements acting on the lichnee."

The beholder drifted away. "I strongly recommend you keep that gem hidden; at all times beware the treachery of Manshoon and the ambitious wizards he commands. I am grateful for the meals you so thoughtfully provided; you should be grateful that I forgive you for the poisons you introduced into the first one; sadly for your ambitions, I have been immune to those particular killers for several centuries. Farewell, priest."

Fzoul stood frozen as the beholder drifted out of the chamber. Whatever unseen barrier had blocked the open doorway was gone now, or had no effect on Xarlraun.

Then the priest suddenly set down the gem and slid it away from him with hasty force. As it skidded into a corner, he hurriedly cast a spell. And stood waiting, tense and watchful, hands raised to cast another spell. Silence. Fzoul let out a heavy breath, and drew in another. Time passed. He drew another breath. Nothing happened. The gem lay quiescent.

Still protected by his spell and looking very thoughtful, Fzoul regarded it. Then he suddenly strode to the door, and called for six upperpriests by name.

Turning, he cast another spell—and the gem was suddenly gone from the room. He nodded, satisfied, and then set off down the passage, snapping orders to the priests at hand; there was much to do.

Five

OLD ALE IN AN OLDER CASK

At last even the old wolf lies down under the weight of his years. He may be strong, but know ye: some years are heavier than others.

Annath of Neverwinter
Sayings of the North
Year of the Cold Soul

"Up, lass. I know you're exhausted, but it's walk exhausted or meet death right soon—so let's see you *up*, lass!" The dwarf's rough voice was close by her ear, one strong hand gentle on her shoulder.

Shandril was adrift in a horrific dream: burning all the friends she'd ever known with runaway spellfire. Writhing and arching in the flames, they melted away to blackened, bare skeletons—except for their heads, screaming at her in anger and agony. She heard the rough burr of Delg's voice from somewhere near and reached out a lazy hand. Her fingers found bristling hair, trailed through it—and caught in a tangle.

"Aaargh! My *beard!*" The dwarf's angry growl was almost drowned out by a shout of laughter from Narm.

Shandril came fully awake, opening her eyes to morning light in the woods and to the angry face of Delg inches from her own, dragged there by her grip on his beard. Horrified, she let go and brought a hand up to cover her mouth in confusion. A breath later, looking at Delg's injured expression, she used that same hand to stifle giggles.

Delg let her laugh until she reached the helpless whooping stage, then sighed, reached out one hairy hand to the front of her tunic, and pulled.

Shandril was dragged bodily up from where she lay slumped against a tree, pillowed on clumps of moss Narm had torn up and arranged for her the night before. They had left the scorched ruin of battle behind and stumbled into the night—the morning, rather—for a good long time before collapsing in a damp hollow, somewhere very dark and near the ever-chuckling sound of running water.

Shandril was a little unsteady on her feet, and the morning—even here, in the dappled shade of the trees—seemed very bright. Delg was glaring up at her, his hand on her arm.

"Can you walk?" he demanded gruffly. "Speak, lass! I need to know you've still got all your wits after last night."

"I—I think so," she managed before Narm approached.

Her husband bowed, reached a hand toward her as a lord grandly leads his lady into a dance—and in his empty palm a dozen roses appeared.

Shandril gasped in surprise, and he put them in her arms with an air of triumph. Their sweet fragrance swirled around her, and she smiled as she felt the magic that formed them surging into her, making spellfire waken and flow. The roses glowed for a moment—and then, with the sound of many tiny bells, faded away and were gone.

Shandril stared at her empty arms a little sadly. "My only regret, love, is that they're gone if I drain them," she said, eyes brimming.

Narm shrugged. "I guess I'll just have to go on studying that spell until I get it right."

"Get it *right?*" Delg's voice was rough with derision. "Gods, but now I know how wizards get all the lasses. . . ." he muttered in a low aside that could be heard at least a hundred trees away.

"Yes," Narm replied with a smile. "I managed the 'no thorns' bit, but the color . . ."

The dwarf squinted at him. "They were red!"

Narm smiled. "I was trying for blue." Shandril laughed delightedly, and drew his face down to hers. His arms were strong and eager, his mouth sweet—and as they embraced, Shandril heard a loud, hawking sound. Delg, standing just behind them, spat far off into the trees in disgust, startling something small into scuttling flight through the fallen forest leaves.

"There'll be time enough for that sort o' thing later, when we're well away from here," the dwarf growled. "One Zhent band found us, and others may know we're here now, but they're all sure to find us if we stay here, right at the end of the trail we left crashing through things in the dark last night—while the two of you cuddle and kiss and whisper sweet secrets. Come *on!*"

Narm lifted his head. "Sorry, Delg. We're—we're with you." And they stepped out amid ferns and tree roots to begin another long march through the dim depths of the endless wood.

"We've got to move far today," the dwarf said, "and not be found by anyone or anything. With no spellfire and your best spells gone, lad, we can't risk any fights. Since your lady's got such a dainty stomach of mornings, I suggest we do without eating until around highsun . . . but drink deep at this stream and fill all our skins while I keep watch."

Narm and Shandril drank, washed, filled their skins, and went off into the bushes. The dwarf meanwhile kept alert, axe in hand as he trotted around, peering suspiciously into the trees.

Shandril took off the spare robe Narm had lent her last night. A few blackened scraps—all that was left of her own clothes—still clung to her here and there. She brushed them off, sighing, and rummaged in her ever-lighter pack.

When she swung the pack onto her shoulder, she was wearing her last intact clothes, inherited when she joined the Company of the Bright Spear—the much-patched homespun tunic and breeches of a down-on-his-luck thief. That bold first step into adventure seemed a long time ago now.

"Why so tense?" Narm asked, coming up beside Delg. "I haven't seen any Zhents about—and I've looked as far off as I can, too."

"Eyes, lad," the dwarf growled up at him. "I can feel them, every moment. We're being watched, again."

"Should I tell Shan?" Narm asked quietly.

"Not just after she's been off in the bushes, lad," the dwarf said, looking critically at the blemishes along the edge of his axe-blade. That Zhent idiot had certainly managed to bring it down on a lot of stones last night. "But soon; I don't want her walking carefree."

Shandril ran despairing fingers through her hair as she came toward them. "Oh, for a bath! I *stink!*"

"We all do, lass," the dwarf told her gravely. "All the easier for dogs to find us, if they've got any more with them."

"Gods," Shandril said, face paling, "don't remind me."

"No, no," Narm said, with feeling. "Don't remind *me*. I can still feel those teeth."

Shandril remembered all too vividly, retched, and turned hastily away. They watched her shoulders shake for a moment, and Narm turned to Delg with a sigh.

"Now look what you've done," he said.

"Nay, lad—yon's your handiwork. Grab her, now, and let's be on our way. We haven't time for foolishness."

"Foolishness?" Shandril's voice was weak but indignant, her face the color of old bone as she rose from her knees.

The dwarf glared at her. "Aye, foolishness. You've several days' march of woods to be sick in—you don't have to *stop* each time you feel ill. On!"

She glared back at him, took a deep breath, wiped her mouth clean, and went on.

* * * * *

"What was that?"

"The sound of your own big feet, Othrogh," the Zhent swordmaster muttered. "Quiet, now—the maid could be the other side of that next tree."

The half-orc sniffed the air, then shook his head with an emphatic grunt. "No. I'd smell her."

Around him, the other members of the patrol rolled their eyes, made various faces, and sighed. Swordmaster Cleuvus looked at Othrogh sourly and said, "Just keep your lips shut for awhile, hey? They gave us all the same orders—and you heard 'em as well as I did." He looked up. "The rest of you," he added shortly, "spread out—now! She hurls fire, remember? If you all crowd together under the same tree like that, how could she miss?"

There were various grumbles and dark looks; he knew

they'd only gathered to hear him berate Othrogh—and they knew he knew. Cleuvus grinned. Ah, well, swordmasters were never loved. Except when they went to town with coins enough to hire—

He was still thinking such vivid, pleasant thoughts when the tree beside him grew a stout arm with a mace at the end of it and rudely crushed the back of his head in. Cleuvus fell on his face like a thrown stone, thinking of love forever.

"Skulk through the forest, would ye? Wear dark armor that offends mine eyes, would ye? Oh, the crimes! The *crimes!*" The voice rose in mock anguish amongst the startled gasps of the Zhents, and its owner lumbered into their midst—and bowed.

"Rathan Thentraver, Knight of Myth Drannor, at thy service. Looking for little girls in the forest, are we? Well, if ye find any, be so good as t—"

"*Get him!*" The eldest Zhent snarled, and swords flashed in a sudden rush of dark armor.

A man dropped heavily, cursed—and then gurgled and fell silent. The object he'd tripped over rose, dusted himself off, and then calmly glided forward to bury his bloodied dagger in the back of another warrior.

Torm of the Knights grinned at his comrade Rathan across the tumult of clashing weapons, then said, "Now is that nice? You could've waited for me to get some blood. You could have let Torm—much thinner, handsomer, and younger than a certain priest of Tymora—strike first! You could have busied yourself at some ritual or other; the one where you wear ladies' underthings and pretend to be a paladin, perhaps—but oh, no! The clarion call of battle was too strong. The—"

He broke off to duck frantically aside as two Zhent blades crossed in the space where the knight's face had been a moment earlier.

Puffing, Rathan smashed his way through another Zhent's guard, shattering the sword raised against him. As the man fell, spraying blood from his crushed face all over the knight's knees, Rathan said, "Oh, aye—let ye strike first and grab all the glory. Betray the commandments of Lady Luck to dare all and leave my life to chance. Let a clever-tongued thief go ahead of a respected, dignified— nay, even rotund—pillar of whatever community I'm currently passing through. Not by the Lady's laughter! When the bards sing ballads of this day, when two knights went up against almost a dozen Zhent sword-swingers in the forest, 'tis Rathan whose deeds will awe. Rathan who'll get the beauteous maiden as his reward. Rathan who'll—"

"Take his usual pratfall," Torm put in, his blade finding the throat of the Zhent whose frantic swing had made Rathan stumble back hastily. The fat priest tripped over a tree root and sat down heavily. "*Oww!*" he complained as the ground shook.

For their next few breaths, the knights were too busy slaying the last few Zhentilar to notice that the tree whose root had felled Rathan shook now in soundless laughter. Two golden eyes high on its trunk watched the last blood spilled, and then closed, just as Torm leaned against the bark below them, breathing hard, and said, "Well, still no sign of what we seek—how many Zhents is that, now?"

"Thirty-three," Rathan's voice came back gloomily to him from the other side of the tree. "*Why* do they always come along just when I need to relieve myself? Tymora, if ye're listening—tell me that!"

* * * * *

The day passed in continuous plodding travel—one weary stride after another, slipping and ducking and scrambling through, around, and over trees—fallen trees, leaning trees, and gnarled, tangled, growing-in-all-directions trees, damp leaf-mold slippery under their feet. Here and there pale brown mushrooms the size of halflings' heads rose up in clumps, and rotting stumps held lush green cushions of moss.

Shandril hadn't thought she could ever tire of trees—but then, she'd never thought she'd see so many trees in her life, let alone in one day. These weren't the beautiful giants of the Elven Court; Hullack Forest was dark and dense and damp, its trees grown thick together.

The three travelers felt like unwelcome intruders; none of them had wanted to stop at highsun to eat. They'd hastened on, instead, searching for higher ground and a clearing where they could camp.

The sun had sunk low by the time the ground began rising again. Here and there, rocks showed through the moss and the fungi-cloaked wreckage of fallen trees. Ravines and gullies appeared more often, and the black pools of standing water were smaller and fewer. As the sun slipped to a last, low red ribbon under the trees, the weary travelers' hearts rose. They were climbing sharply at last.

"Delg," Narm said excitedly from behind the dwarf as they slipped and clambered upward, Shandril between them, "some of these rocks have been cut and dressed. Look: straight edges on this one—this must be some sort of ruin."

"You don't say," the dwarf said softly. "It wouldn't surprise you overmuch, I suppose, if I told you I'd noticed a thing or two about these rocks myself. . . ."

The dwarf's voice died away in wonder as they came out into a height of crumbling stone arches, walls, and broken stairs. Shattered pillars reached like jagged fingers up at the twilight sky. Selune shone faintly just above the horizon as night came down on them.

"Well, here we are for the night, whatever your likings," Delg said, peering all around with keen interest. "This is *old,* old indeed—and not dwarven nor yet elven, either. I'll have a look at this in morning light .. . . I can tell the age of the stonework better then."

"For now," Narm put in firmly, looking at the dark trees behind them, "we'd better find a corner of this we can defend, or we may not live to *see* the morn."

Delg sighed. "Shandril," he said plaintively, "you had a thousand thousand dalesmen to choose from after—after the company fell. Did you *have* to choose a whiner and a worrier?"

Shandril sighed right back. "Delg," she said mildly, "I love this man. Give him at least the respect you'd give a dwarf of his age, will you?"

"I *am*, Lady. I am," Delg replied, and they saw his grinning teeth flash in the growing moonlight. He lurched over to Narm and clapped him low on the back, hard enough to send the young wizard stumbling ahead helplessly.

"Forgive my manner, lad. I don't mean most of it—much. Your lady can tell you how it was in the company. We were swordmates together—and, mind you, she survived it, then. Ferostil was nastier than ever I was, and Rymel more the prankster, too. If mere words are enough to hurt you, lad, grow some armor speedily; it doesn't get any easier on the ears as you get older."

"My thanks, Delg," Narm said shortly, "but I'd be happier if you could tell me what *that* is."

"What, lad?" Delg's axe glinted in the moonlight.

"That thing, there!" Narm said fiercely, pointing. Far away across tumbled arches and broken rubble, something dark and winged seemed to both fly and to *flow* over the stone beneath it, like some sort of giant black snake. A snake with batlike wings, eyes like glimmering rubies, and a cruel snout. It was coming toward them, not hurrying, as though dinner seldom escaped it.

"Shandril!" Narm said commandingly. "Hold still, and I'll cast my light spell." He lowered his voice, and added, "It's my last—to feed your spellfire. . . . Ready?"

Shandril nodded, and Narm hurried through the gestures of casting the spell as the dwarf advanced to stand as foreguard, hefting his axe. "Battle again, is it?" he muttered. "Then let it come! Clanggedin be with me and guide my axe."

Narm's casting ended as the winged thing rose up into the air before them, passing over Delg's reaching axe. No magical radiance appeared beneath Narm's hands, which rested on Shandril's neck. She had willed the light into her, drawing the tingling energy in through the bare skin of her neck. Flames danced briefly in her eyes as she waved him away, then looked up to face the winged horror directly.

It loomed above her. Dark and terrible, its leathery wings beat in eerie silence, its bony jaws spread wide, its red glowing eyes met hers. "Turn back," Shandril said, "and we will not harm you. Turn back!"

* * * * *

Above the glowing crystal ball, a light feminine voice chuckled. "They do *talk* a lot, these fools. Always threatening and declaiming grandly—when they're not pleading, that is."

"True, Mairara," came an older female voice in answer. "Yet I fear this servant creature will fail us as all the others have done."

Gathlarue set her goblet down on the tabletop and stared into the crystal ball that had risen to float just

above it. In its curved depths they both beheld the scene
in the ruins. Both stared so intently into the globe that
neither noticed as one leg of their table grew a silent,
bearded smile for an instant, ere a quiet wisp of a shadow
rose from it and slipped away.

* * * * *

In deadly silence, the dark horror folded its wings and
plunged down on Shandril. Narm cried out and drew his
dagger, and Delg's axe rose as he raced in to swing at the
flank of the descending menace. But there was a sudden
flash and rolling roar of flame.

While backing toward a fallen stone wall, Shandril had
hurled fire into the beast's open mouth.

The man and the dwarf both staggered hastily back
from the rush of flame as the monster, covered with it,
perished in writhing tatters of smoking flesh. It gave off a
horrible smell. With mixed awe and satisfaction, Narm
and Delg watched for a moment while it shriveled and
burned. Then they heard a queer choking sound from
behind the ruined wall.

In three bounds Narm was around the corner, heart in
his mouth. His wife knelt on the stones. Shandril shook
her head, waving him feebly away. She was being thoroughly and wretchedly sick. "The *smell*," she gasped.
"Gods, how vile!"

"Vile, indeed," said a new voice from beyond her.
"Were I younger and less—'hem—stout of stomach, I'd
be doing that too. Which should serve ye as a warning,
girl, not to be hurling flames about at just everything that
moves. Ye'll burn up something ye value, one o' these
days. Phew! Come away, come away, all of ye—that thing
smells as if it did nothing but roll in dung and eat dead
things."

"Who," Delg and Narm demanded together, "are you?"

The stout, dark figure beyond Shandril drew something from its belt—a dagger whose blade glowed with blue fire in the night. Narm stepped quickly in front of Shandril, raising his own dagger, but the man shook his head and brandished the glowing blade to serve as a light.

Its radiance shone down on him, illuminating the grizzled, scarred, and yet somehow good-natured face of a burly man clad in flopping, food-stained leather armor. Fierce brows and mustaches gleamed gray-white on his large and weather-stained face. Huge swash-boots flapped beneath an ample paunch as he stepped forward, handed the glowing dagger to Narm—who juggled it gingerly— then swept around the young mage and grandly offered his hand to Shandril to help her rise.

Warily she avoided it, coming to her feet in a crouch, facing him. "Yes," she said, fire winking in her eyes, "who are you, sir?"

The battered, leonine face wagged sadly from side to side. "An' here I thought I was famous at last, over at least the lands of all the North. Ah, well."

He drew back from Shandril, plucked his dagger deftly from Narm's grasp, and struck a heroic pose, holding the dagger forth as though it were a great battle-sword. "I am Mirt, called the Moneylender, of Waterdeep. Men once called me—'hem—Mirt the Merciless. Some folk call me the Old Wolf."

Delg eyed the stout man sourly. "I am Delg, of the dwarves." It was a gentle dwarven insult, implying that the speaker did not trust the one he addressed enough to furnish his last name.

Mirt bowed in reply, and made a quick, complex sign with one hand.

Delg's eyes widened. "So," he said with new respect,

"you have known others of my race as friends, before. Well met, stout one. What brings you here—to the depths of this forest, and alone?"

"Well met, short one," Mirt replied easily. "I like to pick mushrooms this time of year, and Hullack Forest seemed a nice enough place—quiet an' all, until spellfire started roaring about all over the place, and—well, ne'er mind. Come back to my camp, all of ye, and we can swap stories for a bit. Until dawn, say . . ."

"A moment," Narm said quietly. "Delg's question is a fair one, sir. Before we follow you into gods know what, tell us how you come to be here. We are—suspicious folk, these days. Everyone and everything in Faerûn seems eager to kill us."

"Ye, too?" Mirt replied mildly, raising his brows. "'Tis a plague, it seems. They're always trying to kill me, too."

Narm waited. A breath of silence passed, and Shandril quite deliberately climbed up a ragged edge of stone wall to stand above them. She glanced quickly all around, and then stood facing the man who called himself Mirt, one hand raised. Fire licked along her fingers for a moment.

The stout man watched her, nodded as if in acknowledgment of power, and then turned back to the young mage and smiled winningly. "Well, Narm Tamaraith, ye're right."

Narm frowned. How did this man know his name?

He opened his mouth to ask just that, but the stout man waved him to silence, saying, "Aye, it's rude of me not to congratulate ye on your wise marriage to Shandril Shessair right off, and set ye three at ease."

Mirt smiled up at Shandril and added, "The bride is as beautiful as I've been told, and no mistake. Well met, all of ye." He bowed again, various daggers and scabbards about his belt jangling and ringing, and smoothed his mustaches with broad, hairy fingers.

"I've awaited ye here, in these long-desolate ruins of Tethgard—*there's* a tale I'll have to tell ye some time— because a friend told me ye'd be along, soon, and probably in need of aid. When young folk go blundering about the countryside . . ."

Delg rolled his eyes. "All right," he broke in, "we may as well be finding your camp. I can see there're some good tales to be heard. You wouldn't know a certain mage called Elminster, would you?"

"Or a lady named Storm?" Shandril asked softly.

Mirt chuckled and stepped forward to hand her lightly down from her rocky height. "As it happens, both those names belong to friends of mine," he rumbled. "Convenient, aye?" He passed his dagger to Narm again. "Here, lad—ye hold the light; then perhaps ye can stop looking so suspiciously at me, like I'm aching to put it in yer lady's breast the moment yer back is turned. There is something I was given to show ye. . . ."

He pulled off a worn leather gauntlet. They saw a brass ring around one of the man's fingers and a fine chain encircling his thick, hairy wrist. Something small gleamed as it dangled from the chain: a silver harp. Then it all vanished again beneath the dirty leather; its owner winked and turned with a rolling gait to lead the way past a pile of tumbled stones and into the night.

"You know we have enemies?" Shandril asked him. "Some, I must tell you, are powerful indeed. Their magic—"

Mirt chuckled. "Aye, aye, make me tremble in my boots, girl. Ye've run into those Zhentarim snakes, as do all in the North sooner or later, and some of the crazed-wits that every land in Faerûn is home to; the Cult of the Dragon, in yer case. Worry not. The worst they can do is kill ye." He shrugged. "Besides, their arts cannot spy on us or find us while ye stay close to me. I've magic of my own—a little—that I got from a grateful mage long, long ago. It cloaks me, she said, from scrying and probings of the mind, and suchlike. So we can all sing songs and have too much to drink well into the morning."

"Stout one," Delg murmured, "if you keep on like this, it will *be* morning."

Mirt rolled his eyes in silent reply and waved at them to accompany him. They followed the stout, wheezing old adventurer down into a little gully in the rocks, where several dark doorways opened out of crumbling walls— the cellars of now-vanished buildings. Mirt shambled toward one opening.

Shandril yawned, stumbled, and almost fell. Narm rushed to hold her up and found her swaying with weariness, almost asleep on her feet.

Mirt wheezed up close to them, peered into Shandril's sleepy face, and sighed. "The problem with ladies, lad," he remarked to Narm, "is that they take all the *fun* out o' things. After, that is, they've put most of the fun into things, I grant."

He lurched on into the darkness. "Mind yer step, now. The best adventures begin when yer boots step proper and sure along some path or other to glory. . . ."

* * * * *

When Shandril opened her heavy, sleep-encrusted eyes again, the light told her that it was late afternoon. She sat up with a start, fearing that something had gone very wrong. They should have been up and away from here at the first light of morning. Narm's cloak fell from her; underneath it, she wore only her breeches.

Narm smiled reassuringly at her from nearby, where he sat in the arch of an old, ruined stone window, his spellbook on his lap.

"What happened?" she demanded to know, pulling on her boots and getting up. Where was her tunic?

"You needed sleep—sleep you didn't get enough of, after all your fire-hurling. So we let you sleep. Delg's been fishing most of the day in some pools at the other end of the ruins."

Shandril strode to him. "*Fishing?*"

"Aye—he said he wanted to be done before you were ready to bathe in the same water." Narm grinned—and then ducked aside to get his spellbook out of the way of her friendly fists.

She pummeled him playfully, until he caught her wrists. They rolled over, chuckling and straining to slap and tickle each other—until their struggles took them over the sill of the window, to a hard and graceless landing on the turf below.

Delg stumped toward them in dripping triumph, gleaming fish gasping and flapping in both hands. He raised an eloquent eyebrow.

Shandril met his gaze, blushed, and said, "It's not what you think."

"Oh, no," Mirt said in jolly derision, from behind the dwarf. "Of *course* not . . ."

Shandril scrambled to her feet. "Well, it's *not,*" she said indignantly and marched back to where she'd lain. She turned, a dangerous look in her eye, and stood with hands on hips to glare at them all. "What have you done with my *tunic?*"

Then she met Mirt's appraising eyes, blushed, and covered herself with her arms. Delg kept his eyes carefully on hers, and said, "It's drying, on the rocks yonder. It took me awhile to find the right plants to scrub your smell out of it with."

"My smell?" Shandril sighed; she just didn't have any more energy left to be indignant. She turned to snatch up

Narm's cloak—but stopped, staring.

"Look," she said in tones of wonder, then reached out a hand.

"*Don't!*" Delg flung his fish down and shoved her roughly aside. "In strange places, girl, don't reach for things barehanded."

Fast as the dwarf was, Mirt was faster. The fat merchant strode around them both, boots flapping, and plucked up what had caught Shandril's eye. It had lain among the stones beside where her head had been the night through. They all saw it then—a teardrop-shaped gem, smooth and hard and iridescent, like the still-wet scales of the fish Delg had dropped in his haste to stop Shandril. It winked and sparkled in Mirt's hand.

As he turned it, the colors in the heart of the gem mirrored the rainbow and seemed to flash and swirl like liquid in a glass goblet. "My, but it's a beautiful thing," the fat man said softly. "The gods must have left it here for ye to find, lass."

He held it out toward her; Delg gave a hoarse exclamation and grabbed it from him. "Look!" One stubby finger pointed at a tiny, exquisite engraving on the curving flank of the stone: a harp between the points of a crescent moon, with four stars spaced around. "The sign of the Harpers!"

Shandril reached for it, and he laid it gently in her cupped hands.

"Aye, keep it, lass—it cannot be a bad thing." The dwarf turned to rake Mirt with a keen look. "D'you know what sort of gem it is?"

The fat man nodded. "Aye. A rogue stone."

The dwarf nodded, eyeing him suspiciously. "I wonder how it came to be here?" he asked.

Mirt shrugged, smiled slightly, and looked up at the sky. "The gods work in strange ways, their wisdom hidden from us 'til after they're done," he quoted, in the manner of a pompous priest.

Narm thought Delg would bristle at *that* hoary old saying, but the dwarf only smiled and said, "Keep that stone safe, lass—and not worn openly, for all to see. You'd best leave it with your lad while you wash—if you go down with him now, we'll have these fish ready when you're done."

Shandril smiled happily and did as she was bid.

* * * * *

The fire crackled, dying to hot red-glowing coals. Delg poked at it, and then went to his pack, which lay among the rocks. Well back from the coals, Narm sat beside a small candle-lamp, intent on his spellbook. Mirt stood watch somewhere off in the darkness.

Shandril, comfortable for the first time in what seemed like days, lay at ease in the warmth of the fire. No spellfire roiled or tingled within her; she was at peace with the world. She looked up as Delg bent over her—and sighed at his intent expression. She could hardly believe she'd once been hungry for adventure; now it seemed as if it would never let her alone.

"Lass," the dwarf said in low tones, unwrapping dark cloth from something he'd dredged out of his pack. "We need you to have spellfire. Touch this."

Wondering, Shandril peered at what he held. It was long, massive, and black—a dwarven war hammer. It looked ancient, made for brutal killing. From the deep cracks running across it and the bands of beaten metal that held it together, it looked to have seen use in some mighty battles. Awed, Shandril laid a finger on it to trace a curving crack—and felt the tingling of magic.

She looked up at Delg. "Oh, no. Delg, I couldn't." He

looked back at her, his intent expression unchanged. "It must be old, and precious to you," Shandril added softly. "I've never seen it, not in all the days since you first came to the inn with the company."

"It's a lump of forged metal, lass—my friends are far more precious to me than things I can make, and make again."

"You made this?"

"No—'tis ancient, lass; a war hammer of the Ironstar clan. It's about the only magic I have left."

Shandril looked at him, shocked. "I *can't,* Delg! Not your only magic—it must have cost you dearly."

Delg put a hand on hers. "Do you . . . are you my friend, Shan?" He seemed to find the words difficult.

Shandril reached out a hand to stroke his bearded jaw. "Of course, Delg. You know that." Impulsively, she leaned forward and kissed his grizzled cheek.

The dwarf harrumphed and shifted on his haunches. "Then, please, Shan—take the magic out o' this old thing . . . I've a bad feeling that we'll all be needing it, right soon now. Please?"

Reluctantly, staring into his beseeching eyes, Shandril grasped the cold, heavy head of the war hammer and pulled at its magic with her will, feeling the tingling flow begin.

At that moment, a twig snapped in the woods, not far away. Narm's head jerked up, and he threw down his spellbook to peer into the trees.

Delg closed Shandril's hands firmly around the war hammer and told her, "Keep on at it, lass!" Then he rose, took two rapid, gliding steps to where his axe was propped against a rock, and swung it up to the ready.

The attackers came in a rush once they saw the camp alert: a score or so of Zhentilar warriors, nets and clubs in their hands.

Delg looked around and cursed bitterly. Their fat,

wheezing host was nowhere to be seen.

"So I let my guard drop for once. Just *once!*" he snarled as the Zhents rushed down upon them. "Get your back against a rock, lad! Over *here,* where my axe can guard you!"

Narm had no time to rush across to him, even if he'd wanted to; a Zhent swung a club at his face in the next instant. The young mage ducked coolly, and two pulses of light burst from his hand into the face of the Zhent, who staggered, roared, and clutched at unseeing eyes. An instant later, Narm's dagger was in his throat.

As the Zhent toppled, Narm sprang away—right into the folds of a weighted net, backed up by a flurry of clubs. He went down without a sound.

Delg had time for no more than a glance at the young mage. His axe flashed as fast as his strong shoulders could swing it, but height made it hard for him to cut the nets—nets that were settling over him from above by twos and threes. He was soon entangled. Then the net-hurlers drew the net ropes taut with their own great weight and reach. The dwarf was dragged down.

Shandril dropped the crumbling war hammer—it *had* been old, its enchantments all that still held it together—and rose from behind where Delg was struggling. Flames leapt and raged in her eyes.

The men who hauled on the nets that held Delg down were only two paces away. Without a word she flung herself into them, letting spellfire rage from her hands and mouth. She crashed bruisingly against armor, heard men snarl and then shriek amid the rising, roaring flames—and then they fell silent.

Shandril drew the flames back into herself, and looked down at the blackened, smoking corpses. Beside her, Delg was fighting his way free of the scorched remnants of webbing as the next wave of Zhentilar rushed at them.

Shandril hurled spellfire again—ragged and faltering fire. She swallowed grimly and threw out one hand. Fire streaked from it to lash the Zhents bending over Narm. They staggered and fell, shouting hoarsely amid raging flames. Shandril raised her other hand to burn the warriors charging at her from the edge of the clearing. A moment later, however, they laughed in triumph as her spellfire rushed outward, then sputtered and died away in their faces.

She saw the cause: it came out of the night in front of the warriors, a band of utter darkness like a fence or an impossibly wide shield—a black band floating before them as they came. Just behind the warriors trotted a man in robes—a Zhentarim wizard!—with triumph shining in his dark eyes.

Shandril snarled and lashed out at their feet with spellfire, aiming below the dark band. The wizard hastily lowered his creation—but he was too slow to save the feet of one running Zhentilar. Spellfire blasted, and the man's boots vanished. With a shriek of agony, the charging warrior toppled forward into the darkness and was gone, his cry cut off suddenly. As the wall of darkness advanced, Shandril could see the remains of the man, twitching on the ground—two trunkless, footless legs.

Shandril gasped in horror—and then let her hands fall to her sides as the band of darkness came to a halt an arm's stretch away, right above the still-struggling form of Delg.

"On your knees, wench—or he dies!" The Zhentarim's voice was coldly triumphant.

Shandril looked both ways along the band. It fenced her in against the rocky remnant of an ancient wall, and from only feet away, a dozen or more Zhentilar warriors grinned at her, clubs raised.

She sank down, bitter despair flooding her mouth. The

wizard snapped his fingers, and hurled clubs were suddenly crashing in on her from all sides, even before the magical darkness winked out and was gone . . .

Six

FINDING THE TRUE WAY

*Finding one's true way in life can sometimes take an entire
lifetime, for it is often the hardest task one faces—after finding out where the next meal is coming from, how to keep
from freezing every winter night, where there's a sleeping-
place safe from enemies, and just who one can trust to share
it with, that is. Oh, aye—and finding the time to do all of
these things . . .*

Mirt the Moneylender
Wanderings With Quill and Sword
Year of Rising Mist

 "It *worked!* Hah-*ha!*" Fimril, mage of
the Zhentarim, laughed in glee as the
Zhentilar hastened to truss their senseless captives. They were careful not to
do the three any further damage—the
orders they had been so coldly given
about this came from much higher up
than this capering wizard, and had been most menacingly
specific.

Fimril had spent a long and hard year in private, hurling spells and modifying his castings until he'd fashioned

a shieldlike band of magical annihilation: a deadly magic
that sucked in light, warmth—even campfires and bra-
ziers of fire—and solid things, like stools and unfortunate
captives, too.

All the way here, through the forest, a tiny voice inside
him wailed that his shield wouldn't absorb spellfire after
all, that he was marching to his doom. If the spell failed
him, he was doomed . . . even if he escaped the girl's blazing spellfire, any of the warriors who got away would see
that he paid for his folly—painfully and permanently.
Magelings were not well loved among the Zhentilar fighting men.

But it *had* worked—and now not a one of them dared
betray him; their orders had been very clear about that.
Fimril chortled and gloated, watching the warriors
securely truss their unconscious quarry. Ah, but this was
sweet! At last, he, Fimril of Westgate, would get what he
deserved, rising in the ranks of the Zhentarim . . . perhaps even all the way.

He cast quick glances around, checking his bodyguard. Yes, they were ready—four burly, well-armed
Zhentarim standing in a crescent at his back, making
sure that no harm would come to him until he was safely
back in Zhentil Keep.

Fimril laughed aloud and shouted down to the man
who was busily checking the knots at Shandril's throat,
"Ho! Lyrkon! How are our losses this night?"

The Zhentilar finished his task, controlling his exasperation. The knots seemed tight enough: if she struggled,
she'd strangle herself. Aye, good enough. Slowly the
Zhentilar stood. "A moment, Lord Wizard; I'll see." Gods,
but this mage was going to be *insufferable* now . . .

He dusted his hands and looked around. Four—no,
five; he'd forgotten Duthspurn until his eyes fell on the
poor bastard's legs lying motionless on the ground. And

that should be all. . . . Wait, wasn't there a sixth, over there?

Lyrkon took a stride down the ruined wall—in time to see another of his men fall as silently as a gentle breeze glides through leafless trees. He stared at the hand that had appeared over Glondar's mouth—and as the soldier slumped, the face that came into view behind it: a fat, grinning face adorned with fierce gray-white brows and mustaches. Its blue-gray eyes met his own—and winked. Gods!

"Out swords!" he bellowed, pointing at where Glondar was being killed. "We're under attack!"

Along the wall, his men looked up at him, snatching up their clubs or drawing swords—and the one next to Glondar promptly collapsed, a sword through his armpit. The warrior next to him turned at the muffled groan—in time to get the blade of the fat, mustachioed stranger right through his throat.

"Where?" Fimril shouted, peering down at Lyrkon. "Who's attacking us?"

Lyrkon pointed along the wall with his blade. "*He* is, wizard!" he snarled, making an insult of the last word.

Fimril's nostrils flared in anger, and he felt his face going red. *That* was one soldier he could do without when this was over. Right now, though, he'd show them all.

Drawing himself up, Fimril pointed at the stranger, who was now battling his way along the wall. Turning his finger to keeping it aimed at the moving man, the Zhentarim thumbed open a finger-pouch in the breast pocket of his robe and spilled into his hand a dark powder that had once been a large black pearl. He cast it into the air in front of his lips as he spoke the echoing, awesome words that would bring death to the man—and to the nearest soldiers, but that was the luck the gods gave—

and drew himself up in cruel triumph to watch the slaughter.

Light that was somehow *dark* flashed between wizard and fat man—and back again!

The eyes of Fimril, would-be ruler of the Zhentarim, and those of his bodyguard darkened as one. The mage and his men toppled to the ground like emptied husks, dead upon the instant.

The fat, puffing stranger sighed and shook the smoking remnants of a ring from his finger, saying regretfully, "Watchful Order make . . . they just don't enchant these gewgaws the way they used to, when I was a lad . . ."

The last few Zhents, white to the lips, fell back before his lumbering advance, and as he crossed blades with the first and disarmed the man in a skirl of circling steel, they all turned and ran.

Mirt watched the man he'd disarmed scamper after the rest, and he sighed. When they were gone, he raised his voice in an eerie, singing, wordless call. It echoed mournfully off the tumbled stones of ruined Tethgard, and a long moment later, a soft reply came to him.

Mirt strode toward the origin of the sound. From a pile of rubble before him, a phantom lady slowly rose. She had long, swirling white hair and a beautiful face; her dark eyes stared into his with such sadness that Mirt found himself, as always, on the sudden edge of tears. Buried somewhere far beneath the debris, Mirt knew, lay the crypt where she had been entombed. Lady Duskreene of Tethgard, its door would say. Mirt silently added two words to the inscription he envisioned: Unquiet Spirit.

"Mirt," she said, in that soft, sad voice. "It has been long since you called me."

"Grandlady," Mirt said huskily. "I have need of yer— powers."

The translucent, dead-white watch-ghost frowned, emerging in a smooth, silent flight from the rubble, revealing her skeletal, legless torso. She floated in the air before him.

"Name your desire, son of my blood."

"There are soldiers fleeing this place—Zhentilar. They must be destroyed."

Duskreene smiled. "And your girth makes catching them all a doubtful prospect for you? Will you wait for me? I have been so lonely."

Mirt went heavily to one knee and bowed. "I will," he said formally.

She swirled over his head and arrowed off into the trees. After a moment, a terrified scream—suddenly cut off—came to Mirt's ears. A few breaths later, there was another, fainter and farther away.

Mirt got to his feet, grunting at the effort, and went over to Shandril. Checking that she was still breathing, he cut the knots at her throat with his dagger, and set about unbinding her.

A few breaths later, as he was carrying the freed Narm over to the wall, he heard another scream.

Groggily, Shandril roused. "Whaa—"

"Peace, maid. Lie still while I free Delg, here. He's got more nets on him than several boatloads o' Moonsea fish."

When the ghostly lady at last returned, Mirt and his companions were all awake and were nursing splitting headaches, rubbing at rope burns, and sipping cautiously at firewine from Mirt's belt flask. Mirt had apologized to them for scouting in the wrong direction, and was telling Shandril what he guessed—not much—about magic that could swallow spellfire.

As the glowing apparition flew into view, Delg choked, grabbing Mirt's arm and pointing. "Hast any spellfire left, lass? L—"

"Relax, Delg," Mirt said, pushing him back against the wall with one large and firm hand. "This is a friend—an ancestor of mine—and a lady of high breeding, too. I'd like ye all to meet Duskreene, Lady of Tethgard."

The three stared up at the translucent lady as she smiled and drifted slowly nearer. Long hair swirled about her bare shoulders and breast—and but for the white pallor and translucence of her form, she might have been still a living woman. Below her breasts, however, bare ribs curved from a spine that dwindled away into wisps of glowing radiance.

"Well met, friends of the son of my blood. Be welcome here, in what is left of my home." Her voice was soft, almost a whisper, and her eyes were kind. She looked around at the crumbling ruins and shook her head. "It was once so grand—and now, so little is left."

Then she turned and smiled at Mirt. "For once, you've missed the best accommodation." She pointed. "There's a door, the other side of that pile of stone. Behind it, several rooms are still intact—and safe from falling in on you, I believe."

Mirt bowed. "My thanks, Lady." He turned to the others. "Lady Duskreene ruled in this castle before there was a realm of Cormyr, very long ago. She's now a watchghost—one of the few ghosts who do not always mean swift death to the living."

"Here," Duskreene added, "you sleep under my protection. Relax, and feel safe." She glanced at Mirt, and mischief danced in her eyes. "And please bear with my kin —when he gets no sleep he's apt to be as grouchy as a bear."

"'Gets no sleep,' Lady?" Narm's eyes were wide with wonder as he looked at her. He'd never seen a ghost before—and this gentle, dignified, half-beautiful and half-skeletal woman was nothing like the spectral monsters whispered of in ghost stories.

The lady who had laughed and loved a thousand years before he was born looked into his eyes sadly. "I'm very lonely here—and on the too-rare occasions when Mirt comes to call, he tells me what has befallen in the lands around since last we talked. I take a morbid interest, I'm afraid, in what the remote descendants of those I knew as friends—and rivals, and foes—are doing, and what contemporaries of mine still walk the world today."

"Such as . . . Elminster?" Shandril asked on a hunch, inclining her head to one side.

It was an interesting sight, seeing a watch-ghost blush. "Yes," she said, eyes far away, seeing things long ago. "He was much younger then. Yes," she said again, and laughed, "such as Elminster, indeed."

"Tell me more," Delg said eagerly. "I've *got* to hear *this*. . . ."

* * * * *

"How quaint," murmured one who watched from the darkness of the trees, concealed by layer upon layer of cloaking magics. It listened and spied all through the watch-ghost's long talk with Mirt, and through her silent vigil over the sleeping foursome, in the hours before dawn. All the while, it took care to keep out of her sight.

There was very little in Tethgard that night that Iliph Thraun did not see and hear.

* * * * *

"The trick to finding your way back out of deep woods, look ye," said Mirt to Narm, "is to glance back behind yerself often on the way in. Then ye know what to look for."

"What if you must be leaving by a different way?" Delg asked sourly, almost challengingly.

Mirt froze, and then turned and blinked at the dwarf. His face looked as if he had just been spoken to by a stone, or he'd just seen a bird smoking a pipe. He blinked again and said mildly, "Well, then ye ask the elf who guided ye in to show ye the way out, of course." And with a merry twinkle in his eye he strode on through the deepest stands of Hullack Forest in his relentless, rolling, brush-crashing way.

Delg snorted more than once as he followed. Mirt had urged them up in the chill dawn, bidding a hasty farewell to the wraithlike Duskreene. Without ceremony, he'd led them in a steady tramp through the trees. The going proved agonizing to Narm and Delg; limbs that had stiffened overnight cramped and groaned at the joints.

Mirt kept them moving along with a steady stream of jests and barbed digs directed at lazy dwarves and effete young mages. Shandril shook her head at some of his words, but she wisely kept silent and followed the bobbing axe the stout old merchant adventurer wore at the back of his belt.

Something about Mirt's name was niggling away in her memories, something fleeting that the ranger Florin Falconhand had said, and a reply that Elminster had given, in Shadowdale, at some point in the whirlwind activities of her brief stay there. She looked back at Narm, as if meeting his eyes would bring the memory to her—and it did. She smiled at Narm and turned back to stare at the broad back in front of her. Mirt was one of the Lords of Waterdeep, the not-so-secret band of powerful folk who ruled that great and splendid city.

Striding along at Delg's side, Narm returned Shandril's brief and knowing smile. Her expression had been as bright and beautiful as the rising sun, which had just announced morning through the branches above them. Rosy lances of light struck amid the trees here and there. The sudden, broad dawn reminded Narm that the Realms were beautiful and vast, but of course safer when one walked them with friends. He chuckled his joy aloud and thus earned a sour look from Delg.

"When a lad chuckles like that," the dwarf said gloomily, "it's usually the sound of his wits escaping out his mouth. He's sure to do something wildly stupid, all too soon."

Ahead, Shandril turned, eyes flashing as she laughed. "Why, Delg! And what does a lass's chuckle warn you of?"

The dwarf's beard bristled as he clamped his mouth tightly shut and glared at her. A deep red hue slowly crept up his neck and across his face and balding head as he walked along in the general laughter. Almost thirty paces passed underfoot before a deep rumbling announced that Delg had joined in.

* * * * *

The morning sun was warm on the old wizard's face. Elminster stood conferring with the youngest mage of the Knights of Myth Drannor, one Illistyl. The high balcony of the Twisted Tower in Shadowdale afforded a splendid view of the lush green meadows below.

The old sage's pipe kept going out in the breeze. He tapped it on the stone parapet and said, "Mind ye watch Shaerl while I'm gone . . . she's apt to act ere prudence governs. She's young yet."

Illistyl, who had seen but nineteen winters herself—rather less than the Lady Shaerl—smiled tolerantly. "Impetuous action being the province of the very young *and* the very old, my lord?" she asked, eyes all too innocent.

Elminster snorted. "Now girl, grant ye I could sit here happily amid books and all and let the Realms be hurled down and laid waste around me, but 'tis not impetuous nor foolish to lift a hand to prevent such a thing. Some of thy deeds, and those of thy fellow Knights, may be hastily thought on or taken at whim, but I do consider acts ere I take them—consider them well, as all sh—"

"Aye, aye," Illistyl interrupted him smoothly. "I shall, I shall. As ever." She patted the Old Mage's arm. "I would be more at ease if most of us weren't galloping all over the Dales, distracting those hunting for spellfire . . . and if Dove and Jhessail could spare more time from their little ones, though I know that above all we must keep such younglings safe. Alone, I can give Mourngrym little aid if aught demanding power or influence should befall."

Elminster's eyes were briefly moist. Her softly spoken, archaic words had reminded him of a young maid he had stood with long ago, as beautiful and as skilled in Art, a lady now only ashes. Too many young lasses laughed only in his memories now, gone to dust, naught left of them but their fading writings in spellbooks and his even more faded memories. Abruptly, the Old Mage looked south toward the trees that hid the millpond and the burned flagstones of Sylune's Hut. Gods be struck down, there is *another* lost lady, he thought briefly, then swept aside his dark thoughts angrily. I *must* be getting old!

He raised his eyes to look at lazily drifting clouds and, with an effort he cared not to show, said teasingly, "Perhaps Torm will again come to thy aid."

Beside him, slim Illistyl stiffened. "You jest, I trust," she answered coldly.

The old sage's eyes twinkled merrily as he gravely replied, "Aye. Of course." He turned then, took her hand gently, and kissed it.

Illistyl stared at him, astonished. His mustache rasped across her knuckles like a bristle-brush for a moment, and she found herself staring into very blue, very keen old eyes. She shivered involuntarily; Elminster's gaze made her feel quite naked, and more than a little ashamed. It seemed that he saw into the very depths and corners of her being, parting all the shadowy curtains of old jealousies, regrets, and small deceits. And yet his voice, when it came, was both tender and approving.

"I must go, little one," he said. "I foresee a need to face the archwizards of the Zhentarim before long—and with the spells and monstrous assistance they employ in battles, I've no wish to be anywhere near Shadowdale when the fray begins. Forget not what Jhessail and I have taught thee, and follow thy good sense, and all will be well in the ending of it. Thy good reason is more important than all the power ye will ever wield."

As he released her hand, Illistyl shivered again, closed her eyes briefly as if gathering her strength, and then snorted at him, eyes flashing open. "A lot my good reason will do if Zhentil Keep's soldiers march down that road there!"

Elminster clucked, reprovingly. "Manshoon has other worries, girl, worse than ye know. Myself, for instance. He needs his armies—or thinks he does, and that's all the same to us—to face other foes." He patted her hand. "Abide here and keep the dale safe. Lhaeo will serve thee in need. Mystra shield thee."

"And comfort thee," she replied formally, and added, "mind you return speedily, Old Mage. You will be needed —and missed."

"Many have said so," he said over his shoulder as he swept down the stairs, "over the years. And when I was not there, the will of the gods unfolded anyway."

Illistyl shook her head in amused silence, followed him

down one flight of steps, and then crossed to a gallery with a window over the meadow.

Below, Storm Silverhand sat calmly upon a magnificent black horse and held the reins of a smaller, fatter dapple-gray for Elminster. Her alert eyes saw Illistyl arrive at the window, and she waved.

Illistyl leaned out and called, "Bring him back soon, good lady. And don't let him talk your ears off."

The bard smiled back at her as they both heard Elminster's voice reply, "And why not? Listening does the young good, and makes the patience of the old supple. Besides, my tongue rests more often than it once did."

"Truly?" Illistyl called from the safety of her window. "By the gods, you must have been an endless cataract of nonsense in your youth."

The old sage clambered ungracefully into the saddle, patted the gray reassuringly, and made no answer. The flourishes of his hands as he lit his pipe, however, were eloquent.

He nodded to Storm without looking up, blew a smoke ring in the direction of Illistyl's window, and set off at a trot. Storm followed, raising her hand to Illistyl in salute.

The youngest mage of the knights watched them ride until they were out of sight. Then she sighed and went down to join Mourngrym and Shaerl. She held dark fears about the days ahead.

* * * * *

"Not so long, now," Mirt said. "I never thought I could grow tired of the sight o' trees. Stop me vitals, but this clambering about is hard on old legs!"

"Tell me truth, do," Delg answered sarcastically, sitting down hard on a nearby fallen tree with a sharp whuff of released breath. "Where, by Marthammor Finder-of-

Trails," the dwarf asked as the others took seats around him, "are we going . . . if you don't mind my asking?"

"I don't mind in the least, friend Delg," Mirt said grandly and grinned. "I don't know."

Delg's head came up like that of a dog, bristling to strike at a suddenly seen enemy. "You don't *know?*"

"He says that a lot, doesn't he?" Narm said to Shandril in the silence that followed.

Shandril was too apprehensive to reply. She had been looking constantly here and there into the trees around for signs of the Zhents who must be following them, but Mirt's *I don't know* had snatched her attention back to him.

The wheezing old merchant in tattered leather chuckled easily and pointed ahead into the trees. "It matters not *exactly* where we walk, look ye—as long as we keep alongside the road through the forest toward Arabel, and not too close to it. I hope to come out of the western edge of Hullack as close to deep night as we dare, so that prying eyes are fewer. A certain inn of my acquaintance stands there, *The Wanton Wyvern* by name. We spend a night in cozy luxury, and walk on west in the morning, suitably disguised. Yer way lies in that direction, does it not?"

"It does," Shandril agreed cautiously. "And I would walk it with you, I think. But first tell us, Mirt, Lord of Waterdeep, what you know of us and the many who pursue us. I am tired of always running, and never sure why I must, and what awaits me."

Mirt nodded, not reacting at all to her identification of his rank. "Get used to that feeling, Lady; it's what life becomes for most of us." He grinned and added more softly, "Wise caution, Lady. Forgive me if I am brief. These old bones grow stiff if I sit about too long."

Clearing his throat pompously as if beginning a grand

tale, Mirt said, "Ye are Shandril of Highmoon, raised by an old friend of mine, Gorstag. Ye recently left his inn to join a company of adventurers and therein met this noble and handsome dwarf"—Delg glowered and snorted—"and this young lad of thine, too. Along the way, ye also met Elminster and the Knights of Myth Drannor, first discovered yer power of spellfire—inherited, methinks—and sent to their graves a dragon and no less than three bone dragons, or 'dracoliches,' if ye prefer, as well as the Shadowsil. Ye also sent Manshoon of Zhentil Keep into headlong flight."

Mirt scratched his nose thoughtfully, fixing eyes that were suddenly very blue on her. "All of this tells me Shandril Shessair is rather more than she appears. Elminster has spoken to Khelben Arunsun of thee in some detail, and the Blackstaff in turn has told me something of thy great power and importance. So have others I know who harp. They tell me ye would meet with a certain sister of Storm to learn more about thy powers, and are on the road to her."

He chuckled. "Chasing thee, no doubt, are some self-interested mages and brigands who have heard of thy doings by now. Also at thy heels are the Zhentarim, the Cult of the Dragon, and priests of Bane still loyal to the High Imperceptor, all falling over themselves and each other in their hurry to seize thy spellfire. Behind at least two of these groups are darker foes, shapechanging beings of great power who dwell in a world of shadows. They call themselves 'the Shadowmasters,' and many wizards of Faerûn have fought them down the centuries. They seek to control Toril and other worlds, deciding who may pass from plane to plane. Here they take care to work through others, for when Elminster can catch them in Faerûn, he destroys them."

Mirt leaned forward, his face for once serious. "Ye are

still alive today, Shandril and Narm, because Elminster and the Simbul have been weaving spells, spying, and setting all manner of things to sprawling chaos in order to keep these Shadowmasters from striking ye down."

Shandril, face pale, stared at him numbly. Was *everyone* on all the worlds and planes out looking to kill her? *Why* had the gods given spellfire to Shandril of Highmoon? She had asked herself this, she reflected ruefully, far more than once before.

"After ye were attacked in Shadowdale," Mirt went on, "Torm and Illistyl of the knights took yer shapes, and camped on Harpers' Hill. They were guarded by soldiers, the knight Rathan, and a few Harpers. There was an attack on the hill by things like the one ye fought two nights back—dark horrors, or 'darkenbeasts'—fearsome things created from dogs, sheep, and the like by cruel magic. That attack was set by the two youngest, most reckless Shadowmasters, and they paid for it with their lives."

Mirt sighed. "Elminster's hands have been red with blood, indeed, protecting ye this last tenday; that attack was but one of many. Why, think ye, did he keep ye in a spell-sphere one night?—I hear ye brought it down, too, testing spellfire!—Well, outside the tower, several Harper mages spent much of the night darting all over the sky, trading lightnings—and worse—with these Shadowmasters."

Delg's eyes were large and round; Narm was somehow glad that this was as much news to him as to them.

"One of these dark ones died that night, too," Mirt went on, "when he got past them to strike at ye. Elminster used some sort of spell I've never heard of before to snatch the sphere from around all of ye and hurl it about the Shadowmaster, like a tightening fist, until all its prismatic effects were visited on the creature. It was trapped, unable to escape to another plane, and was destroyed."

Shandril shuddered, and cast a quick look at Narm. His fists were clenched in his lap, and he looked chilled and frightened.

Mirt frowned. "Yer faces say ye've not known of this before. Ah, well—perhaps that was for the best. Terrified folk seldom make wise decisions." He got up with a grunt and added, "Enough talk for now. On, or night'll come long before we see open land beyond these trees."

Shandril nodded, her face rather white. "Why has no one ever told us about these 'Shadowmasters'?" she almost whispered, as they all stood up. "I would rather have known."

Delg shrugged. "What difference could it have made, lass, save to worry you?"

Mirt nodded. "Aye. One thing more, too. Does one put a sword into a child's hand and march her out to face the gathered host of the Flaming Fist, just to see her expression? That's sheer cruelty."

"While standing her in the mist so she can't see the army she faces, is merely slaughter—is that it?" Shandril asked softly, eyes steady on his, flames leaping deep within them.

Mirt held her gaze in silence for two long, slow breaths before he reached out one gnarled hand to touch hers. Then, to the astonishment of the others, he knelt before Shandril, as one does before a king. Looking up over her hand, her fingers still in his gentle grasp, he said roughly, "Aye. Ye have the right of it, Lady. That's why I came here. It's never nice to die alone."

* * * * *

"It always takes longer to get out of a forest than it does to get *in*," Mirt grumbled as the last of the light failed. Dusk hung heavy around them as they made a hasty camp amid the trees.

Delg seemed upset with their route and everything else; when Narm asked him what was amiss, the dwarf turned dark eyes up at him and said, "I feel ill luck ahead, soon."

The gloomy dwarf stood first watch, and Mirt was soon snoring like a contented bear on one side of the fire. Shandril and Narm lay together in their blankets and held each other. After Narm fell asleep, Shandril stared into the fire.

It seemed very long ago that they'd flown over Shadowdale together at their wedding—and longer still since she'd left *The Rising Moon* in search of adventure. And now, folk she hadn't even heard of plotted her death.

The watching skull was patient. It waited, floating low in the concealing darkness while silent tears fell onto Shandril's blanket. It waited, motionless, while she settled herself down against Narm, stroking his cheek tenderly.

It waited, as she fell asleep, and waited still, until Delg's attention was elsewhere. Then, silently, it drifted down to feed.

One bare shoulder had been left exposed as Shandril and Narm lay huddled together. The skull sank down and bit the smooth white flesh. Shandril stirred—and then, with a sort of sigh, relaxed. Spellfire flowed slowly, unseen, out of her.

Delg got up then, as good sentries do, to walk about and check on the safety of those he guarded.

The skull cast a hasty, silent spell to keep Shandril asleep as its fangs withdrew, and then another to quickly heal the wounds it had made.

By the time Delg looked down at Shandril, the skull was gone. Plucky lass. If she'd been a dwarf, now . . . Not for the first time, Delg wished he'd married. This was the sort of daughter he could be proud of. Tenderly he covered her bare arm and shoulder with an edge of the blanket, then stalked on.

The skull watched him go and made no move back to where it had fed. Its memories went back a thousand years. It had learned patience.

Seven

AT THE SIGN OF THE WANTON WYVERN

Do ye remember an inn, Tessyrana? Old and dark and rambling, lost in the arms of the wild woods a long day's ride from anywhere—but warm and firelit within, against the chill winds of the storm. The smoke stung our eyes, and its old and spicy smell enshrouded us as it did everything else in the house. We climbed worn, curving stairs away from the ready laughter and ale, into a candlelit room, a cozy den nestled amid others in the night, carved out of low beams, gentle mutterings and creakings, and uneven floors. And for one night, at least, that plain, tiny, and friendly little room was our home.

Amhritar the Tall
Tall Tales: A Ranger's Life
Year of the Striking Hawk

 Manshoon looked up, unsmiling. Fzoul and two silent upperpriests stood across from him, and two beholders floated overhead. In the air between them all, in an inner chamber in the High Hall of Zhentil Keep, hung a naked man.

It was Simron, late of the Eastern Stonelands Company of the Zhentilar, and he was *very* naked—much of his skin was missing.

Blood flew as Manshoon's invisible spell-claws tore at the veteran warrior's flesh. He screamed hoarsely, the red rain from him being caught below in a huge bowl, for later use in dark, cruel magic. The Zhentarim did not like to waste the talents of their members.

"You *do* still have strength enough to scream," Manshoon said calmly. "Good, Simron—that means you've still strength to speak, too. Tell us more of what happened when the maid unleashed her spellfire."

Simron groaned. Manshoon frowned, and unseen claws raked deep, red furrows across the backs of the old warrior's calves. Simron's legs jerked helplessly, and gore spattered the beholders overhead. They did not seem to mind.

"I—I—Lord Manshoon, mercy!" Simron said thickly, coughing crimson between his words.

"Mercy must be bought, soldier," Manshoon said mildly, "and you've still not told me what I want to know. Now, sh—" There was a commotion at the guarded door of the chamber, and Manshoon turned in some annoyance to see its cause.

A mageling Manshoon had always thought of as more ambitious than sensible stood among the guards, face lit with excitement. "Lord Manshoon!"

The High Lord of Zhentil Keep made a sign, and the guards drew back to let the young wizard rush into the chamber. Silently, Manshoon gestured to the mage to speak—and he did, words tumbling over each other in haste.

"In Sembia, Lord—we've been attacked. Ah, wizards of the Brotherhood, Lord, seeking spellfire as you asked us to . . . they were set upon by some Harpers, and killers

sent by the Cult of the Dragon. We won both battles, but
Arluth is dead, and Chsalbreian, and—"

Manshoon held up his hand, and the mageling fell
silent. "Our thanks for your diligence, Sundarth. We are
pleased. Leave us now; our favor goes with you."

Stammering thanks and farewell, the young mageling
bowed himself out.

When he was gone, Manshoon looked up at the bleeding, moaning man hanging in midair, and he sighed
loudly.

"Too many foes are after spellfire for me to just sit back
and wait for blundering, ambitious underlings to bring it
to us," the High Lord of Zhentil Keep announced. "I'll
have to become directly involved in the hunt for this Shandril."

The beholders, hovering watchfully overhead, said
nothing. Manshoon looked across the chamber to meet
the eyes of the High Priest of the Black Altar.

Fzoul shrugged and said, "That's the way of wizards.
For my part and my counsel, hold back for now, and
watch to see if the claws we've sent out catch anything."

Manshoon rolled his eyes. "I grow no younger," he said
carefully. "What use is spellfire—or the triumph of our
Brotherhood over all—to me, if I'm toothless, blind, and
failing in my dotage before we gain either?"

Fzoul raised an eyebrow. "You may not live to find any
of these things if you move openly now. I hope you've not
forgotten that your open participation in this hunt is sure
to bring out Elminster of Shadowdale—to say nothing of
the Simbul, Khelben Arunsun, and others—against you.
Azoun has already doubled his patrols in eastern Cormyr
and is killing our warriors as fast as he finds them."

Manshoon shrugged. "If I feared danger or opposition,
I would never have come to hold the title I do now, nor to
stand in this place."

A rumbling voice broke in on his words then, from overhead. It sounded amused. "How will you succeed, Lord Manshoon, where others have failed? Finding magic that will stand against spellfire will take time you have too little of, and much luck—or both."

Manshoon shrugged again, giving the eye tyrants overhead a thin smile. "The Brotherhood is often guilty of a fault dear to our natures: in trying to outdo each other, we try to be too clever. A far simpler approach than the schemes we've pursued so far will probably be all that is needed—brute force."

Fzoul raised an eyebrow and gestured for Manshoon to continue.

The High Lord of Zhentil Keep turned expressionless eyes on them all and said, "Club the wench into submission with an army of zombies controlled by underlings using items of power. Bury her under undead, no matter how many she destroys—and bring her down. My magic is strong enough to take care of any Harper or Cult meddling in such a battle."

Manshoon strolled across the room and then turned to look up at the floating body of the Zhentilar. "Then we take the girl someplace secure," he continued, "and let the lich lord drain her—or use magic to bind her wits and will ere she recovers, then study her at leisure." He snapped his fingers. "Whatever plans we pursue, a watch must be kept on Elminster from this moment on to ensure he doesn't show up to rescue her or ruin attempts to take her."

He gestured, and a guard at the door went out, returning in a few breaths with a wizard just old enough to master his awe and fear. After a quick glance at the hovering beholders, the young mage kept his eyes on the floor or on Manshoon.

"Heldiir," Manshoon said in a cold, smooth voice, "you

are to take twenty of your fellow mages, now, and keep a continuous spellwatch over Shadowdale. Monitor all magic wielded there, keep track of the doings of Elminster—and report any major castings or movements on his part to me immediately, whatever the hour. Go, speedily, and do this."

"I-I will," Heldiir managed to croak, then hurried out.

Manshoon looked up in time to see the beholders drifting back toward the arched windows through which they had first entered the room.

"Your plan has some merit," one said.

"We shall watch—and see," the other added in a deep, neutral rumble, as both eye tyrants drifted from view.

Fzoul Chembryl glided to a door, spread his hands, and said simply, "The risk is yours." Then he was gone.

Manshoon watched the door close behind the priest, smiled without humor, and looked up at the silent, dripping soldier.

"Mercy, Simron?" he asked mildly. "Mercy is for the dead." He made a small gesture with one hand, and there was a dull, splintering crack from the body overhead.

Its head jerked, and then dangled limply at an angle, tongue protruding. Manshoon strode toward his own door and did not look back as the floating corpse slowly drifted down toward the bowl of blackening blood.

* * * * *

"Watch sharp, now," Mirt warned as they peered into the last gleams of fading sunset over the Storm Horns, far off on the horizon. "There's sure to be at least one snake hereabouts who seeks Shandril and spellfire."

"Is there? By the ever-observant gods, your perception is keen. You surprise me," Delg muttered sarcastically, keeping a hand over his axe blade to shield it from reflecting any of the sun's failing glow. It was growing dark fast here in the trees, evening descending quickly on the rolling farmlands ahead.

"What, again?" Mirt replied teasingly. "What an exciting life ye must lead."

Delg raised an eloquent eyebrow but thought it wiser to make no reply. Somewhere near at hand, Shandril sighed, and in mimicry of one of the haughty Sembian ladies who used to stop at the *Moon* for a night, she murmured, "*Really,* milord. Must you?" She smiled as Narm's comforting arm closed around her shoulders.

Mirt uttered a satisfied sound, came to a halt, and pointed. "That fence line, there? That's the eastern paddock of the *Wyvern.* Come. My belly tells me it's past time for some hot roast dinner."

"Master, we obey," Narm said in gentle mockery. Mirt sighed heavily, rolled his eyes, and waved at them all to follow him. The stout old merchant pushed past a tangle of wild raspberry canes, creating angry crackling and tearing noises. He waded through the canes toward the road, slipped on a muddy patch of bank—and fell with a heavy splash into the ditch.

For a long, breathless moment, silence descended. Shandril smothered giggles, not very successfully. Delg cut his own way through the canes with a few deft swings of his axe, and then launched himself into an exaggerated pratfall down the bank, coming to rest so that one boot just crashed down into the edge of the water with a splash. The spray drenched Mirt's face, which had just arisen from the muddy waters wearing a dark expression.

"Unusual maneuver," the dwarf remarked cheerfully, "but I can see its virtues now, O Great Warrior. It'll certainly lull any waiting foes into false overconfidence and allow us to make a grand entrance while they're still rolling about on the ground, laughing helplessly."

One muddy paw lashed out from the water, enfolded the dwarf's boot in a loving grip, and pulled. Delg's mirth was cut suddenly and damply short, leaving only bubbles to mark its passing.

"I hope you don't expect us to join you," said Shandril carefully, reaching a hand down to him. Mirt waved it away, spitting muddy water considerately off to one side.

"Nay, nay, lass—if ye gave me yer hand, ye'd end up in the wet here beside me, instead o' getting me out of it. Nay, me an' the intrepid Delg here'll just wallow about for a bit, and then join ye on the far bank. If ye don't feel up to leaping the ditch, any of ye, just step on my shoulder— here—and find yer way across . . . blast it!"

Shandril did giggle then, but made use of his offer. Full darkness had fallen by the time they all reached the road beyond. Mirt and Delg dripped their way to the front and rear of the band, respectively, and both set off in grim silence for their goal.

The farms and woodlots of Cormyr stretched out before them in the gloom, and stars winked overhead. Selune had not yet risen, and the four travelers went over the hill under the cloak of night.

Before them, at the bottom of the slope, two bright pole-lamps flickered on the right-hand side of the road. The lamps flanked a stout gate that led off the road into a high-fenced yard. Up out of the dark shadows of this enclosure rose several large, dark buildings. The nearest one was a rambling place; they could see part of it by the light of another, dimmer lamp on a post near the door.

From a leaning spar that jutted above the closed gate, a rusty shield hung down on a chain. On the shield, the words "Strike to enter" were painted. Under this sign slumped the body of someone filthy, dressed in a very tattered collection of rags, and sitting up against one of the gateposts.

In heavy silence, Mirt went alertly forward, his sword drawn. The figure did not move. As they drew nearer, they heard faint snoring. Nonetheless, Mirt warily faced the fat, unmoving, ragtag figure, and he rapped the shield-gong with the pommel of his raised, ready sword.

The snores broke off abruptly, just as a small wooden window squealed open in the gate above. A face looked out at them. "Travelers?" came a gravelly, not unfriendly voice.

"Aye," Mirt replied. "Two men, one women, and a he-dwarf, on foot. We're armed but come in peace, and prepared to pay well for a warm meal and a good bed—if they're as good at the *Wyvern* as I remember."

"Well met!" The voice was less wary. "Welcome to *The Wanton Wyvern,* then. I'll open the gate." The window closed, and they heard the hollow sounds of wooden bars and props being shifted. Then the gate groaned inward.

The man standing inside looked tall and battered, and so did the stout wooden staff in his hand. They'd scarce got a look at him before he leapt out, past Mirt—who turned automatically to keep his drawn sword facing the man—and raised his staff threateningly over the ragtag, awakened sleeper.

"Be off, you! *Move,* Baergasra! I've told you before—*away* from the gate!" The staff thumped the tattered derelict solidly in the shoulder, and the tall man used it to shove and roll his bedraggled, gruntingly protesting target away from their path.

"Please come in," he puffed over his shoulder. He raised the staff again as the bundle of rags moaned and tumbled hastily out of reach. "This old leper is always hanging about here—but we've never let her inside the gate. The *Wyvern* is clean, I assure you."

Mirt merely nodded and strode into the inn yard. The others followed.

The tall man came after them, closing the gate hurriedly. "Please go within," he said. "There, under the lamp. We've plenty of room tonight; and there's food hot and ready."

"Good, good. My thanks," Mirt called, and waved at Delg to lead the rest in. As Shandril followed, she noticed Mirt's sword was still drawn, and his eyes darted around alertly, peering into the shadows.

Their rooms were simple but warm and clean, clustered together at one end of a low-ceilinged gallery. Broad stairs led down from the center of that passage to a landing overlooking the main taproom of the inn, and from there descended again to a lobby just within the front doors.

The Wanton Wyvern was old and dusty and dark, paneled in fine woods and hung with torn and faded, once-fine tapestries. "Battle spoils," Mirt identified them briefly as they passed; Delg nodded agreement. Everyone noticed the crossbows hanging ready behind the front desk of the *Wyvern*.

The place was warm and friendly, however, with perhaps a dozen other guests—two warriors, a rosy-robed priest of Lathander with two servants, and the rest merchants—already drinking and joking in the taproom. The staff was easygoing and attentive; a serving lass whose girth matched Mirt's own showed them to a table against one wall, near the crackling hearth-fire.

Shandril looked around, taking in the colors and lights and warmth for a while, letting the talk and the strong smells of wood smoke and cooking wash over her. She heard Mirt rumble something about this being one of those inns you could feel at home in, and Delg growling something in reply, about too much wood and not enough honest solid stone, but at least they didn't give dwarves funny looks . . . and suddenly, even before the promised dinner came, Shandril felt something hard touch her fore-head, hard and unmoving and restful. . . .

"Thy lady, lad," Mirt said, reaching over to poke Narm. "She's out dreamstalking already. . . . Nay, nay, don't wake her. Just keep her hair out of the soup when it comes. . . ."

Unmoving, Shandril lay face forward on the table, her hair spread out around her in a swirl of ash-blond tresses. Narm's gentle hands gathered it back to her shoulders, combing out the worst tangles. Shandril slept on, shoulders rising and falling faintly.

She was running barefoot through night-dark woods, flames of spellfire racing up and down her bare body like a beacon. Where her feet came down, flames leapt up and left a fiery trail. Behind her, she could hear wolves running, wolves and men . . . men with dark cloaks and cruel eyes. They rode skeletal dragons that laughed hollowly, even after she blasted them. There were more of them, more and more, and the spellfire in her hands was fading away and failing. . . . They came nearer, the men laughing now along with the bony dragons . . . near, nearer . . . Dark hands shifted suddenly, fingers lengthening horribly into reaching, writhing black tentacles. . . .

"*No!* No, you won't take me!" Shandril screamed, lashing out with her hands. She was somewhere warm and bright, sitting—at a table at the inn. With her friends. Shandril blinked and stared about wildly, breathing hard.

"Easy, Shan, easy," Narm said, holding her. "It was only a dream."

Shandril nodded—but her gaze had settled on a hard-faced man approaching their table. He looked like a warrior, and he strode slowly at the head of four others of similar cut. Mirt turned in his seat to face these strangers, but did not rise.

Delg leaned across the table and hissed, "*No* spellfire unless you have to, Shan. Let us handle this, aye?"

Shandril had no time to reply. The newcomer's voice was already raised in anger. "*You're* the ones who stole my little girl! Thieves! Slavers! You won't get away this time! Innkeeper! Bring your crossbows!" He waved a hand and stepped aside. The warriors behind him, all armed, started menacingly forward.

Mirt rose ponderously from his chair to meet the foremost man, who held a naked scimitar ready.

"You're first, fat one," the man sneered, drawing up his blade for a slash.

Mirt ducked suddenly beneath its bright edge and slammed into the man's midriff. The man flew backward, crashing into another brigand in a confusion of clattering blades, hard knees, and helplessly flailing hands. Mirt continued his lunge, grabbed the belt of yet another man, and flung him sideways into the man who'd first accused them. "The *landing!*" he bellowed as he fell amid a growing hubbub.

Narm and Delg were already looking up. Two more warriors were hurrying down the stairs to the landing, cocked crossbows in their hands. Delg's axe flashed across the room, whirling as it flew. Men shouted in fear, and the tables all around emptied in haste. The axe sailed true, and the next moment one of the archers was slumped on the stairs, whimpering and clutching at the red ruin of his shoulder, where the bright dwarven axe was buried deeply amid the spreading blood.

Narm stood up coolly, shielding Shandril with his body, and raised his hands to cast a spell. Before he could, Delg slapped his leg. Narm looked down—and the dwarf thrust a small, loaded hand-crossbow into his hands. Narm stared at it for a moment, and then took it, aimed it carefully, holding it in both hands, and fired. An arrow thrummed into the floor as the bow from which it had come crashed over the railing. Its owner clutched at

Narm's quarrel in his throat, made strangling noises, and followed his weaponry to the floor below.

Without pause, Delg snatched a handful of quarrels from his belt, thrust them into Narm's hands, and scrambled up onto the table, drawing a long knife from his boot.

Men shouted out in the lobby, and the thunder of running feet answered the call. Blades had been drawn all over the taproom. Some sort of alarm gong rang behind the bar, and there was a momentary lull in its wake—so everyone heard the grisly cracking sound as Mirt calmly broke a man's neck. The attacker's body slumped to the floor like a heavy sack of coal as the old merchant's hairy hands released him. Wheezing, Mirt snatched up a chair and met the charge of the last swordsman, sweeping aside the slashing blade.

All the while, Narm's trembling hands fumbled at reloading the unfamiliar weapon. He wished he knew some better battle spells and cursed himself for not having enough magical strength to protect his lady. The bolt slipped once again from its groove. Narm cursed and looked up in frustration. Over his shoulder, he glimpsed the man who'd accused them all, drawing back his hand and snarling. A dagger glittered in it, a dagger meant for Shandril. Narm roared a warning.

Shandril twisted desperately sideways in her seat to get below the table. The knife came down, leaping through the air at her with frightening speed, twinkling as it came. A straining body leapt to intercept it in midair over the table, shielding her for a crucial instant before crashing heavily down amid the scattered remains of their dinner.

Narm landed with a ragged gasp and lay still.

Shandril stared at him in horror. Fear and anger coiled in her throat with the rising spellfire. Trembling with rage, she stood to lash out at the man—but the warrior no longer stood there.

Delg had leapt from the table where he had been fighting and struck the man squarely in the face—knife first and with all the dwarf's bearded and booted weight behind it. The man was falling with Delg still wrapped around his head, both of them covered in blood that did not belong to the dwarf.

Off to one side, Mirt had just broken his chair over the disarmed swordsman, who was falling now in a strangely boneless, flopping way to the floor.

There was no foe left to smite. Shandril stood there, hands smoldering, facing a frightened innkeeper and two red-faced but rapidly paling cooks with cleavers and crossbows in their hands. Other patrons stood farther back, swords and daggers and eating-forks held outs, fear on their faces. Silence came again to the taproom of *The Wanton Wyvern*.

"No, lass," Mirt rapped out at her, pointing to where Narm lay on the table. The bloody dagger stood out of the young mage's side, just below his left shoulder. "Delg, take his feet, will ye? We've no time to lose!"

Delg got up, dripping his victim's gore and panting. "Anyone else hurt?"

Not pausing to answer, Mirt raised his voice in a bellow addressed to everyone in the taproom. "*All* of ye—stand aside! I've no quarrel with any of ye, but any who bar our way will end as these did, by Tempus! And any who raise blade against us will answer for it to King Azoun!"

In the shocked silence that followed, the frightened onlookers silently parted to make way for them, and Mirt hurried them out to the doors.

"Delg, *scout!*" he barked, and the dwarf lowered Narm's legs to the ground and hurried past them into the night outside. "Shandril," the stout merchant added, holding Narm by the shoulders, "take his feet, gently—but haste matters more than handling, now. . . . Good, good . . . hurry, now. . . ."

Delg was waving them on. They hurried out into the night and across the dark and muddy inn yard. Narm's eyes were closed, and he was breathing raggedly, breath rasping and wet.

"Where are we going?" Narm asked. Mirt's shaggy, lionlike head was looking this way and that. "To the gate," he roared and trotted on. In a few jolting seconds they were there, and the old merchant thrust Narm into Delg's arms.

"Hold him," he panted, "and *don't* let him fall." And he whirled away from the staggering dwarf to attack the props and bars of the gate like an angry bear, snatching and grunting and clawing.

Wooden spars bounced and crashed aside, and before they'd stopped bouncing, he had the gate open. Out into the road he stumbled, looking this way and that.

"Baergasra? *There* ye are! Quickly, we've need of thy healing." Mirt said in a voice halfway between a snarl and a sob. A breath later, the old derelict in tattered rags appeared out of the night, running hard. An astonished Shandril realized she was watching a healthy and fast-moving woman, not a drunken cripple. Mirt waved her in through the open gate and came after, straight to Narm.

"Delg?" Mirt snapped. "All safe?"

"Looks clear," the dwarf replied grimly as he shifted Narm's limp body across his shoulders. Shandril had been holding her man's head tenderly, but she let go in haste as Mirt plucked him from Delg's shoulders and laid him against the base of the high fence. Then the Old Wolf snatched out his dagger.

By the glow from its blade, Shandril saw the stout, filthy beggar woman kneeling beside Narm. The knife stood out of Narm's narrow chest, just forward of the armpit.

Baergasra's grimy fingers plucked the blade deftly out, and Mirt's hand was there to press hard against the blood that followed. The woman waggled the bloody dagger so that its blade caught the light. She stared at it a moment, flung it aside, and spit after it.

Baergasra then laid her hands on Narm and murmured something. Her fingers glowed briefly. When the light died, she slowly sat back, sighed, and rested her hands on her thighs. With careful fingers, Mirt began to unlace and draw off Narm's robes.

The beggar woman helped him. Shandril could hear her talking to the old merchant now. "It went deep, indeed, but it carries only sleep venom, not the usual Zhentarim killing blackslime. He'd have lived, but it's good I was close by . . . so how are you, Old Wolf? It's been awhile, it has. . . ."

Behind her, Shandril heard a sharply indrawn breath. She turned.

"*Who* let *her* in here?" demanded a furious voice. The tall, battered doorguard of the inn stood facing them, staff in hand. Barring his way with drawn knife, Delg squinted up at the man fearlessly.

"I did," Shandril said hotly. "She can heal, and it was needed."

The man strode forward and, with a sweep of his staff, thrust Delg aside into a helpless sprawl. "But she's a *leper!* She's—"

"—Always wanted to pay you back for belting me, Thomd," said the woman in rags, rising with smooth, agile speed to thrust the reaching staff aside and embrace its wielder. They went over together with a splash into the mud, and the filthy lips met his sputtering ones firmly. Then the beggar woman rose atop him and laughed heartily.

"Ah, but it's a good thing I've *not* got the wasting

disease, Thomd, or you'd be sharing it now." She rolled off the panting, frantic man in the mud and winked at Shandril with cool gray eyes. Pulling open the filthy lacings of her bodice for an instant, she revealed a tiny silver harp pendant nestling in the filthy folds of a gargantuan bosom.

Then she turned back to Mirt, shook her head resignedly, and said, "Well, now that you've let the world know I'm not as I seem, perhaps you'll let me use your bath, Mirt, while I watch over the healing of your young man, here. Give me your cloak, Thomd."

The struggling man in the mud looked at Delg's dagger, inches from his nose, and with a helpless grunt unpinned the cloak and rolled out of it.

"Hand it here," Baergasra said merrily, "and don't mind the mud—I'm used to it, gods know." Delicately she began to strip off rag after rag, dropping them all into the trampled mud at her feet.

"One more thing, Thomd," she added, nudging the tall man with her foot as he slowly sat up, "burn these for me, will you? I never want to see any of them again."

Delg and Thomd watched in identical amazement as the barrel-shaped woman stripped off rag after rag, and stood at last clad only in grime. Lots of grime and mud, caked thickly in places. She scratched some of those places, grinned at them both and held out an imperious hand for the cloak.

Delg bowed low and presented it to her as one would to a great lady. She swirled it about her shoulders and reached for the pin. Thomd handed it to Delg with a sigh, and Delg handed it on with a low whistle of appreciation.

The filthy woman stuck her tongue out at him as she pinned the cloak close about her, grinned again, and said to Thomd, "Did you see any leprous bits? Well?"

Thomd shook his head. "N-No," he managed through his teeth. "But the *smell* . . ."

Baergasra sighed. "You know," she said slowly, "one gets used to it?" She scratched again and said, "Well—get *up,* man, and get going! I want that bath."

Mirt looked up from Narm. Shandril could see an ugly purple scar just forward of his armpit, but the skin was whole again, and the blood had stopped. He still slept, presumably from the venom.

Venom. The dagger. Shandril looked in the direction the Harper had thrown it, and saw its glint in the shadows. Carefully she picked it up and stuck it in her belt. You never know. . . .

"Ah, Thomd?" Mirt said. "If ye go in and fill the bath, I'll bar the gate again. Delg, go in and tell them to calm down, hey? We'll clean up, I give my promise. . . . If anyone gives ye trouble, mention my, er, close friendship with King Azoun. Shandril, as much as I hate to ask ye to do it, will *ye* guard *us,* until we're in and settled?"

"Of course, Mirt. It's a pleasure," Shandril said happily, and meant it.

Eight

SOAP, STEAM, AND SOFT CURSES

It's usually around bath time that the tithe collectors come to call. Besieging warriors, on the other hand—now they generally have consideration enough to come early so you know how best to plan your day.

Estimyra of High Horn
Twenty Winters a War Wizard
Year of the Dragon

 "Allow me, Lady," the dwarf said gruffly, handing a brush and a hand-bucket of soap around the edge of the ragged curtain. Steam rose from the other side of it, accompanied by splashing noises and a few groans of pure pleasure. Baergasra the Harper, priestess of Eldath, was joyfully scrubbing away half a year's sweat and dirt.

"My thanks, Sir Dwarf. Well met!"

"Our thanks, Baera," Mirt said feelingly. They were gathered in the inn's largest and best bedroom. Shandril was feeling very sleepy again, but beside her, Narm felt much better—and was hungrily devouring a second serving of

153

the dinner the innkeeper had brought up to them.

From the other side of the curtain, Baergasra chuckled. "Ah, but it was a little thing I did, and in return for it you've given me this. It feels good to be clean again!" There was a rueful pause, and she added despairingly, "But my *hair!*"

"What about yer hair?" Mirt asked carefully. "I've seen far worse, proudly sailing along the streets of Waterdeep, assured of a display of the highest fashion."

The reply was mournful. "Most of this'll have to be cut off to get rid of the worst that's really stuck in the tangles."

"If it's not too personal," Delg asked carefully, sitting down again on his stool beside the curtain, "just why did you choose to wander about in rags, anyway? Is begging so profitable hereabouts?"

"Little man," Baergasra darkly replied, a nasty insult to any dwarf, "I do what I must, whether it's harping or begging, and don't snarl overmuch about it. Orders are orders, and a noble cause is, as they say, a noble cause. But that doesn't mean I enjoy it."

"Ah," said the dwarf, cocking his head at the word *harping.* "Of course. Forgive me, big woman."

There was a sputtering laugh from the other side of the curtain, and it suddenly bulged beside Delg's head as the brush came swiftly back to him—or at least to a momentary embrace with the side of his brow.

"Ooohhh," he commented from the floor a moment later, lying beside the stool. "This one bites."

"As I recall," Mirt rumbled jovially, "yes. It—"

"A gentle reminder, Mirt," the Harper called from her side of the curtain. "I still have the soap bucket to return to someone."

"Ahh, aye—'hem! Ahem," Mirt replied hastily. "To be sure, to be sure. . . . Are ye hungry perchance, Baera? We've food here, and—"

"Thank you, I will. It's been awhile since I've had something properly cooked, and with sauces, to boot. And Narm may need another spell or two; I'd best remain here to be certain. I'll stay the night, if you've room. If he falls asleep, don't try to wake him without me, mind; that venom can't be hurried."

"Yer bed is ready when ye are. How are things in the Hullack wilds, then?"

"Not so bad, yet," was the reply, punctuated by sounds of a scalp being vigorously scrubbed. "But getting worse. Zhentarim and bandits both are multiplying in the Stonelands and raiding farther. That one who called you out, downstairs? He's one of the local Zhentarim rats—a thief by the name of Osber. He was probably so eager to take all the credit for capturing Shandril of the Spellfire that he didn't bother to call on any nearby magelings. Tymora smiled on you there; the Zhentarim spell-hurlers hereabouts lie low and aren't all that strong, but they can lay hands on powerful wands and the like if they've a mind to."

"But he did manage to round up six men-at-arms," Narm protested.

Baergasra chuckled. "Those were his 'fist,' his own little band of bully-boys. They're never far away from him, and tonight three of them were enjoying a quiet evening's entertainment here with several of the local night girls."

"What's that?" Mirt asked, alert. "Shouldn't we—?"

The Harper chuckled again. "No fears there. The girls aren't Zhentarim; two, in fact, like to . . ."

"Harp?" Delg offered, back on his stool again.

"Indeed they do, Sir Dwarf." Her voice changed again. "But there's darker news than that." She coughed briefly and went on. "The real reason I want to see Narm safely back on his feet myself, in fact, is that all across the Realms, these last three rides or so, spells have been going wrong. Going wild, sometimes."

She paused, but no one said anything. Narm stared at the curtain in growing horror. If that was true, what in the name of all the gods was he going to defend Shandril with? And what, a small voice whispered chillingly inside him, will befall if Shandril's spellfire itself becomes unreliable?

"Magic is no longer the sure thing it once was," Baergasra said quietly. "A—A certain friend of mine reminded me of Alaundo the Seer, and his prophecies. Something about 'chaos of Art.' Remember, Mirt?"

"Aye. Aye." The old merchant's voice was rough. "That's part of the one about the gods walking the world and making war, isn't it?"

"Yes," Baergasra said in a near whisper from behind the curtain. She was silent for a long time, and then added, "I knew you'd remember, Old Wolf. It's good to see you again, if Realmsdoom is really upon us. That's another reason I'd like to stay until morn."

Mirt nodded and rose quietly, wheezing only a little. He walked around the curtain and replied, "It's good to see ye again too, Baera. Hmmm—the rags did add a certain something, didn't theee*eaaHHH!*"

He reeled back into view again, doubled over. Mirt, sometimes the Merciless, had ducked too slowly. The soap bucket looked most fetching on his head.

Delg convulsed in silent laughter. Narm and Shandril could not keep so quiet. The dwarf rose amid their mirth and solemnly handed Mirt the brush, pointing meaningfully at the curtain.

Mirt removed the bucket slowly and winced, but took the brush. "I'll save it for later," he muttered, and sat down again. "Thanks, Delg."

"No quarrels," said the dwarf, finding his stool. "You were impressive indeed, downstairs."

Mirt grinned. "So it's my turn to be the giddy-goat here and now, hey?"

"Something like that," Delg agreed, and they laughed.

"You've certainly assembled a band of giggling idiots this time, Mirt," came the sharp voice from the other side of the curtain.

Mirt raised an eyebrow. "What d'ye mean, 'this time'?"

* * * * *

Storm took off her second boot and stretched, catlike. On the other side of their leaping fire, Elminster sat sucking his pipe into life in a cloud of drifting, snapping white sparks and curling green smoke.

"The wards, El?" the silver-haired bard asked.

Elminster nodded. "Set as strong as my Art can make them in these troubled times. None can see us or reach us, short of the gods. Ye can lay blades aside, take thy ease, and undress—if that's what ye're asking."

Storm grinned at him and began unbuckling and unlacing. Then she frowned. "What do you mean, 'in these troubled times'?"

Elminster puffed on his pipe; a small inferno went up. "Magic's not the sure thing it was a winter ago," he said. "It's going wild now sometimes, and not even Mystra herself will answer me over it."

Storm met his eyes for a long breath of silence, then shivered. "Alaundo," she whispered, and he nodded. Storm stared at him a moment longer and then sighed, shrugged, and went on disrobing. Silver hair curled free about her shoulders and down her back; she removed dagger sheaths and safe-pouches from where they were strapped next to her skin, and with obvious pleasure rubbed away the marks they left behind.

The old man across the fire had seen her do this many

a time before, since the days when he himself had changed her, when she was only a babe. He sat and smoked companionably, directing discarded apparel away with magic that spun unseen from one lazy finger. Clothing floated silently through the air in his direction; more than once Storm smiled her thanks at him. When she was done, he said merely, "Ye still look magnificent, lass."

"It's a good thing ye're the great age ye are, isn't it?" Storm teased him, mimicking his own voice and manner before he could utter the same sentence. Elminster chuckled and wiggled his eyebrows. Obediently his pipe extinguished, rose up into the darkness overhead, and vanished.

The fire followed it, leaving behind only a warmth and a glowing in the air.

Storm stared at it, and then looked at Elminster, mouth open. "Ye gods," she whispered, "was that—spellfire? I thought you'd used fire spells to ignite real wood. . . ."

Elminster shrugged. "The little lass isn't the only one alive who can work such tricks. She merely does it naturally. Azuth taught me, long ago. It drains me overmuch, mind; I don't do it lightly."

"But you did it just for me," Storm protested.

"That was not a light thing," Elminster said, deadpan. He winked at her.

Storm reached a hand out through the faint glow to clasp the sage's hand. "You are a delight, El. I love you, Old Mage."

"Oh, good," was the dry reply, and she felt him wriggling closer. "Then ye won't mind if I lie beside ye here. Being old and shy an' all that, I'll be leaving my clothes *on*, though."

"You? Shy?" The bard snorted, and then wrinkled her nose. "I forgot to get our blankets. They're—"

"On the horses where they should be, keeping the faithful beasts warm," Elminster replied tranquilly. "Ye'll find ye won't need blankets—my Art'll keep us as if we were bundled up, but without getting too hot or the like, and make the ground beneath gentle to lie upon, as well. Trust me."

Storm met his eyes and smiled. "I do." They lay side by side in the darkness, holding hands, and looked at the silent stars glimmering high overhead. As Selûne rose and grew bright, Elminster let the faint spell-glow fade until they lay in darkness under the night sky.

They remained together in silence for a time, watching the stars wheel overhead. Although a stranger looking down on them would have placed Storm in her lush late thirties, despite hard muscles and white sword-scars aplenty, and Elminster somewhere the gray side of sixty, both bard and archmage were hundreds of winters older than that.

With his fingers, Elminster stroked the hand that he held, and he thought about the secret he shared with the woman who lay beside him in the grass. The secret that had shaped both their lives.

Both of them carried some of the immortal magefire locked forever inside their bodies, small parts of the divine power of Mystra placed in mortals of Faerûn to maintain some great and mysterious balance. They could be slain, releasing the power of Mystra—as Storm's sister Sylune had been, not long ago—but grew old only slowly, aged more by the care of responsibilities and the grief of outliving even elven friends than by physical causes. Sometimes, they felt very old.

Elminster was wise enough to give Storm this time to drift into slumber under the watching stars. It would ease her heavy heart. For himself, however, it was enough to have her beside him. Of the sisters he'd reared, Storm was the most his friend, even if he loved the Simbul more as mate and companion. Elminster smiled up at the stars and was happy.

"El," the beloved voice beside him came softly, "you know I love riding Faerûn with you . . . but tell me; where are we bound this time, and why?"

"We go to meet a certain old enemy of mine, and do a certain thing," Elminster said carefully. "Is that enough?"

He heard the grin in her voice. "Of course. You phrase *nothing* so eloquently." With easy grace, she rolled up to one elbow and looked down at him. "And the 'why'?"

Elminster looked into her level gaze and melted. "It is part of an ongoing game I play against—certain folk. A very old and deep game, to limit the power of those who watch from shadows in this world. The Malaugrym—aye, ye remember them, I know—are after Shandril of Highmoon. Her affair's by no means clear and done yet. We'll doubtless meet in Silverymoon, these Shadowmasters and I, to do spell-battle over her. . . . What we do now will become important then. 'Tis more important that the Shadowmasters have no benefit from what I've left undone than that the Harpers or Shandril—or Toril itself—gain strength by what we do, if we prevail. . . ."

Storm laughed softly and kissed him. "I love it, Old Mage, when you're so forthcoming and open." She lay down again beside him. "Never change, will you? Promise me that."

"Ah, lass," he said sadly. "That's one of the promises none of us can keep."

He lay there in silence until she slept, holding her hand tightly. When her slumber was deep, he waved his free hand, and a spellbook floated silently out of the night to hang above his nose. Spellfire was but one of Elminster's little secrets; another was the fact that he no longer needed to sleep.

The old, familiar symbols and phrases filled his mind

again as they had so many times before, but he did not let go of Storm's hand, even for a moment. Throughout life, one does not miss any chance to hold onto the things that are really precious, if one is truly wise.

* * * * *

A cool wind whipped around the mages and howled off east, along the old and broken rock ridges of the Stonelands. It brought faint, far-off howls with it.

Ramath involuntarily looked over his shoulder, but the black-robed wizard beside him only smiled.

"Whatever it is would have to travel much of the night to reach us, mageling, even if it knew we stood on this spot. My Art will turn it away if it tries. So stand easy."

Ramath shook his head. "I've tried, Dread Master—but whenever I look where it's dark, I see her."

"Who?" The question was sharp.

Ramath swallowed. "A light-haired girl . . . shrouded in flames."

"What? She's here, and moving about, hidden from all but you by magic? Or can you see rocks and trees through her; do you see something from your dreams?"

"A dream image I suppose, Master—yet I'm not asleep. I see her walking amid trees, with a dwarf, a wizard of about my age, and a fat man in floppy old boots. They're just walking, not seeing me or anything—but they're always heading this way, straight toward us. . . . I walked to the cliff over there—you saw me—and it seemed the same; straight toward me. It's—I've never known anything like this before."

Dread Master Ghaubhan Szaurr regarded him coldly for a moment, and then said very softly, "Who has spoken to you of such a band of travelers?"

Ramath looked startled. "No one, Dread Master. I've

not heard of or seen any of these folk before—I was hoping you'd know what spell or ghost was affecting me."

"I think I do," the Dread Master replied. "Go down to the Zhentilar swordmaster by the fire and tell him to come up to me. And pay close heed to these images you see. When you return, I shall want a full and detailed account of anything new that you've seen. Hasten."

Obediently his apprentice scrambled away along the path. Stroking his sharp-pointed chin thoughtfully, Ghaubhan Szaurr watched him go.

The wind flung the wizard's cloak out behind him like a black sail. Ghaubhan stood on the rocky height feeling its tug and listening to it flapping as excitement rose within him: Ramath had some sort of magesight, the gift of Mystra or Bane or some other dark power—and Shandril of Highmoon was coming this way.

Spellfire would be his soon; Ghaubhan could almost taste it. He thought how best to place the warriors—stupid brutes all, but useful against the maiden's companions—for the battle to come. It was even more crucial to use his magelings so they stood no chance of tricking or turning on their Dread Master. Best if they all died at the maid's hands—men turned to ashes by spellfire could tell no tales to seeking magic, and could not whisper against him. If one ashen corpse wore Ghaubhan's cloak and ring, in fact, they'd think Ghaubhan Szaurr fallen.

And given time to master spellfire while in hiding, this lowly tutor of magelings would become a Dread Master indeed! Then the high lords of the Keep had best look to their Art, for the Zhentarim would soon have a new master. . . . If that book he'd found in old Asklannan's spell library spoke truth, any man whose blood joined with one who wielded spellfire stood a chance of gaining it himself. That joining, moreover, would be a pleasure. . . .

Ghaubhan grinned wolfishly in the dark, and waited for

the hurrying steps of Ramath to announce the mageling's return. He'd bear watching, that one . . . such sight does not come from empty air; how came he by it? Fzoul and his upperpriests thought Ghaubhan Szaurr served the Cult of the Dragon; only Manshoon and a few senior wizards knew he in truth worked for the Zhentarim. . . . Was this Ramath a spy for Fzoul, then? Was he sent by someone in the Cult who'd become suspicious of Ghaubhan's loyalty? What fell and mysterious power moved the young fool? None known to a lowly Dread Master, for sure. . . .

* * * * *

" 'Fell and mysterious power!' I like that," Gathlarue said softly in the night-gloom. "It has a certain ring. . . ."

"It does," Mairara agreed. "This Dread Master is an engaging half-wit all around. Such twisted cruelty . . . such lame deceits."

"Lame they may be," Gathlarue said, "but it is my hope he does gain the spellfire. Not only will he be straw in our hands, but it will be entertaining to the utmost, watching him destroying most of the Brotherhood as he seeks to master it."

"Fun watching, to be sure," came the reply, "so long as he holds the Zhentarim together long enough to destroy Elminster of Shadowdale first. If we feed this Ramath visions for long enough, our ambitious Dread Master will not dare to start the foolishness too early. I would see Elminster perish soon, and the Brotherhood is the only blade we can wield that seems strong enough to slay him."

"There are others," Gathlarue said softly. "If we could turn the one called the Simbul against him . . ."

"They love each other strongly now."

"Precisely," Gathlarue said. The slow smile that stole onto her face then made Mairara shiver despite herself. "Precisely. . . ."

Nine

DEATH BEHIND THEE,
ITS CLAWS UPON THY SHOULDER

Time is the thief that knows no locks.
Faeranduil of Neverwinter, Sage
Sayings of the North
Year of Sunset Smoke

"Fare thee well, too, Baera," Mirt said roughly, and then his arms were tightly wrapped around her, squeezing as though by mere strength he could hold onto some part of her afterwards. The fat Harper, looking somehow sleek and striking this morning after her bath, gripped him back just as hard, and they stood locked like two wrestling bears for a long moment.

"Go, then," Baergasra said finally and pushed him away. Her voice was suddenly husky, and her eyes glimmered like the morning dew. "I fear I'll not see you again, Old Wolf." She waved him away sadly. "So go—quickly, all of you; I hate tears. Let me be lonely again."

"Well," Delg said gruffly, "if you took a bath more often, mayhap you'd be lonely *less* often. . . ."

He ducked under her wild and immediate grab and came running back to his companions, grinning from ear to ear.

"Next time, little man," Baergasra called after him, hands on hips, "I'll have a cake of soap ready for a certain dwarf. Begone, the lot of you!" She snorted, and then waved farewell.

Mirt, shaking his head at Delg, led them over a hill that hid the *Wyvern* from view behind them, and hid Baergasra with it.

The fat old merchant's shaggy head swung to and fro as they walked on. They all went slowly under the weight of much new-bought food as Mirt peered watchfully at every tree and rise around them. At length his gaze came to rest on Narm, striding along beside Shandril in his customary silence. "Are you well enough?" he rumbled anxiously. "Any pain?"

Narm grinned. "I'm . . . well, it seems. Worry not! It's in the past and done."

"As you were nearly in the past and done yestereve," Delg added meaningfully.

Narm sighed, then raised an eyebrow carefully. "Are you always this cheerful," he asked the dwarf, "or is this some sort of special occasion?"

The dwarf shrugged. "I—something's amiss; I feel it in my bones. I'm a little . . . bladesharp, this morn." He shook himself as a dog shakes off water when climbing out of a pond, and went on down the road.

Mirt rolled his eyes and shook his head but said nothing.

Narm and Shandril exchanged glances. "I have a bad feeling about *that*," Shandril said softly. "When Delg senses something amiss, he's usually all too right—something *goes* amiss before the day is out. So please, Narm . . . be careful; watch always for danger."

Narm nodded wryly. "What else do I ever watch for since we first met?" He wrapped an arm about her to show he meant no complaint, and added, "I fear you're right, though. I'll keep wary eyes, as best I can."

"If you two can find the will to leave off cuddling for a breath or two," Delg said sourly from ahead, "your mouths —and brains to guide them, too—are needed in a little dispute. Not our last ere sunset, either, I fear."

Mirt stood at the roadside. He was looking down at the dwarf rather like a bull wearily regards a small, loud dog: as something not yet worth kicking, but that may soon become so if it continues to annoy. "We leave the road here," he said patiently, "and go across the fields. Trust me; I know this land well."

"As do I," the dwarf replied, unmoved. "The more northerly we tend, the closer we get to the Zhentarim and the lawlessness of the Stonelands—where for all we know this Dragon Cult rides freely, too. Short of turning back into the teeth that follow us, this is the worst way we could head."

Mirt sighed. "Aye, so it may seem. But look ye, Sir Dwarf, and heed—in Suzail, or any port on the Inner Sea, the Zhents and the Cult could have a dozen's dozen of agents waiting, an' we'd never know until their blades were in us. More than that; they've hired eyes aplenty watching for the walking source of spellfire, and those known to guard her, in all those places. Moreover they expect Shandril to come that way, and by the roads. These be all good reasons, by my blade, to turn aside and seek the secret way I know."

Delg snorted. "The Stonelands are bandit country, and worse—they hold fearsome beasts and Zhent evil. Enough of both, even *you* must admit, that the Purple Dragons have never been able to hold Azoun's word as law north of the road that links Arabel with High Horn, let alone to Desert's Edge, where earlier kings of Cormyr always claimed to rule. A land of outlaws, breakneck gullies, little hidden cliffs and thornbushes; it crawls with monsters by night and creeps with them by day. Do you think us a band of sword-swinging heroes, bedecked with magic blades and fancy armor? Or have you such a band up your sleeve—or hidden in that capacious belly of yours?"

Mirt sighed again and spoke with exaggerated gentleness. "I have no quarrel with thy glowing description of the land, nor do I have any swordarms to protect us—save the two that come visibly attached to this belly ye're so impressed with. Yet, look ye, I know of a way not known to those who chase at our heels. A way to save Shandril nearly a season of travel-time on her long way to the North, a way to avoid the roads and inns of Cormyr—and the trackless wastes of the Backlands on the western edge of Anauroch, too, where every second merchant could well be a Zhent agent, or someone else who'd just as soon stick a dagger between yer shoulder blades the moment ye turn yer back."

"So what is this magical way, that I've never heard of it?" the dwarf asked suspiciously, brows bristling.

"That's it precisely," Mirt said, lowering his voice. "Magic. That's all I prefer to say."

Delg snorted. "Trust me, then, you're telling us: trust me to lead you into a land of death because I've left some handy, oh-so-reliable magic there, which'll whisk us away from all danger and leave all our foes and cares behind."

Mirt smiled thinly. "I couldn't have put it much better than that—are ye sure ye don't do a rich trade in dealing horses somewhere in Faerûn?" Then he sighed and looked to Narm and Shandril. "Ye've heard Delg, and my words too, about the paths before us. Choose then, whether ye'll follow me. I will say only two things more:

first, that the way through Cormyr's roads and cities is almost certain death, where my way offers death not so sure by a long measure; second, that whate'er yer choice, it must be made speedily, for if we stand here debating in the open all day, death will come up behind us and lay claws on our shoulders while yet we speak."

Shandril stared at him and at Delg, and then looked to Narm, who said, "The decision must be yours, love."

They gazed into each other's eyes for a moment, and then Shandril turned back and said very quietly, "I'm sorry, Delg. Storm and Elminster and the Knights told me some things about gates, and this sounds like one—am I right, Lord Mirt?"

Mirt nodded. "The gate, aye; but not this talk of 'Lord'; ye're no subject to me."

Shandril waved away his words. "I would walk where Mirt leads us now, Delg. Will you come with us? Please?"

Delg growled, looked away, and then spat into the dust slowly and carefully. "Of course I'll come. It's wrong. I can feel it. It'll bring death, but someone's got to be along to see that it isn't yours, Lady. I'll come."

Silence hung heavily around them for what seemed a long time, and then Shandril whispered, "Thank you, Delg. Thank you." Her voice trembled on the last word, and Narm looked to her in alarm; she was close to tears.

His slim lady stood looking at the dwarf, who squinted warily back up at her a moment more, and then smiled, clapped his hands together, and said briskly, "Let's be walking, then! The sun rolls on, and I grow older with it."

Amid a general murmur of agreement, they set off after Mirt. The old merchant's rolling gait was surprisingly fast. He strode purposefully across the field, heading for a distant stile over the rubble fence that separated this field from the next.

Delg, as was his wont, fell back to guard the rear, his ready axe glittering in his hands. He muttered as he walked, words meant for no ears but his own. "Never hurry to your doom, lass. It will come for you soon enough. Too many of my folk have gone looking for their doom— and sure enough, it found them." His knuckles were white where he gripped his axe, and the corded veins in his hairy wrists and forearms stood out darkly as his hands shook.

It is never easy to see your own death close ahead, know there is no escape, and go calmly to meet it.

* * * * *

"They were here, in this village?" The Zhentarim's voice was cold. "And no one knows which way they went?"

"No, Lord Mage," the swordmaster said a little uncertainly. "We've asked everyone."

"Not forcefully enough, I'd say. Start chopping off villagers' fingers until someone *remembers* something."

"Aye, Lord." The warrior's voice was not happy. Needless butchery was never wise. These folk were terrified of the Brotherhood already. Turning that fear to desperate, fighting hatred would be all too easy. The Zhents had to sleep somewhere tonight, whether or not this maniac of a wizard burned the inn to the ground.

"*I've* just remembered something," a voice rumbled from a roof close overhead.

The swordmaster looked up. "Eh?"

"It's Zhent-killing time!" Rathan Thentraver announced gleefully as he launched himself off the edge of the roof. His not inconsiderable bulk crashed down atop the swordmaster, who crumpled to the ground under the knight and did not move again. "Truly, the loads some of us bear in life are heavier than others." Rathan smiled up at the startled Zhentarim wizard as he paraphrased the old maxim.

The wizard, looking at the stout priest in surprise and anger, never saw the slim thief lean down over the edge of the roof, Rathan's borrowed mace in his hand.

"Magusta, dear?" Torm asked interestedly as he clubbed the wizard on the side of the head. Blood flew, and the man fell without a sound. "No," Torm said, watching the mage bounce and sprawl on the ground, arms twitching. "I guess not." He sighed theatrically and slid down from the roof. "When shall I ever catch up with that maiden? My lips ache for her kisses!"

"Not half so much as yon wizard's head aches for another hit o' my mace, I'm thinking," Rathan rumbled, taking it from his fellow knight and bending forward to finish the task.

There was a startled shout from a nearby window, and two Zhents ran around the corner of the *Wyvern*'s front wall, swords drawn.

While Rathan finished the mage, Torm snatched up the sword of the sprawled swordmaster, hefted it critically, and then threw it hard. It flashed end over end through the air and cut a crimson line across one Zhent's face. Torm leapt after it, drawing his own sword with a smile. "*This* is more like it!" he called back as steel rang and he turned aside the first warrior's blade. "Chop and hack merrily, work up an appetite, get a lot of good fresh air. . . ."

"Did ye *have* to mention food? My belly feels like it's been lying starving in a dungeon for a month—and here I am going into battle." Rathan's snort of disgust was matched by a low, ominous rumble from his abdomen. Torm hooted with laughter and killed a Zhent.

Rathan lumbered along the front of the inn as the man fell, calling plaintively, "Wait for *me,* will ye?" At full run, he spread his hands comically and addressed the sky. "Tymora—I *try* to serve ye faithfully, but this selfish thief *never* waits for me. Was ever a priest so put upon as I?"

* * * * *

All that day and the next, they walked farmlands, avoiding bulls and their owners alike and, when necessary, keeping to the shelter of the high stone walls that divided one farm from the next. Mirt led them at a tireless, steady pace across country, always seeming to know exactly where he was going. He kept silence when they walked, but was ready with an endless flood of salty jokes and tales whenever they stopped to eat or rest.

It was on the morning of the third day, after a night whose chill made them all stiff, that Delg asked the stout merchant, "Why, Deeppockets, could you not bring along a nag or six for us to ride? We'll die of gray hair and cold winter catching us in these fields before we see Silverymoon."

Mirt chuckled. "I did ride some of the way in Cormyr before we met. But horses are wiser than those who seek adventure: ye can't get them to go into deep woods, try as ye might. So I bid them a fair gallop and let them loose, and I walked."

"We're not exactly in deep woods *now*," Delg reminded him sourly, waving at the empty fields around them. "Or are there trees on all sides of us that I'm too short, perhaps, to see?"

Mirt sighed. "I've also yet to succeed in getting a horse to climb over a stile—or crawl along a stone wall to escape a farmer's eyes. Walking's better . . . as *most* dwarves are only too quick to tell me."

Delg sighed in his turn. "You're right, as usual," he replied. "I just mistrust all this open sky above, and not a hole to hide in. These bone dragons that attacked Shan before—they always fly, and I've heard of mages flitting about in the sky, too. I feel . . . naked."

Mirt nodded. "I prefer shade, and trees overhead, myself. Yet since I took up the harp, I've learned that all country has a way of its own, and ways in which it serves better than other countryside. This may be open—yet it's more private, look ye, than the roads."

Narm nodded. Shandril eyed the fat lord curiously as he wheezed his cautious way up a creaking stile to peer over its top into the field beyond. He nodded, then waved a hand for them to follow.

Shandril climbed up behind him and asked, "What is it, Lord, to be a Harper?"

Mirt froze, then sighed gustily and went on down the other side of the stile. "*Don't* call me 'Lord,' look ye, lass. I'm not so old as all that." He gained his balance, looked testily all about in the manner of an old and short-sighted lion, and added, "Ye should know, little one, that I'm not a very good Harper."

Shandril smiled. "*Don't* call me 'little one'—and don't try to wriggle out of answering, either." Behind her, she heard Delg's dry chuckle.

Mirt turned slowly and loomed up over her like an angry mountain. Then he grinned. "Right, then, good Lady Shandril. I shall try to tell thee something of what it is to be a Harper." He cleared his throat grandly and waved his hand at the field before them. It was dotted with cow dung. He lofted the nearest pat into the air with the toe of his boot and added, "As we walk, of course."

"A Harper holds peaceful sharing of the lands above all other goals," Mirt declaimed grandly, waving at the rolling fields around them. Several nearby cows turned their heads to stare at him curiously. "By sharing," he added, winking at the nearest cow, "we mean all the races living in and under the land, where each prefers to live, trading together where desire and need stir them to, and respecting each other's holds and ways—without the daily bloodletting that all too often holds sway in the Realms today."

"If you don't mind a word against that," Narm replied carefully, "it seems all too seldom that Harpers manage to avoid indulging in a little bloodletting themselves."

Mirt grinned, rather like a wolf raising bloody jaws from its fallen prey. "True. We must fight, it seems, often enough to keep old blades such as—'hem—myself busy, our swords and our tempers both sharp enough. Yet, know ye; all of us fight when we must, or die. Moreover, ye hear only of blades drawn and death and spells hurled, and never know of the many, many times more that a quiet word and a skillful deal has turned enemies aside from each other, forced a way clear where none was before, or distracted foes from the eager task of tearing each other's throats out. That is the true Harper way, lad: subtle and quiet, behind the shouting. Trust, and wisdom, and outfoxing others is what we deal in."

"Oh," Delg grunted, "how'd *you* get to be a Harper, then?"

Mirt sighed. "My long patience had something to do with it, as I recall," he answered deliberately, drawing a gleaming dagger and, with a single flick of his wrist, casually trimming off the tips of the nails on one hand. Narm stared, fascinated, but Shandril shuddered. If he'd missed by half an inch . . .

But he hadn't. The Old Wolf smiled at her again, a mirthless grin that reminded her of a grinning skull she'd seen—long ago, it seemed—amid the ruins of Myth Drannor. Then he pointed ahead. "We turn here," he said shortly, and then added, looking down, "even if we're clever dwarves."

Delg grunted in reply. "If I hear you tell us we're lost, just once," he threatened, "you'll find yourself rapidly becoming more *my* size." He glared at the tranquil wind-driven clouds that filled the sky and the endless rolling fields and rubble walls around them.

"I've crawled along in the dirt once or twice before, ye know," Mirt told him, and added over his shoulder to Shandril, "that's something else to being a Harper. There's fools' pride—the sort that won't get dirty, an' do this or that—and then there's Harpers' pride: where ye won't quit and won't be scared off. If ye only have the first kind, ye seldom live long enough to learn the second, unless ye leave off being a Harper altogether."

"Do all Harpers talk this much?" Delg asked innocently from somewhere just out of reach.

Mirt sighed again. "It's one way to keep from fighting," he replied patiently, then turned to Narm and Shandril. "Ah—remember *that,* too."

"You'll remind me, from time to time, about all the things I should be remembering?" Shandril asked him dryly, eyes twinkling.

"Certainly," the fat merchant boomed cheerfully. "All the way to Silverymoon, if ye like."

"I was afraid you'd say that," Narm told him as they approached another stile.

Mirt grinned at him. "Ye, lad, are already beginning to speak as a Harper does. If ye can learn some spells to match that mouth, ye'll be a mageling to be reckoned with . . . now, where was I?"

"At the strutting grandly bit, Lord," Shandril told him, so softly that it was almost a full breath later before Delg snorted. Shandril chuckled softly despite herself, and Narm started to laugh. It was another breath after that before Mirt joined in.

* * * * *

Overhead, the moon rode high above dark, ragged, racing clouds that streamed across the stars like tattered banners. Where the moonlight fell between the clouds, it laid bright white strips across the field.

Narm lay drowsily watching the clouds, Shandril asleep on his shoulder. The two of them were buried in a warm haystack, only their shoulders and heads protruding. Beside Narm's face lay Shandril's hair, a swirling mass that smelled faintly of spices. Baergasra had given her some bathing spices to ruin her scent for dogs—and worse things—the Zhents might use to track her.

To his left, Narm could just see the alert shadow that was Delg sitting watch. The dwarf sat with his blanket held over the ready axe in his lap, thereby preventing moongleams from betraying their presence to a watcher in the night. Despite Delg's caution, the deep, rhythmic snores of Mirt the Moneylender—once Mirt the Merciless, mighty Lord of Waterdeep—could tell anyone in this corner of Faerûn right where they were.

To Narm's left, something moved. It was Delg, creeping silently as a cat to peer into the night nearby. He seemed to see nothing amiss, because after a few moments, he turned and looked toward the haystack. His eyes met Narm's. The dwarf nodded and withdrew to his post as silently as he had left it.

Narm thought the dwarf's face looked bitter and drawn in the moonlight. Usually Delg seemed lit by a fierce fire from within, his face like a smithy door, spitting surly sparks with energy to spare. Not now. He looked like a ruined farmer Narm had once seen—beaten, bereft of hope.

The dwarf stared out across the moonlit field again, beaked nose pointing like an accusing finger into the night. Then something cold and wise crept slowly up Narm's spine, and with sudden certainty he knew the look Delg wore. He looked like a man about to leave his friends behind forever and go down into the darkness that does not end.

For all their differences, dwarves and men do look like brothers when their faces wear the same hopeless expression. Delg looked like a man who knew he was about to die.

Ten

A HARD AND STONY PLACE

The Realms hold many a hard and stony place—and the worst of it is, some of them come well furnished with wizards.

Glarthlyn of Silverymoon, Sage
Shadows in the Firelight
Year of Dark Frost

Ahead, the land was rising. "The Stonelands," Mirt announced unnecessarily.

Delg squinted up at him. "It may come as a great surprise to you, large and mighty one, but I'd managed to puzzle that out for myself already."

Mirt sketched a florid bow. "The wits of the dwarves are keen, and the fame of their workings resounds from the Spine of the World to the peaks of the Dustwall."

Delg made a rude sound in reply. The fire-blackened pans he carried clanked slightly as he clambered to the top of a ridge to get a better view ahead.

In the distance, like a row of old and gray teeth, a line of crumbling stone cliffs rose out of the mottled greenery of the forest. The edge of the Stonelands. Between that line and where they now stood stretched a wide expanse of gently rolling pastureland. Down its center, the road that linked Cormyr with Tilverton lay like a dark snake basking in the sun. The Moonsea Ride, it was called. Soldiers of Cormyr kept the brush cleared on either side of the road; a long, long walk across open ground lay between them and the Stonelands.

Delg turned to Mirt. "How d'you propose to get unseen across *that?* Wait for dark, I suppose—or have you some hidden magic at the ready?"

Mirt grinned easily, then lazily reached out one stout, hairy arm to haul the dwarf back from the crest of the ridge. "I've as little liking as ye do for waiting about while foes on our trail grow nearer, friend Delg. Sit ye down for a breath or two, and I'll show ye my hidden magic."

The old merchant wheezed as he bent over and fished in the open top of one of his large, flopping leather boots, dragging a leathern cord into view. It was loosely knotted around his leg; Mirt grunted, drew the knot open, and then pulled on the line. A wrinkled, seemingly empty sack came up from the depths of his boot. "A gift from a lady," he announced with dignity, shaking the hand-sized thing to rid it of folds and wrinkling his nose at the boot smell it gave off. He was not alone in this reaction.

Then the Old Wolf opened the bag's drawstring and plunged his hand in, drawing forth a gown of shimmering, flame-red silk, with a bodice of linked gold chains.

Hastily the old merchant thrust the garment out of view again, chuckling. "Sorry—wrong handful," he explained as Shandril lifted an eyebrow and the other two grinned delightedly. The next thing he drew up was a mesh sack, holding a large bottle filled with something dark. The mesh bag and the bottle both seemed too large to have come out of the wrinkled sack—which still looked and hung as if empty.

Delg's eyes fixed on the bottle and lit up. "Amberjack! Now *that's* worth dragging around one of these magical sacks for."

Mirt had already made it vanish into the depths of the bag again and was feeling around, his arm thrust into the small sack up to the shoulder. Shandril could see that it wasn't half deep enough to swallow the Old Wolf's arm—but . . .

"Ah!" Mirt said in triumph, and drew forth a large bundle of russet cloth, mottled with green, orange, and silver threads that confused the eyes, making one's gaze involuntarily slide away from it. The old adventurer set the bundle carefully on the ground and undid its tied ends, unfolding it to reveal what looked like a stack of shallow, silvery glass bowls inside. With the air of a tavern show wizard, he fanned these curved pieces of glass as one does a hand of cards; they looked like plates or masks to Shandril.

Delg snorted in sudden recognition. "Priests' regalia of Leira," he said. "May I remind you, mighty Lord, that the Lady of the Mists numbers few priests among her faithful? We'll hardly pass unnoticed."

Mirt bowed. "True, but the nasty spells Leirans are known to favor will keep most folk—even Zhents—from bothering us, and we certainly won't be recognized. These all-concealing robes—aye, put it on atop all ye wear, lass; over the head it goes—can shift about to fit the wearer, and even be commanded to hold their shape over emptiness, to conceal the true form and stature beneath. I carry half a dozen about, for—er, the proper occasions."

He showed them how to don the featureless glass masks, pull the cowls over their heads, settle the mantles on their shoulders and chests, and do up the loose, dangling sashes that went on last. Unfamiliar in his own robes, face hidden under unmoving mirrored glass, the merchant laid a hand on the glass orb that adorned his mantle. He seemed suddenly taller.

"Ye do the same, Delg," his voice came to them, hollow through the mask. "Increase yer height, enough so no one will think 'dwarf' when they see you. Shan, the magic works by yer will, when ye touch the orb; make yerself taller—and yer shoulders greater, to hide yer womanly front. That's it, good. . . . These robes were hard to get, mind, so hurl no spellfire unless ye are sore beset." He turned, rummaged in the bag, and suddenly a staff, topped with a multihued, ever-changing orb, was in his hand.

Shandril only had an instant to stare in wonder at its flowing, lazily changing colors before the old merchant swung away, stuffed the bag into his belt, and led the way up over the ridge with a slow, measured stride.

"Keep with me," his muffled voice came back to them, "Brothers of the Mists. In a half-circle, behind me, as is fitting. We go north this day, as the Lady's weird bids us."

Delg fell in behind and to the left and gestured for Narm and Shandril to walk beside him, to the old merchant's right. Matching the old man's stride, they marched slowly down the grassy slopes to the road, the orb-topped staff borne before them, its swirling hues shifting and brightening.

Narm wondered if the goddess Leira would be angered at this false use of her regalia, and bring some capricious doom down on them. Or would this deception delight her?

The young mage looked to either side, but the road seemed empty of life for as far as he could see in either direction. Yet he could feel the sudden weight of cold, unfriendly eyes regarding them from somewhere—and knew by the way her head moved beside him that Shandril felt the scrutiny too.

The uplifted orb flashed and pulsed ahead of them. Mirt said, "Ah! The Lady leads us on." He strode right across the road, heading for the cliffs beyond.

The ground around them was rising now, with rocks rearing out of the grass. There was not a bird in the sky or a beast to be seen anywhere, but the strong feeling of being watched persisted until Mirt led them into the ferny gloom of a little gully that pierced the cliffs.

The orb on the staff suddenly darkened. Mirt regarded it with satisfaction. "Whoever they are," he said, "they're not using magic to send eyes around corners after us. . . . They could see us only when we crossed the open road. Right—get this stuff off, all of ye: haste is what matters now."

After a few frantic minutes of unstrapping and wriggling out from under cloth, Mirt had stuffed the bundles back in the bag, and the bag was restored to its carrying place in Mirt's boot. Delg eyed it suspiciously as it slid out of sight, and said, "How many more tricks do you carry, Mirt? And are all of them as helpful as that one?"

"Many, and of course," Mirt answered smoothly. "Now let's be on—no trails are to be trusted in the Stonelands, and it's a ways yet to the gate I know of."

They scrambled warily along the gully, Mirt in the lead. Delg muttered from the rear, "If it's not betraying too much to tell us, just where *are* we heading?"

"Irondrake Rock," Mirt said, and Delg nodded.

"I've seen it," he said simply as they struggled up to the head of the gully and peered about. Bare shoulders of rock rose all around them in a confusing, broken landscape of rising ridges and plunging ravines. Scrub trees, gnarled and stunted, thrust branches in all directions, and the land ahead was a patchwork of greenery and rocky heights.

Death could lurk anywhere in a land like this, Shandril

thought—and be at your elbow before you saw it. She felt strangely weak and very vulnerable, like a deer surrounded by hunters. She drew a little closer to Narm, who put an arm around her, as if knowing her thoughts.

Delg, seeking any signs of pursuit, was looking suspiciously back the way they'd come. After a long moment, he sniffed, shook his head, turned to follow Mirt over the first ridge, and executed a precarious scramble down the other side into the concealing thickets of the next ravine.

Wary as they were, none of them saw the skull that floated along behind them, for it was cloaked in magics that made it invisible. The lich lord's cold gaze was bent steadily on the small band—in particular, on the slim form of the maid among them. Nightfall approached slowly as the day went on—too slowly, it seemed. Iliph Thraun was getting hungry again.

The day wore on in an endless struggle up and down treacherous slopes and breakneck ravines. Everywhere around the travelers rose the crags and outcrops that gave the Stonelands their name. The Lord of Waterdeep, the dwarf, the bearer of spellfire, and the young mage who'd married her struggled through the broken lands, scraping and bruising elbows and knees on the ever-present rocks.

As they went, Mirt spoke seldom—no surprise, for he was wheezing and puffing like an old and indignant goat. When he did break silence, it was always to cheer them with tales of skeletal trolls, monstrous ettins and hobgoblins, and sly, cruel-fingered goblins who lurked in the Stonelands, dragging intruders down in ambushes or stonefall traps—and feeding on them.

"Do you mind belting up, merchant?" Narm asked at last, exasperated. The young mage was white to the lips from fear, and he cast involuntary glances at every bush and shadow as they walked.

Mirt chuckled and clapped him on the back, a mighty blow that nearly sent the mage sprawling. "Ah, stop me vitals, lad," he rumbled, "but it's good to see some spirit in ye at last."

Delg squinted up at the fat merchant. "Speaking of 'spirit in you,' I recall seeing that bottle of amberjack in your bag—and wondering what else it might be hiding from us, too. Berduskan dark, perhaps? Or have you a little winter wine?"

Mirt chuckled. "I once had a considerable cellar in here, aye—but traveling's thirsty work, and most of the stock's gone now. Moreover, friend Delg, this is *not* the sort of country one should try legging it through with a few skins of wine on board. Falling and breaking bones is easy enough when sober."

"A lecture on morals and practicality from Mirt the Moneylender?" Delg put his hands to his open mouth in mock amazement.

"Stow it, little one," Mirt suggested in kindly tones, then led the way along the winding, snakelike crest of a ridge that headed west, on into the seemingly endless maze of rocky heights and tree-cloaked ravines.

As the group climbed and clambered on, Shandril's fingers went numb from clawing at too many rocks, and she felt a growing weakness—an emptiness—inside. What was wrong with her? She sighed, drawing an anxious look from Narm, which she put off with a smile. Scratching at a scrape on her arm, Shandril wondered how much more of this punishing travel she'd be able to last through.

Overhead, the sun had passed its height, and was beginning the long slide toward sunset. As she squinted at it, Narm voiced the thought that had just come into her own mind.

"I'm not liking the idea of camping in this, somewhere on the side of a rockfall," Narm said to Mirt. "How much farther is it to this gate of yours?"

"If we keep on steadily," Mirt told him gravely, "we should reach it just before nightfall."

Narm rolled his eyes. "Nightfall," he said. "Of course."

The old merchant—as usual, Delg reflected sourly— proved to be right. The sun was low and the depths of the ravines shrouded in purple shadows when Mirt pointed to a tiny spur of rock in the distance. "Yon's Irondrake," he said simply, and hastened on. Despite the chill breezes of twilight, they were all sweating as they clambered up, over, down and through seemingly endless rocks.

Narm could well believe what he'd heard of brigands evading armies of Cormyr in this tortured land; half a hundred men could be waiting on the other side of every ridge, and you'd never know it until y—Suddenly wary, Narm swallowed and suspiciously checked the terrain around them.

Delg, who was climbing in his wake, grunted. "About time you started being scared, lad," the dwarf said. His tones told Narm the dwarf had just deemed him not quite a complete idiot—but still damned-before-all-the-gods close. The young mage sighed and looked at Shandril. The sight of her always cheered him.

As it happened, there weren't a hundred armed brigands waiting around the next ridge. Instead, a grassy meadow opened out in front of them, rising steeply up to tumbled rocks at the base of a lancelike pinnacle of stone. The fire of sunset blazed down one side of this rocky spire.

"Irondrake Rock," Mirt announced as if he'd just put it there himself. "Named for a great wyrm that once laired here."

"Once?" Delg asked suspiciously.

Mirt chuckled and pointed a thick finger at the base of the toothlike spire of stone. "Its grotto lies there, if ye've a mind for fool-headed poking about. Perhaps, if it'd make ye sleep easier, Shan'll hurl a little spellfire in there—and singe whatever calls it home now."

The dwarf squinted up at the stone spire. Save for the calls of birds in the trees below and behind them, all was quiet around it. The tall grass of the meadow, studded with weeds and wildflowers, looked as if nothing had disturbed it all this season. Even so, Delg didn't care much for the way stony walls rose on either side of them to hem the meadow in, forming a great funnel that lead only upward to the Rock. But he could see no sign of danger. Yet.

Grumbling into his beard, Delg led the way up through the thick grass toward the rocky spire. "Where's this gate of yours, then?"

Mirt grimaced. "At the very top—of course."

"You'd need the luck of the gods to get to it in winter," Delg replied, staring up at the crumbling flanks of Irondrake Rock.

Shandril followed his gaze, and swallowed. She'd have to climb *that?* She turned to Narm and found on his face the same growing alarm she felt. Without thinking, they threw comforting arms about each other.

"Last light," Delg said sourly. "Little as I like camping anywhere in these lands, we'd never get more than halfway up before it'd be too dark to climb—even without the two lovejays, here." He cocked his head at Narm and Shandril. They looked back at him with identical expressions that told Delg he might have problems getting them to climb Irondrake Rock even in full sun, and with a whole day to do it.

Delg turned back to Mirt. "Where exactly does this gate of yours take us, anyway?"

"A certain place in the High Forest, south of Stone Stand," Mirt replied, his eyes on the cliffs around them.

"Shall we look at the cave?"

Delg nodded. "After I've looked around behind the Rock first, and had a bit of a peer at those ledges above us, too—or we may find ourselves attacked both in front and behind." He strode on through the grass.

"What a cheery fellow," Mirt observed in the fluting, jolly tones of an effete courtier. Shandril stifled a laugh.

As the merchant strode forward, twilight laid deepening gloom on the meadow. Night came down swiftly on the Stonelands; before Delg had returned to them, it was fully dark. "A fire?" he asked, stumping up to Mirt. "You know better than I how dangerous that is here."

The old merchant adventurer shrugged. "In the cave, we'll need light and can have it. Out here—well, it could be seen a long way." He rummaged in his magical sack for a moment and drew forth a stout, iron-caged lantern. Opening one of its glass panes, he sniffed, pronounced it "full" with a satisfied air, and extended it to Delg with a grand flourish.

The dwarf sighed, took it, and extended his other hand. "Another?" he snapped, looking from Mirt to his empty palm.

It was Mirt's turn to sigh. He rummaged in his bag for a long time and finally held up—another lamp, identical to the first. It came to Delg accompanied by Mirt's triumphant smile.

The dwarf merely snorted, thrust both lanterns into Narm's grasp with a terse, "Here—hold these. No dropping," and extended his empty hands again. "Flint and steel?"

Mirt raised an eyebrow. "Of course—but what happened to yer own, eh?"

Delg chuckled. "Just testing," he replied, hands going to his belt. As he took one lamp from Narm and lit it, and Mirt did the same with the other, Shandril put her hands on her hips and demanded, "Are the two of you going to play these games all the way to Silverymoon?"

"Of course not," a menacing voice purred out of the darkness near at hand. "They'd both have to stay alive to do that."

Mirt spun around with an oath—in time to meet winged death swooping down on him from the night sky. He ducked aside, grabbing for his blades, and stony claws tore at him. The fat merchant turned and smashed the lantern to flaming ruin on a grotesque, leering horned face —and stony wings beat as the thing fled aloft, squalling.

*   *   *   *   *

"Patience," Gathlarue said in that same purring voice. The rings on her fingers glowed with a faint blue light. "We'll strike only when my winged ones get them really dancing."

Mairara stared into the eyes of her mistress and saw a light in them that made her shiver. She looked hastily away, down over the edge of the cliff, to the battle below. "The soldiers, Lady?"

Gathlarue nodded. "Those with Tespril stay up here with us; send the others down. They're getting restless; best give them some blood." She laughed aloud.

Mairara shivered again as she hastened to pass on the orders.

*   *   *   *   *

"Gargoyles!" Delg shouted. "Only magic can harm them. Narm, ge-" The rest of his words were lost in the jarring impact of another winged form. The dwarf's lantern fell to the grass, smoked—and then its flames caught dead weeds, and flared.

In the sudden, flickering blaze, Shandril and Narm saw
Mirt turning toward them, glowing dagger in one hand
and sword in the other. Above and behind him, the gargoyle that had attacked him was turning in the air, wings
beating raggedly. Narm coolly raised his hands and
blasted it with a bolt of force. The stony monster screamed
thinly as it spun end over end away from them, clawing
vainly at the air. Then it leveled, banked, and flew heavily
on; Narm muttered a soft curse. He had no more such
spells.

The other gargoyle was clawing at Delg, who rolled in
the grass, cursing. Shandril lashed out at it with spellfire—a thin tongue of cutting blue-white flame that laid
open the nearest shoulder and flank of the gargoyle, and
sent it over on its back with a scream of pain.

Mirt was on it an instant later, bounding in with flailing
blade and heavy knees, pinning it. The glowing dagger
stabbed down, rose, and thrust again, viciously. Squalling,
the thing convulsed.

Behind Mirt, the other gargoyle was diving in savage
haste. Shandril stepped forward, trembling with sudden
anger and—could it be—pleasure? She shuddered at the
thought, but poured out spellfire in a huge ball of destroying flame. Small stony bits flew in all directions, clattering
wetly off the stones around it.

Mirt rose from the sagging form of the gargoyle. Dark
wetness smoked all down the blade of his glowing dagger.
He looked irritated. "Gods," he snarled, "give me something to *fight!*"

The gods seemed to have heard. A breath later, the
beleaguered travelers saw dark, armored forms charging
out of the night. Dark forms armed with swords.

Mirt's face twisted into a savage smile, and he gave a
satisfied hiss as his blades swept up to meet the foremost
Zhentilar.

The rumble that came from Delg as he bounded past Narm and Shandril also sounded satisfied. "Watch behind us, lad!" he called back, as he rolled under the blade of a Zhentilar, and felled the man with a smashing blow to the side of his knee.

Something small and dark spun out of the night at Narm, and Shandril blasted it into flying dust with a little shriek of anger. The flash of her spellfire showed her the dark helms of half a dozen or more warriors approaching across the meadow. Lips tightening, she hurled a handful of destroying spellfire. If she wasn't quick, the next dart or arrow or stone might get to her beloved.

Narm gave her a quiet smile of thanks before he turned and pointed into the night beyond Delg. Green fire crackled from his hand, and Shandril saw three men in dark armor convulsed in the grip of Narm's magic before it faded. Their screams faded a little more slowly.

* * * * *

"Gods above, Mistress!" Tespril was frightened, her eyes large and dark. "They've destroyed the gargoyles already. Shouldn't we throw spells now, before our soldiers are gone, too?"

Gathlarue was kneeling, nursing fingers that still smoked from where the rings she'd worn had flared and burned away. She looked up and hissed in anger and pain, "Do you command here, Miss?"

Tespril shook her head frantically. "No, no, Mistress," she said, almost pleading in anxious haste. "Yet look! Our best chance slips away."

Leaning over the edge of the rocky height where they crouched, she pointed at the trampled grass below. The meadow was lit up as spellfire lashed out again, and more Zhentilar died.

Gathlarue reached out and caught hold of Tespril's arm and breast with cruel fingers, digging them in bruisingly deep. Tespril hissed in pain, but the sorceress clawed her way up her younger apprentice until she stood upright again. Swaying slightly, Gathlarue stared down at the ruin of her force.

Freed, Tespril sobbed in pain and shrank away. Then Mairara felt the cold eyes of her mistress turn on her.

"The mistake is mine," Gathlarue said in a soft voice. "I was too impatient to get my hands on spellfire." She turned to look at the battle below once more, and spellfire flashed again. "Now, Mairara, is your chance to prove yourself. Use the power you planned to betray me with—show me how good your killing sorcery has become!"

Mairara stiffened, met the cold eyes of her mistress for a long, chilling moment, and then whispered, "I'll make you proud of me, Lady."

Gathlarue raised a hand. "Do nothing—yet—to draw their attention to us up here."

Mairara had already raised her clawed hands to work a spell that would blast the fray below with lightning. At her mistress's words, she lowered them, frowned, and then nodded suddenly in decision. Flicking hair back over her shoulder with one hand, she gestured with the other, muttering.

The sprawled form of the gargoyle Mirt had slain now moved, wriggled, slithered, and seemed to flow, unseen amid the tumult of clashing blades and lumbering Zhentilar. It rose slowly and split, twisting and flowing into sudden sharp definition—becoming the alert, deadly-looking forms of two smaller, unharmed gargoyles.

Mairara made a growling sound deep in her throat, and spread her hands. Gathlarue smiled. Somewhere in the darkness behind them, Tespril whimpered. Mairara, eyes flashing, gestured again, lips drawn back from her teeth in killing laughter.

* * * * *

Delg turned, bloody axe in hand. Something had moved—there! Ye gods! More gargoyles were leaping and flapping out of the night, heading for Shandril. Roaring, the dwarf bounded away from the Zhentilar who'd been cautiously approaching and ran full tilt toward the lass, swinging his axe for momentum as he went.

Narm threw something into the fallen lantern's flames to make them blaze like a bonfire. By its leaping firelight, he spotted the gargoyles. With one hand, he caught Shandril's arm and dragged her around to see this new danger. Small bolts of light streamed from his other hand, but the monster ignored them as it plunged toward the human maid, claws reaching out to rend and slay.

Shandril turned in time to stare into red, baleful eyes close enough to touch easily with her fingertips. Startled, she screamed—spitting spellfire into the face of the thing as it crashed into her, slashing with cruel claws. She screamed again. Spellfire suddenly exploded into a bright ball around her that made Narm stagger back—and the gargoyle disappear forever.

In the wake of her fire-burst, Shandril lay dazed, smoke drifting from her torn clothing. Where the gargoyle's claws had slashed her, ribbons of blood glowed briefly with the same radiance as spellfire, and then faded.

On the trampled grass nearby lay Narm, groaning and clutching at his eyes. The burst of flame must have blinded him, at least for now.

Delg cursed as he ran toward them both. He saw the second gargoyle flying in for the kill, sinuous stone wings beating as it stretched out long-clawed limbs. With a last, desperate bound, Delg leapt at it. It sensed him, and slid aside with frightening speed. Delg found himself about to pitch over its moving body, but he hooked his axe around one of its wings. The shock as he was brought up hard against a stony flank a moment later told him he'd succeeded. The gargoyle had crashed to the ground.

The dwarf kicked and scrabbled against living stone for a few frantic moments, then got to where he'd hoped to be: crouched low astride the back of the gargoyle, with a firm grip on the root of one wing. He raised his axe to hack and hew.

The gargoyle charged at Shandril—and with jarring force Delg brought his axe down on the side and top of its head. Stone chips flew. Beneath him, the monster shook and screamed. It tried to stand up, stony muscles surging—and Delg hacked at it again, putting his whole shoulder behind the blow. Sparks flew from the striking edge of his axe, and the gargoyle shuddered. A good part of its shoulder broke off and fell away—and a maddened instant later, the thing and Delg were both aloft. The beast whirled, buffeting Delg with stony wings, trying to shake him off.

At the stars overhead, Delg snarled, "For the glory of the Ironstars!" and brought his axe crashing down again. The unwilling mount of living stone he rode plunged earthward with terrifying speed.

Rocks rushed up to meet him like hungry teeth. Delg clung to the gargoyle, hacking desperately. Air roared past him in an angry wind—and at the last instant, the gargoyle twisted aside and shook itself, tearing his fingers free.

The impact of the stone, smashing through his chest and guts like a great fist, drove the breath from him, and his axe spun away like a hurled hammer. Delg scarce heard the despairing cry of the Zhentilar it happened to strike, for he himself hung impaled on stone.

Stone—always his friend, something he could work to his bidding, and trust, something solid and dependable.

As if from a great distance, Delg Ironstar heard the voice of one of the elders, telling him long ago—so long ago—*From stone we come, to stone we return, in the end.*

He looked out as the shattering pain rose to choke him, and he saw Shandril's eyes blazing with grief and shock as she screamed his name. She was running toward him through the fray. Dying, Delg of the dwarves of Mintarn Mountain, Harper, and Shield-Son of Clan Ironstar, wondered if the young lass he'd come to love so much would reach him in time.

Eleven

TOO LITTLE TIME, TOO MUCH DEATH

Splendid, heroic deaths? Only in tales, ballads, and books, kitten. Death in battle is always brutal, painful, and messy—and there's never time enough then for those heroic scenes legends tell of. Too little time, too much death. There's never time enough in life for any splendid or heroic things, kitten. Remember that—and make time before you must die. If you do that, you'll have forged a better life than most.

Laeral of Waterdeep, quoted in
Words to an Apprentice
Ithryn Halast, Year of the Weeping Moon

"Delg! *Delg!*" Shandril's eyes spilled over as she ran, heedless, across the trampled grass.

The battle raged around her, Mirt grunting with effort amid the crashes of steel on steel. Unheeding, Shandril wept tears of fire and fell on her knees beside the dwarf.

Delg was reaching a trembling, clenched hand to her, eyes glittering in agony. "Sh-Shan . . ." he gasped faintly, blood on his lips. "For . . ." His eyes were still beseeching hers a breath later, when they went dark.

In his ears, Delg heard the soft crackling of flames. The Lady Sharindlar had come for him, and his time in Faerûn was done. Tears blurred his last sight of the human lass he'd given his life for, and he couldn't even tell her of the love he'd come to feel for her. . . . Raging against the Zhentarim who had brought him death, Delg Ironstar went down into the everlasting darkness, waving his axe.

"*No!*" Shandril threw her arms around the hairy, sweat-soaked body, but the dwarf's eyes stared past her, dull and unmoving. She knew they'd never see her—or anything else—again, and she clutched Delg tightly, her face pressed against his hard, strong-smelling chain mail. And she cried.

In the rocks high above, Mairara curled her lip in the darkness and gestured with both hands. The crippled gargoyle turned on broken wings to swoop down on the unguarded, weeping maiden.

Shandril cried uncontrollably, body shaking.

Mirt roared out as he ran for her. The Old Wolf finally reached her, shook her, and bellowed, "Shan! *Shan!* We need yer spellfire, *now!*"

Shandril stared up through a rain of tears that would not stop falling, and saw the gargoyle veer off for another pass.

Mirt shook her roughly. "No *time*, lass! We've—"

A spell raked them from the rocks above, bolts of crackling lightning that made Mirt grunt and bite his lip as they jolted him. Shuddering, his hand reached out and tightly grasped the haft of Delg's axe.

Shandril was oblivious, her face buried in the old dwarf's sweat-soaked leathers. She wept silently.

"Gods aid me *now!*" Mirt cursed. He hurled the sobbing girl away and spun around.

Just in time. A Zhentilar blade was already cutting the air toward his neck. Mirt raised his left hand, Delg's notched axe in it, and blocked the attacking sword. The impact shook both men, and the old merchant's own curving long saber was in the man's throat and out again while they were both still shaking.

Another Zhent was hurrying at Mirt. The warrior held his blade low and deadly as he charged in, but was still steps away when flame rained down from above, cooking him and sending the old merchant staggering back, eyebrows smoldering.

Thank Tymora and Mystra both for *that* carelessly hurled spell, the Old Wolf thought, wondering just how many Zhent wizards were waiting in the darkness up there. He'd led his friends right into a waiting trap this time . . . all because he'd been foolish enough to think the wizards wouldn't know about the gate here. He quickly retreated to Shandril, glancing back to make sure no new dangers threatened. Only then did he discover where that last gargoyle had gotten to.

There! High above in the night, the dark form of the gargoyle flapped in a tight turn, head leering down, preparing to dive. . . .

"*Shandril!*" Mirt growled, backhanding the weeping maid. "Aid me!"

The sobs broke off just as the gargoyle plummeted out of the night. With a curse, Mirt cast Delg's axe at it and grabbed the magical dagger at his belt. Another Zhentilar warrior was trotting out of the darkness, shield and sword raised; the Old Wolf knew he couldn't escape their blades forever.

Then the air beside him exploded with a roar. Mirt cried out, turning his head away from the bright flash. He didn't see the gargoyle burst into dust and flying stones, or the screaming Zhentilar vanish into ashes and shifting smoke.

Shandril looked around at the ruin she had wrought. Smoke rose in wisps from the blackened turf. A man was crawling slowly through the scorched grass toward her; she raised a hand to destroy him. Then she recognized Narm's head. A cold shiver ran through her as she realized just how close she'd come to slaying him. It could have been done in a moment; he would have been dead forever. It was all too frighteningly *easy.* . . .

"Now! Hit her now—before it's too late!"

Without taking time to look, she hurled spellfire up at that shrill voice and was answered by more despairing screams—followed by a sharp cracking sound as rock shattered and began to slide.

The ground shook. Smoldering figures in dark armor bounced and rolled amid tumbling stones. The ledge above the meadow where the Zhents had been broke off and slid down toward her. One slim figure floated in the air for a moment, rising above the cascading stones, and then flew to another rocky height, robes rippling.

A Zhentarim! Shandril bared her teeth and hurled a gout of spellflame, blasting the rock where the dark-robed mage stood. Her foe rose above the shattered stone and hung in the air, mockingly. Arms raised, the Zhent began the gestures of spellcasting.

With a shriek of fury, Shandril dashed her hands towards the ground, hurling spellfire downward. A moment later, she rose on columns of spellfire that pummeled the rock and turf beneath her, and she raced through the air toward the Zhent. A startled face gaped at her. The Zhent was a woman!

Shandril charged right at her, eyes blazing fire.

Gathlarue knew real fear for the first time in a long, long while. It hurt even to meet the maid's gaze—raw, burning pain that would have torn her apart if she'd not twisted free. Gathlarue turned in the air and fled, flying as fast as she could.

Spellfire tore the night apart above her.

Gathlarue found herself falling. Rocks rushed up to meet her. Her mind snatched desperately at spell phrases; she magically steadied her descent and came to rest on smoking grass. Her hands trembled as she wove a shield-shaped wall of magical force before her, curving it to meet the cliff at her back.

Spellfire struck Gathlarue's shield an instant after she was done. It splashed on bare earth, ignited grass—and then clawed its way along the spell-shield. The flash of its strike left her eyes watering. She closed them hastily as a second attack came, striking with such fury that it shook the shield and Gathlarue beneath it.

Still flying, Shandril screamed with rage, but the magic defied her spellfire. She hurled fiery destruction a third time, feeling the deep ache that told her she had little energy left—and saw that bolt, too, lick harmlessly off the Zhentarim's invisible shield.

Panting, Shandril landed on the smoking meadow, staring at the woman in dark robes. The sorceress turned her cruel, frightened face aside and would not meet her eyes. Breast heaving, Shandril stared at her enemy—and then her eyes narrowed, and she spread her hands over her head. She lashed out at the cliff behind the woman.

Rock cracked, shook, and fell in a gathering roar. Mighty boulders crashed and rolled, and the Zhentarim disappeared beneath them. Dust rose.

Shandril stood ready, eyes hard, until it cleared.

One of the mage's hands protruded from the fallen rocks, straining vainly toward the open air and freedom she'd never reach.

Her fingers reached, twitched feebly, and then fell still.

Puffing, Mirt rose from atop a rocky knob, the blood of Zhents all over him. The meadow was empty of living enemies at last. He raised his eyebrows and spared breath enough to mutter, "So young . . . so much power . . ."

"Gods," Mairara whispered to herself, crouching white-knuckled behind a rock in the heights above the meadow. Then her eyes widened in horror as the veteran Zhentilar beside her stood up and calmly hurled a dagger at the maid below, putting all the strength in his shoulder behind the smooth throw.

Steel spun through the night. The venomed blade had served Unthlar Highsword well over the years, slipping into many a rival's back or unwary eye. Its touch meant death. Unthlar watched his deathfang hurtle toward Shandril's slim, unprotected back, and he started to smile.

Too soon. Mirt saw the flicker of its flight. Groaning in his haste, he leapt between Shandril and the attack, throwing up both his own blades to knock the dagger aside.

At the same time, words of soft anger came out of the night beside the puffing merchant. The strongest spell Narm could hurl—one that always left him utterly drained of wits and strength—rent the night, exploding in the air right in front of Unthlar.

Mairara shut her eyes and flung her head to one side as wetness splattered the rocks around. She looked back in time to see Unthlar's lower half—all that was left of him—stagger backward and fall heavily among the rocks beside her.

She heard curses and scrambling sounds from behind her as the few surviving Zhentilar fled in terror. Then Mairara looked down again—straight into the hard eyes of the maid who bore spellfire.

Shandril stood staring up at the Zhentarim sorceress. Her hair was moving about her shoulders with a life of its own, curling in slow menace.

"By Mystra's mercy," Mairara whispered, looking at

Shandril with wide eyes, "make it quick."

Shandril granted her that last wish. When the roaring had died away, all that was left was drifting smoke and the cracking of overheated rock.

White-faced, Shandril looked down at Delg's still body, and then turned to look east. The tears that fell from her cheeks burned the ground they touched. "Right, then, Lord Manshoon," she said, voice brittle and quavering. "I've done all the running I'm going to do. Now *you* will learn what it is to be hounded!"

A skull that floated unseen in the darkness near the top of Irondrake Rock looked down and chuckled, the teeth of its perpetual grin chattering hollowly.

* * * * *

"It's not as though I've naught else to do, look ye," Elminster said, spreading his hands. Released from his grasp, the pipe floated off by itself to hang ready in the air nearby.

Storm glanced up from the strings of her harp. "More important than spellfire?"

Elminster's expression was sour. "Who's to say what's of more import—my giving a little boy a scroll to play with so he grows up to become an archmage—or passing on word of a foe to a nomad chieftain—or telling a Waterdhavian guildmaster of a plot against him? I've done all these in the last few days, and there's always much more still to do—the untended garden grows weeds best."

"Shandril needs help now," Storm said quietly, her eyes dark and troubled. "I can feel it."

"And she shall have it," Elminster said, hands moving in the opening gestures of a spell. "Why d'ye think we rode out of the dale, if not to keep it safe against spells I might need to hurl—or the careless cruelty of those who might come looking to hurl spells at *me*? But know ye, timing is all-important in affairs of power—and her moment is not come."

He cast a stern look at Storm's harp, and she obediently stilled the strings and shifted it to her shoulder. "I spent much of the night scrying the Realms as ye slept, and saw—too much. Matters that must be dealt with now, I tell thee! The lass must find her own wings to fly with while I deal with Dzuntabbar of Thay—and the wizard Vlumn's plans to create ice golems the size of mountains in the High Ice—and a little matter of twisting awry some poison-creating spells that certain Calimshite satraps are perfecting before they get the idea such deadly craziness might work."

"All that, before highsun?"

"Aye, and more. Come!" The Old Mage squinted at the night sky and muttered, "With luck, we'll have time to look in on Shandril by now tomorrow."

"If she's not dead by then," Storm murmured in reply, just before Elminster's spell swirled around them both.

* * * * *

Irondrake Rock trembled, melted, and slid down into liquid ruin. The stars around it wavered and fell, as Shandril looked away from the spire. She blinked, and fresh tears came. Again.

Mirt knelt beside her. "Thy lad's okay," he said roughly, as he awkwardly put an arm around her shoulders. "But milord dwarf, here . . ."

Shandril nodded. She was crying freely now, tears raining into her empty hands.

Mirt looked at Delg's body, shook his head sadly, and said, "We haven't even time to bury him. Shan, will you take him to ashes? He'd prefer that to Zhentarim spell-pestering, I'm sure."

Shandril nodded, trying to still her tears. "H-He was trying to give me something, when he died . . . in his hand. . . ."

Mirt looked at Delg's fist, outthrust still in the agony of death. The broken ends of a fine golden chain hung from between the tightly clenched fingers. Mirt tried to pry them open, but he could as well have clawed at the fist of an iron statue. Pitting all his strength against the cooling hand, Mirt managed to ease the dwarf's fingers apart. Saying a silent prayer to Moradin in apology for this desecration, he slid out what lay within.

It was a silver harp pendant: the badge of a Harper, torn from around the dwarf's neck. Mirt stared at it, open-mouthed—and his vision blurred.

Shandril looked at the shaggy old warrior sharply. A thin, wheezing noise hissed from his bent head. She realized suddenly that the old merchant was weeping.

At her shoulder, Narm asked wonderingly, "Delg was a Harper, too?"

Shandril nodded slowly. Mirt abruptly thrust the harp pendant into her hand, rose, and said gruffly, "Burn him, will ye?"

Narm reached out a hand to him, and the two men embraced in the night like scared children.

Shandril stared at them for a moment. Then she carefully set down the pendant, raised her hands, and gave Delg a warrior's funeral, engulfing the dwarf's body in a pyre of spellfire lit by the red anger and grief that burned inside her. Flames roared up at the stars, even as the spellfire in Shandril's hands faltered, sputtered, and died.

They watched the dwarf burn to ashes. When all was done, Mirt said grimly, "Now, we walk—before all the rest of the Zhentarim come down on our heads here. I carry a ward that shields us against magical mind-prying and scrying. With that and thy spellfire, we can win our way on, as long as we give them no more chances to gather against us."

"No," Shandril said softly.

"What then, lass?" Mirt asked, peering at her in the night.

"I'm done with running away," Shandril said in a cold, resolute voice. "We stand—and fight."

"Here? Shan, every outlaw and prowling beast in the Stonelands heard the battle—and saw the pillar of flame ye just raised, burning Delg. Yer spellfire's gone for now, an' all Narm's spells—and without Delg, I'm too old and fat to wave swords enough to defend both of ye. We must be gone from this place!"

"Yes. Gone—to Zhentil Keep."

"Lass, are ye *crazy?*"

"Probably," Shandril said, her voice very steady. "Mirt, will you guide me there?"

"Before all the gods, why?"

"My days of running and skulking are done. I'm going to make Manshoon pay for—for Delg, if it's the only thing I do before I die. Manshoon, any other Zhentarim wizards I can find . . . and anyone else in that city who stands in my way. I'll probably have to kill everyone in the whole Brotherhood to make up for Delg's death. They should pay in blood for those soldiers in Thundarlun, too." The eyes that looked up into Mirt's were like cold, dark iron. "Are you with me?"

The old merchant sighed. "Aye, Shan," he growled. "I'll stand with ye. But I'll do it in the morning, mind—and if ye're in such a whirling hurry to get to Zhentil Keep, I know where we can get a teleport there, instead of stamping across the Stonelands and Daggerdale for days upon days, fighting every beast of the wilds and Zhentilar patrol."

"Where?" Shandril's voice was quiet and calm.

Mirt fought back a shiver when he heard it. "In Eveningstar, south and west of here. In the spells of a good lady by the name of Tessaril."

"Another old friend?" Narm sounded on the edge of tears, but managed a hint of the wry tone he usually adopted when sparring with the Old Wolf.

Mirt bowed his head. "Aye, and I am honored she calls me so. No jests now, lad—I'm busy trying to keep yer little one, here, from throwing her life away."

For two long, cold breaths, Shandril stared at him thin-lipped, and then managed a smile, and turned to look west.

"Find Eveningstar for me, then, and Tessaril," she said.

Mirt's gusty sigh of relief echoed off the rocks around. Then they all looked back at the drifting ashes that had been Delg, and there were fresh tears.

Later that night, as Mirt led the way up a narrow cleft, heading west out of the still-smoldering meadow, the Old Wolf said, "Tell me, lass: if ye've any plan for this attack, or if we're all going to rush headlong to our deaths."

"We get there, you show me Manshoon, and I burn him," Shandril said sweetly.

"That's it? No battle plans at all?"

"You're my battle plans, Old Wolf," Shandril told him.

Mirt sighed and stumped onward. The comforting weight of Delg's battered axe rode in his hands, and he stared ahead, looking for certain moonlit crags to guide him to the best way down into Cormyr again.

In his mind, Mirt saw Delg's dead, staring face, and muttered to himself that he really was getting too old for adventuring.

* * * * *

When Mirt fell for the third time, the cold mists and the lightening gloom told them dawn was not far off. The Old Wolf announced wearily that he'd fall asleep walking if they went on. Narm and Shandril both murmured exhausted agreement, and a moment later they slumped together in a little dell, sitting on the turf. Wearily the old merchant wrestled Delg's pack from his back and felt in it for a prickly handful of kindling.

"Is that wise?" Narm was yawning as he spoke.

Mirt managed a shrug in reply—and then stiffened. The other end of the chain Delg had broken must have somehow fallen into the pack. As the Old Wolf's arm came out with kindling, the fine gold lay curving along it. Mirt stared. Dangling from the chain was a tiny four-pointed star fashioned of some white metal, set atop a tiny black anvil. Mirt touched it, shaking his head in wonder. "He was an Ironstar dwarf," he murmured.

"What's that?" Narm bent forward, his voice thick with sleepiness.

"The fabled lost clan of the dwarves," Mirt said, his weary voice echoing with awe. "The mightiest, most noble dwarven house, driven into hiding long ago. They're a legend among the Stout Folk—and among men who delve for metal, too." Tears came into the old adventurer's eyes. "Ah, Delg," he growled and shook his head again.

Shandril began to cry—and in the same instant, Narm began to snore. Mirt looked over at them. The young mage was asleep where he sat, face gray and drawn with exhaustion, eyes open and unseeing, his mouth gaping. Shandril shook, huddled into a ball, beside him.

Long, still moments passed before Mirt went to lay a comforting hand on her head. Tears streamed down the face she lifted to him, and dripped silently from her chin. Shandril's eyes were very gray as she bit her lip to keep from weeping loudly. She looked at Narm anxiously, not wanting to wake him.

Mirt put an awkward arm around her shoulders. They shook, and Shandril whimpered once, deep in her throat, before she thrust her face against his chest and began to sob. Mirt held her tightly and said nothing. He'd done this before in his life, more than once, but still did not know any words to give her that were both comforting and true. Perhaps there were none.

He stared into the little fire he'd kindled and saw places far away and faces from long ago. The Old Wolf barely noticed when the girl in his arms fell into an exhausted sleep. He was still sitting there when the last coals died away to gray ashes and the pale dawn came creeping over the crags.

Twelve

WHAT FOUL WIZARDRY

Raise not thy voice in anger, lest the sleeping dragon wake.
Old saying of Faerûn, set down by
Glarthlyn of Silverymoon, Sage
Shadows in the Firelight
Year of Dark Frost

Somewhere in the Stonelands, Manshoon turned in satisfaction from his scrying ball.

"It's time," he said softly, looking around at the encampment. Fear was in the faces that looked back at him; even the veteran Zhentilar here were wary of the High Lord of Zhentil Keep. Manshoon had spent much of yestereve raising their dead comrades until an army of zombies stood around the clearing, silently waiting.

"The wench's fire has burnt out for now," the high lord said as he strode across the sward to pluck a jack of hot wine-and-mushrooms broth out of the hand of a startled soldier. He drained it, tossed it back, and added, "She'll be easy prey." The soldier nodded uncertainly, not speaking.

Manshoon turned. "Beluard? Where are you?"

"Here, Lord." His latest apprentice trotted hastily up to the master, wiping broth from his lips with the back of one hand. Manshoon favored him with a wolfish smile.

"You recall my discussions with Sarhthor about arranging shortages of pork and sugar in Sembia?"

"To drive prices up just before our caravans arrive, Lord?"

Manshoon nodded. "Do it," he said, and vanished. The last thing Beluard saw was his cold smile.

For a moment the apprentice stared at the spot where Manshoon had stood, and then looked fearfully at the zombies standing all around. They stood in a gray, putrid, unbroken ring—the thin passage he'd threaded through them moments earlier seemed to have disappeared.

Beluard took a deep breath, looked into undead eyes that stared back at him with hundreds of dark, glassy stares, and wondered if he dared to walk through them. The stench of death was very strong, and he stood there a long time licking his lips, face paling, trying to decide.

* * * * *

The ring of stones was old, old beyond the eldest ruined towers Manshoon had seen in Myth Drannor. Perhaps elves had raised it in the dim past—or men who worked magic before Netheril was proud.

The builders had certainly commanded great magic. Down long ages, through gale and blizzard and lightning crashing from the sky, the stones large as giants floated in a ring above the turf and never fell. Some power kept even the smallest birds and wild things away from the silent ring. There was something comforting in such titanic strength of Art—something that awed even Manshoon. He came here when he needed to think, to be alone, and to feel comforted.

It was also the place he knew best in the Stonelands—a sure destination to teleport to. Out of habit, Manshoon put a hand on one of his magical rods as he stepped out of the teleport spell's swirling mists and into the stony ring. From here it would be only a short walk to a height Shandril and her companions would have to pass.

He stiffened. Men were standing by the cliff edge, just beyond the ring. Men in robes, and others in familiar dark armor. Manshoon relaxed just a little. What were mages and soldiers of the Brotherhood doing *here?*

They had seen him. Swords slid out, and one sorcerer reached for a wand. Manshoon recognized him: Ghaubhan Szaurr, his double agent. Another traitor who wanted spellfire for himself.

"Unhand that wand, or die," Manshoon said coldly. He waited until the sounds of surprised recognition had died and the Zhentilar who were readying crossbows had set them down again. Then he favored them all with a wintry smile—and struck.

Lightnings crackled white and terrible from the rod he held, and men died. He lashed out again at the shouting, running men of the Brotherhood. Warriors scrambled for cover, but their armor cooked them, lightnings dancing around the dark metal like swarms of angry insects, and, screaming, they died. A few magelings were robed in the shimmering cloaks of protective spells, and still lived. They made the pitiful beginnings of spells, shouting and stammering incantations so sloppily in their fear that Manshoon winced at the sounds—and then he worked more powerful magic and they died too, jerking and gasping and falling.

So perish all traitors. Manshoon strode forward, plying the rod with cold precision, until only one man was left.

Dread Master Ghaubhan Szaurr stood trembling in his

black cloak at the edge of the cliff, one hand on his wand again. The fading, darkening shimmering of a failing protective spell hung around him.

He did not dare draw forth the wand he held as Manshoon's cold smile and dark, dark eyes held his. The High Lord of Zhentil Keep strode toward him.

"M-Master? Lord, what have we done? Why have you slain all my men?" Ghaubhan's mouth was suddenly very dry. He licked his lips, swallowed, and tried again to speak. "Lord Manshoon? It is you, isn't it?" The sorcerer's eyes narrowed. "Or are you Elminster, using Art to look like my lord?"

Manshoon's lips twisted. "*Elminster!*" he spat. "Try not to insult me more than you have already, Ghaubhan. Traitor."

"Traitor? *Never,* Lord! I swear t—"

Manshoon gave him another wintry smile. "I found Asklannan's book." He watched a sickly look grow on Ghaubhan's face, then added, "I know the orders you've given, and the plans you've made. Ramath was my creature from the beginning."

Ghaubhan stared at him in despair—and then, suddenly, grabbed for the wand at his belt.

With two fingers, Manshoon made a very small gesture.

The Dread Master felt the tingling and twisting, and looked down. His hand was shifting, turning green—and hissing. His arm now ended in the head of a serpent, which rose, reared back, and showed him fangs as it prepared to strike. Ghaubhan stared into its glittering eyes, looked up in horror at Manshoon's grimly smiling face—and then whirled around and ran with a despairing scream.

The edge of the cliff was very near, and in a moment, Ghaubhan Szaurr was gone.

Manshoon walked to the edge, looked out for a moment at Cormyr spread out below him, and then peered down at the broken body on the rocks far, far beneath the height on which he stood.

A dusty gray bone vulture had been disturbed into flight by the sorcerer's dying plunge. It circled, thick wings flapping, and began its slow spiral down to the remains.

Manshoon watched it and sighed. *So we all, in the end, feed the carrion birds . . . or the worms.* Then he stirred, slid the rod into its sheath at his belt, smiled, and turned away. *What need had he of flying skulls, zombie hosts, or incompetent underlings? He'd wasted enough time here. It was past time to seize spellfire.*

The High Lord of Zhentil Keep walked past the sprawled corpses without even looking at them. He had quite enough zombies already.

* * * * *

As they descended through ravine after ravine, Mirt tried again to talk some sense into Shandril. "Will ye not change yer mind about this craziness of going up against Manshoon? Ye'll be killed, lass!"

Shandril stared at him, eyes burning and chin lifted, and said slowly and very clearly, "I will not run away any longer. If foes seek me, they shall find me, before they expect to, and bearing less mercy than they might hope to find. If that is not the Harper way—too *bad!* Now guide me to Zhentil Keep—or I'll *walk* that way, whatever the dangers, and Narm with me."

Narm nodded, and echoed quietly, "I'll be with you."

Mirt shook his shaggy head and sighed. "If you must rush to your death, Shan, the fastest way is still south and west, a little ways more, to Eveningstar. It may take us the rest of this day—but it'll save ye a tenday of walking in dangerous backlands. What say ye?"

For a moment, Shandril stared at him with those blazing eyes, then nodded. "Start walking."

Mirt made a noise that might have been a chuckle, and turned without another word to lead the way to Eveningstar.

* * * * *

Elminster frowned and set down the small crystal orb he'd been staring into. "Hold still, Storm," he said, striding over to where Storm sat by the campfire.

The Bard of Shadowdale froze obediently, the pan she'd been about to pack away still in her hands. Elminster put a hand on her head and muttered a few words.

Storm tingled all over. A whirling light seemed to spin and snap in her mind. When his hand was gone, she looked up cautiously, and asked, "What was that?"

"A spell to make thee more powerful at sorcery. It lasts only a little while—but that's all the time we should need it for." Elminster took hold of her shoulders and knelt facing her. Eyes bent on her own, he uttered some harsh, sliding words, and touched the first two fingers of his left hand to the bridge of her nose.

Force boiled through her, and the silver-haired bard found herself gasping, on her back on the ground, fingers twitching and wriggling as a yellow haze swirled and eddied in her head. "And just what, El, was *that?*" she gasped as her vision cleared.

"A spell that allows ye to shoot forth a ray that'll wipe some of a wizard's spells right out of his mind." Elminster gave her a grin that was not pleasant to look at, then added, "Too powerful for ye to carry normally—but I need ye to hit Manshoon with it, very soon now."

"Manshoon?" The bard was getting a little tired of gasping in surprise, but Elminster had managed to take her breath away again.

"Aye. Now put that pan down, get away from the fire, and belt up! Ye've been after me to aid Shandril—well, now it's time. The Zhentarim have been far too busy for their own good, and they've rushed things a little. Timing, and all that. Stand ye back, roll the drums, and—bring on Manshoon!"

Elminster's severe expression melted into a reassuring smile—just for an instant—and then his hands were moving, and he stared into the fire and mouthed curses Storm could not quite hear. She found herself glad of that.

* * * * *

Ah, this was the place. Manshoon walked the last few steps to the narrow bridge of rock that led to the bare, windswept summit. He risked leaning out to glance down. Yes, there they were. The fat one, the young mage, and Shandril in a gully that turned toward him and passed under the overhanging cliff. Perfect.

Manshoon took a step onto the stone bridge—and then paused as a robed figure suddenly appeared in his way. It was an old man with a mop of white hair and beard, a mockingly raised eyebrow, and features Manshoon knew only too well.

"Well met," Elminster of Shadowdale said wryly, not quite bowing. "Nice weather up here, isn't it, Manshoon?"

Manshoon snarled like one of his own hunting dogs and raised a hand threateningly.

Elminster looked innocently at it, then mildly met Manshoon's angry gaze. "Something troubling ye? Lack of spellfire, perhaps?"

Manshoon hissed the word that unleashed the most

powerful killing spell he carried. There was a flash, and the stones around them rocked and shook.

Below, Mirt looked up and swore. "Manshoon—and Elminster! *Run!* Both of ye—move! There's no telling how much of that mountain'll come down if they start blasting each other in earnest. Come *on!*"

Snatching up Shandril bodily, the Old Wolf broke into a heavy run, Narm at his side. He paid no heed to Shandril's sharp words of protest, but lumbered along like a draft horse gathering speed for a gallop, wheezing lustily in her ears as he went. Furious, Shandril tried to claw at his face and win free of his grip, but Mirt ignored her nails until Narm could cast a hasty magic that slowed and hampered her struggles. Shandril snarled at them both, and then—as the Old Wolf thundered on—gave up, shrugging and spreading her hands with a weary, apologetic smile.

Atop the cliff, Elminster's image only smiled as the spell that should have torn him asunder spiraled into him and roared away into vast distances. Through the dark hole rent in the Old Mage's middle, Manshoon could see the rocks of the summit beyond, could feel a whirling wind drawing him forward.

"Spelltrap," Elminster said mockingly. "Fooled again, Manshoon."

The roar of the vortex grew louder, and Manshoon found himself being sucked off his feet toward the phantom image of his enemy. As Elminster's crooked smile rushed up to meet him, Manshoon had just enough time to speak one word: the one that summoned aid so costly he used it only in dire need.

Now, for instance. . . .

* * * * *

Elminster tossed something small into the fire, stepped back from its flames, and said, "Scratch any itches ye have right now, lass—things're apt to get a mite busy around here in a breath or two."

Storm's hands went to the hilt of her sword.

Elminster nodded, and her long sword slid out. "We were within a breath of losing Shandril," the Old Mage told her, "and from the Zhentarim gaining spellfire. Instead, Manshoon should be paying us a visit any time now."

His hands moved in the intricate gestures of a spell, and a score of silvery spheres sprang into being around him, drifting upward like so many bubbles. Some floated toward Storm. Behind her, the horses snorted. Storm turned from watching Elminster's spheres twirl and rise to see what had startled their mounts. And she froze.

Three huge, dark beings hung in air that had been empty moments before, eyestalks curling malevolently. The trio of beholders were floating behind the High Lord of Zhentil Keep, who stood facing Storm, his eyes dark with fury.

Storm gasped. "Tymora and Mystra, aid us!"

* * * * *

"Have they gone?" Shandril asked softly, lips at his ear.

The Old Wolf shuddered to a stop, breathing heavily, and turned.

"Set me *down*," Shandril added—and was alarmed to feel him stagger under her as he bent to let her feet touch the ground. The Old Wolf was wheezing like a lustily plied bellows . . . she'd heard more than one fat man breathing like that back at the inn in her youth, just before they dropped dead.

The Old Wolf gasped fast and often as he looked back

the way they'd come. "I can't see them, lass," he replied at last. "And more . . . than that; even if they both appeared right here . . . in front of us . . . I can't run a step more . . . for a bit . . ." His breath came in gasps, and he put a hand to his chest before he noticed her anxious gaze—and angrily snatched his hand away again.

Shandril watched the sweat roll down his face and said gently, "Sit easy for a bit, Old Wolf. I have to—er, visit the bushes. I don't think we'll see two mages of that power again until their battle's done—and a spell-fight like that might have no survivor."

"Or it might have a winner," Narm said grimly, staring back up at the bare peak where they'd seen the two wizards outlined by a spell-flash. "I just hope it's the right one."

"I've always thought . . . Elminster could handle Manshoon . . . any day," Mirt puffed, "but in things . . . of magic . . . nothing is certain." He struggled to get up. "We must be . . . away from here, while we can! There's—"

Shandril pushed him back down again. "Today still holds plenty of time for walking, when you've breath enough to do it. I need you."

Mirt stared at her, sweat dripping off the end of his large, red nose. "Lass," he asked quietly, "what for?"

Shandril looked fondly at the fat old man, and her mouth crooked into a smile. "To protect me, of course."

Mirt's snort would have been louder if he'd had the breath to put behind it, but it was still impressive.

* * * * *

The fire crackled and flickered calmly in the aftermath of the reflective magic Elminster had cast into it. It had no way of knowing what was about to erupt around it.

Manshoon sneered at the archmage and the bard and

snatched a wand from his belt. Behind him, the three beholders were drifting apart, moving to the sides of the fray where nothing could get in the way of their magical gazes.

Elminster's hands were moving. Storm looked to him for instructions, but he paid her no heed. A dozen of his spheres were drifting around her now.

Manshoon's wand spat lightning. The bolt writhed and stabbed through the air—until it reached the fire. There it dipped sharply into the burning wood, as if dragged down by something unseen. Flames crackled; sparks flew in all directions. Then the bolt of lightning leapt up out of the fire again, arrowing back at the leader of the Zhentarim. Storm raised her blade as she heard him gasp. Lightnings whirled and struck home; Manshoon staggered.

The air was suddenly full of humming, bone-shaking beams of force as the eye-powers of one of the beholders lashed out at both Elminster and Storm.

The silver spheres created by Elminster's earlier spell were everywhere—darting and whirling to intercept the magics hurled at the bard and the old archmage. Whenever a sphere came into contact with magic, it flared in a sudden, silent pulse of silver-blue light—before sphere and spell disappeared together. Elminster finished his magic and nodded in satisfaction. Feeling Storm's eyes upon him, he turned his head and wiggled his eyebrows at her. Then his hands were moving again.

The air in front of Manshoon was abruptly cut by a crooked line of snaking darkness as wide as a man's head. Wind whirled violently toward this rift. The advancing darkness approached the frantically casting Zhentarim, and then the dark vortex split into two ebony, reaching arms. The newly formed fork of whirling chaos lashed out past Manshoon, stabbing at the drifting eye tyrants. Their eyestalks bent in chorus to gaze upon it, but the advancing lines of darkness never slowed. The rifts widened. Glimpses of a whirling, winking other-where were visible within them. Wind rushed into them with the quickening roar of thunder, and the bladelike points of the rifts each touched a beholder.

The eye tyrants whirled and spun helplessly, eyestalks flailing the air with frantic futility as they were dragged into the planar rifts. Amid flashes and angry, ground-shaking rolls of thunder, they spun faster and faster, until Storm could no longer distinguish them from the whirling chaos of the rifts; they were gone.

The vortices promptly collapsed and vanished. Man-shoon snatched time enough to glance back over his shoulder, and his jaw dropped. Only one eye tyrant remained, rising above him to gain a clear path to strike down at Elminster.

The Old Mage smiled tightly and let his hands fall again, his next spell done.

Zulthondre was an old and powerful eye tyrant; its chitinous body plates reflected the firelight in dancing green tongues of radiance. It knew the scent of the old, bearded man facing it across the small campfire. That smell had emanated from the very floor of the chamber in the Citadel of the Raven, where it had met with Man-shoon and Sarhthor. Zulthondre seethed with rage. No human had ever outwitted it before.

The beholder ceased its futile eyestalk attacks; each beam it had lashed out had been absorbed by a silvery sphere and utterly wasted. Instead, Zulthondre bent its large, rage-reddened central eye balefully on those sil-very spheres. The power of the eye destroyed the old man's spheres one by one, and each winked out of exis-tence.

And then Zulthondre's world exploded in flames.

The Old Mage watched in satisfaction as eight blazing fireballs spun into being around the beholder—and then burst in unison, with a roar that made Storm's ears ring. The eye tyrant darkened, writhing in obvious agony. Plates of chitin were flung away from its convulsing body as its skin wrinkled, melted, and burst open. Jets of bodily fluids boiled forth from within. Mouth gaping in a soundless scream, the beholder crashed to earth, flames rising from its body.

Manshoon had been frantically snarling spells, two wands crossed over his head. They flickered and vanished an instant after the beholder's death crash, leaving the sorcerer's hands empty, but outlined in dancing sparks. Ignoring the tumult behind him, Manshoon straightened in triumph, eyes flashing, and snarled, "*Now* you'll pay, Old Mage! *Die!*" Many lightning bolts raced from his crossed hands then, tearing the air with vicious snarls of their own to strike at the Old Mage.

Elminster stood unmoving as they came. An arm's length in front of him, the bolts struck an invisible, protective shield of force, and crawled futilely over its surface.

"One day," Elminster replied calmly, "ye'll anger me overmuch, Lord High and Mighty—and I'll make time enough to hunt down and blast to nothingness every last crawling clone of thine, thy every last hiding-hole—and wipe ye from the Realms entire; aye, and all the other worlds, too. So take care, Manshoon, to ne'er grow *too* powerful or *too* persistent in angering me—or I'll lose my temper, and it'll be too late for thee."

He turned deliberately to the bard and said, "Now, Storm."

Storm let fall her sword, and spun to face the High Lord of Zhentil Keep.

Manshoon's hands were already darting through the

gestures of a spell, obviously aimed at the Old Mage. But the Zhentarim gaped in surprise as a spell leapt first from Storm's hands.

Storm felt an exultant thrill as the tingling magic rolled out of her, more power than she'd ever felt before. She laughed in pleasure. It felt good to finally be able to lash out with magic at a man whose spells would normally easily hold her at bay, however hot her hatred of him.

Radiance danced around Manshoon briefly and then disappeared. Had the spell failed? Storm bent anxiously to snatch up her sword, all her exultation gone.

The Zhentarim's hands faltered and fell, and he seemed to stagger for a moment. "What—what have you done?" he roared.

Elminster grinned. "Charge at him, Storm."

Storm launched into a run.

The Old Mage smiled at Manshoon and waved a hand. His pipe obediently rose from the ground where it had been quietly smoking by itself, and drifted toward his lips.

"I held down thy defenses, idiot," Elminster told him calmly, "while Storm wiped out half thy spells, or so. Oh, by the way: I'm still doing so. If ye try to use a spell against her, ye'll end up feeble-witted, and we'll just leave ye here." He smiled. "I *know* ye won't be able to resist trying some magic now."

The Old Mage puffed on his pipe and added, "Ah, yes: Storm may want to cut off thy hands, too, to keep ye from casting too many spells if ye ever recover."

The Zhentarim looked open-mouthed at Storm. A blank expression washed over his face.

Storm knew from the horror that replaced this look that Manshoon had tried to use a spell to whisk himself away from the battle—and had discovered it was gone.

The High Lord of Zhentil Keep grabbed at a rod at his

belt, saw how close Storm was, and tried to turn and run at the same time. Storm's blade caught him under one armpit and spun him around.

"Defend yourself, wizard!" Storm spat at him.

Manshoon stared at her for a moment, then snatched something from his belt, leapt back, and hurled it at her.

Storm's blade struck it aside. The bard saw the Zhentarim's dagger flash with a dull green light as it spun away.

"Poisoned?" she said contemptuously. "You snake!" Her long sword slashed out.

Manshoon shrieked as some of his fingers went flying.

Elminster called, "Ware, Storm—his contingencies are likely to harm ye and save him!"

Storm ruined Manshoon's other hand with a quick chop.

"Kill him from a distance, eh?" she replied, stepping away. Manshoon fumbled a wand out of his belt—but Storm cut it out of his bloody hand, and her backhand slash laid open Manshoon's face. Her eyes were hot, and with terrible speed that bright blade was reaching for him again. The High Lord of Zhentil Keep staggered back, coughed wetly, and, snarling, aimed another wand at her. An instant later, he was gone—leaving behind a burst of black, evil-looking flames that reached hungrily from the wand for Storm.

She fled, dived past the fire, rolled, and fetched up at Elminster's feet, panting.

"Easy now," Elminster said, "Ye hurt him badly enough that ye triggered one of his contingency spells; it whisked him away. I've raised a spell-shield around us. Whatever else he planned, we're safe here, for now."

Storm looked up at him, shaking silver hair out of her face. "You seem to take this very calmly."

Elminster watched the beholder burn. As the oily

smoke drifted away from them over the hills, he said softly, "It never lasts, ye see. . . . I've had to kill him—oh, is it twenty-and-one, by now? Aye—that many times."

"Why didn't you slay him again this time?"

Elminster shook his head. "He's prepared for that—half a day after he dies, his next clone's skulking about somewhere in the Dales, and death's hardly a setback at all. This way, I pulled him across Faerûn, away from Shandril and the spellfire he's so hungry for, hurt him, and broke his power for a time . . . a good afternoon's work, I'd say. Besides, a certain lady has a prior claim on Manshoon's life—and I'd hate to deprive her of a chance to do some real good with her spellfire."

* * * * *

For the first time in years, Manshoon knew fear. Maimed, wincing at the burning pain from his hands, he whirled through mists and shadows for a moment, and then the world rocked and changed again. He found himself back on the clifftop where Elminster had first spell-trapped him.

Manshoon staggered and raised hands to his dazed head. Only a last defense had saved him: the contingency spell he'd worked long ago, which whisked him away when death came too close. It took him back to the last place he'd left by any sort of traveling spell. It was a powerful, expensive magic that had snatched him back from certain death only three times in all the years he'd ruled Zhentil Keep.

Well, four times, now. Or so he thought for the space of slightly more than one deep breath.

"Well *met,* butcher," came a cold, clear voice from close at hand.

Manshoon turned in time to see Shandril standing

amid the rocks nearby. Her eyes kindled into twin flames. "For Delg," she whispered fiercely. Her lips curved into a wolfish smile as she raised flaming hands.

He did not even have time to scream.

Thirteen

DARKER DREAMS THAN THIS

Weep not, child—whatever terrors your night dreams hold, someone somewhere in the Realms has faced and fought worse. Wizards who raise monsters from nothing, or twist them from simpler beasts, or call them from far and strange places, you see, are tormented by the evil they work—and all of them dream darker than you can. That is their worst punishment—no matter what horrors keep you awake, all of them must nightly face darker dreams than this.

Laeral of Waterdeep, quoted in
Words to an Apprentice
Ithryn Halast, Year of the Weeping Moon

You will be subject to my will, Iliph Thraun. You will follow and feed only as I direct, and you will challenge no one. You will take care not to be seen or felt by the one you drain. You will . . .

The voice that Iliph Thraun had come to hate so much in these last few days, the voice that had echoed through its being, leashing it with irresistible authority, faded at last—forever stilled. The speaker was dead, and the lich lord was free.

"And," the hollow voice hissed, rising in triumph, "so passes Manshoon of the Zhentarim—and I am free again."

The skull rose so suddenly out of a tangled ravine deep in the Stonelands that a dunwing flying past squawked and shed feathers as it darted away in fear. The skull laughed. The chilling sound trailed behind it as it flew, breaking free of the last, fading traces of Manshoon's control, and racing west—heading for Shandril, filled with hunger.

* * * * *

Thrulgar, the older of the two doorguards, stiffened and brought his spear down, and its tip caught the lamplight in a gleaming arc as it moved.

Azatlim, the guard who stood at the other end of the porch, turned when he saw the flash.

Out of the night, three folk were approaching Eveningstar. A fat, aging rogue with a disquieting look about him; a young man in the robes of a mage; and a bedraggled wisp of a girl in torn clothing. Travelers, aye—but were they fallen afoul of brigands? Were they beggars? Pilgrims—or thieves themselves?

Thrulgar made sure his back was against the double doors that led into the main hall of Tessaril's Tower, braced his spear against the bronze door plates behind him, and cast a quick look down the porch to make sure Azatlim had seen them, too.

Azatlim was hastening toward the tower doors, spear at the ready. Good. This could mean trouble. Thrulgar cast a glance in the other direction, judging just where the alarm gong was in case he had to strike it in a hurry.

Then the three stepped up onto the porch.

"Who are you three, and why come you here by night?"

Thrulgar kept his voice calm and his eyes on the empty hands of the intruders.

The fat man rumbled, "We've come to see Tessaril Winter, Lord of Eveningstar, on a most urgent matter. We cannot wait until morning, and must see her now." When these words were out, the man shut his mouth as if it were a steel trap.

A little silence followed; Thrulgar let it stretch as he peered long and consideringly at the three of them, then said, "You cannot pass. Go up the road, and take rooms at the inn. The lord will see you in the morning."

"We will see her now," the fat man repeated patiently.

Thrulgar locked gazes with him and was surprised at the wisdom—and the steel—in the eyes that met and held his. He had to muster all his will to pull his gaze free, and shake his head.

"No one disturbs the lord at this hour," he said flatly.

"I do," the big man levelly replied, "just as Azoun does." The Purple Dragons stiffened at that, but their spear points did not come down.

"Go away until morning," Azatlim said. "And take care to speak with respect when you name the king."

"I did," growled the man, "considering—ah, ne'er mind. We must speak with Tessaril, man, and speedily! We'll not go away, I warn ye."

"You *warn* me?" Thrulgar repeated, voice rising. "Who are you, stout one, to stand on the soil of Cormyr and 'warn' a Purple Dragon of anything?"

"Guards," the slight lass said quietly, "if you can spare a moment from blustering, look at me."

Two startled sets of eyes did so, but Azatlim was moved to ask, "Why?" in tones that were just on the proper side of a sneer.

"Because of *this*," she told them evenly, then raised one arm slowly to point at the sky behind her.

Without taking her eyes off the guards, she let flames crawl slowly from her shoulder to her fingertips, and then explode with a sudden roar into a bright pillar of fire, raging skyward. In the next moment, it was gone. She closed her hand and said in the same calm voice, "I'd hate to have to use it on you to get in that door—but I've just used it on Manshoon of the Zhentarim, and he died *very* easily."

The guards in chain mail stared at her, and their faces grew pale. They hastily yanked down their visors and raised their shields.

"Come ahead, then," Thrulgar's voice came hollowly from within the all-concealing war-helm. It trembled only slightly. "For Azoun we stand, and for Azoun we'll fall."

The woman hesitated. These men clearly meant her no harm, and she had no love for slaughter. Both their spear points were leveled at her breast now—and as she waited, one of them reached out and slapped at a gong behind him.

Struck glancingly in frantic haste, the gong made only a sort of clank, but the doors behind the men opened almost immediately. An unshaven man clad only in boots and a night robe looked out, a drawn sword in his hand. "What befalls here?" he asked, peering over the shoulders of the guards.

"These three demand immediate audience with Lord Tessaril," said Thrulgar without turning around. "The maid threatened us with conjured fire if we didn't let her pass."

"I saw and heard the flames out the windows of my room," the man with the sword said dryly. He straightened. "Outlanders, I am Tzin Tzummer, Herald to the Lord Tessaril and king's man. More guards await within, and I can call on many others if need be. Even using magic, you cannot prevail here by force of arms. Tell me your names, and why you are so set on seeing the lord now."

"I am Mirt," the fat old man said, waving at his companions to keep silent, "and as a Lord of Waterdeep, I demand audience with Lord Tessaril Winter."

The herald frowned. "None know the identities of those who wear the masks of the Lords of Waterdeep, save for the Lord Piergeiron of that city. Anyone could come to this door claiming to be a Lord of Waterdeep. Besides, it's highly unlikely a Lord of Waterdeep would ever come to Cormyr without a large escort, an invitation from the king, and—ah, rather more splendid clothing."

"You don't know Waterdeep very well," Mirt murmured.

"Whether I do or not," Tzin Tzummer replied coolly, "your claim is not going to move me to let you in, especially given the magic the maid among you wields—all here will resist to the death, if need be. If you'd prefer, one of the guards can escort you to the inn— *The Lonesome Tankard,* just up the road, there—and see that you get comfortable rooms. Come back in the morning."

Mirt inclined his head. "Reasonable words, herald—yet we can no longer afford to be reasonable. D'ye know what this is?" Slowly his hands went to his belt, opened a pouch there, and drew forth a Harper pendant, on its broken chain.

The herald's eyes widened, but he said slowly, "That device is welcome here, as are those who bear it. Yet we serve Azoun here, not the silver harp. Could you not come back in the morning—and unarmed?"

Mirt sighed. "Azoun, is it? Well, then. Hold yer blades back a moment." He turned and waved his companions back off the porch, followed them, and turned as his boots touched the dirt of the road. There, in the full light of the porch lamps, he slowly drew a dagger that glowed

—the guards traded glances—and he dropped it point-down in the earth at his feet. Upending the empty sheath, the old man twisted it in a certain deft, delicate way. Its steel tip slid sideways and open, revealing a tiny cavity; out of this Mirt plucked something and held it up. It was a ring.

"In Azoun's name," he rumbled formally, holding the ring up between finger and thumb so they could all see it in the flickering light of the lamps, "I ask immediate audience with Tessaril Winter, Lord of Eveningstar."

"A Purple Dragon ring," the herald said wonderingly. "I've never seen one in the hands of an outlander before."

"Well, now you have," Mirt said testily, "and no, I didn't steal it. Azoun gave it to me when I guarded his two infant daughters, years ago, when—but that's not for me to tell without his word. Well? What's it to be? Defy Azoun or let us in to talk to Tessar? By the burning lashes of Bane, I've kissed her often enough!"

* * * * *

As the full darkness of night descended softly on Eveningstar, Lord Tessaril Winter lay abed, lounging in the warmth of the dying fire. King Azoun ruled this pretty village through her, and matters both great and small sometimes weighed heavily on her mind. Today, it had been Lord's Court, and she'd had to disentangle several nasty trade disputes and sit through much blustering. She cared nothing for the threats, but the shouting had given her a headache that had taken three hot mugs of soup and much quiet to quell.

She yawned and shook her head ruefully, set aside the spellbook she read every night after she'd used a spell, blew out the lamp, and waited for slumber to take her.

The four chains her bed hung from creaked once as

she settled down, and then all was dark and silent. For a time. . . .

The roar of spellfire awakened Tessaril. She sat up in the hanging bed and looked out her west window in time to see flames licking at the night sky. Snatching up a wand in one hand and her sword in the other, she strode to the north window, using the tip of her scabbarded blade to hook down a robe from a peg along the way.

It was a long way down from her chambers at the top of the tower, and a wizard going into battle should never get out of breath. Tessaril tossed the wand and blade ahead of her as she vaulted the windowsill, whispering the word that evoked a spell that let her fall the three floors to the ground slowly and gently. By the time her feet touched the grass just outside the tower, she was dressed.

Snatching up wand and blade, Tessaril let herself into the ground floor of the tower through a secret door that would open only for her and trotted to the main hall, shaking the sword free of her scabbard as she went. She burst out the front door with wand and blade both held high, expecting trouble.

* * * * *

Mirt's words still hung in the air as Lord Tessaril herself strode out into the light. All around her, her men stiffened, and the herald said, "Lord, you should not—"

The rest of his words were lost as Tessaril tossed sword and wand aside with a clatter and ran across the porch to kiss the fat man who held the ring. Even in her bare feet, the slim, ash-blond Lord of Eveningstar stood taller than everyone else present, and she moved with fluid grace and a warrior's speed.

Tessaril flung her arms around the old merchant.

"Mirt! Old Wolf, I'd never thought to see you here in Eveningstar! Come in, come in! Who are your friends?"

Mirt managed to keep a grin off his face as she dragged him into her tower, through a throng of astonished Cormyrean faces. Narm didn't.

Goblets of wine were in their hands a moment later as Tessaril waved them toward her audience chamber.

"Come in here and tell me what business presses you so urgently," she said, making signs to the guards—who scattered in all directions, one darting up the stairs with her sword and wand.

"Teleport me to Zhentil Keep," Shandril burst out. "I . . . I have to destroy the Zhentarim, now!"

Tessaril smiled. "Some of us have been trying to do that for years," she said, "and they still sit in Zhentil Keep tonight."

Shandril looked at her with eyes that blazed, just for an instant, and fought to control her voice. When the words came out, they were low and angry. "Lady, those snakes killed our friend and have hunted me like game across the Dales. Today, I burned Manshoon to bones and ashes—and I want to go after the rest of the Zhentarim before . . . before my nerve fails me." Her words ended with a sob.

Tessaril stared at her. "You're serious," she said quietly. Then, slowly, she shook her head. "I'd be sending you to your deaths."

Narm looked quickly at Shandril. On the verge of tears, Shandril pleaded, "Please, Lady? Please? I must go *now!*" Her voice rose. "I can't go on like this, every day, wondering how soon we'll be killed!"

Tessaril looked at her and asked softly, "Are you in the right state of mind, now, to go up against any Zhentarim—and live?"

Shandril glared at her. "By the gods, *get me to Zhentil*

Keep!" she cried, then held up a hand that blazed with spellfire. Around her, men cried out, weapons rang as they were drawn, and she heard running feet approaching.

Tessaril was on her feet facing Shandril, flinging up her hand in a restraining signal. Silence fell.

Shandril looked around at all the scared faces and raised blades and saw the herald holding a sword warningly at Narm's throat. She shook her head wearily and dissolved into tears, turning to Mirt's arms. "I'm sick of all this killing and fighting and running," she sobbed. "When will it all *end?*"

"It never does, lass," Mirt said softly, holding her. The words summoned to his mind memories of burning cities, spilled blood slowly running out and down stone steps underfoot, and corpses—fields of sprawled, contorted corpses—all around. "It never does."

Mirt and Tessaril exchanged glances, and the Lord of Eveningstar said quietly, "You'd best bring her in and tell me what this is all about. I can see this is going to be one of those evenings when the gods turn us on our heads a time or two. . . ."

* * * * *

Storm looked up at the stars sailing endlessly overhead. They glittered softly through a thin veil of scudding clouds. She said, "I can't sleep, Old Mage."

"What's amiss?" A wrinkled hand came out of the darkness to pat her own comfortingly.

"Manshoon. What's he up to, now?" After a moment, she added, "I hate leaving things unfinished."

"Lass," Elminster told her gently, "nothing is ever finished. Do what ye can, when ye can, and go on to the next thing. Some folk never learn that, all their lives long—and never do anything, spending their time worrying away at something they should have set by long ago."

Storm sighed. "You're right." She watched the stars for a while, then whispered, "Old Mage, remember when I was young? You used to hold me until I fell asleep, and tell me wondrous tales of when Faerûn was new . . . ?"

The old, familiar arms went around her, bringing with them the faint reek of old pipesmoke. "Would ye like a story now?"

"Please," she whispered, and covered his hands with her own.

"Well, now," Elminster said slowly. "Ye see those stars, up there? I recall a time when . . ."

* * * * *

Firespark rode on her shoulders as Tessaril walked silently down the street toward the *Tankard*. Her tressym was restless and ill at ease; it answered her only with a wary little mew when she stroked it. The winged cat could smell trouble before she could, so Tessaril went well armed now.

She'd turned the tower over to her three guests for the night, telling them to get some sleep while she went out to 'confer with someone.' All nine of her Purple Dragons were already gathered to guard them, and she'd used a sending to call in war wizards from High Horn. That aid would not be here until midmorning at the earliest. She herself would sit guard over them until the wizards arrived—once she'd told Dunman at the *Tankard* to alert the local Harpers. If she knew Zhentarim, this night would bring an attack from some fell wizard or other.

Behind her there came a peculiar hissing sound, a groan, and the thud of someone falling.

Turning, she calmly drew a wand. In the end, until she

died or Azoun gave her other orders, Eveningstar was hers to defend. Trying to see the cause of the commotion, Tessaril peered back into the nightgloom in front of the tower, a bare thirty paces behind her. With one bound, Firespark was gone from her shoulders.

Something small and white floated in the air beside the tower porch. One of her guards lay sprawled in the dirt beneath it. As Tessaril stepped forward, raising the wand, the eyes of the floating thing—a human skull, by the gods!—flashed, and part of the front wall of her tower simply vanished with a little sighing sound. Lamplight spilled out through the breach, accompanied by frightened curses. The Purple Dragons within hauled out blades and peered out into the night.

A sudden bright bolt of lightning spat from the skull. Trailing sparks, the bolt danced from man to man, making each in turn convulse, stagger, and fall. Smoke rose from their armor.

Tessaril mouthed a curse and triggered her wand. Fire shot through the night, shrouding the skull in bright flames. It turned slowly to face her, quivering in the air as flames raced over it. Then its eyes flickered, and it spat another bolt of lightning from its bony jaws.

Tessaril dived to one side, but no one in the Realms could have dodged that leaping lightning. With an angry snapping sound, the bolt struck her, and she reeled, gasping, and fell. Her veins crawled. She could not breathe. White needles pierced her eyes, and the smell of burnt cloth and hair was strong in her nostrils. Only the hard dirt against her cheek told her she was still alive.

The bolt that had almost slain Tessaril awoke the slumbering Mirt. He sleepily shuffled out of the audience chamber, blade in hand, then skidded to a halt when he saw that the entire front wall of the entry hall was gone—and that a skull floated in the night outside. Purple

Dragons lay sprawled about the room amid fallen blades and splintered furniture.

Mirt snatched up a discarded sword and hefted it to throw. As he moved, the skull turned to confront him, fire flashing where its eyes should have been. With a chill, Mirt recognized the same leaping flames in its empty sockets that he saw in Shandril's eyes when she was angry. Spellfire lived in this undead thing.

The skull laughed hollowly as it drifted slowly into the room, the twin, coiling flames of its gaze bent on him.

"I'm getting *much* too old for all this," Mirt grunted sourly, squinting up at the glowing skull.

On the road below, a weak and dazed Tessaril fought her way slowly to hands and knees. Pain raged inside her, and from somewhere nearby, she heard a frightened, querying mew. With weary detachment, she looked down at herself and saw the cause of her tressym's alarm: smoke was rising in lazy curls from her body. Biting her lip, the Lord of Eveningstar caught her breath, struggled to a sitting position, and frowned in concentration to gather her wits for another spell. As she fought to make the intricate gestures, she heard and saw the battle above.

"All right!" Mirt growled, waving both blades. "Come on, then! Let's be at it!" A voice from his memory—female, and mocking, but he was damned if he could recall just who, at this tense moment—echoed in his head:

Heroes can't choose which fights they will win.
That is why all of them die in the end.

The light within the skull flickered. The air was suddenly full of the bright, deadly pulses of flame the Old Wolf had seen many mages hurl down the years—the bolts that cannot miss.

So this damned dead thing could work spells. Thanks be to the gods! Mirt held that sour thought as he steeled himself against the pain he knew would come, and threw his borrowed sword at the skull as hard as he could.

The bolts struck him, lancing into his body with shuddering pain. As always, their energy made his limbs tremble violently. The Old Wolf set his teeth, staggering back under the force of the attack, and blinked back tears to see what happened to his hurled blade. It missed, whirling away harmlessly into the night as the skull rose smoothly up out of its path.

Mirt snarled, plucked up a stool from the wreckage nearby, and hurled it at the skull, lurching into an ungainly charge in its wake. His eerie foe bobbed again, and the stool hurtled harmlessly past it and shattered against a wall. The skull's hollow laughter rang out around the old, wheezing merchant.

Then the skull spat something at him that glowed with tiny, sparkling motes of light. Panting in his haste, Mirt dived aside and rolled on the floor—but not fast enough: some of the spittle struck his arm and shoulder.

Aaargh—acid! *Gods,* but it burned! Roaring in pain, the Old Wolf twisted on the floor and clutched his shoulder. It felt like slow-moving fire was crawling along his flesh; Mirt whimpered at the pain and writhed helplessly.

Unseen, the skull soared past him, heading for the stairs. The grand stair climbed from the entry hall to a gallery on the floor above, where many statues stood. Among them were warriors of Cormyr, a mermaid rampant upon a wave, and a sleeping dragon. As the skull floated amid these, a dagger suddenly spun at it, striking chips from the curved bone of its jaw before glancing off.

The lich lord turned menacingly and saw a servant-woman on the landing, her face white with fear. She was frantically trying to raise a sword that was far too heavy for her.

A tongue of flame slid out of one of the skull's eye sockets, and the woman moaned in fear. She swung the sword weakly at the flames, shrank back, and cried, "Tempus aid me!"

Iliph Thraun laughed aloud and struck at the woman with its whip of flames. She screamed, waving the sword ineffectually as the fire raged around her. The lich lord lashed the woman with flames until she crumpled and fell, hair smoldering. Then it flew on into the upper levels of Tessaril's Tower.

At the top of the next flight of stairs, Narm and Shandril sat together on a bench, weapons in hand, uncertain of what to do as crashes and cries came up to them from below. At first, they didn't see the silently floating skull drifting up the darkened stairs. Then Narm scrambled up with a startled curse and hurled a hasty swarm of bright bolts at it.

Shandril stared at the skull. "What *is* it?" she asked of the world at large as Narm's missiles hit home. Bright pulses struck bone and burst and flared around the skull, but it seemed to ignore them. It opened its mouth and spat spellfire at Shandril.

Narm leapt between Shandril and the reaching spellflames, shuddering as spellfire struck him and swirled around his shoulder. The young mage staggered, but the skull rose quickly to direct its stream of flames over him—and into Shandril's breast.

Shandril gasped in surprise. It *was* spellfire! Then her face hardened, and her eyes and hands began to flame.

"Yes! *Yesss!*" the skull hissed, as she hurled the conflagration back at it. Narm lifted a face tight with pain to peer at the skull, and he gasped—it was *feeding* on the spellfire Shan was using on it.

Shandril hurled streams of spellfire at the thing. It chuckled, teeth clattering hollowly. She set her jaw and wove the blaze into a bright net of flames, cutting the air with so many arcs of fire that the skull could not avoid them.

The skull plunged into the fiery net and spun there among the strongest flames. Where spellfire touched it, the burning fury darkened and died. The residue slid weirdly into the fissures and gaps in the bones—all except the eye sockets and gaping mouth, which poured an ever-increasing stream of spellfire back at her.

Spellflames engulfed the girl, raging and roaring. Shandril shuddered under the attack—every inch of her seemed to be trembling uncontrollably—and then struggled to advance against the skull's stream of spellfire. Her eyes were narrowed to slits, her face contorted with pain.

"Shan! *Nooo!*" Narm screamed, but she seemed not to hear. He gulped, took two running steps, and leapt, reaching for the skull. His hands slid over smooth hardness and into the eye sockets. There they found burning, excruciating pain. Narm threw back his head and howled, as roaring blackness rushed up to claim him. Despairing, wreathed in the skull's fire—Shandril's stolen spellfire—Narm fell screaming into that onrushing darkness.

Shandril stared as Narm toppled heavily to the floor, body blazing. His screams ceased abruptly as his limbs flopped loosely on the stone. Then he lay very still.

Silence fell. The skull's attack had ceased even as Shandril's did. In horror, she stared down at her husband. The skull glided slowly forward to hang over her. It leered down, glowing, opened its mouth in echoing mirth—and then fell suddenly quiet, hanging motionless, its flames flickering and fading.

* * * * *

In a dark room deep in the High Hall of Zhentil Keep, Sarhthor, mage of the Zhentarim, sat at a black table and stared at a tiny skull that hovered above it. The skull was carved from human bone—from a bone of one Iliph Thraun, lord among liches. Small radiances swirled around it, chasing each other in little currents and eddies as Sarhthor bent his will against the far-off lich lord.

Sweat ran down his face, and his hands trembled as he stared fixedly at the carved skull. Wrestling with the cold will of Iliph Thraun across a great and echoing distance, Sarhthor reached deep and found strength he hadn't known was there— and held the lich lord from attacking Shandril.

* * * * *

Weeping, Shandril hurled herself on Narm, as she had done long ago in Thunder Gap. Dragonfire had ravaged him then—but this was spellfire. Lips to lips, flesh to flesh, she embraced him frantically, pouring healing spellfire into him.

Above them, the skull quivered, and its eyes flashed flame. Then it shook again, more feebly, and hung motionless.

* * * * *

The door opened suddenly without a knock, and Fzoul Chembryl, High Priest of the Black Altar of Bane, strode in. "What are you doing?" he asked coldly.

The miniature skull sank down to land softly on the table, and a weary Sarhthor looked up at him. "Lord Manshoon left this means to compel the lich lord with Art, and gave me orders to use it in his absence to prevent the lichnee from passing out of our control," he explained.

The wizard shook his head and wiped sweat out of his eyes. "I'm not the mage he is—and perhaps I lack some detail or secret to make this work, too; I can't seem to contact Iliph Thraun properly. The lich is there, all right—but it seems almost as though something greater stands against us, fighting me."

"Elminster?" Fzoul snapped, wondering who *else* could be interfering with the skull in Manshoon's absence.

"Nay, nay; something greater. Bane, perhaps." Sarhthor said that with a straight face but inner pleasure; the priests of the Black Altar never like to be reminded of their rebellion against church authority—and how the Dark One himself might feel about it.

"Our Lord?" Fzoul's voice was harsh. He tried to scoff, but it didn't sound convincing. The two men stared coldly at each other for a breath or two.

Then Sarhthor shrugged, and waved at the miniature skull lying motionless on the tabletop. "Try for yourself. My skill is not great enough to know clearly who it is."

Sarhthor took care to hide all signs of his inward smile as Fzoul silently but savagely spun around and stalked out.

* * * * *

The lich lord hissed suddenly, and its eyes lit with flame. Freed of the restraint from afar, it sank down to bite into Shandril's shoulder as she lay atop her husband. The spellfire that blazed from her pulsed and flickered as the skull began to drain her, hauling energy out of her reluctant body slowly at first, and then with greater speed.

A grim and blackened Thrulgar burst into the room then, at the head of a handful of white-faced but grimly loyal Evenor farmers. They clutched pikes and pitchforks, and sleepiness battled horror in their eyes as they stared at the skull.

By then, the lich lord was strong enough to rise from Shandril and lash out with rays of stolen spellfire. The sudden flames hurled the men to blazing and broken deaths against the walls of the room.

Weeping amid the dying shouts and screams, Shandril lay sprawled atop Narm, feeling spellfire flowing steadily out of her. Twisting feebly, she tried to gather her will but could not stop the flow. The skull was draining her with frightening speed. A bright path of radiance, spellfire being sucked out of her forever, now linked her with the grisly thing as it floated low overhead, chuckling. Shandril struggled to pull free by willing a sudden surge of spellfire into the bone thing. It hissed at her in anger—but the steady flow of its draining continued, and the fire within her was fading fast.

Narm lay lifeless beneath her. Shandril stared up at the grinning skull, and cold fear crawled along her spine. The only way to stop this skull slaughtering everyone in this town—in Cormyr, and even in Faerûn—was to cut off its supply of spellfire.

And the only way to do that was to end her own life.

Shuddering, Shandril crawled toward a dagger, fallen beside Thrulgar's hand. The lich's spellfire suddenly flailed her as the skull realized her intent. It wanted all she had; she must not die yet. Tears nearly blinding her, Shandril gripped the weapon and slowly, determinedly, brought it to herself. Would dying hurt much? She swallowed, shut her eyes against sudden tears, and pressed the keen, cold edge against her throat. . . .

The roar of spellfire that rose around her now was deafening, numbing; it shook her like a leaf. . . . Could she complete the task? Angry spellfire thundered around her. Tears sizzled on her cheeks as the white heat dried them. She felt a sudden, chilling jab at her shoulder: the skull had set its teeth in her again. In the storm of flames, Shandril struggled on, trying to die. . . .

Fourteen

SKULL UNLAID FORBEAR THEE

When death comes unlooked-for, it finds a way into the strongest fortress. It does no good to set extra guards at the gates.

Asargrym of Baldur's Gate
A Merchant Master's Life
Year of the Blue Flame

 "Ah, now we come to it, lass; 'tis time."

"Time for what?" Storm Silverhand had been drifting off pleasantly to that place of dreams where gods whispered to mortals. Elminster had finished his tale, and the stars still glimmered watchfully overhead.

"For ye to guard me—remember, ye came on this ride to guard me?"

Storm rolled over and smiled sleepily at him. "I still can't imagine what I can protect you against that you can't guard against better yourself."

Elminster patted her bare shoulder affectionately and said, "Stand guard over my body while I go dreamweaving."

244

"Dreamweaving? You?"

"I know no better way of putting ideas into the minds of sleeping folk to sway them into doing certain things without clumsy coercion or betraying my hand in it."

Storm nodded, stretched, and got up, shrugging on her leather jacket. "I *knew* it was too soon to take off my boots," she said sweetly, stepping back into them with a sigh.

Elminster waved a hand. "Ye won't need them—who's to see thy bare feet, out here in the night?"

Storm smiled. "The ones who'll be attacking, of course."

Elminster shook his head at that, and smiled. "Ah, ye al—"

Then he broke off, swayed, and turned to her, his face suddenly grim. "I must attend to things, it seems," he said, snatching up his staff.

"Shandril?" Storm asked, her long sword already in her hands.

Elminster shook his head. "Narm. When I trained him, I linked to him—and I've just felt him die."

Storm's face paled. "Old Mage," she said quickly, "may I?"

Elminster inclined his head. "Of course." The mists took them.

* * * * *

They were in a room of stone, strewn with fallen farmers, splintered and tumbled furniture, and small plumes of smoke and dying flames. Elminster seemed to know where they were. He was staring not at Narm's sprawled body, but at who lay atop him: Shandril Shessair.

She lay curled on her side, unmoving. A human skull hovered over her, its teeth locked on her shoulder. The flesh there shrank as they watched, dwindling toward bare bones. There was a line of blood at Shandril's throat, and the knife that had made it lay fallen by her open hand.

"By Mystra's bloody beauty!" Eyes blazing, Elminster was hurrying across the room.

The skull rose from its feeding, fixed its gaze on him—and opened its bony jaws to hurl spellfire. The angry blast of spellfire tore *through* the Old Mage; its flames leapt out of his back and scorched the wall beyond.

Shocked, Storm saw him stagger, tremble, and then struggle on toward the skull. Elminster's body seemed to be alive with flames. He advanced slowly, fighting against the flowing spellfire like a man walking against a deep, fast stream. As he went, his staff blazed into life. Pulses of radiance raced along it to where the Old Mage's hands held it. When they reached his hands, he tossed the staff aside, grunting in pain. Storm thought he looked suddenly *very* old.

Elminster reached the skull, took it firmly in hands that caught fire, and hurled it against a wall. There was a roar of spellfire. Sparks as big as a man's hand—bigger by far than the blackened, smoking, ruined extremities the Old Mage was now holding up, groaning in pain—winked and leapt around the room. Smoke rose where they touched.

Elminster's staff shattered with a noise like thunder, and the room was suddenly dark. A single, glowing light remained against the wall, growing slowly brighter.

The skull was cracked but still hung together, spellfire swirling around it. Storm swallowed, and then set her teeth and leapt at it, bringing her blade down.

The skull darted to one side. She pivoted and lashed out at it again. This time her blade just caught the edge of its jaw, and sent it tumbling end over end through the air.

Desperately Storm ran after the skull, trying to hit it before it could spit spellfire at her.

She failed. Flames roared out at her—and the bard flung herself frantically to the floor, landing hard on the cold flagstones. Then she was up, scant inches in front of the hungry blaze and dodging around the room, hacking at the darting, spinning skull as it spat swirling flames at her. She groaned, then screamed as spellfire burned her. Staggered, she slipped on a fallen sword and was burned again. The pain made her gasp, but she leapt over fallen townsfolk and fought on. She was burned again and again, the smell of her charred leathers growing ever stronger. Sweat ran down her limbs with the fury of her leaps and twists. She battled both the laughing skull, which hung always out of reach, and the agony inside her, which grew all too powerful as time went on.

Storm smelled her own cooked flesh as she raised a burned arm to drag her long sword around for yet another strike, trying to smash the skull in a corner. It ducked and weaved under her blade, and shot free—only to spin about and spit gouts of spellfire at her as she ran desperately along a wall. Fire was suddenly all around her again, and Storm rolled, scraping over an armored body she couldn't see. She fought to keep control of her stomach against the sickening pain of fresh burns. Though the pain made her weak, she kept up her attacks, trying to buy time for the radiance growing at her feet:

Shandril, whose body was glowing ever brighter.

Shandril's eyelids fluttered as Storm rolled past her, and spellfire rained down all around. The bard staggered to her feet and faced the lich lord once more, circling to keep it from seeing Shandril. Storm's heart soared as she slashed the air and forced the skull to back hastily away. Behind them both, Shandril stirred.

The bard could barely stand now. Spellfire roared past

her ears, and she heard her hair sizzle. Storm stumbled, moaning in her agony, bracing herself against the fresh pain she knew would come tearing into her.

But it did not come. Blinking, Storm stared at the skull—and saw Shandril's arm raised from the floor in front of her, gathering in all the spellfire that was meant to slay Storm. Shuddering in relief, the bard fell to her knees, leaning on her sword in exhaustion. Her silver hair swept down over her burned body, and she whimpered.

Shandril looked at her once, and her eyes flamed. She rose, struggling against the stream of spellfire as Elminster had done, and snarled in sudden defiance. Spellfire roared out of her eyes, white-hot and destroying. The force of her blasts hurled the skull back against the farthest wall of the room and held it there. The skull tried to break free of the streaming flames, but could not. It tried to scrape along the wall, but she forced it into stillness, pinning it against the cracking and protesting stones with the continuous force of her blasting fire. She knew how to destroy it now—she hoped. When she'd willingly given it that surge of fire, it had been angry, and its draining hadn't quickened. . . .

A tongue of darker force curled out from the skull, reaching for her. Shandril watched it come, knowing that it would drain her of spellfire again if it reached her. She snarled and pounded the skull with her spellflames.

The bony jaw moved, and the skull spoke. "Why do you tolerate these fools, child? How do you endure the stupidity of Those Who Harp? They *waste* their power helping others—craven weaklings, all. As are you, little one, for aiding them and consorting with such dross."

"And you, skull," Shandril replied in a voice of cold, biting iron, "are too selfish to find any joy in aiding others, or in what good might befall them. If you think kindness and love are marks of weakness, *you* are the stupid one."

She strode forward. "I am tired of pain—and of what you have done to my friends. You want my spellfire so much—well then: Take it! *Take it all!*"

And she leaned forward to embrace the dark tentacle of flame that was straining to reach her. Spellfire rolled out of her—but this time, she did not fight it. Instead, she forced the energy out of her in waves, hurling it through the linkage at the ever-brighter skull that bobbed against the wall.

A holocaust swirled around the skull, white and bright. The thing of bone shook, teeth chattering, and then a keening, rising wail escaped it: "*NnnnooooooOOO!*" The wail ended abruptly in a burst of flame.

Shandril felt the brief, stinging rain of powdered bone on her cheeks—and then the room fell silent.

In the sudden quiet, both women heard the Old Mage groan.

* * * * *

In an inner chamber of the temple, Fzoul Chembryl reeled back from a font of water that still flashed and bubbled, and he howled in pain.

The lich lord was gone—destroyed while it was linked to him. Fzoul clutched his head and shrieked. An upper-priest rushed in.

"Master?" he asked hesitantly. Fzoul was crouched against the wall, whimpering.

At the sound of his voice, the Master of the Black Altar turned his head and looked up. He stared at the upper-priest but did not see him—and small wonder: smoke was curling up from his eyes in two thin, gray plumes. . . .

* * * * *

"Old Mage," Storm whispered, "are you—all right?"

"Of *course* I'm not all right," Elminster replied as the bard rushed toward him. He tried to rise, and then reeled back, fires rising from his body. "Stay back!" he ordered Storm weakly, waving a hand. "There's still enough spell-fire in me to kill ye!"

The Old Mage groaned, then raised his head, cleared his throat, and said testily, "Must I do everything, look ye? Can no one else save the Realms this time?" He seemed to be speaking not to the two women, but to someone else. Though no one answered him, Elminster nodded as though satisfied.

He thumped a flagstone with his fist and tried to rise. Halfway upright, he grunted, stiffened, and sank back down. Flames tumbled out of his mouth in a little, rolling puff. He fell back full length on the blackened flagstones, fires flickering here and there along his body. Then there was a sudden whirlwind of blue-white flame where the Old Mage lay—and he vanished, leaving the bare floor behind.

Shandril made a small, startled sound in her throat. The two women stared at the empty place where Elminster had been, and then at each other. Storm shook her head.

"Gods . . . to see the Old Mage so hurt; does your power challenge the gods, Shan?"

Shandril turned to her and began to cry. "No, Storm. No. If it did, *I'd still have my Narm!*"

Narm lay sprawled on the floor, face gray, hands spread in a last, futile effort to help her.

Shandril looked at him once and then buried herself in Storm's embrace. It was all over; Narm dead, Delg gone, her dreams shattered, Manshoon's slaying only a passing satisfaction, this place and her newfound friends here destroyed, even Elminster laid low . . . how could the gods be so cruel?

Shandril was sobbing bitterly against Storm's chest when priests in the robes of Lathander burst up the stairs into the room, led by a soot-smudged Tessaril and a pair of Purple Dragon guards with frightened, grim faces and drawn swords.

Storm, in her burnt leathers, knelt with arms around the sobbing wielder of spellfire. She nodded at Tessaril in recognition and then said quietly, "There is nothing you can do here, now; all of you save Lord Tessaril, please leave us."

Tessaril gestured silently to her soldiers in confirmation of these orders, and the men obediently filed back down the stairs. Their shocked expressions told Storm what the room around her must look like to those who hadn't seen the battle.

When they were gone, Storm reached out to pat Tessaril's shoulder in thanks and said quietly, "Shandril, there is something we must do."

The Lord of Eveningstar looked down, unsmiling. She shuddered and reached out her hands.

Storm shook Shandril until she looked up through her bitter tears. The bard stared into her eyes and said, "There's a chance we can save your Narm. Only a chance. We need your aid."

Shandril nodded numbly, and the two women took hold of her hands and formed a kneeling ring around Narm's body. They laid their free hands on her husband's chest.

Then Storm looked up and said gravely, "We need your power, little one—slowly and steadily at first. Then give us more, carefully, and we shall see if your spellfire matches the fabled fire of old."

White-faced and trembling, Shandril nodded. Tears of fire rained from her cheeks as the spellfire slowly curled down her arms.

As they knelt together over Narm, his body began to glow.

* * * * *

"The collective performance of the Brotherhood thus far has been a source of some amusement," Xarlraun said, its deep voice cutting across the chamber, "but hardly effective."

The beholder floated above the human Zhentarim gathered in the room. Deep in its shadow, Fzoul replied, "Aye. Manshoon is dead."

"For how long, this time?"

"Forever, we believe." Fzoul blinked his newly healed eyes, but was unable to keep a smile entirely from his face. "He may find it difficult to come back from death without any bodies to possess."

"He had six or seven waiting."

"Aye." Fzoul bowed. "Unfortunately for our esteemed high lord, 'had' is the correct word."

"I see," the beholder said softly, drifting away. "The price of spellfire grows high indeed."

Fzoul nodded. "I've ordered Sarhthor to call our magelings back from pursuing spellfire. Brotherhood trading concerns have been neglected, and immediate steps should be taken. Certain trade officials in Melvaunt, Ordulin, and Priapurl, for example, have lived too long."

"Undoubtedly," said the beholder. It sounded amused. "Is the hunt for spellfire over then?"

"Rather than becoming an attractive addition to our power, spellfire could well become the doom of the entire Brotherhood. It would certainly have done so, the way Manshoon was going about it. Its capture became his private obsession."

Fzoul paused and looked around the chamber—at the upperpriests and Sarhthor, at the head of the surviving senior mages. His mouth tightened as he recalled Manshoon's traitor agent, Ghaubhan Szaurr. He wondered briefly if the wizards had discovered his own agents among their ranks.

"Nonetheless, spellfire is too important to ignore. At the very least, we must destroy its source—how much longer can one young girl have such luck, after all?—or prevent our rivals in Mulmaster, Thay, Calimshan, and the Cult of the Dragon from seizing it. With or without us, the hunt for spellfire will continue."

Fzoul turned and pointed at a certain mage as if coming to a sudden decision. Let them all think him as headstrong and arbitrary as Manshoon; it would lead to traitors revealing themselves before their plans were ready. The wizard Beliarge was too ambitious by far—and capable, too. It would be best to eliminate him now.

"You are our next chance, Beliarge. This Shandril is weaker now than she has ever been—and word has come to me that Elminster and the Harpers are no longer guarding her. All you need overcome is the Lord of Eveningstar, a woman who thinks herself something of a wizard. I'm sure you can prevail against the likes of *her.*"

Sarhthor stirred, but said nothing. Beliarge bowed and smiled.

With cold pride, the High Priest of the Black Altar looked around the chamber. At last the Brotherhood was under his command. It would be best not to make the same mistakes Manshoon's arrogance had led him into. He gave them all a cold smile and asked, "Is there counsel anyone here would like to add? Ideas, disputes, or other business? I would like everyone to speak freely, without fear of reprisal—for we are truly a Brotherhood, not a tyranny."

There was a moment of silence, and then Sarhthor spoke. "There is one thing more: a report from one who survived the failed attempt for spellfire in the Stonelands."

Fzoul raised an eyebrow. "I did not know anyone *had* survived."

Sarhthor nodded and gestured, dismissing a spell. The features of a mage standing behind him flowed and shifted—and Fzoul found himself looking at a woman who must have been stunningly beautiful before she became so burned and disheveled. Now she looked like a victim of a leprous infection that had eaten cruelly at her. Bristles of short hair adorned one side of that ruined head and locks hung long and silky down the other. Someone in the room hissed in revulsion.

"Who are you?" Fzoul asked briskly. Frightened eyes met his for a moment.

"Tespril, Lord. I'm—I was apprenticed to Gathlarue."

Fzoul nodded. *Gathlarue the Wonder Wizard,* he'd heard that one called, who thought women should rule the Brotherhood but was so feeble-witted that she thought she could conceal her gender from her fellow Zhentarim. She'd led the attack at Irondrake Rock, hadn't she?

"Greetings, Tespril," he said coldly. "Tell us what befell at Irondrake Rock."

She raised startled eyes for a moment—did the high priest know *everything?*—and began. "My mistress, accompanied by myself and her other apprentice, Mairara, was in Marsember on Brotherhood business, with ten and six Zhentilar as escort. We received orders to hunt Shandril Shessair after she entered Cormyr, and chased her through the Hullack Forest. She reached Irondrake Rock in the Stonelands before we caught up with her. It seemed to be her destination; I don't know why."

Fzoul raised his eyebrows but silently waited for her to continue.

Tespril stared at him uncertainly, then said, "My mistress decided the confined area Shandril and her companions had reached offered an excellent chance to defeat them."

"How many companions had she?" an upperpriest asked sharply.

Tespril turned tired eyes on him. "Three," she said. "The young mage who is her mate—he has no power to speak of—a dwarf, and a man named Mirt, whom we believe to be the same Mirt widely believed to be a Lord of Waterdeep."

Fzoul's eyes gleamed. Here was a chance for a fat ransom—or better, an agent in the City of Splendors under the magical control of the Brotherhood. He asked calmly, "Did they speak of meeting anyone?"

Tespril spread her hands. "Not that I heard. Dusk fell while they were still exploring the area, and my mistress decided to attack."

"You failed," Fzoul said flatly. "Why?"

"My mistress believed that the gargoyles she commanded—by means of rings she'd crafted—could defeat Shandril and her companions. Only Mirt, we believed, carried an enspelled weapon." Tespril shook her head, remembering the horrors of the fight. "I—I fled after my mistress was slain. I think we killed the dwarf, and the Brotherhood should know that Gathlarue's forcewall spell seemed to thwart the spellfire for a time. I saw most of the warriors killed; I doubt any of the Brotherhood survived but me."

"How did you escape?" Sarhthor asked coldly. "You don't have the power to use a teleport spell."

Tespril looked at the floor. "I—I used one of the Brotherhood's teleport rings."

"Only Gathlarue among you was given such a device,"

Fzoul said softly.

Tespril nodded. "I . . . stole it from her, before the fight. I was sure we'd lose." Her gaze fell to the floor.

Fzoul turned away. "The Brotherhood thanks you for your foresight and your report. Sarhthor, you know what to do."

Sarhthor nodded, face expressionless, and turned, waggling only one finger. Tespril made a short strangling sound in her throat before her body hit the floor.

"This meeting is ended," Fzoul said smoothly. "I thank you for your attendance and your efforts thus far. Diligence in the service of the Brotherhood is always"—he paused to give everyone time to look down at Tespril's sprawled body—"*justly* rewarded."

* * * * *

"It *worked!*" Shandril said through delighted tears, embracing Storm. Narm's chest rose and fell again steadily. "Gods thank you! Was this your idea?"

"No," the bard replied very softly. "It was Sylune's."

Shandril's eyes widened. "That long ago you spoke of me?"

"No," Storm said. "Sylune does not live as she did before, but her spirit is sometimes with me." She smiled slowly. "Harpers have secrets upon secrets—do you think it was an accident you were married on the site of her home?"

Tessaril bent and kissed Shandril. Her eyes were very sad. "It would be best, child, if you got pregnant again as soon as possible."

"Again?" Then the blood drained from Shandril's face, and she whispered, "What's happened to my baby?"

"The skull's draining," Storm said gently, "was too much for the life inside you. Iliph Thraun killed your unborn child."

Shandril stared at her in horror. "Gods aid me." Her words were so faint that they could scarcely be heard. Wordlessly, the women embraced her. They stood pressed together for a long time, but Shandril did not cry. For now, at least, she had no tears left.

At last, Shandril sank back and looked down at Narm, who lay breathing quietly, his face no longer gray. She sighed, and her lip trembled. She bit it, and then stood up, lifting her chin.

"Well," Shandril said, "at least I have my Narm again." She looked around at the cracked, blackened walls, and added, "And another score to settle with those of Zhentil Keep."

The air in front of her flickered, and suddenly a man in dark robes stood there, rings gleaming on his hands. He bowed and smiled at them. "A nice cue, that. Thank you. Beliarge of the Zhentarim, at your service," he said.

Storm's eyes blazed. She shoved Shandril away, and dived for her sword. Beliarge watched her with a mirthless smile, as his fingers moved in the intricate gestures of a spell.

Tessaril stepped forward suddenly and caught hold of Shandril. Turning the startled maid around, she hissed a word. A floating, shimmering, upright oval of light appeared in the air in front of Shandril—and she felt Tessaril's hands at her back, shoving her through it.

Abruptly the stone-lined chamber disappeared, and she was somewhere else. Somewhere grand and dark, where she'd never been before.

* * * * *

In Tessaril's Tower, Storm whirled up from the floor, long sword in hand.

The Lord of Eveningstar had raised her hands to cast a spell at the smiling intruder. Her face sharpened in anger.

The Zhentarim smiled politely at them both and crooked a finger. The spell he'd cast took effect—and both women froze, unable to move.

"Delighted to make your acquaintance, ladies," he said, bowing. "I hope you enjoy my little achievement; a more powerful holding spell than I think you'll find anywhere else. If I didn't have more pressing concerns, I'd tarry and get to know you both better—but my business is with Shandril Shessair, and since your gate helped her leave so abruptly before my spell was done . . ."

He stepped forward and twisted the sword from Storm's grasp. Choosing a place where her leathers were burned away, he idly drew a scarlet line across her belly with the keen tip of the blade.

Storm's eyes glittered at him in helpless anger. "The spell won't let you go free, no matter what I do, you see?" Beliarge said pleasantly, holding up the blade in front of the bard's nose so she could see her own blood glistening on it.

"I could carve my name in you both with a dagger, and take quite a lot of time and trouble over it, too, without your being able to move, or even make a sound. Were I a cruel man, I could toss you down the stairs—or even out a window—and you'd land all rigid. It shatters bones like glass, I'm told." He sighed theatrically. "Spellfire, however, is more important even than this, so I must leave you. Perhaps we'll have an opportunity to spend some time—truly enjoyable, leisure time—together, in the future."

With cruel fingers, he pried open Tessaril's mouth and put the bloody tip of the blade between her teeth. Supporting the naked steel lightly on his fingers, the wizard yanked Storm into place at the other end of the blade. A moment later, the hilt was deep in her own mouth, the quillons just in front of her lips.

With a satisfied smile, the Zhentarim mage stepped back and surveyed the two helpless women and the blade suspended between them. He waved them a cheery farewell, favored them with one last cruel grin . . . and stepped through the gate.

Fifteen

IN THE HIDDEN HOUSE

All of us need a hidden, private place, a little refuge all our own where we can shut out the cares of the world for a while. It's why we build play-huts when we're young and love-nests when we're old—but those can be lost forever if the love fails. Those of us wise enough or lucky enough to have such a place as we grow older will keep our wits longer and laugh more than others.

Laeral of Waterdeep, quoted in
Words to an Apprentice
Ithryn Halast, Year of the Weeping Moon

 Shandril stood in a grand hall of dark, carved wood and oval mirrors. They reflected back the room behind her— but without any trace of her own reflection in them. She looked down at her hands wonderingly, but they were visible enough. What sort of place was this?

A place Tessaril knew, that was certain. Shandril looked behind her; the flickering oval of radiance was still there, hanging in midair. What would happen if she stepped back through it? She'd walk straight into the arms of that Zhentarim and another battle—and the bone-deep ache told her she had too little spellfire left for such a fray.

Shandril ran weary fingers through her hair and looked down a long, unlit, carpeted hallway in front of her. It ran straight out of the chamber where she stood and into distant darkness. Shandril was reluctant to leave this room and perhaps get lost in a place full of dangers she did not know. It might go on forever like the dungeons under Waterdeep, and she'd starve or die in a trap before finding a way out or seeing the sun again.

She glanced back at the magical gate and wondered if she'd be able to see back into Tessaril's Tower if she went around behind the oval of light and looked through it. Behind the gate was a wall, and against it stood many dark, heavy wooden tables and tall chests, all of different heights. One of them proudly displayed the Purple Dragon, but bore several heavy padlocks. On another lay a slim, glowing sword, small enough for her to comfortably lift. Wondering, Shandril approached it and hefted its cool weight in her hands. She was still holding it as she turned to look at the back of the gate.

She saw nothing through the oval of light except the other side of the room she stood in. Shandril sighed—and then froze, hardly daring to breathe, as a man's back appeared in front of her. The dark figure of the Zhentarim, striding out of nothingness beyond the gate into the room with her. He turned his head to look about, and she saw his cruel smile. In a moment he'd turn and see her. She glided forward.

It was hideously *easy*.

He turned, almost touching her. His eyes lit up as he saw her, he started to smile—and she thrust the sword up, into his throat.

Beliarge of the Zhentarim choked and sputtered. His

eyes bulged, and as Shandril tore her blade free, blood rained everywhere. With futile fingers, the wizard clawed the air and his throat, the rings on them powerless to save him. Blood spattered on the floor and on Shandril. Some sprinkled the oval radiance of the gate—and it rippled like water and disappeared. The Zhentarim staggered, fell clutching at his gullet, made a horrible gurgling sound as he kicked at the floor, and then went limp.

Shandril was alone again. She shivered.

For a moment she stared down at the rings on his fingers, but decided she did not want to touch those bloodied hands or search him for anything else, either. Using a corner of his robes to wipe the worst of the blood from her arms and the sword, she looked around the room once more, sighed, and walked to the hallway. She was not going to stand here beside a dead Zhent. . . . The gods alone knew what spells might be set off by his death. Elminster had warned her about that once. Even the magical gate was likely trapped somehow to keep Storm and Tessaril from coming through, or Shandril from returning.

So where had the good fortune of the gods landed her *now?* A short flight of steps led down into the hallway, and from where they ended the passage ran straight and narrow to the remote distance, from which she now glimpsed some sort of light. Dark rectangles lined its walls—shuttered windows? No . . . paintings.

Shandril went toward the light, glancing up at the pictures as she passed. They were hard to see in the dimness, but the first few seemed to be portraits of noble folk, staring haughtily out of the frames at her. Then she came to one that was blank, as if nothing had ever been painted on it. The picture after that was covered with a sort of fluffy white mold that smelled of old, long-dead, spices. All that showed through it of the portrait beneath were two large and piercing dark eyes.

Shandril shuddered at their glare and walked on. The next painting was bare—except for a large, dark stain near its bottom. Shandril drew back. The stain surrounded a slit in the canvas; it looked as if someone had thrust a sword through the painting. From that gash, the darkness ran down the wall, like blood flowing to the floor.

A small sound came from back down the hallway behind her. A scraping sound, like a boot at a careless step. It echoed slightly around her. Shandril looked back—but the hall was empty.

Silence fell. When she stepped forward again, the echo returned. Her own footfalls were now reverberating through the hall, though she'd walked down the first stretch of it without raising any echoes. Magic? A trick of the air? Or was someone really pursuing her? Shandril frowned again. What *was* this place?

She stopped, looked back again, and decided the likelihood of pursuit was all too possible. She turned and went on again toward the light she'd been heading for—the end of the hall, a small, lit area where there were three closed doors. The warm yellow radiance seemed to be coming from the walls; she couldn't see any torches or lanterns. The dark-paneled wooden doors looked old—and all the same. None bore any marks or labels, and no sound came from behind any of them.

After a moment, Shandril took firm hold of the cold brass knob of the door on her left, turned it, and pushed. The door opened into darkness. Something small and winged whirred out past her head, circling her for a frightening moment, and then was gone down the hallway. Shandril looked at where it had come from, but the room was too dark to see anything. She listened. Nothing. She closed the door and turned to the portal on its right.

It opened into a dim, dusty room with a worn wooden floor. As she looked in, the light inside seemed to grow stronger. The room stretched off to her left; she saw ceiling beams and a confusing array of crates, barrels, and boxes covered with draped cloth.

She closed the door and tried the center one. It opened easily, revealing dark emptiness. Cold night breezes wafted in around her; the doorsill seemed to be on the edge of a cliff, with jagged rock walls descending on her left to black depths far below. What looked like a village lay in the distance beneath her, judging by the number of scattered fires and points of lamplight. The scene looked like the view from the edge of the Stonelands, a view she'd seen not so long ago—but in the dark night, the cliff might have been anywhere. On an impulse, she dug a copper coin out of a slit in her belt and tossed it through the door. It dropped, bounced off rock somewhere nearby with a tiny clinking sound, and was gone. The cliff, at least, was real—and there was no sign of any rope, or steps, or safe way down.

Shandril closed the door.

Behind her, the scraping sound came again. She spun around—to see the Zhentarim wizard walking slowly and confidently down the hall toward her. There was no blood on him; he looked unhurt and very much alive. He smiled at her as he came. "Well met, Shandril Shessair," he said lightly. "You bear a sharp sword, I see. Shall we try it against my spells?"

His smile was steady and confident. Fear touched Shandril. Trembling, she hurriedly opened the door on the right again—but the crates and dusty cloths were gone. This time, the door opened into a brilliantly lit hall of polished marble and hanging candle clusters.

Shandril swallowed. Cold sweat ran down her back. If she stepped through that door, would she ever find her way out again?

She looked back down the dark hallway to see how close the Zhent had come—and found herself staring at a stone wall that hadn't been there before, blocking the hall only a few paces away. The carved stone face of a lion stood out in relief in its center, and seemed to smile mockingly at her.

Despite the wall, she could hear the scraping sound of the wizard's boots coming nearer, somewhere on the other side of the stones. He was striding confidently, not slowing or seeming uncertain about his way. She tossed another coin—and it vanished into the lion's smile without a sound. An illusion.

There was no Narm or Mirt or anyone else here to help her now. Whether she lived or died was up to her. *Damn* all Zhent wizards! Shandril took a deep breath, turned back to the well-lit marble hall, and went in, sword ready.

The marble hall was large and empty. It stretched away for many paces on all sides, dwarfing Mourngrym's feast hall in Shadowdale. The ceiling was lost in darkness high overhead, and the polished floor gleamed under her boots. Shandril hurried forward, trying to get as far away from the door—and the wizard pursuing her—as possible.

There was a hint of movement on either side as Shandril hurried past, as if phantoms were locked together in stately dances—but whenever she looked directly to either side, where she thought she'd seen movement, all was still.

The hall was wider and longer than any room Shandril had ever seen—probably larger than the hall she'd run through in the dark in Myth Drannor—but now she could see its other end. Stairs led up to a dais there, and a single dark door. She was about halfway there when the music began.

Soft, sweet piping and harping. Intricate and mournful—and like nothing she'd ever heard before. She looked all around, but no musicians were to be seen. The music seemed to wash around her, coming from everywhere and nowhere. A trick sent by the wizard—or something else? Far behind her, she heard the door where she'd entered swing open, and the scrape of boots sounded again on marble.

Shandril set her teeth and strode on. The music faded as she reached the steps. By the time she had ascended to the top and looked back along the hall, all was silent—except for the sounds of the striding wizard. He was coming toward her, a small figure in the distance, and Shandril knew he was smiling. She could feel it.

Behind the approaching wizard, the hall had changed. At that end now were stone pillars and archways, brilliantly lit by flickering torches, which showed her at least four stone-lined passages running off at various angles. They certainly hadn't been there when she'd come into the hall.

Shandril sighed and turned back to the door in front of her. At least *it* hadn't changed on her—yet.

It opened easily, but made a long groaning sound. The room beyond was dark except for a small glowing sphere that hovered just within—a sphere about as big across as a shield . . . magic, no doubt. Shandril studied it narrowly for a moment, looked back at the steadily approaching wizard, and then shrugged and stepped into the room.

The glowing area flared around her, growing both bright and purplish. The radiance seemed to have no source, but clung to her as she walked on, and revealed faint aspects of the room. She was in a long, narrow, low-ceilinged chamber crowded with chairs, chests, and cabinets. As she peered ahead, the outlines of the dark furniture seemed to flow and shift for a moment, as though they sometimes held other shapes. Behind her, the darkness closed in again.

The room ended in a white door. Shandril opened it—and leapt back as it swung open to reveal a hissing, coiling mass of snakes. The writhing serpents filled a small cubicle lit by a ruby-red glow, their entwined, slithering bodies piled atop each other in a wriggling heap taller than Shandril herself.

Sweating, she slammed the door, encountering rubbery resistance for one horrifying moment. As its lock clicked shut, many similar clicking sounds came from around her. Shandril turned in her little purple glow, and saw other doors shining palely in the darkness. She was sure they had not been there before.

She heard the wizard's boots scraping on the marble outside the room. In sudden panic, she ran to one of the shining doors and wrenched it open. Beyond lay a short hall containing a small table and a shabby green carpet.

She ran down it and whirled through another door to find herself in a small, musty, octagonal room. All of its eight walls were doors. She opened one, and cold mist eddied out, rising off black water that lapped at the other side of the doorsill and ran back into starlit darkness. She could not see the other shore of what seemed to be a huge lake. As she looked out, mist damp on her cheeks, a strange, ululating cry echoed from far away across the water. Shandril shut the door hastily and stepped back.

Another door, to her left, opened by itself. She screamed and jumped away—but nothing emerged. Keeping her eyes on that door, she backed hastily away, found another door behind her, and opened it.

Now she was looking into a hall hung with old tapestries. At its far end, there was moonlight—coming from where, she couldn't tell—gleaming on something that moved. Armor! A man in a full suit of plate armor stepped away from the wall as she watched, and he walked to a door. Shandril made a small sound of surprise.

The armored figure whirled around. It took a slow step toward her, then reached up and raised its visor—showing the dark, empty interior of its helm. Abruptly it turned away, walked to another wall, and took up a stance there, hand on spear, as if it had never moved.

Shandril stepped back out of the hall into the octagonal room of many doors, and looked around warily. The door that had opened by itself before was closed again now—and several of the other doors had changed their sizes and shapes; they were no longer identical.

Breathing quickly, Shandril opened a door at random—and found herself face-to-face with the Zhentarim mage, his hand already extended to open the door from his side. He laughed, and brought his other hand up, reaching forward—

She slammed the door on him, hard. It smashed into his arm with a solid thud. Shandril snatched open the next door without waiting to find out how badly she'd hurt the wizard. The chamber beyond was fiery. She tried the next. The moment she saw a room with a floor in the proper place beyond the doorsill, she fled through it.

This room was small and bare, furnished only with a stool and a single door at the far end. Shandril ran to it and plucked it open in breathless haste, her sword up and ready this time.

"Well *met,* Shan!" The merry voice on the other side of the door was accompanied by a slim, curving sword that deflected her own blade deftly aside. Then its owner tumbled out, swept her close, and kissed her heartily.

Shandril found herself in the arms of Torm, Knight of Myth Drannor and Engaging Rogue. Behind him loomed the large, bearlike form of Rathan Thentraver, priest of Tymora. She blinked at them, dumbfounded.

"Hey! Save some o' her kisses for me, ye sly dog," Rathan rumbled, lurching into the room to tap Torm's shoulder.

Torm broke free of Shandril to draw breath, then grinned back at his fellow knight. "Why?" he asked innocently. "You've a *good* reason?"

Without waiting for an answer, he turned back to Shandril, who still stood dazed. If Torm hadn't kissed her, she'd have thought him some phantom conjured by this place. Perhaps he was some sort of magically disguised monster. . . . The young thief swept her back into an embrace. "What brings you here?" he asked cheerfully. "And where's Narm?"

Shandril's answer was lost in the sound of the door behind her opening. They all turned in time to see the Zhentarim raise his hands. The wizard wore a wolfish grin.

"By the luck of the Laughing Lady," Rathan said in delight, "he's got golden eyes!" An amulet at the priest's throat winked with sudden light.

In response to the priest's words, the wizard's smile fell away in an instant. Shandril watched in horror as the face beneath twisted and bulged, shifting into something fanged and horrid. The man—if it was a man—charged them, waving hands that, as he came, stretched impossibly into long, raking claws.

"Nice nails, too," Rathan observed, drawing a mace from his belt and hefting it as he met the rushing monster.

Torm whirled away from Shandril and waved grandly at the open door he'd come in by. "Your way lies clear before you, Lady," he said. "I look forward to a chance to taste your sweet lips again when next we meet—hopefully at an occasion of rather more leisure—"

"Are ye going to fight, Torm?" Rathan demanded,

smashing his mace into something that reeled back and
promptly grew tentacles. "Or are ye just going to *talk* us
all to death?"

Torm turned back to the fray, plucking something that
looked like a gilded rose from his belt. Shandril watched
him bound toward the monster, calling briskly, "Next
dance, please!"

Rathan struggled amid clinging, tightening tentacles,
and bellowed to her, "*Run,* lass! Through that door—look
for banners, and ye'll be safe!"

Shandril shook her head, still astonished by the speedy
appearance of the knights. Then Torm swung the fragile-
looking rose at the monster—and the room exploded in
golden light.

Pulses of radiance spun ever faster and brighter
around the three struggling forms. Shandril shaded her
eyes against the brilliance, and thought she saw Torm's
blade thrust right through the still-changing monster
before the knights and the thing faded amid a cloud of
rushing golden light . . . and she was alone again.

The room was suddenly empty—and very quiet. All
that remained to mark the passage of the knights were a
few golden rose petals. Shandril stared down at them and
swallowed. Then, holding her sword ready, she went to
the open door Rathan had bid her use.

It led into another many-sided room of doors. There
were six this time. Shandril sighed again and opened one
at random. The scene beyond was one of cold, blowing
snow, somewhere wintry with mountains in the distance—and the sprawled, gnawed bones of a recently
slain orc lying right in front of her. It still clutched a cruel
black scimitar. Shandril heard something growling in the
distance, and she hastily closed the door.

Banners, Rathan had said. Shandril gently opened the
next door to the right. The room it opened into was

choked with banners. They hung everywhere, almost
touching, and the air was thick with their dust and old
smells. Shandril recognized none of them, but she did
think one—a black wyvern on purple silk faded almost to
pink—was very striking. Another displayed three golden
crowns on a royal blue field. It caught her eye because
some old enchantment made the crowns move, each one
winking in and out by itself to reappear in different
spots. Shandril watched it warily as she stepped into the
room.

It was small and square; behind the banners she found
another door. Opening it, she found a short, featureless
hall with another door at the other end. Shandril
shrugged and entered. She'd gone three paces into the
room when a sudden thought struck her; she turned
back and opened the door again, hoping to find Deeping-
dale's colors among the banners. But the room was
empty now, a place of dark, polished floors and cobwebs
in the corners. She shuddered and closed the door again
very carefully.

"Tessaril," she said aloud, almost crying in fear and
frustration, "what have you *done* to me?"

As she spoke, the door at the other end of the hall
swung open. Beyond lay the grand hall, with the Zhentarim she'd slain lying dead on the floor and Tessaril
standing beside him. The Lord of Eveningstar's soot-
smudged face broke into a smile at the sight of her.

Shandril ran to her—and then came to an abrupt halt.
"Tessaril?" she asked suspiciously, her sword up. "Is that
really you?"

The Lord of Eveningstar smiled. "Yes, Shandril." Then
her smile turned a little sad, and she added, "I can tell
wandering in my House has unsettled you."

Shandril rolled her eyes. "Just a touch . . . what *is* this
place?"

Tessaril slipped past her blade and hugged her reassuringly. "This is the Hidden House," she said softly. "It's been here a very long time—since the towers of Myth Drannor stood tall and proud and new, at least."

Shandril glanced at the room around them. *That* old? "Who made it?"

Tessaril shrugged. "An archmage of very great power . . . some tales say Azuth himself."

" 'Some tales'? I've never heard of it."

"Few folk know that it is anything more than a tale—and very few know how to get to it. These days, it serves as my refuge. Sometimes I hide important things here for Azoun. Sometimes those who are hurt—or hunted—spend time here."

Shandril looked down at the bloody corpse of the man she'd slain. "If he died when I thought I killed him," she said slowly, "who was chasing me?"

Tessaril stroked her cheek reassuringly. "A shapeshifting being that Torm and Rathan are after. Did Elminster ever tell you about the Malaugrym?"

Shandril frowned at her. "I—I think so, in Shadowdale. Very briefly. He said I must beware 'Those Who Watch,' but we were interrupted then, and he never told me more."

Tessaril nodded. "They're very dangerous. Certainly too powerful for Torm and Rathan." Shandril's face grew pale, and the Lord of Eveningstar patted it. "Don't worry —did they fight it with what looked like a golden rose?"

Shandril nodded.

Tessaril smiled. "That's a mazetrap I gave them," she said. "It'll whirl them all away into separate mists, tearing them apart even if they're clawing at each other. It'll be awhile before the Malaugrym can find you again."

Shandril looked at her. "Find me?"

"It's after your spellfire, like everyone else on Toril,"

Tessaril said lightly, then added more seriously, "There's not much you can do about the Masters of Shadow—except use your spellfire on anything that has golden eyes . . . really gold, like shining metal, I mean."

Shandril sighed and looked down at the dead Zhentarim again. Then she lifted her head, wearing a determined look. "All right."

Tessaril chuckled. "That's the spirit, Shan." She gently took the sword from Shandril's hands and laid it on a nearby chest. "How did you like my House?"

Shandril looked at her. "When you're alone, it's . . . frightening."

Tessaril nodded. "It can be. Those who don't know the words to say can get lost and wander endlessly, or step through a gate into a far more dangerous place than this—or than Zhentil Keep, for that matter."

"How did you find it?"

"I didn't; I was given custody of it when I took the lordship of Eveningstar. The only easy entrance to find is the one you came by, and it opens only from the room you came from. The Hidden House is part of the wardship of the Lord of Eveningstar. Those who don't know that—including most noble families of Cormyr—have always been puzzled by the high rank given to this post. They usually put it down to Azoun and my being very old friends."

Tessaril smiled and waved a hand. In response, a bearskin rug rippled in through a doorway that had not been there before, glided to a smooth stop by Shandril's feet, and settled to the floor. An instant later, two large and soft chairs glided in through the door after it, and arranged themselves on the rug, facing each other.

The Lord of Eveningstar sank into one of them, drew her feet up under her, and waved at Shandril to sit in the other. "This place once belonged to the legendary sorceress Phaeryl, in the days of Netheril."

Shandril nodded. "I've heard of her—she bred dragons."

"That's the one. No one knew where Phaeryl's lost abode lay; most thought it was somewhere in the Stonelands, and more than one band of greedy adventurers clambered all over the Haunted Halls looking for it. By chance, a warrior of the Harpers stumbled on the entrance you used, too many years ago to want to keep count of. She's a friend of mine, and we explored this place together. It was a lot of fun."

"Fun?" Shandril's tone was disbelieving.

"We learned a lot, talking to the ghosts—"

Shandril's expression told the lord what she thought of *that* experience.

Tessaril shook her head in mock reproof and went on: "—and we got to see a lot of faraway places, and put on the most amazing gowns; you've no idea what crazy things folk used to wear. Oh, and we used to play hide and seek here. We were young, then. Later, we played it with our suitors."

Shandril rolled her eyes and in response heard the deep warm sound of Tessaril chuckling.

"I didn't like it, much, wandering around here alone," the Lord of Eveningstar added softly. "It would have been much worse, though, if a Malaugrym had been chasing me."

Then Tessaril made a clucking sound and waved a hand. Almost immediately, two dark figures in armor—Shandril stiffened involuntarily—clanked into the room, picked up the Zhent's body, and walked out. Empty helms gaped, the visors raised; these suits of armor, too, were empty.

"My guards," Tessaril explained. "They would offer you harm only if I willed them to." Her face changed. "I'm sorry your first taste of the House was fleeing a Zhent and a Malaugrym. The Zhentarim was not supposed to be able to follow you, but I was overconfident. His spells were stronger than Storm or I could resist; I'm glad you slew him when you did, or we'd be standing there like statues still."

She stretched in her chair, looked around at the hall of oval mirrors, and said, "Though if you have to hide from anyone, this is the best place I know of to do it in."

"How so?" Shandril asked, "I'd always be afraid I'd open a door and find myself face-to-face with someone I thought I'd slipped away from, six rooms back."

Tessaril smiled at her. "Yes, the doors do not always open into the same rooms you have found behind them before." Her smile changed, touched by sympathy. "You've already found that out, I see."

She made a peculiar wriggling gesture with her fingers, and a cabinet nearby swung open. A bottle and two glass flagons floated out of it, heading for her hands.

"There's a much greater benefit to this place," the Lord of Eveningstar said as she poured a glass of frosty-cold green wine and handed it to Shandril. "I can feel the presence of any intruder and where they're lurking."

"Me, for instance?"

Tessaril grinned. "We're going to get along fine, Shan. I hope you'll have patience enough to stay here for a bit in hiding while you and Narm and Mirt all get fully healed. There's even a place where you can safely hurl spellfire and make sure you've built it to its height before you venture out again to face the Zhentarim."

Shandril sipped the wine and found it warm and very good. She drank deeply and said, "Thanks, Lord Tessaril. I accept."

Tessaril chuckled again. "Call me 'Tess,' please—and think about one other thing." Her face grew serious

again. "A wielder of spellfire may find fewer hiding places
in all vast Faerûn than she expected. This is one of them.
Think of it when you're looking for a home; neither
Azoun or I will try to command you if you choose to stay
here. We consider it one of Cormyr's treasures—but not
part of Cormyr."

Shandril looked at her in disbelief. "Here?"

"I'm not expecting you to prefer it to freely roaming
Faerûn," Tessaril replied. "I'm suggesting it as the best
refuge I know."

"Umm," Shandril said, resting her chin on her glass
and staring at the opposite wall. The painting on it oblig-
ingly flickered and changed shape.

Tessaril held out the bottle to refill Shandril's glass.
"Narm and Mirt both seem all right," she said. "The
priests of Lathander are in awe of you, by the way, over
what you did to Narm. Storm's gone back to Shadowdale,
we've not seen the Old Mage again, and we've not seen or
heard anything more from the Zhentarim. I've spoken
with Vangerdahast—without revealing that any of you
were still here—and he's of the opinion that you fought
something called a 'lich lord,' more powerful at sorcery
than most archmages living today. *He's* mightily impressed with you, too."

Shandril smiled wearily. "So's everyone else I meet—
but then they usually try to kill me." She was suddenly
very tired, and felt something moving through her fingers. She looked down—in time to see the glass fall from
her hand.

Shandril watched it shatter on the floor, stared at the
bouncing fragments dully, and then raised slow and
angry eyes to look at Tessaril. Flames leapt in them as
she said bitterly, "You put something in the wine. I
trusted you, too."

"I hope you'll go on trusting me, Shan," Tessaril said

sadly as she got up and put her arms around Shandril. "Now you need to sleep—or you'll soon kill yourself. You've been hurling spellfire without rest or food or water. Each time you call on it, it's eating you inside to get its energy. Rest now; you're safe here."

The last thing Shandril felt was a gentle kiss on her cheek. She fell asleep wearing a curious expression. To Tessaril, it looked as if she was trying to frown, but smiling in relief.

* * * * *

"Well?" Fzoul slowly turned from the papers he'd been studying and raised cold eyes to fix Sarhthor with a challenging gaze.

The sorcerer looked back at him expressionlessly. "He failed. Through our spell-link, I felt him die."

Fzoul studied the wizard's stony face. "You're no more surprised than I am."

Sarhthor shrugged. "He was an overconfident, arrogant fool. One more we're better off without."

"You don't approve of cruelty or pride?" Fzoul asked flatly.

The sorcerer seemed almost to smile. "I see no reason to laud villainy just because the Brotherhood uses might and pays no heed to the moral judgments of others. If I have a flaw, it should be something I work against to make me better in the service of the Brotherhood—not something I take pride in and show to all as a weakness of the Brotherhood, ready to be taken advantage of."

Fzoul nodded. "Wisely said." He paused, toying with the tiny skull carved from Iliph Thraun's thighbone. The high priest leaned forward. "Tell me, Sarhthor—what are your own thoughts on this matter of spellfire?"

Sarhthor shrugged. "A formidable weapon, something of almost irresistible power—but not something to tear apart the Brotherhood over."

Fzoul leaned back. "Oh? Tell me, then, what—in your view—are the more important matters facing the Brotherhood now."

Sarhthor nodded. He went to the row of chairs along one side of the room and picked one up. Though it was large and heavy, the slightly built wizard lifted it as if it were made of paper.

Fzoul's eyes narrowed. Sarhthor met the high priest's gaze mildly, carried the chair to the table, and without invitation, sat down opposite Fzoul.

"First," the wizard said calmly, "we must foil Thay's growing influence in Calaunt and Westgate."

"First?" Fzoul's voice was silky.

Sarhthor looked at him expressionlessly and said, "You told me to state my view. If you'd prefer to fence, Fzoul, I can oblige."

Fzoul held his gaze for a long, chilly time, then silently waved him to continue.

Sarhthor inclined his head and went on. "Then there's the matter of Maalthiir of Hillsfar. If he were dead, we could take advantage of instability there to place a large number of agents—and slay those Mulmaster has established there."

The wizard shrugged. "I'd also like to see more of the soft word and hidden agreement in the way we work in days ahead—and fewer marching armies and indiscriminate spell-hurling. We're making enemies at far too fast a rate, and making too many rulers uncomfortable. I don't want to see armies from several realms besieging our walls in a year or two."

Fzoul nodded slowly. "This is more sense than I've heard from the mouth of a wizard of the Brotherhood in several winters."

Sarhthor nodded, the ghost of a smile on his face. "They're all too eager to topple towers and twist the world overnight, aren't they?"

Fzoul lifted his lip in a cruel parody of a smile. "Exactly. I'm hoping we can see eye to eye on more things, Sarhthor, than your predecessor and I ever did. It would be a pleasure to work together to make the Brotherhood great for once rather than spending our best energies in fighting each other, wizards against priests, and cabal against cabal."

Sarhthor smiled thinly. "I'm sure it's afforded the Great Lord Bane—and foes such as Elminster—much entertainment over the years."

Fzoul's smile vanished at those words, but he said only, "Say on."

Sarhthor shrugged. "I'd like to build Zhentil Keep into something greater than a fortress of fear, Fzoul—an empire ruling all Dragon Reach and the Moonsea. Whatever our individual dreams, there'll be more room for ambitious Brothers who wear the robes of Bane or who walk as wizards to find their own desires fulfilled if we grow larger and more powerful. I know Great Lord Bane wants to see such an empire loyal to him, because I've heard your underpriests chanting the Words of Bane often enough. The sorcerers under me provide you with wilder magic than other priesthoods can match—we need each other."

Fzoul's face was grim, but there was a light in his eyes as he asked, "What, then, do you think we should do first?"

Sarhthor did not quite smile. "Well," he said. . . .

* * * * *

Narm came into the hall of mirrors in the Hidden House, went to where Shandril sat, and bent over her. "What're you eating? It smells wonderful."

With an impish smile, Shandril looked up at him over her shoulder, shifted what she was chewing to one cheek, and replied, "Fried snake."

Narm choked.

Mirt chuckled wickedly across the table and said, "Well done, Shan. Ah, to see wizards wearing that sort of expression more often." He lifted his own steaming plate to Narm and said, "Cooked it meself, lad—try it; 'tis good!"

Ignoring Narm's expression of disgust, the old merchant went on jovially, "One must have the right sort of snake, of course, and prepare it just so . . . or it's best to stay with chicken instead, roasted with almonds. That comes close to the same taste, but falls short."

"I'm certain you're right," Narm said in a voice that indicated nothing of the sort. Then the young mage peered suspiciously at Mirt. "Where'd you get the snake, anyway? I'm sure Tessaril doesn't have them stacked up in *her* larder."

Mirt smiled at him and pointed at a door. "I found it in one of the rooms—the one with the bones an' open graves. . . ."

Narm wandered away, waving dismissive hands at the proffered plate and looking rather green.

"Mirt! Stop it!" Tessaril's voice was reproving. "I've brought friends to visit." From behind her, Storm grinned at Mirt, eyes twinkling.

"Mmm," Mirt said in welcome, holding his rejected plate of fried snake up toward her. "The Bard of Shadowdale—and me without anything to plug my ears."

Storm stuck her tongue out at him and took the plate. Out from behind her stepped a familiar figure that made

Shandril squeal with delight and bounce up from the table.

"Elminster!" she cried. "Are you well?"

A flicker of a smile crossed the bearded face as Shandril threw her arms around him and embraced him tightly.

Warm, avid lips met hers, and she pulled her head back, startled. "*You're* not Elminster!"

"No," Torm said with a grin as his magical disguise melted away, "but there's no need to stop giving me that sort of enthusiastic welcome; I'm much prettier than he is."

Shandril whirled free of his arms and flounced away; the punch she threw in the process left Torm doubled over and breathless.

Narm hooted with laughter at the sight and asked, "Why the disguise?"

"Torm's been fooling a dozen or so Zhentarim into thinking Elminster's enjoying a quiet rest in Shadowdale," Storm told him, and looked teasingly at the thief. "It's been a terrible strain on Torm, though; he hasn't been able to get in any philandering, robbing cradles, or lightening purses for almost a tenday now."

The chorus of mock-sympathetic groans was momentarily deafening; Torm hung his head just long enough to drift close to Mirt and deftly snatch a bottle of wine from the Old Wolf's grasp.

Tessaril pursed her lips and wiggled a finger; the bottle promptly shot up out of Torm's fingers and curved down smoothly in a return journey to Mirt's hand. The Old Wolf chuckled, saluted her, and drank. As usual, he didn't bother with a glass.

"Tess," Shandril said in a low voice amid the general hilarity, "I don't mean to sound ungrateful, but I'm getting very restless here." She grinned. "Am I healed enough, yet?"

The Lord of Eveningstar smiled at her. "I think you are," she replied, "and I've something to show you." Tessaril led her through several rooms into the small, cozy, tapestry-hung bedroom Shandril had adopted during her stay in the Hidden House. There, she indicated a window.

Shandril looked at her curiously. "I've looked out it many times," she said, "but it always shows the same thing." She turned to the window—and saw the scene she expected to see.

It was winter outside the panes she was looking through. She could feel the cold coming off the glass. She was looking at a crossroads, somewhere, with high banks and bare-limbed trees all around. As always, there was snow, falling softly and endlessly. In its midst, where the roads met, stood a leaning stone marker with letters up and down the sides. Whenever Shandril stared at the stone pillar, she had the curious impression it was looking back at her.

She turned to Tessaril. "That's what I always see. . . . Where is it?"

"Another world entirely," her hostess replied softly. "But that's not what I want you to see. Have you ever tried to picture someone while standing at this window?"

Shandril stared at her, and then looked at the window and frowned.

Snow swirled outside the glass for a moment and seemed to turn to fog—and then, through a slowly widening gap in the smoky swirling, she saw Gorstag and Lureene sitting wearily in the taproom of *The Rising Moon*. Hot mugs stood by their hands, and they were smiling at each other. Lureene's bare feet—dirty, as usual—were propped one on each of Gorstag's massive shoulders, and he was gently and deftly massaging one of her calves with his powerful hands. Shandril smiled, and found her eyes full of tears.

Tessaril put a hand on her shoulder. "They're well and happy, yes." She stroked Shandril's hair gently. "Are you sorry you ever left the *Moon?*"

Shandril looked up at her. "Once I would have answered you very differently, but—no, I'm not sorry." She laughed shortly. "I always wondered what adventure would be like, and what the other Dales looked like . . . and now I know."

Tessaril nodded. "Look out my window again," she said softly. Shandril saw a very different scene this time.

It was a large but dark chamber with stone walls. A man in a black, high-collared robe sat at a table of ebony marble and seemed to speak to someone who wasn't there. His hands were clasped; Shandril realized suddenly that he was praying.

She turned to Tessaril in wonder. "Who is he?"

"If you plan to have any dealings with the Zhentarim," Tess told her, "you'll be facing the wits of this man: Fzoul Chembryl, High Priest of the Black Altar, the temple of Bane in Zhentil Keep—and leader of the Zhentarim at present. Watch him for a few days, please, before you leave the Hidden House. If you really must walk into the lair of a snake, 'tis best to know what he plans for you—and which is the safe way back out."

Shandril watched the black-robed man. "Where is he?" she asked softly.

"Someplace that surprises me a little," Tessaril replied. "He's not in Zhentil Keep at all—but instead in the Citadel of the Raven, well to the north. It's a huge fortress that the Zhents took over by trickery years ago. The room you're looking at is one I usually see when spying on Manshoon. It's in Wizards' Watch Tower." She smiled. "Some folk of the citadel call it the Old Fools' Tower."

"He's taking over Manshoon's items and places of power," Shandril said slowly, "now that I've destroyed Manshoon."

Tessaril looked sidelong at her and murmured, "Be not so sure Manshoon's gone, Shan. Others have been sure they destroyed him before."

Shandril turned. "Then where is he?"

Tessaril shrugged. "Perhaps you succeeded, at that. Fzoul's never been this bold before."

The man in black seemed to suddenly become aware of their scrutiny. He rose and came around the table toward them, his face angry. With glittering eyes, he suspiciously looked their way.

His hands came up, and Tessaril's face suddenly tightened. She took a wand from her belt and held it in front of Shandril, drawing her back a step from the window.

White lines of force sprang from Fzoul's hands, spiraling toward them across that far-off room—and then there was a sudden flash of blinding white. The window in front of them suddenly burst asunder. Glass shards flew in all directions, parting in front of Tessaril's wand as if before the prow of a ship.

In the empty, dark frame, only smoking ruin was left. The two women stood together looking at it for a long moment, and then sighed heavily.

Amid the broken glass that scrunched underfoot as they moved was something slippery. Shandril bent to look at the floor. Molten glass from the window had already hardened into droplets on the flagstones. A few were rather beautiful; they knelt to look at them together. Tessaril touched one, and then snatched scorched fingers back from it.

"I'm sorry about your window," Shandril said as the Lord of Eveningstar sucked her burned fingertips. "But there's nothing to keep me here longer, now. I'd like to strike at this Fzoul right away."

Tessaril sat up and looked at her gravely. "Shan, you're not ready yet."

Shandril nodded, smiled softly, and inclined her head toward the ruined window. "Neither," she said quietly, "is he."

Sixteen

BLOOD, BLADES, AND BITTER WORDS

Some kings sit upon more bloody thrones than this one, mind. When they talk business, 'tis all blood, blades, and bitter words.

Mirt the Moneylender
Wanderings With Quill and Sword
Year of Rising Mist

 "Ill-prepared Fzoul may or may not be," the Lord of Eveningstar said quietly, "but if you rush in without plans and swords at your side, you will certainly be ill-prepared—and doomed."

"I think not," Shandril replied, eyes flashing. "Forgive me, Tess, but that's where you—and Storm, and everyone else except maybe Elminster—make a mistake. You think of going up against Zhentil Keep with an army. That sort of thing the Zhents know well. They've had much practice smashing down such attacks. I'll do much better if I go alone."

She strode to the bedroom closet and took out her battered pack. The few clothes she had left hung forlornly above it. With a determined air, she started to take them down.

"Alone? It'll mean your *death,* Shan." Tessaril shook her head. "Aren't you even going to take Narm and Mirt with you?"

"No," Shandril said quietly. "You and Storm just gave him back to me—I'm never going to lose him again if I can help it. I'm certainly not going to drag him to his certain death." She turned, a patched and dirt-stained gown in her hands, and added with the ghost of a smile, "And I can't sneak anywhere or do anything agile without a lot of noise if I'm saddled with the Old Wolf."

An involuntary smile came and went across Tessaril's features. "I'm not sure he'd be pleased to hear that," she said slyly. "Shall I go tell him?"

"*No!*" Shandril whirled and took the Lord of Eveningstar by the shoulders, flames leaping in her eyes. "Don't tell any of them, or I'll never be able to go."

Her hands fell away, and she stepped back, drew a deep breath, and then looked up at the lord.

"Forgive me, Tess—after all you've done for me, I hate to—to do this. But I *must* go, now, while I still have nerve enough. Before Fzoul's arranged things just as he wants them and I'm doomed to die in the thirtieth trap he set for me, or the sixty-fifth ambush, or the—"

"Shandril," Tessaril said, looking into her eyes, "calm down, and *think*—is this wise? Well, is it?"

Spellfire blazed in the depths of Shandril's eyes, which were so close to hers that Tessaril gasped, shuddered, and drew back, face pinched in pain.

Shandril gulped. She let go of her and turned her head away. "I'm sorry, Tess—I didn't mean to hurt you. I'm as dangerous to you as to my foes." Tears shone in her eyes as she turned back to the white-faced Lord of Eveningstar. Impulsively, Shandril threw her arms around Tessaril and kissed her. "You must realize, Tess—wisdom is something for priests, and sages, and wizards, and—normal folk. It's no good to me."

"Are you that lonely, Shan?" Tessaril whispered, holding her.

Shandril angrily shook tears away and said, "No. Not anymore. You—and Mirt, and Elminster, and Storm, and the knights—and most of all, Narm—have given me friends along my road. That's why I must go up against the Zhentarim *now*. If I run and hide again, they'll come after you and all my other friends, to draw me out into battle . . . like they did to those poor soldiers at Thundarlun."

She stuffed the gown into her pack in a wadded, wrinkled mass and said angrily, "I have all this *power*—and I can't do anything with it but fend off wizards who toy with me, attacking whenever they feel especially cruel. What good is spellfire if I can't strike at *them* when *I* want to?"

"Shandril," the Lord of Eveningstar whispered. "Be careful. Very careful. The last time I heard words like that, they came from the lips of the sorceress who trapped you in Myth Drannor—Symgharyl Maruel."

"The Shadowsil?"

Tessaril nodded. "Whom you slew."

Shandril shook her head angrily. "I am *not* like her. Never. She enjoyed killing."

"Do you?"

Shandril stared at her, white-lipped. Then she bent forward, eyes blazing again. "Get me to that citadel!" she snapped. "*Now!*"

"Or?" Tessaril stared sadly into her eyes. "Will you use spellfire on me?" she asked quietly, sitting motionless. "Here I am," she added, gesturing at her breast. "Strike me down." Unshed tears glimmered in her eyes as she added softly, "Like the lich lord did."

Shandril snarled in frustration. Flames chased briefly around one of her hands as she clenched it into a fist. "No," she said, turning away, "I will not—and you know it." She drew breath, let it out in a shuddering sigh, and then asked quietly, "Must I beg you to help me, Tess?"

"No," Tessaril said quietly. "I just don't want to lose a friend so quickly. . . . I'll be sending you to your doom."

"Please," Shandril hissed. "Just do it!"

"Why?"

Shandril swallowed. "For the first time in my life," she said, in a voice that trembled, "I want to be *free!* Spellfire has ruled me—and I'll never learn to master it unless I use it as and when I want to . . . just once." She glared at the Lord of Eveningstar and shouted, "Weren't you ever young? Didn't you ever want to do as you pleased?"

Tessaril shook her head. "That's no good reason," she said with quiet scorn. "Every child wants to have her own way."

"I've another reason," Shandril said coldly, bringing her chin up. "The Zhents killed Delg. My last companion from the Company of the Bright Spear, a Harper who laid down his life for me. I swore to avenge him. And my unborn child. And by the gods, *I will!*"

Her shout echoed in the small room. She stared at the Lord of Eveningstar, eyes blazing, panting with emotion, her backpack twisted and forgotten in her hands.

Tessaril nodded slowly, her eyes grave. "All right," she whispered, voice unsteady. "Stand back. I'll aid you."

"You will?"

Sorrow stole like a shadow across the Lord of Eveningstar's face. "I know what it is like to be ruled by the need for revenge, Shan. You must be set free—as I was, long ago."

"You were?"

Tessaril looked at her, face a white mask, and said in a voice of iron, "I will not say more. We *all* have our limits."

Shandril looked at the lord in sympathy, and then her eyes slowly hardened. "Help me, then—and no more tricks, like your wine."

The Lord of Eveningstar lifted her chin, and said, "I'll not betray you, Shan. Ever." She took a deep, trembling breath, managed a little smile, and went on. "I dare not teleport you into so small and crowded a room as the one Fzoul was in—and Wizards' Watch Tower has magical traps built into it to prevent teleportation in or out. I'll send you to the nearest courtyard, Spell Court."

She waved a hand, and an image of a tall, many-spired city appeared in midair across the room. In the foreground was a large, flagstone-paved open area.

"Spell Court?"

Tessaril nodded. "Yes. The entire citadel is linked fortresses and courtyards. Strike quickly, save your fire for Zhents and not their buildings—and when you need to hide, get up into the highest spires you can find and look for wizards' spell-casting chambers. Many have powerful warding spells against magical scrying and also hold stores of healing potions; Zhentarim who've been too bold and gotten hurt run to them when they must."

Shandril stared at the scene and said slowly, her voice almost a whisper, "I want to slay at least five wizards and see fear on Fzoul's face—Delg's life must be worth at least that much. Is the large tower Wizards' Watch?"

Tessaril nodded and sighed. "Yes. Are you certain you want to do this, Shan? Now?"

Shandril turned and simply nodded.

Tessaril bowed her head in response. "Go with my share of Tymora's luck, Shan." She raised her hand, murmured a word, and touched Shandril.

Then Tessaril stood alone in the room with the broken

window, her hands balled into fists. Before she realized how tightly her trembling hands were clenched, blood was running down her palms from where her nails cut into flesh. She turned and ran as she had never run before, racing back through the rooms of the Hidden House.

Abruptly, Shandril was somewhere else. Spell Court, yes, by the look of it: a grim, gray courtyard of dusty stones. Spired buildings rose all around her, the largest one at her back. She turned and stared up, recognizing the tower she was seeking.

She strode toward it, ignoring the dark-armored warriors who stood at its gates. They frowned and reached for their swords—and then shrank back away from her, moving hastily sideways along the wall. Shandril stared at their frightened faces and then glanced behind her to see what they were staring at.

All around her, in a dark and deadly ring, beholders were rising up silently. She'd teleported into a trap.

Shandril swallowed hard. Her eyes began to flame. This had been her choice, well enough. "May all the gods damn you," she said, voice trembling. Her words rose into a sudden scream—a scream that spewed fire as red dragons do.

"Damn you all!" she spat amid flames. Suddenly she was too bright to look at. Flames of death reached out for the eye tyrants around her.

* * * * *

Torm's tabletop dance in imitation of Elminster came to an abrupt halt as the Lord of Eveningstar burst into the room. "She's gone," Tessaril said, panting. "Gone to kill all the Zhentarim."

Everyone gaped at her, wide-eyed. Narm stood up so

fast his chair bounced on the floor behind him. The young mage stared at the Lord of Eveningstar and shouted, "*Why* did you let her go?"

Tessaril Winter looked at him, her eyes dark with sorrow, and said quietly, "I didn't let her go. I sent her there myself."

"Spellfire," Torm said bitterly. "She threatened you."

Tessaril looked at him and shook her head. "No. She was a caged animal, Torm. I had to open the gate and let her out."

Narm stared at her, face wild, and then burst into tears. "She'll *die!*" he sobbed, pounding the table with his fists. "She'll die—and I can't *save her!*" He looked up at Tessaril through streaming tears and struggled to control his voice. "Where is she?"

Torm snatched up a goblet. "Drink this, Narm! You'll feel better."

Storm shook her head. "It's not the universal cure you think it is, Torm." The bard put her arms comfortingly on Narm's shoulders, but the young mage seemed not to feel them.

"Where is she?" Narm almost screamed, and then went on, voice trembling, "We must go to her. *Now!*"

Storm looked at the Lord of Eveningstar. "Have you spells enough?"

Torm asked quickly, "And what should I do?"

"Belt up before any more time's wasted," Mirt said roughly, "and ye, Tess, go and get me one or two o' them healing potions ye keep stowed away. *Hurry!*"

They all looked at him, and then Tessaril nodded and rushed out. Mirt drew his sword and slashed at the air. The blade gleamed in the light.

Narm's reddened eyes followed it, and the young mage clenched his jaw. "What's your plan?"

The Old Wolf grinned at him but said nothing. Then

Mirt's smile turned rather grim as he brought out the notched and battered axe that had been Delg's. He hefted it in his other hand. "Where're those potions?" he bellowed.

Tessaril ran in, hair streaming behind her in her haste. "Here," she gasped, thrusting two steel vials into his hand. Mirt jammed them into his belt, sighed heavily, and gestured at Narm. "Guard him here, lass."

Tessaril nodded, and came forward to kiss him. "Guard yourself, Old Wolf," she said, eyes bright. "I'd like to see you—alive—again."

Mirt laughed, accepted her quick peck on his grizzled cheek, and said, "Ye will, lass. Ye will.

"If I've got to die," he roared at them all, "I'd like to have a kiss to remember, at the last. Pray to Tymora for me!"

Torm spread his arms pleadingly. "Kiss me, Old Wolf," he trilled in mocking imitation of a swooning maiden. "Oh, kiss *me!*"

Mirt glared at him and backhanded his almost empty goblet off the table. It sailed into Torm's face. The thief was still sputtering when the old merchant bowed to them all, murmured something, and vanished.

Narm looked around the room and said grimly, "Can *everyone* here cast a teleport spell except me?"

Storm gathered him into her arms. "That was no teleport, Narm. Do you remember the gem Shandril found in Tethgard—the rogue stone?"

Narm nodded, frowning, tears still bright on his cheeks. "Delg and Mirt knew something about it that they weren't telling."

"Undoubtedly," Storm said dryly. "Mirt put it there for her to find. It was prepared by Khelben the Blackstaff and linked to a spell that many a thief has used down the years, which lets one who speaks the right words teleport to wherever the stone is, long after the spell is cast. Mirt's at Shandril's side right now."

Narm looked at her and asked very softly, "And why not me?"

"You'd be killed, idiot," Torm told him, "unless you've learned a god's ransom of spells since I saw you last. Those Zhentarim'd blast you to ash before you could draw breath to cast your first spell."

Narm stared at him.

"Blunt," Storm told the young mage gently, "but true."

"Besides, you can't follow her until I memorize another teleport spell," Tessaril said, "and I'm reluctant to do that."

"Why not?" Narm almost screamed.

Tessaril turned her back. "I won't send you to certain death," she said, voice trembling.

"You sent *Shan!*"

"I—couldn't stop her, Narm. I can stop you."

Narm stared at her back, fresh tears on his face. "Let me be with Shan!" he cried in anguish. "*Please!*"

Sadly, Tessaril shook her head and turned to meet his gaze with dark eyes that held tears of their own. "Shandril and Mirt can both withstand far more than you can, Narm. You'd wind up a hostage in Fzoul's hands, one he could use to compel Shandril to surrender. Then spellfire would be his, after all."

Narm's eyes blazed. Abruptly he whirled away from her gaze to stamp the length of the chamber and back again. "I should be there!" he protested and turned away again.

"Gods look down damnation," he cursed. Then he pivoted slowly to face the Lord of Eveningstar again. "There's another reason, isn't there?" he asked softly, almost whispering.

Tessaril nodded. "Shandril may fall under Fzoul's control, or be twisted by Zhentarim magic—or spellfire itself—once she uses it in unbridled anger rather than to defend. If she becomes something akin to a Zhentarim, we must try to control her power by using you as hostage to her good behavior." She turned away, sighed, and said to the wall, "As Manshoon would have."

* * * * *

Mirt saw swirling mists for a moment, and then his boots struck something hard. Flagstones. He staggered, and waved his weapons out of habit. They struck nothing.

He stood in a courtyard somewhere in the Citadel of the Raven—he could see raven banners flapping overhead. There were folk screaming and running through the courtyard nearby, and the ground suddenly heaved underneath him. Mirt crouched to keep his balance. He watched in amazement as flagstones rippled and heaved, as if a giant wave were passing underneath them.

All around him soldiers were fleeing, running away from a lone figure standing not far away, near the gates of a tall tower. Shandril, of course; the spell on the gem was set to deliver him about twenty paces from her. Mirt's eyes widened as he saw what she was fighting: a ring of beholders.

Ye gods! Couldn't the lass just have a nice, comfortable fight with half-a-dozen evil archmages? Or a dragon or two? Liches, now—aye, liches were good, even mind flayers. . . .

The Old Wolf was running toward her by then, boots skidding on the broken flagstones of the courtyard. What use he'd be to her, the gods alone knew; he could barely see the lass now, outlined in a white halo of fire. Streamers of spellfire lashed out from it—and beholders died, or reeled back in a shower of sparks, blackened and burning.

The beholders drifted above her like angry dragons,

baffled. They were used to foiling the magic of foes with
the large eyes in their bodies—but spellfire tore through
their anti-magic fields as if nothing were there. They had
magic of their own that lashed out from the snakelike eyestalks writhing atop their bodies. But spellfire drained
away or boiled into nothingness the rays from their eyes,
and it stabbed out at them in return. When their own dis-
integrating gazes were not brought to bear quickly
enough, spellfire lashed through their defenses, and they
died.

The Old Wolf's ears were ringing by the time he got
close to her; the din of shrieking, air-ripping, crashing
magic was incredible. A particularly violent spellblast
shook the courtyard and threw him to his knees—and
that saved his life. A beholder that would have crushed
him with its fall crashed down in front of him instead,
body blazing. Mirt got a good whiff of the reek of burning
beholder, and was violently, uncontrollably sick. As he
raised his head, the eye tyrant's body plates shattered
from the heat within, and their darkened shards bounced
past him.

Mages of the Zhentarim saw Mirt, a lone man in the
midst of that field of ruin and magical chaos, but they
could not have done anything to aid or attack him, even if
they'd known who he was: a whirling spellstorm had
begun to form over the courtyard, created by the struggle
between magic and spellfire. Mages who tried to cast
spells screamed, their minds burned to cinders—or they
watched in horror as their magic went wild, creating mis-
shapen flowers or rains of frogs or worse.

Spell-lightning arced repeatedly from the gathering
storm cloud to the tallest spires of the citadel around,
humming and crackling. Men plunged to their deaths
from those heights, cooked alive, or fell into piles of bone
and ash where they stood. And still the battle raged on.

Such a mighty outpouring of wild magic had to go somewhere—and it did:

Far to the west of the citadel, near the Border Forest, a great meadow of red-petaled flowers quivered, bowed slowly in a spreading ripple that washed from one end of the scarlet field to the other, and then straightened again. One after another, the flowers all quietly turned blue.

In the woods near the shaking citadel, along the foot of the Dragonspine Mountains, a small tree tore itself up bodily, scattering soil in all directions, and shot up into the sky. The branches of the trees around it splintered and crackled and were utterly destroyed by its passage. A startled satyr who looked up through the newly created clearing saw the tree heading west high in the air, tumbling and spinning as it went.

One of the smaller towers along the south wall of the citadel simply vanished. With a groan like a dying dragon, another citadel tower grew a crack as wide as a man's hand from top to bottom. At the same time, smoke billowed suddenly out of the highest windows of Wizards' Watch Tower, followed by stray bolts of lightning, shadowy apparitions, and many-hued, winking spell-sparks. Startled Zhentilar warriors, arming hastily in their barracks, found themselves floating near the ceiling, their flesh glowing a brilliant blue.

One of the flagpoles overlooking Spell Court toppled suddenly, sizzling from end to end with lightning. Beside it, a beholder suddenly caught fire and spun away into the sky northward. A moment later, the horizon was lit by a brilliant burst of flame as the distant beholder exploded.

Wheezing, Mirt found his feet again and lumbered across the courtyard. The aura of spellfire around Shandril was noticeably feebler now. She still stood tall and proud, hair lashing her shoulders as if a high wind raged around her, arms raised to hurl spellfire. Her eyes were two raging flames.

A horrible bubbling sound came to Mirt's ears from overhead. It erupted from a beholder that hung, smoking, in midair, its glazed eyes rolling wildly about on writhing, cooked eyestalks.

Mirt ran on. At the edges of the courtyard, now, he could see many armored Zhentilar soldiers coming out of doors and rushing about wildly. They began hacking at folk who fled past them toward those same doorways. Through the archways that led off Spell Court, Mirt saw soldiers pursuing citizens off down the streets, their swords raised. He began to wish Khelben had never given him that rogue stone.

There came crashing sounds from overhead, as if huge wine bottles were bursting. The Old Wolf looked up and saw balls of lightning forming in midair and streaming in all directions. The leaping lightning struck two beholders and drove them into each other. They reeled apart, and Shandril cut one of them in half with a ragged, faltering bolt of spellfire. Mirt looked on anxiously. She staggered as she brought both hands together and pointed them at the last eye tyrant, and for the first time in his long life, Mirt the Moneylender heard a beholder scream.

Shandril stood alone in the courtyard, her hands smoking, as the last of the beholders crashed to the earth in flames.

"Magnificent, lass! I've never seen such power. Well done!" Like a joyful buffalo, Mirt galloped toward Shandril through the wreckage of beholder bits and fallen stones.

She turned and looked at him, and it was a moment before her dull eyes lit with recognition. Shandril smiled wanly, lifted a hand that trembled—and then her eyes went dark, and she fell to the ground in a limp and sudden heap.

Mirt's old legs got him there a breath or two later. Shandril lay on her face on the stones. Mirt rolled her over; she was still breathing. Thank the gods!

Then he heard shouts, and the clank and clatter of metal. He looked up from Shandril's crumpled form, then slowly all around.

The Old Wolf crouched at the center of a grim, closing circle of Zhentilar warriors. Their drawn blades flashed as they came, and Mirt saw teeth flash in smiles of relief as they realized they'd not have to fight the maid who brought down beholders.

Well, perhaps he shouldn't have thanked the gods all that loudly. The Old Wolf snarled his defiance, beard bristling, and waved his saber at them. None of them turned and fled. Mirt sighed, straightened, and then just waited as they slowly closed in.

* * * * *

Narm paced back and forth under Storm's watchful eye. "I wish I was with her, right now. I feel so *helpless!*" he burst out, hurling the words at Tessaril.

She sat at the far end of the chamber, staring at nothing. Her hands were in her lap, and they trembled.

"Lord Tessaril," Narm said again, urgently, striding nearer.

Storm got up, a warning in her eyes, and blocked his path to the Lord of Eveningstar.

They both heard Tessaril say softly, "I know just how you feel, Narm. Go with Torm and get a good meal into you, whether you feel hungry now or not. Come back when you're done—and I'll have your teleport spell ready."

Narm could hardly believe he'd heard her say the words. "Thank you! *Thank you!*"

"I can't let one go, and then build a cage around its mate," Tessaril said softly, "but you may not thank me so fervently in the end, Narm—nor may that end be far off."

Narm bowed to her and said, "That's a chance I'll take, Lady—one all who live must take. My thanks for giving me the freedom to take it."

As he and Torm went out, Storm and Tessaril watched the young mage go. Then they looked at each other; new respect for Narm Tamaraith shone in both their gazes.

Seventeen

BUSINESS BEFORE PLEASURE

Now in that grim, gray city are women called pleasure-queens, *who keep house amid furs and silks and perfumes and have mastered the art of snaring a man in the street with one dark glance of promise. Disgusting enchantresses—they're the only reason I ever ride north of Selgaunt, I tell you.*

Oblut Thoim, Master Merchant of Teziir
Letters to a Sheltered Son
Year of the Striking Falcon

 Mirt waved his saber; sunlight flashed and glimmered along its edge. More than one Zhentilar eyed that blade warily. The fat man obviously knew how to use it, and the bare fist that held it was as large as some men's heads. Yet there were over sixty blades set against it, and nothing to protect the old one's back. The outcome was certain; he and Shandril were doomed.

A Zhentilar officer muttered, "Easy, now—strike all at once, and we'll run him through from all sides like a pleasure-queen's pincushion."

301

There were scattered chuckles as the Zhentilar took
the last few steps they'd need. Mirt stared around at
them, wild-eyed, sword waving desperately. And then he
smiled and flung himself backward, arching over Shandril's body. He raised his arm as the warriors rushed in,
and the plain brass ring on it flashed, once.

The air was suddenly full of whirling, deadly steel. As
the blood spattered him and the screams sounded all
around, Mirt drew back his arm and felt for the hilt of his
saber. Only a short time passed before the blades vanished again, but the screams ended even sooner. The
courtyard around him ran with blood; it looked like a
butcher's back-room floor.

Mirt grinned and clambered to his feet. "Handy things,
blade barriers," he said, surveying the carnage. His eyes
searched the walls for archers or overenthusiastic mages.
Tymora smiled on him, for once.

"Up, lass," Mirt growled, and plucked Shandril's limp
form up from the flagstones. He draped her over his
arms, his saber still held securely in one hand, and staggered across the courtyard, wheezing under his load.

The maid in his arms grew no lighter as he lumbered
out through an archway, down a lane strewn with bodies
of citizens the Zhents had slain, and turned left at the first
cross street. Smoke rose from shattered towers here and
there; fallen stone was everywhere, and priests and wizards rushed wildly in all directions, each accompanied by
a trotting bodyguard. "The high priest is dead!" one mage
shouted excitedly to another.

"Blasphemous nonsense!" another shrieked back, and
the two men's bodyguards surged into each other in a
crash and skirl of viciously plied weapons.

Whether Fzoul was dead or not, the spell-battle had
reduced the Zhents to a state of chaos.

Mirt was glad he saw no Zhentilar patrols as he made

his way down the ruined streets, turning right then left. He trotted down avenues and up short rises, and still no soldiers blocked his way. A few folk gave him startled glances, and one warrior did step out of a tavern as he passed. But the soldier took one look at the blood-covered warrior with a drawn sword and a woman dangling in his arms—Mirt gave him a fierce grin—and his face paled. He hastily drew back out of sight.

"Tymora, I owe you one—or even two," Mirt gasped, as he sighted the purple door he was looking for and crossed to it.

The door was closed, and the iron-caged lamps on either side of it had burned low. But Mirt kicked out hard, and the door boomed satisfyingly. Once, twice, and a third and fourth time his boot found its mark.

His toes were beginning to feel a little the worse for wear, but as he drew back his foot for another assault, the door swung open as far as its safe-chains would allow. A painted, pouting lady looked disapprovingly out. She surveyed Mirt up and down—blood, Shandril, and all—and her expression did not improve.

"We've had all the trade we can handle for the night, thank you—you'll just have to come back morrow-even, and—"

Mirt handed her his sword. "Here—hold this."

The lady hesitated, then took it, staggering for a moment under the weight of the old, massive saber. Mirt shifted Shandril more fully into his freed hand, and shoved his other hand under the pleasure-queen's nose. The small silver harp winked at her, catching the light. Her eyes rose slowly from it to his blood-spattered face, and then she undid the chains hurriedly, whispering, "Come in!"

* * * * *

"Oh, Great Dark One, lord of the heights and depths, hear us!"

Elthaulin was in his element, intoning the ritual in the deepest, grandest voice he could manage, his words rolling into the farthest echoing corners of the Grand Chancel of the Black Altar.

"Lord Bane, hear us," the thunderous murmur of half a hundred underpriests and postulants answered.

Elthaulin raised his hands slowly, trembling for maximum effect. "Bane, hear us!"

"Lord Bane, hear us," came the massed response. Elthaulin let the dark purple faerie fire radiance ripple into view at the tips of his fingers and crawl slowly down his upraised arms. There were a few gasps from the assembled worshippers; the upperpriest hid his smile. That trick got some of the innocents, every time.

He drew breath for the Great Invocation. Only Fzoul could speak it, by tradition, but Fzoul had neglected to forbid Elthaulin from doing it in his absence, and Lord Bane would not be pleased by its omission. Then he stopped in confusion, peering at the back of the chancel. Underpriests had left their places by the doors and were running in the gloom of the sanctuary, stopping to bend over priests in the congregation. Priests were rising and leaving their places.

What is going on?

In shock, he realized he'd asked that question aloud—and grins were forming on more than one of the uplifted faces below. Fury washed over him, and Elthaulin strode to the edge of the raised dais and sent his voice booming out over the confusion. "Who dares disturb the worship of Bane, Lord Over All?" Abruptly he recognized the face of one of the priests hurrying up the central aisle, and his expression grew pale.

Fzoul snapped at him in a voice that carried to the far corners of the chancel, "Oh, stop that nonsense, Elthaulin. Bane has heard you and is deeply appreciative. This service of worship is now at an end. I need all priests of the rank of Trusted Servant or greater to assemble in the Robing Room. Watchful Brothers, guard the doors of the temple; all who have not taken the robes of Bane are to be escorted out. The Deadly Adepts are in charge. Haste—or perish!"

There were raised voices, and even screams, from the lay worshippers, but others left as slowly as they were allowed, enjoying the sight of priests of Bane actually *running* and looking startled and upset. Elthaulin let his faerie fire slowly fade, and he stood watching.

Fzoul turned on his heel without another word to his Priest of the Chancel, and headed for the Robing Room, priests thickly clustered around him.

Elthaulin kept his face carefully calm, but no one who looked at his eyes could have missed his murderous glare, directed at the retreating Fzoul. His dark eyes flamed almost as fiercely as the Black Hand of Bane behind him over the lesser altar. The altar was giving off black fire, the first direct sign from Dread Lord Bane in over a year. It was a pity no one noticed it.

* * * * *

In the Robing Room, Fzoul turned and held up his hands for silence. His head still throbbed painfully; the wild spellblast that had brought his bookcase crashing down on him had been one of the last hurled by the beholders in Spell Court. By the time he'd come to on the floor beside his desk, it was all over—the maid Shandril had vanished, beholders lay dead everywhere, and the citadel was in tumult.

Fzoul watched coldly as some of the priests in the rear of the rushing throng ran into the backs of their fellows before they realized the room was packed. When order and silence held sway, Fzoul said, "A terrible threat to our Brotherhood is attacking the Citadel of the Raven. I need all of you to help; the eye tyrants were in grave trouble when I left."

If anything, the hush grew even greater. Fzoul could even hear the nearest Brother breathing.

The high priest looked around with cold eyes and added, "The Lord Manshoon recently established a gate magically linking the citadel with the High Tower. All of you, come with me now. We're going to a place normally reserved for our brothers of Art—the Wizards' Watch Tower. Beware—touch nothing and work no magic without my prior approval. There may be many magical defenses. We go to gain what magic we can seize, not to be caught in magical traps or mistaken castings. I shall go through the gate first. Orders are to be followed without question from this moment on—death shall be dealt on the spot for disobedience."

He turned toward the nearest door and, without another word, led the way to the gate. Time enough for them to learn about spellfire when they were dying under it.

* * * * *

There was murmuring all around. Shandril seemed to be rising up through warm water toward a lighted place. Not far away, someone was talking. Soothing female tones, mingled with a deeper man's growl—she knew that voice! Mirt!

Shandril opened her eyes and found herself looking at a truly amazing painted ceiling. Her eyes hadn't wandered very far along its curves and colors before she felt her cheeks burning. Where *was* she?

She turned her head. Lacy undergarments hung on a rail on the back of a half-open door—with a whip dangling beside them. The voices were coming in through the doorway from somewhere below. She lay still in the lush boudoir and listened.

"I wish I'd seen that," came one wistful female voice.

"Ye could hardly have missed it," Mirt protested. "Beholders crashing from the sky, lightning flashing from tower to tower right over ye, here! Ye—"

The female voice that cut in then sounded rather crisp. "We were *busy*, Old Wolf. Busy at something that, if done well, rather holds sway over our attention and senses. Or have you never known the attentions of a lady?"

"No, Belarla," Mirt rumbled, "I could never afford ladies, myself. I always had to settle for women!"

He was answered by one dry chuckle, and one sniff.

Then Belarla's voice said, "Pass the ointment, Oelae—I feel rubbed raw. Aren't those towels dry *yet*, Old Wolf?"

"They're hurrying, they're hurrying," Mirt said. "I'm not used to thy stone irons . . . and besides, these towels got so excited, sliding over ye—"

"Enough! It may surprise you, Mirt, but when you've done this for a year or three, you've heard all the jokes and smart remarks so many times over that any feeble humor they might once have had is gone—*quite* gone."

"Don't ye *love* me any more?" Mirt asked in mock sobs.

"That's another remark of the same sort," was the dry reply. "Hurry up with those towels . . . we've got to be ready to leave the moment your maid is awake—or if she wakes not, whene'er we dare move her."

"Where to?" Mirt rumbled.

"We've got to get her out of the city," the other pleasure-queen said. "There's no place to hide a woman in a house of pleasure."

"Don't ye have cellars?"

"The busiest places of all," Belarla told him crisply. "Too many men like to pretend they're in a dungeon—gods know why! No, Oelaerone's right, Old Wolf. We've got to move her from here. Half the soldiers in the citadel will be in and out of here by next morning. My younger girls start coming in just after evenfeast—and the first customers hot on their heels."

"Or something," Oelaerone said quickly before Mirt could. "I've been in better places to defend against the Zhentarim than this old breeze-box, too."

"If the Zhentarim discover Shandril's here," Belarla responded, "it's not defending the place we'll have to worry about—it's dying well in the few breaths we'll have left."

A chill ran through Shandril. Here were yet more folk she'd pulled into danger. Mirt must have followed her to the citadel, somehow, and rescued her . . . she had hazy memories of seeing him running toward her after the last beholder had finally gone down. He'd brought her to a house of pleasure. . . . Typical of Mirt.

Her lips quirked, but she was too horrified to smile. These two ladies could be dead before night fell if the Zhentarim found her here. . . . And who can hide from the magic archmages wield?

The voices downstairs went on. As quietly as she could, Shandril swung her legs over the side of the couch. She felt empty and weak inside, and her arms and one hip were stiff, but she was whole and everything moved properly. Someone had sponged her face and hands clean, but she was still dressed. Experimentally, she held up a hand and gathered her will.

A dull ache instantly smote the back of her head from within—but her hand flamed with spellfire. She was ready for a fight. Stretching and wiggling her fingers, Shandril gathered her courage and slipped out of the room. If she

could help it, she'd never bring death to any friends again
. . . the way Delg had found death. Her lips moved in a
soundless prayer: gods will it so.

* * * * *

With the air of a man who had expected to ruin a task
but had triumphed instead, Mirt passed warm, fluffy towels to Oelaerone. She merely raised amused eyebrows,
and Mirt harrumphed at her and reached for the bottle of
wine they'd brought him. He took a swig of the ruby red
Westgate vintage, sighed lustily, and took another. His lips
were still at the mouth of the raised bottle when he saw
movement out of the corner of one eye—Shandril, passing the doorway like a wind-driven ghost, on her way to
the front entrance.

Mirt choked, coughed good Westgate Ruby all down
the front of his clothes, and bellowed, "Shan! *Stop!*" The
answering bang of the door told him she was out onto the
street. Mirt groaned, pulled on his boots, stamping in
haste, and snatched up his saber as he hurried for the
door. "She'll be needing me," he said.

Belarla looked at the drawn blade and reached under
the table.

There was a snapping sound as she twisted something
free, followed by a grating noise as she slid a long, needle-
like blade into view. It gleamed blue in her hand. "Where
are we bound?" she asked calmly.

"The Wizards' Watch Tower," Mirt rumbled from the
doorway.

Belarla raised her eyebrows and sighed. "Ah, well," she
said, as they hurried out. "I was getting tired of Zhentilar
men, anyway."

"A good life, while it lasted," Oelaerone agreed, slam-
ming the purple door behind them. "Lead on, Old Wolf."

* * * * *

The time for secrecy was past. Fzoul strode across the antechamber. By the flickering light of the gate behind him, he pushed the eyes of the gasping maiden carved on the wall. Her ivory tongue slid out from between the parted lips, and he pressed it down with one finger. There was a dull grating sound, and the rest of the carved wall—satyrs, nymphs, and all—slid inward and sideways, revealing a dark opening. Fzoul snapped his fingers, and glowfire swirled into being around that hand. Holding his arm high like a torch to light the way, he set off down the secret passage, excited underpriests hurrying behind him.

The passage was long, cold, and damp. Where it dipped in the center of its run, shallow puddles glistened on the floor. Fzoul ignored them, and the illusion of the lich rising from its coffin to stare at the intruders. He strode on past it—and right through the stone wall behind it. The passage continued into a round room somewhere beneath Wizards' Watch Tower.

Fzoul set off briskly up the spiral stair there, passing the many closed doors that led off its steps. He climbed round and round until he was quite out of breath—and the stair ended at a door inset with a palely glowing white orb. He touched the door, hissed the word that opened it, and the light in the orb faded away. When it was dark and the door was safe to open, he waved a silent order to the priests behind him. Strong, eager hands slid the heavy stone sideways, and Fzoul stepped into the spell chamber he'd met Manshoon in, once or twice.

A man, the only occupant of the room, turned from studying glowing symbols on the floor. Orbs of shimmering glass floated above the runes, drifting in slow orbits above the symbols they were linked to. Fzoul came to an abrupt halt and said coldly, "I did not expect to find you here, Sarhthor."

Sarhthor nodded, not smiling. "I could say the same of you, Lord Priest." He waved at the floor. "I've been working spells, trying to trace the maid Shandril—she must be in the citadel still, cloaked by the scrying defenses we've built up so carefully. Otherwise, I'd surely have found her by now."

"Have you set the magelings to searching in person?"

"That's why you find me alone," Sarhthor replied calmly. "My time for spitting orders is past."

Fzoul gave him a sharp look but said nothing. The high priest looked down at the winking runes inset into the floor, and up at the orrery turning ponderously overhead, and finally said, "Well, I suggest we begin to work together, tracking Shandril by magic." He turned. "Ansiber—you and all other Brothers of Striking Hand rank and greater, attend here to me. The rest of you—split into sixes and eights and search the citadel. Instant elevation to the Inner Ring awaits any priest who brings Shandril to me alive. Rouse the citadel against her!"

There was an excited murmur and a rushing of robes until only a dozen or so priests remained. Fzoul looked at them, nodded, and said to Sarhthor, "Have you any water?"

"The quenching-pool, there; the drinking-ewer, there— and, somewhat used, in the chamber pot behind that screen."

"The pool will do." The Master of the Black Altar turned to the priests. "Attend!" he commanded, and they hastened to his side. He pointed at the pool and ordered, "Prepare it for scrying."

The priests bent to their work, and soon a thin, dripping disc of water as large across as the span of seven men's arms floated at waist height in the spell chamber, rippling and glowing faintly.

As he stepped forward to look into it, Fzoul smiled.

"She cannot escape us now," he said in satisfaction.

Beside him, Sarhthor shrugged. "I've thought that before. Yet perhaps this time, we can make sure."

Eighteen

SEWERS, SWORDS, AND SPELLS

Gone to the city to seek great adventure, is he? I wager he'll see more of stinking sewers and swords in the dark than ever he does of splendor and spells.

> Overheard in a tavern, and quoted by
> Tasagar Winterwind, Scribe to the Guilds of Selgaunt
> ***Talk of the Taverns***
> Year of the Lost Helm

 By the time he caught up with Shandril, three streets away, Mirt was puffing like an old and irritated walrus. He came around a corner to find her surrounded by wary Zhentilar warriors. A patrol, by the black backside of Bane! Well, he reflected sourly, the best thief that ever lived couldn't wander the streets of the citadel and avoid them forever.

The soldiers must have stepped out of doorways and side alleys; they'd managed to form a ring around Shandril. She was walking unhurriedly on, toward two anxious-looking Zhentilar whose blades were raised. The others were drawing in around her as she walked, their swords ready.

Finally one of the warriors in her path said uncertainly, "We have you, woman. Kneel and surrender, in the name of the Raven!"

Shandril raised a hand and burned him like a torch. The other soldiers backed away, blanching. Oily smoke rose up from the huddled form in the street—and then Zhentish boots echoed on the cobblestones as they broke and fled. As they went, they tugged horns from their belts, and ragged calls went up, echoing off the grim towers around.

"By my halidom!" Mirt snarled. "Now ye've roused the whole place." He laid a hand on Shandril's shoulder.

She whirled. Spellfire blazed before his eyes, and he danced away with a startled cry. Shandril looked stricken. "Sorry, Mirt—I didn't mean to . . ."

"But you almost did, anyway," he growled. "Come *on*, lass—we've got to get out of here before all the Zhentarim in Faerûn come down on us."

Shandril shook her head, her face white to the lips. "I'm not running anymore. Go if you wish—I'll stay and fight, as long as there're fools to challenge me."

Mirt rolled his eyes. "Ye'll find no shortage of battle, then." He looked over his shoulder at the two Harper women and moved his fingers in a certain sign.

The pleasure-queens traded glances. Belarla swallowed, looked at Oelaerone with an unspoken prayer in her eyes, and glided forward with silent speed. From behind she slid one slim, skilled hand over Shandril's nose and mouth, and her other arm around Shandril's throat.

Shandril stiffened. Spellfire flashed, and Belarla hissed in pain as it cooked her arm and fingers. She was sobbing by the time Shandril's eyes dimmed and she went limp. The Harper made sure she was senseless, and then lowered her gently to the street.

The Old Wolf bent over Belarla. Tears of pain ran down her cheeks as she knelt on the cobbles, Shandril across her lap. Mirt handed two steel vials to Oelaerone, gesturing for her to pour it down Belarla's throat. "Healing potions," he said gruffly. "See that she drinks them both—every drop."

Then he scooped up Shandril, grunted as he heaved her onto his shoulders, and said gruffly, "Thanks, Belarla. Myrintara should be able to set things right for you again, if we can reach her."

Belarla swallowed, shuddered as the potions took effect, and said faintly, "I—I can manage." Then her gaze rose from an empty vial to fix Mirt with a different pained expression. " 'By my halidom'?"

Mirt spread his hands. "Eh . . . heroes say it in all the best bardic tales," he said sheepishly.

Belarla made a rude sound. Oelaerone pointed silently.

Mirt glanced along her arm and saw perhaps twenty— no, more—Zhentilar warriors approaching warily down the street. He eyed them and asked quietly, "Know you any hiding-holes? They'd come in mighty helpful, about now."

"Isn't it a bit late to be thinking about that?" Belarla asked him, but Oelaerone pointed again—this time, at the stones under their feet.

"The sewers," she said simply, then turned. "This way."

They hurried after her shapely form. She led through a short alley and then across a broad street. Another alley led them out onto a long, winding lane. Oelaerone turned down it, ducked into a warehouse, and slipped through a dim maze of high-stacked crates and curious men, to yet another street.

Mirt shifted Shandril over one shoulder, drew his sword, and trotted after her.

Belarla watched behind.

As Oelaerone crept into another alley, Belarla said in satisfaction, "We must have lost them by now—nicely done, Oelae."

They were all startled when a tall, burly Zhentarim mage appeared in their path on the next street. In addition to robes rolled up at the sleeve, the wizard wore a single metal gauntlet that winked with spell lights. For a moment, Mirt and the pleasure queens blinked abruptly at him. The street had been empty moments before.

The mage took one huge step and viciously swung his studded gauntlet backhanded at Oelaerone. She dived headlong to avoid being struck. He ignored her, striding on toward the Old Wolf and his burden.

Mirt raised the tip of his sword, but the wizard darted to the Old Wolf's burdened side, keeping Shandril between himself and Mirt's blade.

"It's past time for you to lie down and die, old man," the Zhentarim snarled contemptuously, leaning in to smash Mirt across the face with the gauntlet. The enchanted weapon was hard, and its magic numbed and froze the victim for an instant so that the full force of its blow struck home. Mirt staggered.

Belarla's blade sang in at the wizard. The sudden sparks of a protective spell spat and shimmered where the blade touched the wizard, then the knife tumbled away. The Zhentarim stiffened, hissed a word, and a web of radiant bolts flared out. Belarla reeled back, clutching her breast in pain, and fell heavily to her knees, her sword clattering on the cobbles.

Then the Zhent turned and ran after Mirt, grabbing at Shandril's dangling throat with the gauntlet. Mirt snarled and thrust with his blade, but Shandril's body hampered his weapon; he could not get a good strike at the mage without carving her, too. He lowered her to the ground so that he could battle this wizard—but the Zhentarim already had his gauntlet locked around her throat in a strangling grip, and had begun to mouth the words of another spell.

Mirt dropped both Shandril and his sword. His fist crashed into the man's mouth—and the wizard's head snapped back, spun, and slumped. Sightless, fading eyes swung past him as the man dropped to the street.

"Getting old, am I?" Mirt growled as he hoisted Shandril onto his shoulders again. With great satisfaction, he kicked the Zhent's body, hard.

Oelaerone was helping Belarla up.

"How much farther is this way to the sewers?" Mirt snarled, looking around for other Zhents. He saw none— only curious citizens glancing up from their daily business. Thank Tymora for that. Oelaerone was pointing again, and Mirt anxiously lumbered in the indicated direction.

"I've run down more streets in the Realms. . . ." he muttered as they turned another corner. This street was narrower, and it smelled; strewn garbage and pools of water were frequent, and Mirt's boots skidded more than once.

"Not far now, Old Wolf," Belarla said from somewhere near his elbow.

Mirt looked around at the squalid street and replied, "You know this area? I just hope he was worth it, Belarla— whoever he was."

"If you weren't carrying the most important being in Faerûn right now," Belarla replied calmly, "I'd trip you into that next pool."

Mirt grunted, swayed, and managed to get through it upright. "I always wondered what pleasure-queens did for entertainment."

"Go down sewers, of course," Oelaerone said sweetly, from just ahead. "After all, folk say our morals belong in the sewer—why shouldn't our bodies keep them company?" She led the way into a short, stinking alley and, with a grand flourish, indicated a pile of dung.

Mirt set Shandril gently down in the crook of his arm, and stared at it. "I was picturing something a little closer to a door," he rumbled.

Belarla sighed and dug into the pile with both hands. "Come on," she said over her shoulder. "We'll have plenty of chances to wash all this off, down below."

"I was afraid of that," Mirt growled, handing Shandril's limp form to Oelaerone.

* * * * *

Water dripped, echoing somewhere in the dim distance. The archways overhead were old and cracked and covered with slimy growths. Here and there, the ends of pipes dripped filth down into the thick, oily brown waters they toiled through. The muck was chest high.

Mirt ducked under a sagging pipe and muttered, "No sneezing, now."

Belarla struggled along at his elbow, helping to keep Shandril's face out of the grime. "Could this be the world-famous Mirt the Moneylender I see? Lord of Waterdeep? Harper Lord? Scourge of the Sea of Swords? Mirt the Merciless, Old Wolf of the North? This same old man, plastered with excrement?"

"I'm in disguise," Mirt growled, squeezing under another pipe. The smell was indescribable; as far as he could tell, the sewers here never drained out except during snowmelt. This would be a great place for a gulguthra lair . . . and as soon as that thought occurred to him, he wished it hadn't.

He peered around in the gloom; light drifted down from street-gratings high overhead—sometimes accompanied by brief deluges as citadel folk dumped chamber pots or washtubs.

"Are we heading anywhere in particular—" he asked "—besides toward our graves, I mean?"

"You mentioned Myrintara, earlier," Belarla answered carefully, keeping her chin up as she walked over an uneven spot and the filth rose to her lower lip. Bubbles broke on the dark brown surface all around her, and she gagged.

"Not in *my* direction, thank you," Oelaerone told her, edging away. "Ah, we're getting into the older part."

Ahead, a noisome waterfall carried the waters they were sloshing through down a short cascade to plunge into the blacker waters of a larger channel. A mist hung in the air. As they went down the falls Mirt exclaimed; the darker water, at the bottom, was noticeably colder. Much colder, in fact.

On his arm, Shandril stirred. "Not *now,* lass," Mirt growled at her. "If you make us fall in this filth, I swear I'll take my hand to your bottom."

"Uhmm?" her sleepy voice responded. "Is that you, dear?"

The Harper ladies giggled; Mirt snorted, and shook the weight in his arms. A moment later, Shandril's eyes fluttered, opened—and met his. Then she looked around.

"Where are we?" she asked and frowned. "And what happened?" Then—the Old Wolf could tell by her face—the smell hit her.

"We're with friends," Mirt said, "in the sewers of the citadel."

"I'd worked that much out already," Shandril replied, wrinkling her nose.

"We're trying to get to the house of Myrintara of the Masks."

"Who's she?"

"A noted perfumer," Mirt panted, as they turned through an arch and into an unexpectedly strong flow of effluent, heading in the other direction. "And an old friend."

"A perfumer would come in very handy about now," Shandril observed faintly. "I think I'm going to be sick."

"Over my shoulder, lass," Mirt grunted, as they struggled on. "Just keep it over my shoulder."

After a moment, Shandril said in a small voice, "I burned one of you ladies; I'm sorry."

Belarla flashed a smile at Shandril and held up one hand to wiggle dung-covered fingers cheerfully at her. "All better, lass—no lasting harm done."

"If we can ever scrub this stuff off us, that is," Oelaerone said ruefully. "The last time we traveled the sewers, we had a boat."

Mirt looked around. "Folk have boats down here?"

"Yes—and rafts, and mushroom beds, and lots of little caches where they hide things, too."

"Treasure?"

"Aye, and the bodies of rivals or rich older relatives, and suchlike."

A sudden outflow from above drenched them all. They gasped and sputtered and swore; the Harper ladies proved they knew expressions every bit as colorful as Mirt did.

"If we ever get out of here, Shandril-my-lass," Mirt said through clenched teeth, "I'm going to give ye a few choice words about what it means to be a Harper—notably, of considering consequences *before* ye act."

Shandril leaned against the comforting bulk of his shoulder as he forged on through the stinking muck, and she said in a small voice, "I guess you mean I shouldn't have come here at all."

Mirt shrugged. "Well, not so fast, lass—'twas high time *someone* gave the Zhentarim something to think about. And ye've certainly found the knack of giving everyone around a wild time, indeed."

Shandril grinned, a little lopsidedly—and then Delg's agonized, dying face swam into her mind, and she burst into sudden tears.

Mirt rolled his eyes and wrapped his excrement-smeared arms more tightly around her, murmuring soothingly.

Oelaerone turned and reproved him mildly. "You've certainly cultivated an expert boudoir manner, Mirt of Waterdeep."

"Only a little way, now," Belarla added, turning into a side channel. It was shallower; as she went along it, her body rose out of the water as far as her waist. Her robes, plastered to her, glistened brown and yellow.

Shandril looked at Belarla, down at her own body hidden under the roiling brown sludge, and involuntarily glanced back at the pleasure-queen's robes. She gagged.

Mirt threw her expertly over his shoulder, but she struggled free and glared at him. "I'm *not* a little girl!"

"Aye," he said dryly. "I'd noticed. Little girls are never *this* much trouble."

Belarla came to a stop, waters swirling around her, and looked up at the vaulted stone ceiling just above her. "This is the one," she announced, pointing at a rune burned into a dark wooden hatch overhead.

Dripping, she and Oelaerone reached up and hauled on its heavy bolt together, their hair plastered down their backs and matted with filth. The door fell open, suddenly, and they splashed and staggered in the water, struggling for balance.

Mirt blinked sewer water from his eyes, thanked the two Harpers gravely, and then heaved himself like an angry whale up out of the water and through the hatch. Grunting, he caught hold of the lowest rung of an old, massive iron ladder. "This must have been used as a well, long ago," his voice echoed back to them.

"No wonder they all died of fevers back then," Oelaerone said disgustedly to Belarla.

"No doubt folk an age from now will wonder at all the barbaric things we do, too," Belarla replied.

"Going through the sewers ranks right up there," Oelaerone agreed, as they boosted Shandril up the ladder.

"Hmmm," Belarla responded, " 'rank' is the right word, yes."

After a short, unpleasant climb, the three ladies found themselves facing a closed door in a small, round room crowded with old buckets. Mirt's arrival had evidently awakened some magic here: a faint, yellow-white glow was emanating from the door and growing steadily brighter.

Mirt rapped on the glowing door with his fist, snatched his hand back, and shook his fingers to clear away the tingling pain. "Strong wards," he commented, eyeing it and wondering if he'd have to knock again.

A breath or two later, the center of the door began to glow brightly, and then something swam out of that radiance, spun together, thickened like rising smoke, and suddenly coalesced into a floating, glowing eye.

The orb regarded them all, bobbing slightly as it turned. Mirt held up his Harper pendant in front of it. The eye blinked, peered at it for a moment, and then drew back to look around at them all again. Then it abruptly swooped back to the door, vanishing into the radiance once more.

Almost immediately, they heard bars fall and chains rattle, and then the door grated open. A young lady in a dark court dress with full skirts, a low bodice, and high shoulders stood looking at them. A wand was held ready in her hand, and her eyes were dark with fear. "Who are you, and why have you come here?" she asked.

Mirt was dripping sewage only a pace away from her.

He bent in a low bow and said gravely, "It grieves us deeply to trouble you at this hour and in this manner, great lady, but we are in desperate straits, and beg immediate audience with thy lady master."

The apprentice stared at him in disbelief for a moment, and then stifled a sudden giggle. "Lady!" she called over her shoulder, and a moment later, another face appeared.

It belonged to a tall, very beautiful lady with huge dark green eyes and glossy black hair.

"Ladies," Mirt said to Shandril and the Harpers, as he went to one knee, "may I present to you—Myrintara of the Masks."

Those beautiful eyes looked at the bedraggled old merchant and blinked in sudden recognition. She groaned, "Not you *again!*"

Mirt grinned wolfishly and replied, "Just get us out of here."

"To do so speedily will be my distinct pleasure," Myrintara replied, ushering the filthy foursome up narrow stone steps. Her apprentice, eyes still wide with wonder, stood at the far end of the cellar they emerged into and held a lamp to light their way.

As they ascended from the cellar to the floor above, a richly decorated dwelling opened around them. A floor higher up, Shandril amended that first judgment to 'palatial.' She tried not to look back at the interesting trail they were leaving in their wake, all over the carpets.

"You're sure you don't want to bathe?" Myrintara asked as she ushered them up another broad, gilded flight of stairs.

Mirt shook his head. "Not unless you feel like fighting off all the Zhentarim in the citadel."

Myrintara leaned her head to one side as if considering his suggestion rather longingly, and then shook her head with regret. "We'd never get the place cleaned up again before business hours."

On the upper landing, several men were cleaning and polishing the marble and carved, gilded railings. They broke off their work to stare at the four filthy guests.

Shandril's eyes widened. So far, she'd counted sixteen servants in their brief climb through the house.

"You must be very rich," she said.

Myrintara laughed. "My girls often say that, too—usually just before asking for money."

"She's generally thought to be the most successful pleasure-queen in all the Moonsea North," Oelaerone told Shandril.

Myrintara looked pleased. "I'm also a Harper and a sorceress, though I'd prefer if both those things were kept from the ears of the Zhentarim."

"How do the masks come into it—in your name, I mean?" Shandril asked curiously.

"She's an expert at cloaking magic; such spells used to be called 'masks' in the Old Empires," Mirt said.

Shandril looked at him. "How is it you know all about her?"

Myrintara laughed again. "We were lovers, girl. Years ago." She looked fondly at Mirt, and added, "Before he got fat."

Mirt looked injured; Shandril giggled at his expression. Myrintara glanced teasingly at him and sang a snatch of an old song: "Go upstairs, take off your armor. . . ."

"No time now," Mirt growled at her. "But if there were, Myrin, ye'd have to watch sharp—or I'd slide ye down the stair rail again."

Shandril looked back down the long, gleaming bannister of the stairs in wonder. At her expression, both Mirt and Myrintara exploded in laughter.

They were still laughing when Myrintara ushered them through an arched doorway into a small room that was bare except for what looked like a massive stone coffin filled with water. Then she turned, face suddenly serious, and asked, "My dear, will you submit to one of my masking spells?"

"Will it make me subject to someone else's will?" Shandril asked quietly.

"No," Myrintara assured her, and Shandril nodded. "Step into the tub," Myrintara directed, "and lie down."

Belarla and Oelaerone looked down at their soiled clothes and peered longingly at the water but said nothing.

Shandril looked up at Myrintara. "Like this?"

Myrintara nodded. "I'll cast the spell on the water and then push you under the surface. Hold your breath and don't be alarmed; I'll let you rise very soon."

A few breaths later, it was done, and a dripping Shandril rose from the tub. Its once-clear water was now a muddy brown; Myrintara looked at it and sighed as she helped Shandril out. "Immersing you ensures you're completely covered," she said, "cloaked from all detecting magics. When you use spellfire again, my mask will be destroyed, but until then—no magic can find you, or see you if it is bent on someone or something known to be with you."

She led them down a passage and through an ornate archway into a chamber that took Shandril's breath away. Under her dripping feet were white fur rugs—whole pelts of northern snow bears. Each one stretched a good six paces in length; they formed a path toward a shallow stairway. The steps led to a raised area where a circular bed floated in midair. Polished, curved mirrors floated around it and spells made stars seem to glimmer in a night sky.

Belarla whistled, looking up. "That's nice."

Myrintara smiled. "The moon rises to match the real Selune in the sky outside—Tears and all."

Oelaerone made an acquisitive, purring sound in her

throat, and turned on her heel to survey the rest of the room—a gleaming, luxurious array of smooth-finished chairs, dangling chains, restraining rings, and statues that were astonishingly lifelike, exquisitely beautiful, and breathtakingly explicit. Mirt was looking around with a sly smile and a raised eyebrow.

"See something you like, Old Wolf?" Myrintara asked him challengingly, an eyebrow raised.

"I should have stayed," Mirt said regretfully.

Myrintara laughed again and led them to a screen at the back of her huge boudoir. Behind it, another archway led into her wardrobe. Shandril had never seen so many clothes in one place before—racks and racks of them, some hanging on wooden forms that dangled from the ceiling on chains. She stared around as Myrintara took them briskly through the corridor of clothes into dimness at the back of the room. There, for the first time, they found dust—and a few discarded chairs, with folded draperies piled atop them. Beyond was a small, plain door. Myrintara swung it open; it led into a small, dusty, empty closet.

"My quick way out," she said with a smile. "Touch the back wall and you'll be taken to my favorite inn, where I go to rest from time to time. I fear the trip, for you, works only in one direction."

"We can force ourselves to be content with that," Mirt assured her sagely. "I'd kiss ye farewell, Myrin, but ye might catch something." He waved at her, and stepped into the closet. The others followed.

The world seemed to blink for a moment, then Shandril found herself standing on a grassy bank with trees all around her. The sun was high and warm; it was just before highsun.

"Where are we?" Belarla asked before Shandril could.

Mirt waved an expansive hand. "Step around those

trees, ladies, and cross the road. Ye'll see."

They all went together. Shandril found herself looking at the village of Eveningstar, at the spot where the overland roads met, by the bridge over the River Starwater. Across the way rose the friendly, ramshackle bulk of *The Lonesome Tankard*, its signboard creaking slightly in the breeze.

"Ah, the *Tankard*," Belarla said with pleasure. "Well, Myrintara certainly knows the good places to stay."

"Hot bath," was all Oelaerone said, fishing around for her purse in the bodice of her soaked, stained, ruined gown.

Mirt chuckled. "We've business with Tessaril, ladies," he said. "My thanks—perhaps we'll talk, this even or on the morrow."

The Harper pleasure-queens rolled their eyes. "Just don't knock on our doors and demand aid or a rescue," Belarla said. "We've done our share for a tenday or so."

"Or so, indeed," Oelaerone echoed. "Gods smile, you two." They waved farewell, crossed the road, and went into the *Tankard*.

As they went up the road together, Shandril tried not to smell the reek coming off them both. She looked at Mirt curiously and asked, "Why didn't you stay with Myrintara, Old Wolf?"

Mirt looked at her sidelong. "I was young and restless, lass. Besides," he added, "did ye not notice—she never stops *laughing!* In bed, at table, in the bath—my ears grew sore, in the end."

Shandril stared at him—and then started to laugh helplessly.

Mirt looked hurt. "I don't look *that* funny," he complained. She was still laughing as they came to the porch of Tessaril's Tower.

One of the guards looked at them, peered a second

time, and then turned and called, "They're back! And—"

He staggered hastily out of the way as a white-faced Narm and a broadly smiling Storm charged out of the tower to embrace the two, heedless of the stench and dirt.

Narm kissed Shandril repeatedly. "Gods, I was scared, Shan. Are you all right?"

Shandril found herself suddenly crying into his chest. "I—I don't know," she managed to say, between happy sobs.

"Well, come in, and we'll find out," Tessaril said from the doorway, and wrinkled her nose. "And you can both have a bath—or three."

Nineteen

SPELLSTORM COMING

Dragons, lad? Let me sleep . . . no, I'm not impressed—not even if the sky was full of 'em. I've seen a spellstorm, lad— and I'd have to see gods walking the Realms to top that.

> The character Nimrith the Old Warrior,
> in the play ***Much Ado in Sembia***
> Malarkin Norlbertusz of Ordulin
> Year of the Prince

 Tessaril's bathroom was surprisingly luxurious. Shandril sighed blissfully as the warm, scented water sluiced away the filth of the citadel's sewers. She ran weary fingers back through her hair, opened her eyes, and found Belarla grinning at her in shared contentment from the next tub, soap suds sliding slowly down her front.

"What made you choose to become Harpers?" Shandril asked curiously.

Belarla smiled. The two Harpers had been delighted at Tessaril's invitation. Across the room, Oelaerone was soaping her hair with quick, expert motions. She flung her head back to keep soap out of her eyes, turned, and said, "We wanted a taste of adventure."

"Adventure? But you're"—Shandril fumbled for words for a moment—"pleasure-queens."

Belarla raised an eyebrow. "Any task grows boring, Shan, if you do it over and over again." With a contented sigh she settled back down into the water and added, "How can we make others excited and give pleasure if we're not excited and enjoying it ourselves?" She nodded at the door they'd entered the baths by. "Tessaril casts spells. We're pleasure-queens; we work magic of another sort."

"And who's to say which of us makes the most changes in Faerûn?" Tessaril put in as she swung the door open, hung her robe by it, and joined them.

A moment later, Shandril was groaning in satisfaction as the Lord of Eveningstar scrubbed at the small of her back. Tessaril looked over at Belarla, and drew down her brows in a mock frown. "Going to the *Tankard* when you could have come straight here to me! I'm hurt."

Belarla spread her hands. "Lady—oops, Lord; I'll never get used to that—you have a lovely bath, here. My heart-felt thanks. We needed a dip in the river first, though, and a horse trough—and Dunman's inn has both of those."

Tessaril chuckled. "So," she said to Shandril, as her skillful fingers kneaded knots and sore spots on the maiden's back, "are you going to tell me what happened in the citadel?"

"Start with the beholders," Oelaerone teased, soap running down her shoulders.

"Well," Shandril said, taking a deep breath, "I'm going back."

The echoing chorus of groans that greeted this was so loud the servants came running to see if anything was amiss.

* * * * *

Sarhthor and Fzoul wearily turned away from the watery scrying disc. The high priest gestured, and there was a collective gasp from the white-faced, exhausted underpriests as they released their concentration.

The disc collapsed. Water crashed to the floor, and smoke rose where it hit some of the runes. Sarhthor and Fzoul strode through the resulting sparks and dancing radiances without even looking down. The wizard wiggled a finger, and a pair of stools glided out from the corners of the room. The two rulers of the Brotherhood sat down, not happily.

"We lost all trace very suddenly," Sarhthor said.

Fzoul nodded grimly. "She—or someone aiding her, more likely—has used magic to cloak her." He turned to the underpriests, who leaned wearily against the walls of the room, and demanded angrily, "Why hasn't the roused might of the citadel brought Shandril to us yet? This is our fortress, not an open city—no one here should defy us." He glared around at them. "Thousands of Zhentilar, scores of priests—and we haven't even brought her to bay, cornered somewhere?"

Priests traded unhappy glances and spread their hands helplessly, not daring to speak.

"Must I do everything *myself*?" Sarhthor and Fzoul snarled in unison. They stopped and looked at each other in the sudden silence. Then, very slowly, they traded cold smiles, and strode to the door together.

* * * * *

"Are you resolved then, lass?"

"I am," Shandril said firmly.

Narm looked at her with pleading eyes. "You've killed

Manshoon and other Zhentarim galore and half a hundred beholders. Isn't it time to stop?"

He looked around Tessaril's audience chamber for support, but found none. Mirt sat with a friendly arm about each of the Harper pleasure-queens, Tessaril was behind her desk—and Shandril sat on it in their midst. Her long hair tossed behind her as she shook her head and leaned forward.

"I want to stop, love—you know how much I do—but they'll never leave us alone as long as they can put this defeat down to a mageling's carelessness, that defeat down to ill luck, and everything else down to Elminster's aid." She waved one hand in exasperation. "None of them saw Manshoon die—even Mirt and Tess keep telling me he'll be back from the grave in a few days. And all of them still think they can get spellfire if they can only catch me asleep or worn out or with my pants down in a privy. The worst of it is, they're right. I've got to strike at them first, before they can spin another dozen traps and plans for me."

"There's no place you can run to that the Zhentarim can't find you," Tessaril added softly. The three Harpers nodded.

"All right," Narm said grimly, "we'll see this through. I just wish you'd never had spellfire, and the Zhentarim had never even *heard* of us."

"My, lad, but don't ye wear the crown of martyrdom well," Mirt said sarcastically. "All of us gripe at what the gods have given us in life—but the best of us go out and do something about it. Can't ye see yer lady's trying to do just that?"

Narm glared at him and then nodded reluctantly. "I still think it'd be wiser to run for Silverymoon now—our best chance for a safe trip is while the Zhentarim are still disorganized."

"Giving them time to rebuild and try for you again," Oelaerone put in, "as Shan says."

"A new leader will take them after new things—not throw more wizards away in going after spellfire when it's cost them so much already," Narm argued.

Mirt growled. "Bah! Where's Elminster, now that we need him to talk some sense into ye? *Ye* would turn down spellfire if ye led the Zhents—but power draws them, as moths flutter about a flame, and they will snatch again and again at the flame, even after they've been burned a time or two."

Narm looked thoughtful. "After all the deaths and the citadel laid waste around them? You really think so?"

Mirt's expression was exasperated. "Lad, lad—*never* credit the Zhents with too much good sense. *What* have they been doing to ye since Shadowdale, eh? Trying for ye again and again, whate'er their losses."

Narm stared at the far wall for a moment and then said, "You're right. That's exactly what they've been doing." He looked at Mirt. "I'm sorry—I haven't your experience, and shouldn't be arguing with what you've seen to be true."

Mirt reached a long arm around Belarla and clapped Narm's shoulder with enough force to make the young mage bounce in his chair. "That's all right, lad. Never known a young wizard that didn't argue. Besides," he rumbled gently, "I lost ye Delg. The least I can do is give ye half the good advice he would have."

"Come what may," Shandril said to her husband, "I'm going back to the citadel—now, while most of the Zhentarim are gathered there hunting for my blood—and bring all this harrying to an end once and for all. This time, at least, I'll have some friends with me."

"Aye," Mirt rumbled. "We're all coming." There was a general chorus of agreement.

Narm nodded finally and said, "Agreed." Then he looked at Tessaril, a question in his eyes.

The Lord of Eveningstar nodded. "I have teleport scrolls ready for all of us, including you—and a sorceress once showed me how to work what she called a 'mass teleport,' where we all go together. This time," she added simply, "the battle must be for all—or nothing."

Mirt nodded. "Let's eat first," he growled.

As the group rose and began filing out toward the kitchen, Mirt steered the young mage by one elbow out the door, across the entry hall, and up the grand stair. When they'd reached the seclusion of the statues above, Mirt stopped among them and said grimly, "Listen, lad. We Harpers're along to see to the Zhents that Shan can't stop in time. There'll be bowmen, priests, and wizards behind every door and tapestry, trust me. Stopping *her,* if she should go out of control and start behaving like another Manshoon, is yer task."

"*What?*" Narm's face was white with anger. "You want me to slay the lady I love? Why of all folk in Faerûn did you dare to ask *me?*"

"Ye married her," was the gruff reply as the Old Wolf stalked away and started back down the stairs.

"Yes, but—" Narm found himself arguing with empty air. He took a few quick steps after Mirt and demanded, "Even if I wanted to, how could I stop Shan? *How?*"

The old merchant swung around and fixed Narm with one gimlet eye. "I know not, lad, but ye'd best be learning. As I said, ye married her."

* * * * *

"My thanks, Sarhthor, for a very good hunch as to where they'd be." Fzoul lifted his gaze from the new disc of water that he and his underpriests had conjured in

Wizards' Watch Tower. He moved away, and Tessaril's features in the scrying pool wavered and disappeared as the magic faded.

He signaled the priests to let it collapse, then snapped at Sarhthor, "Go—ready our warriors!"

Sarhthor only nodded, and Fzoul saw the weariness in his face. "Get some rest," the high priest added. "I'll be needing you soon."

"You will indeed," Sarhthor replied, so quietly that Fzoul's next coldly spoken orders drowned out the sound.

Finished with his lackeys, the high priest strode out the room, down the stairs, and to the Spell Court.

"Who speaks for Bane?" Elthaulin's voice rang out, echoing from the towers around the courtyard as Fzoul came in. The upperpriest held the scepter of Bane high above his head. Sunlight gleamed on the glossy-smooth black hand at its tip.

"The darkness of night," half a hundred throats replied.

"Who walks the night?"

"Those who are faithful," came the unison response.

"How shall they be known?"

"By the blood they spill," the assembly thundered.

Elthaulin brought the scepter down into the shield-sized bowl of black blood in front of him. Its level of liquid began to drop immediately. "Behold our sacrifice to the Dread Lord! Behold, the Great Lord Bane drinks the blood we have given! Behold!"

In triumph, he held up the empty bowl. "Bane is satis—"

"I'm sure," Fzoul's dry voice cut in, and sudden silence fell. The Master of the Black Altar added, "Enough, Elthaulin. Have done with ritual, Brothers—I need you all ready for battle within the hour. This Shandril is coming for me, and she'll find her way here, no doubt, all too soon."

A rush of shocked, obedient priests followed. Amid the hurrying clamor, Fzoul stopped a servant and murmured

some commands. The servant rushed off, and Fzoul
strolled unconcernedly across the courtyard.

Wondering priests, on their knees to pray to Bane for
spells, looked up in awe at his cool and calm manner. Only
when he was well inside the tower again and sure they
could no longer see him did Fzoul break into a run, taking
the stairs in frantic haste.

* * * * *

Tessaril came out onto the porch and found her herald
sitting with the guards, correcting a blazon with careful
strokes of his brush.

"I'm sorry to disturb you, Tzin," she said quietly, and
the tone of her voice made him look up quickly. "I charge
you to assume command of the king's affairs and of justice in Eveningstar for a time. I'm going to the Citadel of
the Raven—to war."

Mouths dropped open all down the porch. The blood
drained from the herald's face, and he started to say
something.

Tessaril held up a hand to forestall the torrent of words
she knew was coming, then said, "If I do not come back,
tell Azoun I did what I had to do—and that I have always
loved him." Her voice trembled, and fell to a whisper. "It
has been an honor to serve the Purple Dragon."

She turned away quickly then, before her voice broke,
and hurried back inside her tower. She did not want to
look even once at the beautiful village around her—in
case it should prove to be the last time.

* * * * *

Fzoul found the room he was looking for. He chose a
mace, a weighty hammer, and a javelin from the racks

around its walls. The weapons hefted well in his hands. Next he turned his attention to the wall, where he knew a secret rune was hidden. The high priest smiled as he found it, pushed and turned the rune-adorned panel, and watched part of the wall swing open.

The niche within held a skull, a mummified hand, and several bottles of brown glass. He chose one bottle, wiped the dust from it, undid the seal, and experimentally licked the yellow liquid within.

The burning sensation on his tongue made him nod with satisfaction; it was still deadly—to others, at least. Over years of careful exposure, he'd built up a resistance to this particular poison. Carefully the high priest anointed the weapons he'd chosen, girded himself about with them, replaced the bottle, and closed the door of its hiding place.

Then he descended to the forehall of the tower, stood on a paving stone that had been enchanted by Manshoon years ago, and spoke one of the words the mage had taught him. An almost inaudible singing sound answered him as the hidden spell engine Manshoon had prepared spun silently out of another plane and into solid existence in Faerûn. It could appear only in this place, but Fzoul—being the spellfire maid's target—was just the bait to bring her here to face it.

Fzoul could not see the spell engine, but he knew that it now filled most of the room behind him: a great wheel that would begin to spin if spells struck it, absorbing the magic to power itself. Manshoon's greatest work. It drank all magic cast at it.

Fzoul smiled tightly, opened the front door of the tower, and waited.

As though on cue, a man appeared in the doorway—a man in dark leathers, a bow slung at his back. He panted briefly, then caught his breath. "You sent for us, Lord?"

"Aye," Fzoul said, looking out at the score of Zhentilar archers gathered there. "Thank you for your promptness; it is appreciated. Do any of you bear any sort of magic item with you? Anything that carries an enchantment?"

One man held up a dagger.

"Leave it outside," Fzoul ordered, "and retrieve it later. To carry it into this chamber could mean your doom."

Several other archers hastily divested themselves of small items; Fzoul hid a smile by turning away and saying, "Come!"

In the forehall, he turned to face them. "Ready bows, and conceal yourselves behind the tapestries in this room, and in doorways and entries all around the Spell Court. I want you hidden, mind, and silent until I give the signal, thus. Respond only to this signal: other archers will be stationed openly in the court. Orders to them to loose shafts, or their doing so, are *not* orders for you to fire."

The high priest looked at them coldly. "When your signal does come, you are to fire at the intruders—not to kill, whatever they do, but only to bring down your targets. I will inform you verbally if there are any changes in these orders once battle begins."

His face melted into a slow, soft smile that held no mirth or friendliness, and he added, "I don't need to warn you what your fate will be if you should happen to send an arrow my way. The wizards of our Brotherhood *are* running short of people to test new spells on."

He looked around briskly. "Any questions?" Silence. He clapped his hands. "Right—string bows, and hide yourselves! Be ready!"

When they were hidden, Fzoul strolled quickly around Spell Court, nodded his satisfaction, and went back to the forehall.

Standing not far inside the doors, he drew a deck of cards from a pocket in his robes, and idly began to play a

betting game he was fond of. Without other players, he
merely dealt two cards off the top of the deck to see what
hand Tymora, the goddess of luck—or his own lord,
Bane—had given him.

The first two cards were a magician and a priestess, one
of the two best hands in the game. Fzoul smiled in satisfaction. The second hand consisted of two priest cards,
and his smile faded. They were the weakest hand one
could draw. Whoever devised the game had not been fond
of priests, he thought darkly, and drew another hand.

This time, he drew the other highest possible hand, and
hummed to himself contentedly as he shuffled the deck.

He'd barely finished humming that first song when suddenly, figures appeared in Spell Court, very near the Wizards' Watch Tower. Fzoul recognized the slim, curvaceous
Lord of Eveningstar; a fat, aging man whom Fzoul knew
to be a Lord of Waterdeep; two pleasure-queens of the
citadel; the young mage—and his mate, the lass who
wielded spellfire. An odd band of heroes, to be sure.

Fzoul smiled tightly and gestured with his free hand.
Arrows sang as they flew.

Twenty

CROWN OF FIRE

There is no greater glory in the Realms than winning—or defending—a crown. Never forget that.
. . . Even wizards can surprise ye.

Mirt the Moneylender
Wanderings With Quill and Sword
Year of Rising Mist

Shandril, behind her companions, raised her hands, and spellfire poured out. A bright net of spellflame suddenly surrounded the party. The arrows striking it burst into white pulses of light, hissing, and were gone.

"Come!" she cried, and strode to the door of Wizards' Watch Tower, keeping the bright net of flames behind them all. The Zhentilar soldiers around the edges of the courtyard did not follow, their faces fearful.

From where he stood near the door, Fzoul watched her come, and he knew his own moment of fear. The maid's spellfire seemed stronger than ever. Her eyes blazed like two small stars, and her feet left flaming footprints in the spell-guarded stone. He dragged his glance up from that astonishing sight and managed to greet her with a polite smile on his face.

"Welcome, Shandril Shessair. I've been waiting for you. Fzoul Chembryl, at your service."

Fzoul willed the playing card in his right hand to melt into its true shape: a wand. It fired. He was still smiling as its radiant bolts leapt out to strike Belarla, Oelaerone, Tessaril—and Narm.

Shandril snarled at him wordlessly, and her spellfire roared out to form another defensive net. She glanced behind her to see if her companions were within her shield of flames. Narm was crumpling to his knees, face twisted in pain, and Tessaril was staggering as she tried to hold a swaying Belarla upright.

Shandril also saw Zhentilar guards in black leather as they stepped out from behind tapestries to block the doorway behind her. Beyond them, the archers whose arrows had greeted their arrival were closing in across Spell Court, bows in their hands.

Anger rose and coiled like spellfire within her. "You're good at trapping things, Zhentarim," she spat angrily, "but let's see if you're any better than Manshoon at holding them." She drew back her hand and hurled a blazing ball of spellfire at Fzoul.

He stood watching calmly as it roared toward him, spitting flames. Then it seemed to swerve sideways, smashing into—a great, shining wheel of translucent force that appeared behind Fzoul. Spellfire splashed furiously along its edge, glowed, and was absorbed.

Fzoul bowed mockingly. "I'm sorry for any humiliation this might cause you, Shandril—but I fear I must ask you to kneel and cast away any weapons you may be carrying. Or die, of course."

* * * * *

Elthaulin strode angrily into the nave of the Black Altar, his soft shoes slipping on the polished marble underfoot.

"Neaveil! Oprion!" he called, his voice echoing irreverently in the lofty darkness. Startled heads turned, but he paid them no heed. If Fzoul was going to interrupt devout rituals, Elthaulin could trample on a few meaningless traditions.

"Yes, Master of Doom?" Oprion was at his side swiftly, as always.

Elthaulin smiled approvingly at him. "Assemble all temple troops here, and any underpriests you deem more loyal to me than to Fzoul."

Oprion's eyes widened. "What has befallen?"

"Fzoul's facing the wench with spellfire in the citadel— right now! He may well perish, or be left so weak we can seize power once and for all. Assemble everyone you can! *Haste,* for the love of Bane! All of you!"

Priests scrambled away at his bidding. Unseen, one dodged out an archway and took a hidden way to the street. There his features changed, melting into those of a powerful and well-known wizard. Sarhthor was an old hand at quickly and quietly slipping away.

* * * * *

"Kneel before *you?*" Shandril flung the incredulous question like a weapon at the high priest as she leapt toward him, tugging out her dagger.

Fzoul gestured with one hand.

Shandril heard bows twang. She screamed as a shaft took her in the shoulder with numbing force, spinning her around. A second shaft that would have found her breast missed as she fell, humming over her straight into the throat of a Zhentilar warrior blocking the doorway—just as the bloody point of Mirt's sword burst through the man's black leather tunic.

Grunting with the effort, Mirt snatched up the guard's body and staggered forward, using it as a shield.

Fzoul shouted orders. Arrows whipped and whirred around the room. The guard's body was rapidly transfixed with shafts that leapt, hissing, into the limp flesh as Mirt slowly advanced.

Long paces in front of him, alone on the forehall floor, Shandril yanked the shaft from her shoulder and writhed in agony, trying to master enough will to use spellfire to heal herself. Radiance leaked out between her fingers as she clutched her shoulder and groaned, thrashing back and forth on the tiles. Each time spellfire pulsed, some of it drifted away from her like glowing threads of smoke, drawn inexorably into the slowly turning wheel of the spell engine.

"Cease firing! No more shafts!" Fzoul snapped, and strode toward Shandril, a javelin raised in one hand.

Narm rose from his knees and, through clenched teeth, hissed the words of a spell. Lightning flashed and flickered around the room, and Zhentilar archers groaned as they fell. Behind the charred and toppled bodies, the blue-white bolts crackled along the walls and into the spell engine. Most of the Zhents lay still; others were moaning and moving feebly; perhaps six still stood, and few of them held bows.

Trembling uncontrollably, Narm fell, lifeless, onto his face.

Fzoul's angry counterspell lashed past him and out the open doors, striking harmless smoke and sparks from the flagstones of Spell Court. Snarling in disgust, the high priest hefted his javelin and strode down the long forehall to slay Shandril.

Face twisted in pain, Shandril Shessair slithered on the tiles, crawling back toward the door, trying to get away from the strange glowing wheel that was drawing spellfire from her. It was turning slightly faster now, its pull slightly stronger, a wheel that spun for her death.

Through a haze of pain, Shandril saw Sarhthor standing in the doorway, face unreadable. Crumpled on the floor in front of him was Oelaerone, curled around the black arrow that had felled her.

From the floor beside Belarla's senseless form, Tessaril yelled, "*Old Wolf, your dagger!*"

"Of course," Mirt rumbled, dumping the body he'd been using as a shield atop a Zhent clawing at him from the floor. Coolly he ran the buried warrior through with his saber, turned, and held his own dagger up. Obliging his will, it glowed.

Fzoul stopped and flung another spell. It flashed at the Old Wolf, trailing streams of magical radiance as the spell engine's draining tugged at it. The weakened spell reached Mirt's dagger—and was absorbed into it. The Old Wolf gave the high priest a triumphant smile. Then he tossed the dagger and, in the same motion, swung back with a snarl to smash aside the reaching blade of the next Zhentilar.

The dagger sparkled end-over-end through the air and into Tessaril's sure grasp. The Lord of Eveningstar came up from the floor in a run, black skirts streaming, heading for Fzoul and the great wheel.

A Zhentilar shaft hummed from near the door and caught her in the back.

Tessaril gasped, staggered, and fell, twisting in agony. "Strike the wheel with this, Old Wolf," she gasped, holding up the glowing dagger in a hand that trembled, "or we're all doomed!"

Mirt growled at the Zhentilar he was fencing with, and

then reached over their singing blades to punch the man in the throat. Catching the strangling warrior's neck, he shoved the man aside, into the path of an arrow meant for him. As the corpse spun away, Mirt lumbered across the tiled floor like a angry bear. Arrows flew. Fzoul ducked one, only paces away from Shandril, and went hastily to his knees, bellowing, *"No more arrows!"*

Mirt fell onto his knees and skidded the last few feet to Tessaril's side. He yanked a steel vial from his belt and forced it to her lips—spilling most of it down her chin as an arrow tore into him and he jerked involuntarily.

Roaring in pain, he snatched the glowing dagger from the floor, staggered to his feet, coming almost face-to-face with Fzoul—and hurled the trusty little blade over the high priest's shoulder. Dagger and wheel touched.

The flash and roar struck eyes and ears like a solid blow.

Wizards' Watch Tower rocked. The blast hurled dust and fragments of riven furniture and chipped walls the length of the forehall. In the gale, helplessly tumbling Zhents shrieked in fear, arrows and bows splintering around them as they came tumbling across the floor. Mirt was flung back into a decorative suit of armor that stood against one wall of the forehall, and together they tumbled ingloriously to the tiles.

Shandril's body burst into bright radiance as the spell engine's energy flooded into her. An arrow in her shoulder glowed, melted, and was gone. She shuddered, still racked with pain—and Fzoul was upon her, snarling, javelin descending.

The air flickered suddenly, and Sarhthor was there between them, a dagger in hand.

Fzoul's javelin plunged down—through the wizard's body. He stiffened as it pierced him, drove his dagger weakly into the high priest's neck, and gasped, "For

Those Who Harp!"

Mirt stared at Sarhthor, open-mouthed. "A Harper? *You?*"

Fzoul lurched backward, gasping and tugging at the dagger in his neck.

Shandril pounced on him furiously. Spellfire blazed down her arms as she got both hands on the high priest's throat. His flesh sizzled, and he screamed, eyes locked on hers. Shandril glared at him, flames rising from her eyes—and into his open mouth she spat a tongue of fire that went down to his vitals.

The high priest shuddered in her grip, clawing feebly at his weapons belt, and Shandril spat more fire. Fzoul's head arched back. He made a horrible rattling sound as spellfire exploded within him. Ribs burst out through his robes, and flames rose from his shattered body as Shandril shook him, still angry, and then shoved him away.

The body of the high priest of the Black Altar crashed to the floor in flames. The raging fire that consumed him was very hungry. Oily smoke rose from the tangled bones.

Behind Shandril, Sarhthor staggered upright and gasped bloodily, "Sh-Shandril, listen. Touch my head. . . . Use my life . . . and raise a crown of fire—the most powerful spellfire. . . . Shatter towers. . . . Take beholders. . . . *Hurry!*"

As his words trailed away, the Zhentarim wizard convulsed around the javelin, falling to his knees.

"Do it!" Tessaril groaned from the floor. "He speaks truth!"

Astonished, Shandril reached out and touched the wizard's head. They knelt together on the tiles. Sarhthor's eyes, red with pain but bright with a fierce will, stared steadily into hers. Shandril felt the wizard urge his fading life-energy into her. It flowed through her fingers with an uneven tingling, and red-hued spellfire crawled slowly out of her, enveloping them both in a flickering aura.

The spellfire grew stronger. It brightened to blinding whiteness as the wizard's eyes darkened. He fell back, dead, mouth open and contorted. Shandril looked down at him sadly, then rose from her knees.

Roaring spellflames curled to form a crown around her head as she turned, white-lipped and terrible. Her eyes were two leaping flames. Spellfire surged out from her in beams that stabbed at the Zhentilar warriors all around the room. Men screamed as they died, but she did not seem to hear.

When no foes remained in the chamber, Shandril walked out into the Spell Court. Many of the Zhents had already fled, hearing and seeing the holocaust within the tower. Those brave or stupid few who had stayed at their posts realized their mistake immediately. Shandril's crown of spellfire lashed out again. A web of fiery rays leapt around the courtyard, felling the warriors there. The power roared out of her—and wherever she looked, men died.

In moments, Spell Court was cleared except for smoldering corpses. Shandril turned toward the nearest wall, her eyes blazing, and blasted the first doorway she found. Inside was a hallway filled with burnt bodies—wizards who'd been watching through slits in the door, no doubt. With roaring spellflames, Shandril sheared a way through the corpse pile and stepped into the hall beyond. The heads of many an evil wizard peered out of doors and then hastily vanished. There were shrieks of fear.

Shandril smiled and sent killing spellfire after them. Faerûn would be a better place without the Zhentarim. She strode on, sending flames swirling around the walls of every room she came to.

Ahead of her, a door slammed. Shandril sneered at it

and let fly. The door and the man hiding behind it were immediately wreathed in spellflames. They turned to outlines of ash and fell—first the door, crumbling away like a torn curtain, and then the outline of the terrified man behind it.

Shandril shivered at what she'd done—and then remembered Delg, and the men of the Company of the Bright Spear who'd fallen before him. Laid low by wizards' spells. Deliberately she walked on, hurling balls of roiling spellfire into rooms right and left.

She came to the end of the hall; stone stairs ascended in a dark spiral, and she went up. The crown of fire still raged around her head and lit the way.

Dark armor gleamed in the light of her flames. A desperate Zhentilar suddenly leaned down from around the curve of the stairs, swinging a heavy morningstar. Spelllight twinkled and pulsed along its length; Shandril threw her hands upward and embraced the spiked end as it came. The weapon smashed her against the wall. She crashed hard into the stone. Breath hissed out of her in plumes of flame, but still she clung to the weapon. The soldier above tried to tug the morningstar free, but Shandril smiled grimly at him and held on.

The magic of the enspelled weapon surged into her; the metal in her hands glowed white, melted, and ran through her fingers.

Cloaked in rising spellflames, she melted the sword that the terrified Zhentilar now swung at her—and then blasted into his helm, leaving it empty, blackened metal. The headless body fell limply to the stairs and rolled past her. She climbed on, hurling fire in all directions.

Fresh shrieking told her she'd come to another floor full of wizards. Futile spells lashed out, clawing at her in vain attempts to take her life; arrows of magic sizzled into nothingness as they leapt at her; balls of acid hissed into

ash; and illusions of snarling dragons and diving beholders lunged at her, thrown by those who had nothing else
to fight with. She blasted their upraised, spell-casting
hands, the doors they tried to hide behind, and the floor
they stood on, sparing none of them.

One overconfident Zhent flung open a door and flashed
a sinister smile. Dark beams leapt at Shandril from his leveled wand. The spellfire Shandril unleashed swept away
beams, wand, wizard, and all, smashing a hole in the side
of the building. Flames rolled out of the fortress in a boil-
ing ball. The torn and smoking contents of the room fell
from the scattering flames and rained down on Spell
Court.

Zhentilar warriors had been flooding into the courtyard, frightened officers snarling orders and lashing
those who lagged. In awed unison, they stared up at the
rolling flames.

Something black and burning fell from the midst of
the scattering fire and landed at one warrior's feet. It
was a shriveled human hand, smoke rising from the
exposed bones of its fingertips. The Zhentarim ring that
had adorned one finger was only a melted star of metal
now. The Zhentilar warrior looked up at the jagged hole
in the side of the fortress, shivered, turned, and started
to run.

An officer snarled an order, but the arrow that should
have taken the fleeing soldier's life was never fired. The
archer, too, turned and ran—and then another, and
another, until the square was emptying—shouting, fleeing
men spilling out into the streets.

An explosion rocked a nearby spire of the citadel. It
slowly cracked and fell, to shatter on the stones of the
courtyard. Nearby, an old and crumbling balcony was
jarred loose by the impact and broke off. Screaming
priests tumbled into Spell Court with it.

Inside the citadel, Shandril climbed on. A group of desperate wizards took a stand on the stairs, using spells to hurl stone blocks down on her. As Shandril smashed the first few blocks to hot, flying sand, an avalanche of stones thundered down the stairs and swept her away.

Wizards cheered. Shandril cascaded helplessly down the stairs, fetching up against the wall after tumbling a floor or two. Blood ran from her mouth and from a gash on her forehead; her face and arms were dark red with bruises. Finding her feet among the tumbling stones, she snarled and held up her hands. Spellfire blazed; her blood turned to flame, and her cuts sizzled, glowed, and were gone. Then she waved both hands angrily, and a column of spellfire roared up the spiral stair.

In its smoking wake Shandril climbed again, on steps that cracked and groaned with heat. Teeth crunched underfoot as she reached the place where the wizards had been; the only other trace left of them were ashes, spattered thickly on the walls. Shandril saw the outline of an outflung hand, a dark bulk that must have been a spread-eagled body, and a large area of black, oily ashes where many hands and bodies had thudded into the wall together. The smell of cooked human flesh was strong in her nostrils.

She shook her head and climbed on, emerging in a high hallway that led to the next tower of the fortress. She followed it to a high-vaulted room where beholders floated down out of the darkness to hurl futile magic against her. Shandril sent them spinning in flames. They one by one shattered against the walls of their chamber and fell, eyestalks writhing feebly. From there she followed the stink of burning flesh down a passage—and found herself again in Spell Court.

Frightened citizens of the fortress-city were staring in awe at the devastation there. So many of the cruel men who'd lorded it over them lay dead and broken, so suddenly laid low. Carrion birds were already wheeling watchfully in the sky high above.

Shandril surveyed the death she had wrought, then pointed at a few men who were going through the clothing of the sprawled Zhentilar archers.

"You," she said. They looked up, blanched, and fell on their knees, crying for mercy. "I don't want to kill you," she said wearily. "I want your service." She pointed into Wizards' Watch Tower and said, "Inside that place, you'll find three women, a young man, and an older, stouter man who are not clad as Zhentarim. You'll also find the wizard Sarhthor; he's dead. Bring all of them out to me, as carefully as you can—your lives depend on it." She watched them scramble up eagerly. "Oh—and take nothing from their pockets."

This was done, Mirt and company removed well away from the Tower. Then Shandril raised her hands—and blasted Wizards' Watch Tower.

Her fire roared into the open doors of the forehall and burst out of a hundred windows. The tower shook. Cracks appeared here and there, widening with frightening speed as smoke spewed out of them. There were small green and pink explosions of flame in upper windows as the flames reached magic items there. And then the tower came apart.

The stone spire shifted, flung aside huge pieces of the upper floors, and hurled itself down into the courtyard below. The rolling sound was like angry thunder. Men in windows around the court stared open-mouthed at the tumbling stone. Most of them were too tired to scream. Others seemed to take some satisfaction in seeing the tower fall. The last of its walls toppled into ruin, and dust rose up as the tortured stones of the courtyard heaved one last time.

Shandril looked around the court, spellflames dancing in her hair, breast heaving. Another turret toppled. It shattered on impact and sent stones bouncing and rolling almost to her feet.

Once the dust settled, she stood back, satisfied—and then frowned. Wizards' Watch Tower had been only one in a forest of gray fortress towers, most of which still stood. She raised her hands to bring the whole lot of them tumbling down . . . and then paused: a frightened dunwing was flying past her, calling to a mate it could not find.

Shandril watched it go, sighed, and shook her head. Life went on, towers rose and fell—and who noticed? What difference did it all make? She spread her hands and saw the spellfire rippling along her skin. What good was all this power to hurt and kill and compel? It was empty. Well, at least she could also heal.

Shandril turned to where her companions lay, and spellfire flared in her hands again. Narm's body was still, his lips twisted in a snarl of agony. Shandril looked down at him, and the face of Delg came into her mind.

Her eyes blurred with sudden tears. She knelt and kissed those twisted lips gently, and felt them move under hers as spellfire slid slowly out of her. Carefully she held its flow in check, pressing herself against the body of her man, willing his hurts to fade away. Spellfire rushed through him, clearing away burns and clotted blood, scars and contaminated flesh. Narm groaned weakly, shifting under her, and Shandril shared her spellfire, letting it run into him in a pool of fiery force. Narm stiffened.

"Ohh!" he gasped. "Gods, but that *burns!*" His eyes flew open.

Shandril smiled down into his bruised face and kissed him, taking her spellfire back. Flames leaked around their lips as he smiled in grateful relief from the pain, then hugged her happily.

When Shandril broke free to breathe, Narm grinned up at her. "You've won! You did it!" he said.

Shandril crooked an eyebrow. "*We* did it," she replied, almost disapprovingly. "Without you—and the others—I'd be so much meat on Fzoul's floor right now."

She sighed and glanced up. A Zhentilar who'd been cautiously approaching across the courtyard turned and fled. Shandril chuckled.

"Fzoul and most of the wizards here are dead—and I think I'm done with killing Zhents for a bit . . . unless they try to bother us again before we leave." She stood up. "How do you feel?"

"Weak, but whole," he said with a smile. He tried futilely to smooth down his hair with his fingers; it stood out straight from his scalp. "I've had enough of a taste of spellfire to know I never want such power," he added. "How are *you*, Shan?"

Shandril smiled at him. "Never better, lord of my heart." Spellfire danced in her eyes for a moment.

Narm shrank away with an involuntary shiver.

Sadness touched Shandril's eyes as they stared at each other. Narm reached out to lay his hand firmly on her arm. "It's not—I don't fear *you*, my love; it's just the fire—"

"I know," she said softly. "You, at least, don't think of me as a prize to be fought over, or a goddess of fire to be feared."

Narm looked at the motionless forms lying nearby. "Neither do these Harpers, love," he said.

She turned to Narm and replied, "Yes, time to wake these dear friends—all but Sarhthor, I fear." She stared at the wizard's sharp features and impulsively bent and kissed his cheek. He did not stir. Sad and sober, Shandril turned to heal her other friends with a kiss. . . .

The last tingling of the spellfire left Mirt, and the gentle healing hands withdrew. The Old Wolf growled and tried to struggle to his feet. The world swam, and his knees gave way. He fell back, too weak and dazed to rise yet. . . .

Tessaril sighed and fought her own weakness. Dragging herself upright, she leaned on her sword for support. "Come, Lord," she said quietly, extending a hand. Mirt groaned again, and struggled to reach her slim fingers. . . .

"Mmm. That was a nice kiss," Belarla said, stretching, as she lay on her back on the flagstones. Shandril watched the wrinkles of pain fading away from the Harper's beautiful face and smiled down at her. Belarla smiled back.

"Yes, she's much better than most of our clients," a still groggy Oelaerone commented from nearby. She sat idly turning something in her fingers: a few scorched feathers clinging to a blackened wooden shaft—all that was left of the arrow that had nearly claimed her life. "But then— they're men . . . and what do men know of kissing?"

Belarla rolled up to one elbow. She stiffened and put a warning hand on Shandril's arm. "Speaking of men," she murmured, pointing.

Shandril looked up quickly and saw men with grim faces—priests in the black robes of Bane—coming into the courtyard. The Holy of Bane were more than a score strong, and some of them held glowing staves and maces. A tall man at their head raised his staff, pointed at Shandril and her companions, and shouted, "For the glory of Bane, *slay them!*"

"*Slay them!*" thundered thirty throats as one, and the priests loyal to Elthaulin, the New Voice of Bane, followed him forward.

With a dark look in her eyes, Shandril rose from the Harpers. Spellfire swirled around her hands and ran swiftly along her hair—and then she sent it lashing out. Elthaulin blazed up in front of her like a dry torch.

Healing took far more spellfire than smiting, Shandril realized wearily. *Must I go on killing forever?* "Halt, men of Bane!" she cried. "Let me be, and I'll leave you alive. Or strike at me—and taste *this!*"

Shandril let flames roar up into the sky and forced a savage smile onto her weary lips. The priests' charge ended. They screamed and pushed at each other in a mad retreat. Shandril followed, grimly determined to make the city safe by nightfall.

No, they'd not soon forget Shandril Shessair in *this* city.

* * * * *

By the time Shandril returned to Spell Court, the sun was setting over the Citadel of the Raven. In the gloaming, she saw winking spell lights beside the cluster of her friends. The lights faded, and a single figure stood where they'd been—the Bard of Shadowdale. Shandril ran joyously to meet Storm, who had begun conversing with Mirt and the others.

As Shandril approached, Storm turned and called out warmly, "I wondered when you'd grow tired of devastating the place."

They hugged each other. "Belarla and Oelaerone send you their heartfelt thanks and their congratulations," Storm said. "Mirt tells me they had to get back to their house, before the customers started to come calling—and before you got them into another fight they might not walk away from."

Shandril had started to laugh, but she fell silent at those last words. She looked past the bard at the body of Sarhthor of the Zhentarim lying still on the flagstones. Shivering, she clutched Storm's strong, reassuring body harder and quietly told the bard what the wizard had done before he died.

Storm drew back in surprise, staring alternately at Shandril and Sarhthor. "I don't recognize him," she said, "but I don't know all the Harpers in Faerûn, after all." Her face darkened. "Come; let's be gone from here before Manshoon regains control."

"Manshoon?"

Storm smiled ruefully. "Manshoon is always less dead than he appears. Elminster's slain him more than once before—quite thoroughly—only to have to do it again a winter later. Manshoon has his secrets." She smiled more broadly and dropped something into Shandril's hand. "And now you do, too."

Shandril looked down. In her hand was a small silver harp on a chain. She touched it in wonder. Its tiny strings stirred in a mournful, somehow proud tune.

"If you both don't mind," Storm added softly, "Mirt wants to give Delg's badge to Narm. You're both Harpers now."

Epilogue

 Lighting crashed and staggered across the sky far to the east. The guard watched it, thankful for the momentary entertainment. No duty post in Zhentil Keep was more mind-numbing than this one. He hefted his halberd wearily and yawned. Rubbing his cheek, he watched lightning crack the dome of night again, and was briefly thankful that the storm was far off; otherwise he'd have to huddle against the door of the crypt to keep dry.

Hours to go until dawn.

"Gods deliver me from this everlasting boredom," he muttered.

"The gods have heard you, fool—to your cost."

The guard tried to spin, but the hand that clasped his neck was very strong. Struggling wildly, he glimpsed the crypt's doorway, dark and open, but he couldn't see his attacker. He didn't need to. Fear lashing his heart, the guard went down into the last darkness, and he knew who had killed him.

Manshoon looked down at the sprawled body. "Yawning when you were supposed to be guarding *my* future is a crime punishable by death. Had I forgotten to warn you of that? Life is *so* unfair."

He carefully closed the door of the crypt, glancing at the four bodies lying ready there . . . four? Gods, he'd best be preparing others; how many had he gone through now? He turned away to start the long walk home across Zhentil Keep. The way was long, and the boots this body wore had started to crumble; he walked slowly, thankful that the storm had emptied the night streets. The few guards who saw him carefully looked away; Manshoon passed them with a grim smile.

Fzoul obviously hadn't known about all of his crypts. Sloppy work, unfortunately typical of the more devout—or ostensibly devout—side of the Brotherhood. He looked up at the spires of the Black Altar as a lightning flash outlined them, and nodded.

"I have a score to settle there." There were advantages to staying dead for a tenday or so—it gave traitors time to show their true colors, get their hands properly dirty and their plans half-hatched. . . . Smashing them then was most satisfying. He was looking forward to it.

He turned away. The High Tower beckoned. He needed a bath, a drink, and a warm body beside his in bed, before dawn. For the first time, Manshoon wondered why he had ever begun to strive for more than such things . . . after all, what more could a man achieve? He shrugged and put such thoughts from his mind. He'd feel more himself in the morning.

* * * * *

Shandril and Narm lay curled up together in front of the crackling fire, a bearskin rug soft and warm around them. Narm glanced up at the walls and ceiling and said thankfully, "Well, at least this room hasn't grown any new doors or corners tonight."

Shandril chuckled softly, took her own look at the Hidden House around her, and said, "I don't know . . . I think I've almost grown used to it." She reached out and turned Narm's chin until his eyes met hers, and then asked quietly, "Don't you think it would make a great home for us? The Zhents would never find us here."

"That was my suggestion, too," a calm voice agreed, "and I still think it's a good one."

Narm and Shandril turned their heads in surprise. A moment later, Shandril leapt up out of the furs to embrace their visitor.

Tessaril winked at Narm. "I come bearing gifts."

"Though not baring them as much as certain folk," Mirt grunted, stepping into view behind her and eyeing Shandril's naked form, still pressed against the Lord of Eveningstar. Shandril stuck her tongue out at him.

Narm got up, holding the rug around him, and cleared his throat. "Er—welcome! Will you have wine?"

Mirt swung a huge bottle into view from behind his back and grinned at him.

"Thank ye, lad, I will," he said, striding forward. He'd brought his own huge pewter tankard, carrying it in the same large, hairy hand that held the bottle. The Old Wolf lowered himself to the floor with a grunt, stretched out on the rug before the fire, wheezed, snatched the fur from Narm's startled grasp, and draped it over himself coyly.

"Oh, *Shan*-dril," he trilled in mimicry of a young suitor. "I'm over *here!* You can come back and lie down by the fire now."

Shandril looked at him, the firelight dancing on her smooth curves, and then walked deliberately to him,

turned a corner of the furs over the Old Wolf's face, and
sat firmly on him. "So, what gift?" she asked, ignoring
the muffled protests from beneath her.

Mirt started to reach his hands up to tickle her, but
Narm grabbed them and ended up on the floor wrestling
with the Old Wolf. Though her seat started to jerk back
and forth beneath her, Shandril sat serenely atop the
shifting and curling bear rug. Mirt's muted voice roared,
"*Don't* break my bottle!"

At that, Tessaril looked up from her belt pouch. She
took in the scene, put her hands on her hips, and
whooped with laughter. When her mirth had died, the
Lord of Eveningstar extended a hand and drew Shandril
to her feet. Then, lips quirked in a wry smile, she plucked
the bearskin out of the struggling pile and put it around
Shandril. "This gift is somewhat serious," Tessaril said,
"so we'd best calm the Old Wolf down a bit."

Narm, who'd found himself in a headlock several
moments earlier and was now unable to get free, agreed
as audibly as possible.

When some order had been restored, Tessaril drew
forth a sparkling gem from her belt pouch. "This is your
gift," she said, "but I advise you not to touch it, or even
keep it on your person—you can probably be traced by
it, and there may be worse things magic can work
through it. I've had the stone tested by the strongest wizards of Cormyr, and we think it's safe for you to see it.
Remember: *don't* touch it!"

Shandril looked at her quizzically.

"It's a speaking stone," Tessaril said, releasing the
gem. It floated in the air by itself, turning slightly, innocently winking back the light at them all. "It came to me
in Eveningstar—borne by a merchant who'd come from
Zhentil Keep."

In the silence that followed her words, she stretched

forth a finger and touched the stone. Light winked within it, and then a voice spoke, cold and clear and very close, as if the speaker were in the room with them.

"To Shandril Shessair, greetings from Manshoon, and a promise: I and those I command will make no further moves against you and yours. Nor will we try again to gain spellfire. You may well mistrust this promise, but I assure you I'll keep it."

The light in the stone died, and the gem sank slowly to the floor, landing on the rug without a sound.

The stunned group stared down at it in silence, and then Tessaril bent over, took it up, and pocketed it.

Shandril shook her head. "I know I'll never be able to trust those words, but—somehow—I believe him. When he said that, he meant it."

"Being killed can have that effect on ye," Mirt rumbled. "What puzzles me is how Sarhthor—Harper or no—knew about this 'crown of fire' bit."

Tessaril looked up. "He was a Harper indeed, Mirt; High Lady Alustriel confirmed it. She tutored him in the Art and recruited him, years ago, but no longer knew if he held himself a Harper or followed his own path of power and evil. At Manshoon's command, Sarhthor did a lot of research on spellfire, devouring entire libraries of spell-lore. In a diary kept in Candlekeep, he read the same passage I have: 'If someone freely gives his life-force to a wielder of spellfire, it powers the spellfire to truly awesome heights, causing a crownlike halo of flame around the spellfire-hurler.' "

Mirt looked at her. "This happened before? Someone willingly gave his life for a brighter flame?" He shook his shaggy head. "Ah, well, I suppose there's no shortage of crazed-wits in Faerûn."

The tankard in front of him grew a mouth, and in the dry tones of Elminster, it said, "And few, indeed, are better able to speak of craziness than Mirt of Waterdeep."

Mirt had flung the nearly empty tankard away—and the old sword on his hip had made it into his hand—before he growled, "Elminster?"

The tankard landed with a clang, rolled over, and stopped. "None other," it said with dignity. "How many archmages do ye throw around, anyway?"

"Elminster!" Shandril leaned forward to peer at the tankard. "Have you—recovered? How are you?"

The tankard looked somehow testy. "Aye, forget about me for days, lass, and then recall old Elminster as if he were a favorite puppy—or some disease—ye'd forgotten ye had. I'm doing just fine, thank ye all, not dead yet."

Narm laughed. "He hasn't changed."

"More respect, youngling," the tankard growled.

"Elminster," Shandril said eagerly, "we're going to have a baby." Her face clouded over for a moment, and she added quietly, "Again."

Mirt looked at her. "Aye, and tankard or no, this calls for a toast or three! Mind ye not fight over its naming, now—if it's a boy, call it after me, not him." He jerked his head toward the stein on the floor.

The tankard spoke again. Shandril was surprised to hear how soft and gentle Elminster's voice could be when he dropped his testy blustering. "It's not a boy, Old Wolf. I know already that thy babe will be a girl, Shandril. The blessing of Mystra upon ye and Narm—and upon her."

"Thanks, Old Mage," Shandril said, touched.

"Ye'll both be needing it—and Narm, too," Elminster added, in his customary sharper tones. "For in the visions Mystra sends me, I've seen that thy lass will have the power of spellfire, too."

* * * * *

Oprion Blackstone sat alone in a high, locked chamber in the Black Altar, staring into a scrying bowl as Fzoul had taught him to do. His false Manshoon speech sounded even better to his ears now than when he'd laid the enchantment, but that accursed Tessaril had put the speaking stone back in her pouch—so he could see nothing of what was happening in the Hidden House. Making the stone burn its way out of the pouch now would certainly be a mistake.

He could, though, hear everything. Oprion raised his head to stare at the carved Black Hand of Bane that hung on the wall, and he said to it grimly, "And that child will be mine. If need be, I'll take the form of a younger man and woo it. For I will have spellfire for my own, whatever befalls gods and men in the days ahead. The gods have twisted humors, indeed, to give a silly, soft slip of a girl such power. Spellfire will be mine."

His face paled, then, as if he was seeing more in the Black Hand than a carving, and his voice deepened into the echoing tones of prophecy. "No struggle is ever done; no matter is ever closed. As long as gods and men strive on Toril, there is no 'forever.' "

* * * * *

"I must go now, lass," Elminster's voice came again. "There are others who'd speak with ye, though."

Another, rougher voice came from the tankard. "Shandril? Lass?"

Shandril was up out of Narm's arms in a rush, reaching toward the tankard. "*Gorstag?*" she cried, and happy tears wet her cheeks.

"Aye, lass; gods smile on you. Lureene has a word for

you, too—"

The voice changed again. "Shan! Are you well?"

On her knees before the tankard, Shandril laughed. "Very happy, Lureene. Safe in hiding, both of us, and with a babe on the way."

"Good! Give it a kiss for me—and mind you stop at two babes, Shan: the gods give us only two hands to hold them with. Keep smiling, little one."

"My thanks." Through her tears, Shandril was seeing again *The Rising Moon,* the inn where she'd grown up. . . . the place she'd run away from so long ago. So long—and so few actual days ago.

"Fair fortune, lass," the tankard said gruffly.

"You fare well, too, Gorstag," Shandril replied almost fiercely. "Both of you!"

And then, before her eyes, the tankard shattered with the sound of a ringing bell, its shards dancing on the stones.

Tessaril shook her head. "That magic eats away at whatever is the focus for farspeaking," she said. "I'm surprised it held together this long." She leaned forward to touch Shandril's shoulder. "No harm has befallen any of them," she said reassuringly. "The magic just overwhelmed the tankard."

Mirt looked at its ruins, then sadly surveyed the empty depths of his bottle. "Is there more to be had anywhere about?"

Tessaril indicated a door. "I took the liberty of bringing in a keg of ale, a little while back." Her nose wrinkled. "About the time I knew you'd be coming."

Mirt threw her a look as he shambled toward the door.

She smiled sweetly and added, "On a shelf on the left, you'll find a selection of tankards for the rest of us to use. You're welcome."

Still on her knees on the floor, Shandril found herself

laughing helplessly. By the gods! Did they never stop teasing each other? And a small voice inside her promptly asked: Why should they?

* * * * *

"Oprion Blackstone?" the cold voice said in derisive surprise. "The priesthood of the Dread Lord flourishes indeed."

Oprion scrambled up. How had anyone passed the guards and locks to reach this room? And that voice. He spun around, and his face went as white as polished bone. "Manshoon!" he gasped, when he could speak. "You're alive!" He stared at the High Lord of Zhentil Keep, looking up and down, and then turned away in confusion. "I'm—I'm delighted."

Manshoon's smile was crooked. "You mean, you're surprised I still have clones left."

Oprion stuttered for a moment, and then said rather desperately, "No, no. But when so much time had passed, we—"

"Assumed you were finally rid of me. Have you raised Fzoul yet?"

Oprion's mouth dropped open. "W-Why?"

"He's thrice the administrator you'll ever be—and a capable schemer, too, if not my equal. The Brotherhood needs him. I hear you've been rather careless with our— ah, human resources, since I was last here. Sarhthor, Elthaulin, and about two hundred others, as I recall; the list made both long and distressing reading."

Oprion's hand tensed as he eyed a sideboard and the magical mace that lay upon it. It winked back at him, brimming with power. Mageslayer was its name; Fzoul had told him what it could do. His gaze flickered away from it, and Manshoon smiled.

"Is it to be war between us, then?" Manshoon's voice was soft and level; he might have been asking what color cloak his colleague intended to wear.

Oprion's wintry gaze met his own silently for a long time, and then the priest shook his head with careful slowness. "No. We work together—as always. It is the best way."

Manshoon nodded. "Perhaps, one day, with trust," he murmured.

Oprion looked at him sharply, but said nothing.

There was a faint smell of pipesmoke in the air, but neither of them recognized it for what it was.

* * * * *

"Be damned to trotting back an' forth all night!" Mirt growled, coming back into the room with the keg on his shoulder. He staggered as he came; it wasn't a hand-keg, but a barrel almost as large around as he was.

Shandril looked at Tessaril. "You think we'll drink all *that?* Lords of Cormyr must be optimists, indeed!"

Tessaril looked at her dryly. "No," she replied, "I think *Mirt* will drink all that—if we want any, we'd best pull a tankard each now, before it's gone." She watched Mirt, wheezing and grunting, set the keg onto a couch. "Tankards, Old Wolf?" she called.

Mirt gave her what some folk in Faerûn call 'a dirty look,' and set off toward the door again. He'd got about six steps away from the couch before it collapsed with a groan, settling the keg nearer the floor, but thankfully not dumping it. Tessaril surveyed it and said, "I've a feeling this is going to be a long night. You'd better put something other than that bearskin on, Shan."

Shan was nodding as the Lord of Eveningstar looked across the room and added, "And so should your h—"

Tessaril's words broke off and, frowning, she glanced from one of them to the other.

Shandril and Narm both followed her gaze, then looked down at themselves. Both wore identical bearskin rugs.

"What's the matter, Tess?" Shandril asked quietly.

The Lord of Eveningstar's eyes were troubled. "Throw those furs off, *right now!* There should only be one of them!"

Shandril and Narm stared at her for one shocked moment, then Shan saw a gold light glowing in the eyes of the dead bear. She shrieked and tried to throw off the skin. Narm's fur fell lifeless and heavy to the stone floor, but Shandril's felt suddenly wet and glistening, and it slapped at her breast and flank as she snatched at the fur around her. Frantically she flung it away, just as it grew a long, hooked claw—that tore a thin ribbon of flesh from her ribs. Dancing backward, Shandril stared down at the blood.

The fur on the floor in front of her gathered itself, shifting, and scuttled toward her.

Shandril had the brief impression of tentacles as she backed away. Her hands flamed.

"*No!*" Tessaril shouted at her. "No spellfire in here!"

Shandril rushed to her discarded clothes and snatched up the Zhent dagger she'd picked up in the courtyard of the *Wyvern*—the one that had come so close to taking Narm's life. With a snarl, she turned back to the thing that wasn't a bearskin rug, and drove the blade deep into it. Warm, pink liquid as thick as honey gushed out, and the flesh seemed to quiver under her thrust.

The thing had grown, rising to about the height of a large dog. It was moving away from her, slashing with clawed, humanlike hands at Tessaril, who was angrily hacking at it with a belt dagger of her own. The Lord of

Eveningstar turned her head then and called, "*Knights!*"

Her words were still echoing in the room when a door appeared in the ceiling and promptly fell open. Torm and Rathan plunged into the room through it, calling, "A rescue! A rescue!" as they came.

Torm hit the floor in a roll, bounced up, and slashed at the moving rug with the slim blade in his hand. Rathan landed hard on the thing with both feet, grunted as it convulsed and threw him off, and staggered back to fetch up hard against the wall. With a flourish he brought a mace out of his belt and swung it down to thump solidly in the middle of the shapeshifting fur.

Mirt rolled back in through the door at that moment. "Ye gods!" he said, looking hurt. "I leave for a moment an' ye start the fun *without* me!"

Tossing tankards in all directions, he snatched out his blade and lumbered forward, bellowing, "*My* turn, blast ye! Out o' the way, Torm!"

The rug was bleeding freely now under their blows, but rising into a man-high form. Tentacles emerged and coiled and shifted back into the main bulk of the thing; the fur broke into shifting patches that floated atop a rippling, glistening, flesh-colored bulk.

Shandril stared at it in horror, then found Narm at her side, his hands raised to cast a spell if need be.

Tessaril stood beside them, her own hands also raised. "Kill it swiftly!" she said urgently, eyes on the thing. "Its magic can overmaster all of us!"

Torm laughed as he leapt over tentacles and repeatedly thrust his blade to the hilt. "Not so long as Elminster's spell lasts!"

"The Old Mage's spell *ended* when he was laid low fighting the lich lord!" Tessaril screamed. "*Beware!*"

"So *that's* what's making my amulet burn!" Rathan said, bringing his mace down with renewed vigor.

"Hurry, lads—it won't last much longer!"

"It may surprise ye to learn that I *am* hurrying!" Mirt puffed as ichor of many colors splashed around him, driven by the force of his blows.

"You *must* be old," Torm remarked, as he hacked away a tentacle that threatened to grip his throat. The rising column in front of him had grown a head now, and its featureless front began to twist and shift, swimming into—Delg's face.

"No!" Shandril stared at it. "Torm—*stop!* What if—?"

"Shandril," the face said, in Delg's familiar rumble, turning beseeching eyes to meet her gaze. "Stop them, lass! They'r—"

"Not a chance," Torm said coldly, running his blade through the open dwarven mouth in front of him. "*Die, Magusta of the Malaugrym!*"

Delg's eyes turned to flaming gold, gazed at the knight, and spat feeble jets of flame at him.

Torm leapt back and crashed against the wall of the room—but the eyes were already flickering and fading. Wearing Torm's sword, the shapeshifting bulk sank down, coiling and sliding into a sickening puddle of flesh. Mirt and Rathan backed away from it, sweating, and watched it die.

As the first whiff of its death reek came to them, Torm picked himself up from the floor, rubbed at one elbow gingerly, and said, "Gods above! What a knight has to do to get a drink around here! Throw us a tankard, will you, Shan? Be useful for once."

Shandril glared at him, opened her mouth to make a sharp reply . . . and then closed it again, smiled grimly, and went to get him a tankard. After today, she could wait to take her revenges. . . .

* * * * *

Much later that night, when they were alone at last, Narm pushed their bed over to where they could look out the newly repaired magical window, and see the ever-changing scenes of Faerûn that appeared beyond.

They lay in bed together and saw stars falling over the dark, dead ruins of an empty city; wolves howling on moonlit moors; men huddled around campfires in high mountain valleys; and a grim place that could only have been Zhentil Keep. Beholders floated menacingly there above a dark altar, where bowls of blood were cast into fires by horn-masked priests clad all in black. A priest they did not know lifted his head and cried some unheard invocation to Bane.

Shandril shivered at the sight. "Narm, hold me," she said softly, trembling. "I'm afraid. So many folk want us dead."

Narm put his arms around her and held her tightly, as if the fierceness of his grip could keep enemies from her. He knew he must be strong when she needed him. It was the least he could do.

"No, my lady," he said firmly into the darkness, "this is where we live happily ever after, as the tales say. . . ."

"Tell me one of those tales, my lord," said Shandril in a small voice. Narm looked up into the darkness overhead—and for just an instant, he could have sworn he saw Elminster's face winking at him, pipe in mouth. He blinked, and it was gone.

Narm cleared his throat, settled his lady's head close beneath his chin, and said firmly, "Later. First, tell me what you plan for us both in the days ahead. How are you going to use your spellfire to remake Faerûn?"

"Well," she said, in a small, quavering voice that gathered strength and humor as she went on, "first there're the rest of the Zhentarim to roast—and then the Cult of the Dragon and their dracoliches. I'd *still* like to get to

Silverymoon—remember?—and meet Alustriel. After that . . . well, we'll see."

Narm shook his head; his nose told him he was indeed smelling a faint whiff of pipesmoke. . . .

Ed's (Elminster's) Afterword

Hello. Well Met! Welcome to my world. This book has been long requested by many patient fans of the FORGOTTEN REALMS® world. Here it is—and I hope it's just the book you've been waiting for.

I've been waiting even longer. I began the Realms circa 1967 as a setting for fantasy stories. When the ADVANCED DUNGEONS & DRAGONS® game first appeared, I was impressed by its precise detailing of magic and monster abilities, so I recast the ever-growing Realms to match its rules. Game play followed, with a band of loyal friends who demanded a logical, detailed, colorful world—and set high standards of role-playing. The events we spun together and the rooms full of Realmslore notes—heraldry, history, genealogy, recipes, fashion notes, and more—have piled up steadily.

About twenty years after I created the world, TSR adopted it as an official home of the 2nd Edition AD&D® game. From sporadic articles in DRAGON® Magazine beginning in Issue 30, the published Realms has grown into a huge line of novels, boxed game sets, adventure modules, rule books, sourcebooks . . . and now even travel books!

Dozens of creative folks have joined me in writing

about the Realms—*often surprising and delighting me with their work.* If you play games set in the Realms or read its tales, it's your world too. You are one of the authors of a rich, continuing chronicle that details what is now the largest, most written-about fantasy world ever.

Hmm. . . . I could almost hear trumpets there.

I'd best calm down a bit and settle back into my armchair with a good book . . . about the Realms, of course.

I've read, reread, and enjoyed every Realms novel so far. They each show very different folk and very different corners of the Realms, but are all the more interesting for being so varied. The Realms is a world in which lots of folk live, not just a small band of heroes who constantly save the world from villains (sound familiar?). Thus, the Realms has lots of stories to be told.

Among the most interesting Realms tales are the Harper books, a series of self-contained stories about folk associated with a mysterious "good" organization: Those Who Harp. (Game rules and additional information about the Harpers can be found in the *Code of the Harpers* sourcebook [FOR4]. I could say it's excellent, but I won't because I wrote it and Elminster spends a lot of time chiding me for what I left out!)

As a Harper novel, *Crown of Fire* is a direct sequel to *Spellfire,* published by TSR in 1987. In *Spellfire,* the saga of Shandril Shessair, wielder of spellfire, began, but either book can be enjoyed without reading the other.

When I set about writing *Spellfire,* I wanted to give readers a taste of what it would be like to dream of adventure and then suddenly be thrust into it, with all its discomfort, worry, and excitement. I also wanted to turn some fantasy cliches on their ears. For instance, at the book's beginning we see a band of adventurers too inept for their own good. Instead of miraculously winning through, they all get slaughtered! Similarly, since guys always get to be the heroes in fantasy, I chose a heroine instead.

About the heroine: I needed her to be powerful enough to meet hostile wizards and monsters and survive, so I gave her spellfire. Only a rare few folk in the Realms can call forth spellfire, and it can cleave through or consume most magic it encounters. Since the Realms are ruled by magic, spellfire is very powerful and very important, indeed. Its precise limits aren't yet known, but all "power groups" in Faerûn see spellfire as an extremely potent weapon they must at all costs possess, control, or destroy to keep it out of the hands of their enemies.

But a character with ultimate power is boring. What could challenge her? I needed my heroine to be naive about the real world, physically weak, and lacking a family to call on for aid. Out stepped Shandril, a dreamy orphan girl who's grown up drudging in one place.

(While we're on the subject of place, let me say I was tired of fantasy books in which a hero wanders calmly through a lifeless landscape and thus comes to rule the world [or defeat its evil ruler] without anyone else noticing, caring, or even seeming alive. So in both *Spellfire* and *Crown of Fire,* a host of other folk are always busily at work, swirling around the main characters. Sometimes this supporting cast is more powerful and important than the heroes. As I said, the Realms is a place where *lots* of people live.)

Spellfire ran longer than was convenient—if bits of it seem choppy, well . . . bits were chopped—and I felt Shandril's story was unfinished. I lamented most the loss of the main villains—the sinister Shadowmasters, who keep Elminster and the Simbul too busy to aid Shandril directly. The Shadowmasters manipulate many of Shandril's foes throughout *Spellfire.* Elminster and his lady protect Shandril offstage by fighting these evil beings for the latter half of *Spellfire,* and by the time *Crown of Fire* begins, the younger, more reckless Shadowmasters have decided to strike openly. Hence the mayhem in the previous pages.

Will there be another tale of Shandril? Who knows? There are so many other tales of the Realms to be told that I don't know what we'll get to read next! Elminster grumbles that we've only scratched the surface; almost nothing of the grand past history of the Realms has seen print yet, and only a bare few tales of here-and-now. I'll be reading along, though . . . and I hope you will be, too.

See you by a fireside, somewhere in the Forgotten Realms!

Ed Greenwood
Realmskeep
July 1993

FANTASY ADVENTURE

Elminster:
The Making of a Mage

Ed Greenwood

From the creator of the FORGOTTEN REALMS® world comes the epic story of the Realms' greatest wizard!

Elminster. No other wizard wields such power. No other wizard has lived as long. No other book tells you the story of his origins. Born into humble circumstances, Elminster begins his life of magic in an odd way – by fleeing from it. When his village and his family are destroyed by a being of sorcerous might, young Elminster eschews the arcane arts. Instead, he becomes a journeyman warrior and embarks on a mission of revenge . . . until his destiny turns in on itself and he embraces the magic he once despised.

Elminster: The Making of a Mage, in hardcover, is coming to book, game, and hobby stores everywhere in December 1994!

TSR #8548

ISBN 1-56076-936-X

Sug. Retail $16.95; CAN $21.95; £10.50 U. K.

DRAGONLANCE® Saga

The sweeping saga of honor, courage, and
companions begins with . . .

The Chronicles Trilogy

By *The New York Times* best-selling authors
Margaret Weis & Tracy Hickman

Dragons of Autumn Twilight
Volume One
Dragons have returned to Krynn with a vengeance.
An unlikely band of heroes embarks on a perilous
quest for the legendary *Dragonlance!*
TSR #8300
ISBN 0-88038-173-6

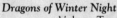

Dragons of Winter Night
Volume Two
The adventure continues . . . Treachery,
intrigue, and despair threaten to overcome
the Heroes of the Lance in their epic quest!
TSR #8301
ISBN 0-88038-174-4

Dragons of Spring Dawning
Volume Three
Hope dawns with the coming of spring, but then
the heroes find themselves in a titanic battle
against Takhisis, Queen of Darkness!
TSR #8302
ISBN 0-88038-175-2

Sug. Retail Each $4.95; CAN $5.95; £4.99 U.K.